Trail of Tears

The Story of John Ross

Based on Historical Events

To From!

Thanks for your help!

Anne Greene

ENDORSEMENTS

I burned with anger at the cruelty of U.S. troops, turned the page and wept with the hero's anguish, opened the next chapter and laughed out loud at the trick played by his friend.

While troops push their people from their homeland onto a tragic journey of starvation and disease, John Ross and Bold Hunter show desperate deeds of faithfulness and love.

Set against the backdrop of the Cherokee removal, *Trail of Tears* brings us close to the suffering and gives us glimpses of hope. This story is history in its finest fictional form, a strong tale, told by a master storyteller.

—**David Warner Parks**, PhD

What if you were uprooted by the government, had your land and home seized, and were forced under armed guard to make a grueling, dangerous and insulting journey to a strange and wild region?

In *Trail of Tears*, Anne Greene well captures this tragedy that was inflicted on the Cherokee people in the southern Appalachians in the early 19th century. The story of main character young John Ross is remarkable—proudly suffering and resisting his condition, sacrificing and putting his people before himself, unexpectedly encountering kindness in the midst of chaos, strengthening his faith, and meeting and growing close to a special young lady.

Unfortunately, *Trail of Tears* is not at all pure fiction—it's a story based on real, historical events. Anne Greene's

tale is one you cannot get out of your head, nor should we forget the history behind it.
—**James Yarbrough**, author of *Liquid Moon* and *You Can't Be Serious.*

Anne Greene's *Trail of Tears* is gut-wrenching, captivating book rich with historical accuracy and detail that could have only been obtained with extensive research on the author's part. Greene manages to masterfully weave the gospel message in this story of a proud nation struggling to survive the forced exodus from their homeland across miles and miles of hardship, cruel atrocities, sickness, and death. It's a love story and The Greatest Love Story poured out with blood and tears and sacrifice on the trail to a new home. I was captivated with the characters from page one and couldn't put it down until I came to the end!
—**Julie Lavender,** author of *365 Ways to Love Your Child: Turning Little Moments into Lasting Memories* (Revell/Baker Publishing Group)

I confess this was my first novel on this subject and it both drew me in and horrified me—doubly so, because I knew this was a real event. Yikes! My heart about stopped during that first chapter.
Trail of Tears is a story of faith in the crucible of suffering. Anne Greene finds a silver thread of redemption in a dark and brutal episode of American history.
—**Lynne Basham Tagawa**, author of *The Shenandoah Road*

Trail of Tears is a heartbreaking yet inspiring tale of history, mistreatment, and love. Greene expertly weaves the facts into a story that touches the heart and makes the reader want to ensure nothing like this happens again. I enjoyed the romance and the realism, and particularly thought the twist at the end for the villain immensely satisfying. Highly recommended.
—**Donna Schlachter,** author of *Double Jeopardy* and other historical fiction.

I can't tell you how much I enjoyed *Trail of Tears*. Only God could have given Anne Greene the heart to tell this story. With every word I felt like I was with John Ross. This historic novel allows you to step back in time to journey with John Ross and the Cherokee people as they are forced to be removed from their land. With every word you can almost hear Anne's compassionate heart telling their story and feel the emotions in the pain they endured. Your faith will be strengthened as you understand the ultimate meaning of dependence on God for every moment of life. And you will rejoice with the prayers of each new believer. This book is timeless and should be shared with all future generations. May Anne's story of John Ross and the Cherokee people never be forgotten.

—Billie Fulton, author of Selah award-winning *Faith Is Not Silent* and newly released *Just A Moment* ... Changes life forever.

Anne Greene deftly weaves a compelling love story pitched against the chilling backdrop of the Native American death march of the 1830's.

—Catherine Finger, award-winning author of the Jo Oliver thriller series.

Trail of Tears
The Story of John Ross
Based on Historical Events

ANNE GREENE

PUBLISHING THE POSITIVE
Plymouth, Massachusetts

Cover and Interior Design: Derinda Babcock

Editor(s): Linda Rondeau, Linda Farmer Harris, Deb Haggerty

PUBLISHED BY: Elk Lake Publishing, Inc., 35 Dogwood Drive, Plymouth, MA 02360, 2021

Library Cataloging Data

Names: Greene, Anne (Anne Greene)

Trail of Tears / Anne Greene

350 p. 23cm × 15cm (9in × 6 in.)

ISBN-13: 978-1-64949-149-7 (paperback) | 978-1-64949-150-3 (trade paperback) | 978-1-64949-151-0 (e-book)

Key Words: Cherokee Indians, Georgia, Romance, Historical, Indian Territory, Survival Stories, Adventure

LCCN: 2021932521 Fiction

DEDICATION

I dedicate this book to Larry, my wonderful husband. Thank you for our love story. Thank you for supporting me in this great adventure of being an author. You are a gift from heaven.

And to my daughter, Michelle, who said this is her favorite book.

And to my dear Lord Jesus Christ who gave his life so I might live.

And to you, my readers, I pray you will love this book.

But as for you, you thought evil against me; but God meant it unto good (Genesis 50:20 KJV).

ACKNOWLEDGMENTS

Thank you ... Deb Haggerty, my publisher; Linda Rondeau and Linda Farmer Harris my editors; Derinda Babcock, my cover designer.

Thanks so much for the help of my dedicated critique partners:

My dear friends: June Foster and Carol McCain as well as the ACFW Scribes Group: April Kidwell, Christina Lombardi, and Tabitha Bouldin.

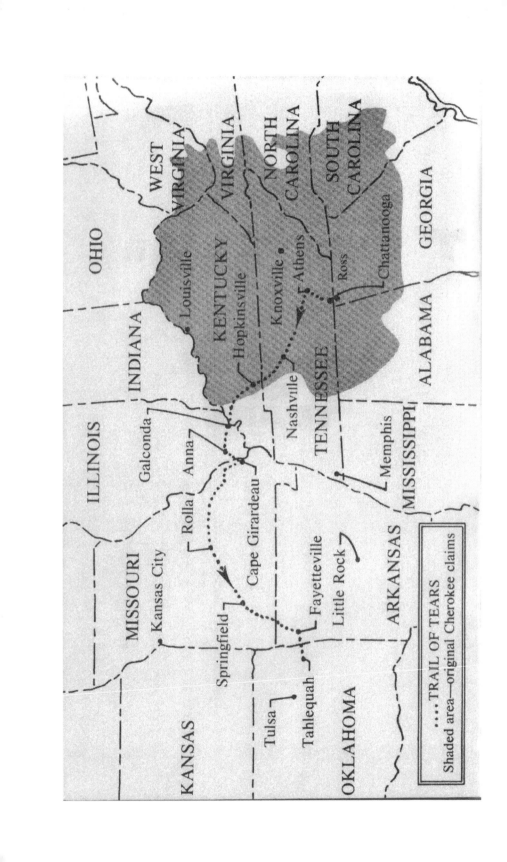

TRAIL OF TEARS
Shaded area—original Cherokee claims

PREFACE

In 1838 when the US seized Cherokee land, the Cherokee Nation split into two factions.

The Ross Faction, headed by Chief John R. Ross, labored to keep Cherokee Appalachian land and fought the federal government using legal methods and passive resistance to retain their ancient homeland.

The Ridge-Boudinot Faction, led by Major Ridge, his son John Ridge, Elias Boudinot, and Stand Watie, reasoned the future of the Cherokee lay in removal of the Nation to Indian Territory, Oklahoma. So, the Ridge-Boudinot faction signed the illegal Treaty of New Echota in 1835. The faction represented only a tiny portion of the Cherokee people. The majority considered the treaty treason.

The Cherokee people executed Major Ridge, John Ridge, and Elias Boudinot for signing the Treaty. Stand Watie escaped. He appears in the Trail of Tears sequel.

My book, *Trail of Tears*, tells the story of the Cherokee Removal.

Bitter feeling continued between both parties during the long lives of both Chief Ross and Stand Watie. The rift resulted in great suffering for all the Cherokee. Ironically, both Ross and Watie claimed to be Christians.

All characters in this book are fictitious. I used the name John Ross to show his ancestry to the actual historical person, John Ross. The brave missionary who accompanied the Indians over the trail is based on the historic missionary who spent his life among the Cherokee and traveled the trail with them.

CHAPTER 1

John Ross walked with a confident stride, sure of his place in the world. He swung his arms, relishing the freedom of his buckskin shirt, so different from the confining claw-hammer coat dictated by his aristocratic status. His long steps covered ground fast. He wiped perspiration from his forehead and couldn't wait to strip and dive into the cool lake.

Today, Father had released him from his responsibilities. Father would not admit to giving John a day off because he needed one. But Father wasn't blind. Last night, John dragged one foot after another when he trudged up to his bedroom. Learning to oversee the Ross plantation hadn't been easy. Without resorting to whips, he used sweat and guile to motivate their slaves.

"Gain their respect. Show them you can do any job better than the best of them." Father's hand had been warm on John's shoulder. "Make them hustle to keep up with you."

John hadn't been certain he could obey Father's orders. But he stood in line beneath the blistering sun for hours loading wagons with heavy bales of cotton to be driven north from their plantation to what had been called Ross's Landing, last year renamed Chattanooga.

Many times, only his pride kept him working. He couldn't quit with the slaves watching. If he gave up, they would dub him a lily-livered silk stocking and wouldn't work.

He flexed his calloused hands. All the suffering had paid off. He was in top shape, his muscles toned ... lean and hard, and his pale skin tanned golden.

A strange rustle disturbed the leaves ahead. What? His moccasins skidded as he slid to a stop on the dewy grass. A huge fallen oak blocked his path, and the scent of fresh sawdust filled the air. He touched the still-living end of the hewn-down tree. Who dared remove their boundary oak?

Every nerve prickled. He rubbed a hand across the back of his neck where short hairs bristled.

He had been born here where the wind blew free, his father before him, and his father before him. John knew every stream and every wood. The land would one day be his, and he would never let anyone steal this property.

He glanced around, scanning the countryside. The small lake sparkled, serene in the early morning sunlight. Across the water, familiar farmland rolled toward foothills. Mountains rose above the hills, following each other in stately procession, peaks shadowed with smoky haze. No movement. No enemy.

He shifted his feet. What should he do? In the distance, a horse neighed—answered by another. He stiffened and clenched his fists. He had to get home. Something was wrong.

He spun back the way he had come and ran. In the still, muggy air, his moccasins made no sound as he bolted down a path beneath trees festooned with ivy. Hearing sharpened for danger, but only the shrill chirp of an occasional bird, bees buzzing among wildflowers, and the whisper of squirrels foraging for nuts broke the silence.

Humid air hung a damp coat of perspiration, wetting the buckskin on his shoulders and chest. Swiping a sweaty arm across his brow, he raced on. He leaped a clump of wild raspberry branches reaching across the trail to rip at his buckskins.

Suddenly, gunfire rattled from the direction of the house. He veered into a shortcut, pounding off the narrow path, shielding his face as he plowed through tangled briars and bushes. Shot after shot crackled through the still morning.

He bounded into a sprint. Must be an army. Why hadn't he carried his rifle? The woods thinned and acrid smoke floated in to sting his nostrils. Fear iced his heart. Gasping for breath, dull pain racked his side as he broke free of the woods and dropped behind a large magnolia tree.

High on a hill at the end of an avenue of oaks, puffs of smoke erupted from rifles dotting the perimeter of the lawn surrounding his parents' white-pillared mansion. Flames licked through two of the downstairs windows.

John's stomach cramped into a hard knot.

Bands of men concealed themselves behind the trimmed hedges. Judging by the baggy broadcloth trousers, the attackers resembled bandits rather than an army of trained soldiers. Their heavy boots crushed Mother's summer flowers.

He set his jaw and gripped the rough trunk. How could he rescue his family? Gulping in deep breaths, he hunched over and crept up the hill, darting behind trees. When he reached the huge tree fifty yards from the wide veranda encircling the house, he crouched and poked his head around.

Barricaded behind a dozen shade trees, attackers peppered gunfire at an upstairs window. One shooter hid behind the nymph in their fountain. Another ruffian stooped on the veranda below the parlor window. A spark flickered as the assailant ignited a bundle of twisted straw. Glass tinkled and the blazing straw arched inside the parlor.

John swallowed the lump clogging his throat. How could he stop so many invaders? He gritted his teeth and dug his fingers into the rough tree trunk. Suicide to go out there.

Thick smoke billowed from the lower windows, blackening the white boards of their home. Just above the blazing parlor, from an upstairs window, shots thundered down on the bandits swarming the house. Through the smoky haze, a lone gunman faced the open window and tried to reload.

Father!

He stood framed against the window, his grim, determined face pallid through the smoke. Fire spurted

3

from half a dozen guns below. Father dropped his rifle, clutched his head with both hands, fell against the high chest behind him, and then his body hurtled through the open window. He plunged through space and thudded on the grass.

Blast the danger! John bolted across the lawn to his father's side, dove to his knees, and cradled his father's gray head. Blood dripped, spreading a warm pool over John's cold hands.

"Father, can you hear me?" John forced the words through his tight throat. This nightmare couldn't be real.

He stared at his father's blood-spattered face. The man who had loved him and guided him as long as he could remember had a frozen look of surprise. John closed his eyes, the sight too horrible to accept. Warm, sticky liquid leaked on his hands. Hot tears forced their way down his cheeks. He'd make Father's killer pay. He'd exact vengeance.

Footsteps clumped through the grass. Father's body limp in his arms, he glanced up.

A stocky man with a crooked nose raced from the shadow of the veranda, and a rifle butt descended. John raised his arms to protect his head, but pain exploded in his skull ... darkness threatened to close over him. He fell to his hands and knees almost on top of his father's body and fought to clear his vision.

This couldn't happen. He had to rescue Mother and Pris. Stop these insane men.

Flames jumped through the windows, singed his shirt, and set fire to the grass. A burning timber fell across his father's body. Violent hands grabbed John's arms and dragged him away from the blazing building. Gravel tore his knees. Rough hands jerked his wrists behind his back and rawhide bit into his flesh. He blinked hard and glared up at the man who rifle-butted him. John shook his head, too groggy to fight the soldier tying his wrists together.

Another ruffian shoved John, and he landed on his back. Drifting on the edge of consciousness, head exploding with pain, John caught scattered glimpses of the marauders' relentless work.

Looters smashed in the windows with their weapons and squirmed through jagged glass to crawl into the unburned portion of his home. Soot-faced thugs, armed with muskets, pistols, and knives, made repeated trips into the flaming house. They emerged, booty loaded on their backs and straining their arms. The raiders grabbed everything from family heirlooms to copper spittoons. One fat man carried a bronze chamber pot on his head.

John tried to squirm into a sitting position. He had to save Mother and Pris. Dizziness forced him to slide down to his side and lower his head. Through tear-blurred eyes, he recognized two of the robbers as neighbors.

Three husky marauders, their calico shirts dark with sweat, strained to steal Mother's rosewood spinet but jammed the beautiful piece in the open front door. As flames devoured the polished wood, the thieves scrambled outside.

Tremors spiked inside John's chest and burst firebrands through the pounding in his head.

Where were Mother and Pris? How could he get to them? When he left this morning, Mother had been sleeping. He hadn't seen her or his baby sister escape. Could she have grabbed Pris and slipped out the back door while Father held off the looters? Or were they still trapped inside their flaming home?

He must help them. Must get them out. He jerked his arms, struggling with the rawhide, but the thongs cut into his wrists and pinned his arms behind his back.

"Dang it. I sure did hanker for thet big house of yourn, but this riffraff they call the Georgia Militia don't obey orders." The man with the crooked nose stood over John. He scowled, seized John's arms, yanked him to his feet, and shook him until John's teeth snapped together. "Your stupid old man put up a fight. He'd still be alive if he'd a come along peaceable." He shoved John hard.

John fell and cracked his left knee against one of the rocks lining the drive. Sharp pain streaked from his knee to his ankle. He grunted.

The man shook his fist at the pillaging troops and kicked the gravel in the driveway. "Dang it! You sorry excuses for soldiers owe me a mansion."

John struggled to his knees, but the world dissolved into blackness. When the darkness receded, intense heat from the inferno scorched his view—or was the fog thick smoke? He didn't know. Nightmarish figures scattered from the house and headed toward the stables.

John felt detached, as though he were somebody else, standing remote above the body lying in the drive. Was he dead? Had his spirit escaped his body? A sense of duty compelled him to mentally record what the soldiers inflicted on the Ross family. He no longer saw the invaders but heard them even above the crackling fire and falling timbers.

"I git that there Jasper. Never did see no horse flesh could beat thatun!" howled a voice rising above the tumult.

Frightened horses neighed and pranced. Then they were loose, galloping down the drive toward where John lay. Eyes wild, they stampeded from the hooting men. The ground trembled beneath John's head with the roar of their escape.

In the lead, the Ross's high-strung chestnut broodmare fell. A loud snap and he knew her leg had broken. She landed so close the bone protruding at an angle almost caught him in the eye. She squirmed, screaming, pawing the earth, unable to regain her feet. One hoof struck John's shoulder and the next few horses sailed over her, but one that followed too closely trampled her. The chestnut's screams echoed in his ears. With a sudden rush of wind, two other animals jumped him.

Sharp pebbles struck his chest and cheeks. Sweat trickled down other horses' legs as they vaulted over him or galloped by.

Greedy men risked being trampled as each tried to rope a blooded horse, some of the fastest in Georgia. Two rough-looking thieves fought for Jasper, John's black stallion. *Lord, please let them fail.* Much better to see his horse run wild than belong to bushwhackers.

Rolling together in the gravel, the bandits bit, kicked, and gouged each other.

John tried to whistle for Jasper. If his horse stopped near enough, he might get a leg over Jasper's bare back. But his lips were dried prunes, his tongue plastered to the roof of his mouth. Even as the two brutes tussled on the path, clawing at each other's eyes, a third man leaped upon John's quarter horse and headed for the woods. John groaned. He loved that horse.

A flying ember landed on his neck, searing his flesh. Each time he inhaled, hot air scorched his lungs. More sparks branded exposed skin. He jerked his hands, but the thongs only cut deeper into his wrists.

He struggled to his knees, but the dizzy blackness returned. Collapsing onto his chest, he wormed over the sharp gravel and reached singed grass, hard and prickly against his body. He rolled over and over until the pressure of a tree against his back stopped him. Here the grass felt soft, the shade cool. He rested his aching head against the lush green carpet, his eyes streaming water.

Shoving each other, the thieving mob broke open the doors of the wooden structures housing the Ross slaves. Looters dragged screaming, fighting, and cringing black women and children outside. A babble of voices merged, with one loud enough to challenge. "I'm gittin' me a slave gal. Take yer hands off her. I had her first. I git her if I got to rip her arm clean off! Leggo, 'fore I shoot you!"

A fox-faced man, greasy hair straggling to his shoulders, tore a crying infant from his mother's arms as another thief dragged the woman onto his horse.

"Hey, Jake, what you want that chile fer?" A nasal Southern voice rose above the tumult.

"My ole lady hankers fer a slave, even iffin she gotta hand raise it." The man cradled the screaming child to his chest and ran for the woods.

Old Mammy Jolene attempted to stand against the mob. "If my man was here, you wouldn't be takin' me nowheres."

"We got them husky field hands 'fore we came here. Surprised 'em. They's tied up safe in them trees yonder. We done put our names on 'em with our knives," a gleeful voice declared.

"Hollingshead, you git these here slaves housed up real good, so's we can pick 'em up when we git back. Rest of you men, c'mon, we cain't play here all day," ordered the crooked nose man who seemed to be in charge. He and another man strode past the flaming ruins of John's home.

Smoke cast a heavy shadow, turning the sky dirty brown and shutting out the sun. The stench of charred wood seared John's nostrils and every breath hurt. Flakes of soot floated thick as rain, to settle in a thin layer over the grass, over the trees, over everything that didn't move.

As though separated from him by a long tunnel, voices echoed strangely before they penetrated his mind.

"Ho, Sergeant. What are we going to do with the lad?"

The rogue turned toward John. "Huh, he still alive? Git him on his feet. He'll be shipped to Indian Territory with the rest of 'em."

The smaller man squatted in front of John. "He don't look any too chipper."

"Dump some water on him an let's git goin'. If he don't git up, shoot him," snarled the man in charge. "Won't git no medals from Gen'l Scott iffen we're late."

"Won't get no medals from Gen'l Scott anyways 'cause of this day's work." The other man muttered and prodded John with a booted foot. "You better git up, kid."

The shock of water drenching his head and face cleared away wisps of the fog. Looking up through a wet film, John shook his head. Pain wrenched a moan from his dry lips. Through the brilliant sparkle of a million spots dancing before his eyes, he strained to see the two men.

"Listen, boy, I want you to hear this. This is from Gov'nor Gilmer, Georgia's finest." The looter pulled a folded paper from inside his butternut linsey-woolsey shirt and unfolded the sheet as formally as an orator. "To Thomas J. Worthington." He patted his broad chest. "That's me, boy. 'For meritorious service in the Georgia Guard: the plantation, Pleasant Acres, now owned by one Elias A. Ross, consisting of 700 acres of tillable plantation land and forest. Signed, Governor George Gilmer, Georgia.'" He waved the paper in front of John's nose. "Deed's all legal and proper, boy."

"Legal? You thieves." John tried to bellow, but his voice rasped. "You're stealing our plantation." He tugged against his ropes.

Sergeant Worthington assumed a brisk, businesslike manner. "Up on your hind legs!"

When John made no move to obey, the sergeant seized John's arm and dragged him upright.

The ground whirled beneath John's moccasins, and he would have fallen without the support of Sergeant Worthington's sweaty arm. John fought bile rising into his throat, hating his weakness in front of these plunderers.

The sergeant shoved him toward the line of trees marking the gravel drive descending to the road. "Git movin', kid."

An acid hole formed inside John's chest as he gazed back over his shoulder. Water dripped from his hair, and his eyes smarted. He'd failed to get Mother and Pris out of the house. The Militia murdered Father, and the US Government stole their land.

A wave of grief slipped through John's anger shield. He gazed at the smoldering gash between two ghostly chimneys where wisps of smoke spiraled from glowing ashes. The black hole had been home these nineteen years and yet, he would not give way to anguish. John stiffened his spine, jutted his chin, and glared at Sergeant Worthington.

"I'll make the Governor of Georgia sorry for this day's work! He'll pay for my father's murder. And you'll hand me back the deed to our property."

CHAPTER 2

His family had expected trouble, but nothing like this nightmare. John set his jaw and narrowed his lips into a rigid line. He clenched his fists against the hate flaming inside his heart. He'd never let Worthington steal this plantation. Never.

The scoundrel curled his lip, spat on the ground, and ran dirty fingers through long, greasy hair.

"Sarge, what makes a man fight when he knows he cain't win?" The sergeant's sidekick scratched his balding head. "The old man must a know'd he was a gone gosling. Him fightin' our whole company. Hard not to admire a fellow like that." He slapped John's back. "But he'd still be alive if he'd a come peaceable."

As if under a wizard's spell, Sergeant Worthington ignored his men and stared wide-eyed at the burned mansion.

John's parallel kick smacked the sergeant in the chest, knocking him flat. His mouth opened like a fish caught on a rock, sucking for air. Off-balance from his kick, John stumbled and fell. Sideways in the dust, he fought the leather cords binding his wrists, squirmed to his knees, and lurched to his feet.

"Sorry, kid." Worthington's sidekick rammed John in the stomach with his rifle butt. "Cain't let you get away."

John doubled, gasped, and struggled to pull in a breath. He groaned, and then retched on the soot-blackened grass.

Black spots shuttered his vision. His heart pumped, but he couldn't catch a breath.

"If I didn't have orders to bring you in, you'd sure as shootin' be gettin' a bullet in your gut." Face red and contorted, Sergeant Worthington lumbered to his feet. "Too bad you weren't gunning at us from inside the house." He rubbed the front of his faded calico shirt with meaty hands. "Then we could've kilt you like we did your old man."

John writhed in the grass. Seconds passed before his breath returned, and new pain stabbed his insides. The sergeant, legs spread, glowered down. "Hear me good, Injin. Even if you ain't got a weapon, you so much as look like you're gonna try anything, it'll be my pleasure to see to it you don't get to drag yourself into the stockade!" He grabbed John's hair and jerked him to his feet. "Orders or no orders."

Sergeant Worthington gave a shrill whistle, and the company of seedy volunteers ranged around John and the sergeant. A soldier, whiskers to his chest, poked John's back with a rifle butt, while a pimply-faced youth aimed a rifle at John's head.

"Lad's spitting image of his old man. Don't know when to give up." The sergeant's sidekick shook his head, his whiskers brushing his chest.

"I'll wager you twenty-to-one this kid don't live long." Sergeant Worthington pulled ten dollars from his pocket, paced around the circle of soot-faced men, and waved the bill.

Hunched over his hurting stomach, John groaned. He was a prisoner. Not a role he'd been groomed for, but he'd do his utmost to disappoint Sergeant Worthington. He would live.

"Okay, you men. This here prisoner is Chief Ross's nephew. Make sure he don't escape." Sergeant Worthington glared at his scruffy volunteers. "And don't give me no more reason to hate y'all." He slammed his rifle butt on the ground. "You fellas on horseback mosey on ahead. Carry as much of this stuff as y'all can. And you, Taylor, get off that black stallion. He's mine."

The sergeant pointed to a group of other men, hands wrapped around their pick of the slaves. "Y'all take charge of them there females and kids and keep 'em here with this here stuff till I get back. We gotta round up the rest of them Injins." He pulled out a bandana and wiped his dripping forehead. "The rest of y'all get your worthless backsides over here and take charge of this here prisoner."

The militia volunteers scattered. Several dozen heavily armed men stayed, their stench gagging John as he fought off their rough hands. They herded him along the carriage drive to the post road.

He recognized one of them. Jeb Taylor. The shiftless man shuffled over and slapped John on the side of his head. John grunted. His ears rang. He blinked to stop the black spots flashing before his eyes.

Oh yes, the Ross family all knew Taylor. The stoop-shouldered man's father and older brother had ignored the boundary between white and Indian land and staked out a homestead on Dragging Canoe's property a year previously. They were just one of the families who moved in and squatted on Indian land. Taylor had tried to court Melissa McIntire. Oh, yes, he knew Jeb.

John's head hurt too much to pay much heed to the squatter, except to note Taylor's bulging forehead veins betrayed his anger about losing Jasper to Sergeant Worthington.

"Ho, Ross, you don't look so high and mighty now." Taylor planted his fists on his waist. "Matter of fact, you don't look no better than any ole slave. How's it feel to be walkin' 'sted of riding that fancy black stallion of yourn?"

The other men chortled as they plodded along the road.

John winced. The thought of another man riding Jasper showed his own helplessness and pushed him to the edge of endurance. He fisted his hands, ignored the pain ripping through his head, and tried to shut out Jeb Taylor's voice.

Another man, his buckteeth chawing on a wad of tobacco, riled up the taunting. "Jebby boy, young Ross can still send Melissa McIntire's heart aflutter. What you gonna do about thet?"

John hauled in a deep breath. His silence wouldn't defuse the situation. Still, he clamped his lips.

Tobacco dribbled down the buck-toothed man's chin. "Even covered with dirt, hands tied behind his back, and walkin' purty, Miss Melissa would likely choose Ross's good-lookin' puss to your ornery one any day. And look at that there physique!" The man drew out the modern word. "Why, it's like comparin' a bull moose with a cow."

The other soldiers guffawed. Didn't appear Taylor was popular with the men. Ribbing him seemed hilarious to them. The soldiers marched faster.

"No man's gonna call me a cow." Taylor, rather than attack the soldier, made a vicious noise and stuck his foot between John's moccasins.

John sprawled onto the road, his chin cracking on the hard-red clay. A savage thrust smashed into his back, and his breath whooshed out.

Jeb Taylor raised his rifle again and shoved John's face into the road. Taylor's heavy boot jammed John's neck, pinning him down.

Dust filled John's mouth, and he fought to breathe.

"Seems to me high and mighty Ross looks more like a worm burrowin' in the dirt than a bull moose. If I cut off your tail, can you grow another?" Taylor's high-pitched voice rose another decibel.

The company of men, drunk with excitement, egged on John's tormentor while John squirmed and fought to rise.

Jeb Taylor ground his boot harder. From what seemed a great distance, a chorus of voices hooted, "I'm bettin' Melissa'd still take Ross!"

From the corner of one teary eye, John glimpsed Taylor's skinny face turn purple as he raised his rifle butt. John lifted a defending shoulder and tucked his head but was helpless to stop the ruthless man's assault.

CHAPTER 3

John gasped for air and swallowed another mouthful of dust.

An authoritative voice spoke, "Hold it right there. Take your foot off the prisoner, you jealous pup. I don't cotton to any man being tormented when he can't defend himself. You want to vent your spleen, William Ambrose's your man."

John recognized Ambrose's voice. He was a white planter who worked his own land adjacent to Indian lands. Most men respected Ambrose for his fairness as much as for his strength.

Taylor ground his boot before he stepped back.

John gasped in a breath, and a groan forced its way up from deep inside. He wheezed and spat out a wad of dirt.

"Jist seemed like a good chance to even scores. Ain't often a fellow like me gets a chance to even scores with a rich bugger."

John pushed himself to a sitting position. His ears rang, and the back of his neck felt raw.

"Help him up." Ambrose jutted his jaw.

"He can get up hisself!"

"I won't tell you again."

Taylor hunkered away from Ambrose, a scowl contorting his face, but he reached down, grabbed John beneath both arms, and yanked him to his feet.

Sergeant Worthington stood by, hands on hips, leering, sweat dripping from his face.

When John straightened, the world spun. He spit more grit, then lowered his head and charged Jeb Taylor. Before he connected with the bully's midsection, several militiamen seized his bound arms and hauled him away.

A huge grin cracked Sergeant Worthington's face as he resumed command. "Cut the funnin' men. We got to get to town afore dark. I want Ross walkin' in, not dragged."

If the militia didn't rest soon, John doubted he'd be walking anywhere. They'd marched through the spongy heat for hours, each step jolting pain through his head. As they trudged through the hot countryside, the motley volunteer soldiers disputed booty and slaves, bickering among themselves, and cursing the heat. Sergeant Worthington rode John's horse ahead of the unruly column.

As the day grew hotter, dust and humidity slowed the jabber until only the scuffle of feet broke the silence. Though his head pounded, John kept every sense alert. The longer his guards walked, the more carelessly the men carried their weapons. Could he find an escape? His gaze darted toward the woods. Too far. Better places waited ahead. Thicker woods. Wider rivers.

"Chow break." Sergeant Worthington pulled Jasper to a halt.

"'Bout time." A chorus of voices called.

Soldiers dropped to the ground where they lounged beneath trees shading the road. They broke rations out of knapsacks or pockets.

One man tugged off his boots. "My feet are swole so big I cain't hardly get my boots off."

"Dratted flies. Pesky things keep swarming on a body when he's sticky." The soldier-for-a-day whisked his floppy-brimmed hat through the air. "Flies are big as June bugs." He pulled his dingy shirt, clinging with sweat, away from his chest. "Must be ninety-eight degrees in the shade."

"Yep. Air's so wet I don't know whether it's sweatin' or I am," Jeb Taylor used his hat to fan his face. "Cain't see why I couldn't have one of them horses. There better be one for me at the next place."

No one offered John water or food. Not that he expected them to. He slumped beneath a tree, unable to find a comfortable position to rest with his hands trussed behind his back. Every bruise ranging up and down his long frame throbbed, and every heartbeat brought a surge of pain to his temples.

He thought of Mother and Pris. Had they survived the fire? Neither Sergeant Worthington nor Jeb Taylor would tell him, and Ambrose sat too far away to ask. John searched his guards for a friendly face.

He turned to a boy—couldn't be more than sixteen—who'd been eating steadily, gun laid across his legs, not saying a word. "Did you see my mother or baby sister?" Silently John cursed his voice for trembling.

"Nobody got out of thet house," Sergeant Worthington interrupted. "When it started burning, it were a tinderbox."

Vomit rose in his throat and flush heated John's sweaty face. He sank back against the tree. The man had to be lying. He had to be.

"If I ever find the rapscallion that set fire to Ross's house, I'm goin' to tar and feather him, after I hamstring him." Sergeant Worthington rubbed the blade of his knife with his thumb and glared at his men through narrowed eyes. "I've been dreamin' of settin' up housekeeping in that mansion for two years. Gilmer and me, we had us a deal ...."

Soldiers yanked their attention up from their food and stared. Sergeant Worthington lowered his head.

Ambrose stooped near John and pressed his water canteen to John's lips. "Don't worry. Your mother and the baby are alive. The pony soldiers waiting at the rear of the house took 'em down the back road short cut."

Thank you, God. The regular army wouldn't molest Mother. Or torture her or Pris with thirst. Since Mother was a gentlewoman, maybe the soldiers gave her a horse to ride.

17

"Ambrose, don't you give that Injin more than a few sips of water." Sergeant Worthington patted some crooked stripes on his calico sleeve. "If you got more water than you need, trot on over here and give it to my horse." He gurgled water from his own canteen, then tipped the brim over his head, and let the liquid splash through his long, sweat-matted hair.

John's tongue felt large and fuzzy against his gritty teeth. Swallowing brought little relief to his parched throat. Yet, tension leaked out of his shoulders—Mother and Pris were alive.

One step at a time, he'd get through this. He leaned against the tree, closed his stinging eyes, and gazed into the mirror of his memory.

Father had been lounging behind his desk in the library and John had folded his six-foot frame onto the horsehair sofa. Mother carried in a tray of mint juleps and iced cakes, her hair shimmering in the light from the chandelier of candles. Tall and slender, she wore a blue silk dress just the color of her eyes. Mother's long skirt rustled when she glided across their Brussels carpet, her flowery fragrance trailing her steps.

She handed John a glass. "No mistaking you and I are kin."

He often mimicked the soft Scotch burr that made her speech so charming. "Aye, we do look related."

Father raised his drink in salute. "Your mother was sweet sixteen when her family left Sutherlandshire, Scotland, and moved to the Virginias. Charity doesn't look a day older tonight."

True enough. Though her honey-blond hair and sapphire eyes sometimes evoked some individuals to envy, Mother had a way of giving her complete attention, making any person she spoke with feel she cared. When she entered a room, conversation gained sparkle and glow.

She moved to the couch, bent, and touched John's cheek. "Seems like only yesterday you hung onto my skirt. Now look at you." She ruffled a hand through his freshly groomed hair.

"Those broad shoulders"—she whisked imaginary dust from his linen shirt—"and you tied your cravat with just the proper careless elegance. You're so strong and confident. Only that reckless light in your eyes betrays your youth. You cut a figure no man in the country can best. You're a McCormac through and through."

John's cheeks burned.

Mother raised her julep in a toast. "To Princeton. Our son will show you what a Southern Scotsman can accomplish."

Smiling, his face alight with love, Father reached for her hand. "No, indeed. Our John's going to show those intellectuals at Princeton what a Cherokee has inside him."

Mother set her glass on the marble mantle, gazed at Father, and showed her dimples. "Elias Ross, we shall not discuss the issue again."

"Your long-nosed ancestors aren't any more honorable than mine!" Father banged his fist on the end table, making the astro lamp jump. "Did you have a better house in the Virginias? Did you own more slaves?"

"Now, Elias," Mother crooned. She knew how to charm his fiery father out of his quick temper. "Our home's the showplace of Georgia ... as elegant as any in Virginia. Otherwise my parents wouldn't have consented to our marriage." Her smile sparkled.

"Hang your parents! I would have married you if I had to kidnap you." Father settled back in his chair and smiled. "Just made life more pleasant with their permission."

Uncomfortable with his parents' words, John jumped up to pace. "Forget all that ancestor nonsense." He added an edge to his Georgian drawl. "I'm as proud of being Cherokee as I am of being descended from Scottish lairds."

Mother, as per usual, had the last word. "John, flaunting your Cherokee blood can only hinder your social life."

Had the conversation been only last night? John opened his eyes to reality and heaved a sigh as he pulled on the thongs binding his wrists. No glossing over his Indian lineage now. To the United States, he was a Cherokee Indian—an unwanted alien. Like snow melting before the spring sun, the white man forced his people off their own land.

Strange to think of himself as Indian. Up to now he'd thought of himself as John McCormac Ross, a young man comfortable in both White and Indian worlds. He tried to shrug away the ache in his shoulders and neck. Like it or not, he was Cherokee ... one-sixteenth, his name on the rolls. No hiding the fact of his heritage.

Sergeant Worthington's voice barged into his thoughts. "Up and at 'em, men. We've got us a whole passel of redskins to capture." Buttons bulging over his outsized paunch, the sergeant wiped his perspiring red face on his dirty sleeve, clutched the pommel of Jasper's saddle, and heaved himself onto the sidestepping horse.

Jeb Taylor bounded up from where he sat behind Ambrose's back, then strode over and gripped John's buckskin shirt. With a jerk that twisted John's neck, Taylor hauled John to his feet and shoved him toward the road.

Ambrose moved to intervene. "Hold on there—"

"Shut up, Ambrose." Sergeant Worthington jabbed his forefinger at William Ambrose. "You go with me." He pointed to half of his soldiers. "And you twenty men come with us. We're splitting up here. We're taking the main road to New Echota."

Worthington turned to Jeb Taylor. "I'm putting you in charge of these twenty rag-tag men who call themselves militia. You head on down the branch road. Take Ross with you. I'm lettin' you have the plum McIntire pickins, so you owe me."

William Ambrose frowned. "That road meanders ten miles farther across country before it intersects again with the main road just outside New Echota. We should take Ross with us."

"That extra hike'll be good for Ross." Sergeant Worthington turned Jasper toward the main road. "I'll meet up with you in New Echota." The sergeant called back over his shoulder, "Make sure Ross's still walkin' when you get to the stockade." He gave Jeb Taylor a broad wink.

The hair on John's nape rose as if he stood too near a lightning strike. He worked at the rawhide binding his wrists, but the sweat-damp thongs tightened.

Taylor ordered, "Okay men, double-time."

"But it's blazing hot."

"March!"

John's body reeked with sweat when they arrived at the first farm on Pine Grove Road belonging to the Raincrow family.

Taylor backed John against a tree and thrust a bayonet against his chest. "Jist so you don't get no idea of being a hero and warning them Injins." He turned to a cohort. "Guard him. If Ross so much as whispers, stuff your bandana into his mouth and use your bayonet on him!" He stuck his face into John's. "Don't you move a hair." Taylor turned away and motioned with a skinny arm, "Follow me men."

John sagged against the tree, his heart beating like a wild thing. What would happen to the Raincrows?

The troops deployed around the building and then burst through the front door. They dragged the aged Grandfather Raincrow into the sunlight, a man revered for his knowledge of ancient legends and who, as a young man, had been a renowned warrior.

Tottering on his cane and looking bewildered, Grandfather blinked at the soldiers. He held up a shaking hand and called a grandchild to translate into Cherokee the unknown English the militia yelled at him. His brown, wrinkled face, impassive as his native Georgian hills, he knelt on the red clay dirt. His six grandchildren slipped to their knees in front of him. In Cherokee singsong style, Grandfather prayed. His quivering voice rang in the hot, still air.

Perhaps because of the old man's dignity or because he didn't resist, the troops handled the man gently when he finished praying.

The soldier guarding John shared water from his almost empty canteen. "If your father hadn't shot at us, you'd not have your hands tied. We don't want to hurt you people. We just need to move you to the stockade."

"Let's go, men." Taylor raised his rifle in a sweeping motion.

The irregulars marched at a fast pace along Pine Grove Road while the old man and the children straggled behind.

Taylor glanced back. "Everett, you lag after us and bring Raincrow and his grandchildren to New Echota. They cain't keep up."

John's guard nodded, trotted back, and took control of the Raincrows.

Prodding John in the side with his rifle butt, Jeb Taylor and the rest of his men marched down the meandering road through a long valley between low, rolling hills. As they came to each farm, the soldiers plundered and took prisoners. During each raid, Taylor ordered John shoved against a tree and guarded with a bayonet.

Hands numb, rawhide cutting into his wrists, John plodded along like a leashed sheep dog watching the wolves ravish the lambs he longed to help.

The ruthless prisoner-taking and house-plundering contrasted starkly with the fertile farms and sturdy cabins, surrounded with post and rail fences that pastured cows and held orchards, they passed. The marchers and prisoners left behind neat barns, pigpens, and poultry yards with animals that looked content and unaware.

At one farm, thirsty soldiers looted a spring house and gulped all the buttermilk and sweet milk cooling inside the clay brick building. They dipped perspiring faces into the cold water that flowed under the spring house. John dropped to his knees and plunged his face into the water.

At each farm, Taylor ran to the stables, swearing if they came up empty. Red-faced, he kicked anything in his path.

John suffered Taylor's hard boot kick his shins more than once.

At each plundered home, Taylor ordered the men to move on and left a guard behind for the slower women and children. He hurried the rest toward Mill Creek Road.

Some Indians hid amid high-tasseled corn. John's heart jumped. Maybe the men would escape. But the irregulars discovered them. Face grim, jaw set, one Cherokee surrendered his hoe—most likely the man had planned to fight off the invaders.

"I obey Chief Ross's command to my Nation not to resist if soldiers came." Bill Talking Tall, the other farmer signaled his son to hand over his gun and surrender.

Exchanging sullen glances with John, they joined him. Bill's small daughter, who must have been carrying water to her father when the soldiers arrived, slipped her hand into her father's and ran beside his long steps, her eyes big with unasked questions.

Surrounded by soldiers, John and the other prisoners crossed Mill Creek. The rickety bridge groaned under their weight. They passed the new gristmill, its immense wooden wheel paddling placidly in the creek, turning the great stone grinding wheels inside.

Miles later, they reached the Echohawk house. Their small son had just died. Through the open cabin door, John saw the child's body lying on a bearskin-covered rope bed. His mother sat beside her baby, smoothing his hair, touching his cheek, caressing his tiny hand. John ducked his head and blinked hard. The militia arrested Mrs. Echohawk and left her child's body in the cabin.

Taylor pranced and scuttled in front of his men and looked to be in a fever. "Get a move on. We've got to reach the McIntire mansion." He walked along the line, tapping the strongest-looking men on the shoulder. "You twelve come with me." He narrowed his eyes and thinned his lips. "You too, Ross." He pointed to his remaining soldiers. "Y'all guard the other prisoners and meet up with me at New Echota. I can't wait around all day with these women and children slowin' me down." He slapped a battered hat against filthy britches.

A shiver spidered John's backbone. Taylor must be after more than a horse. The tough, wiry tyrant sought Melissa. He'd always wanted her. But she would have nothing to do with the squatter. *God, I pray the McIntires got wind of this roundup and fled.*

"Step it up, men. We ain't got all day." Taylor began to jog. Booty and guns rattling, the whole group of them ran the last two miles to the McIntires' plantation.

John had often visited the two-story, white-pillared, colonial structure. After a congenial meal, he'd sat with the family on the lower veranda and enjoyed their view overlooking the valley. Melissa's parents considered John a match for their pretty girl. He liked Melissa just fine but had no intention of settling on one girl for years to come.

As the armed crew approached, the house looked empty.

The stable door stood wide open. Their carriage was missing. Being of mixed blood as was John, the McIntires must have been warned, taken what they could carry, and headed north to live as white people.

When Taylor found there were no horses on the estate, he stomped over to where John stood backed against a tree. Jeb's face had turned purple.

John rolled with the punch Taylor smashed into his mouth. Another busted him in his eye.

John's guard grabbed Jeb's hand. "The men are getting good stuff from the house. You be missin' out."

Jeb turned on his boot heel and sped for the mansion.

John slid down the tree into blessed numbness. Better he took the brunt of Jeb Taylor's wrath than if they'd found Melissa. Pain smarted from so many places. To take his mind off the throbbing, he concentrated on what was happening around him.

His guard sat in the grass, his brooding gaze taking in the looting. "Makes a man ashamed to be part of this outfit." He rubbed a hand over his beard. "If I hadn't stopped Jeb, he would've beat you to death. He sure is mad, and he hates you."

"Yeah. Thanks." John squinted against his pain and watched Taylor carry so much loot from the McIntire house his back hunched like a turtle's shell.

Finally finished, he left a man to guard the booty the marauders couldn't carry with them and headed toward John.

John struggled to his feet.

Taylor laughed. "You gettin' the idea you ain't gonna make it to the stockade?"

John clamped his lips.

Taylor turned to his remaining soldiers. "Let's make up lost time!"

Backs loaded with plunder, the grinning Militia surrounded John and forced him to keep pace.

They reached the farm owned by the Widow Takatokoh. After surrounding the house, the soldiers pounded on the front door. "Come on out."

Mrs. Takatokoh opened the door.

"Surrender and no one gets hurt."

John's heart beat fast. Mrs. Takatokoh had been sick for a long time. The frail widow limped out into the yard, strapped her small son on her back, and patted her old dog goodbye. She took a child by each hand and stumbled away from her home.

They'd only walked a few yards when Widow Takatokoh clutched her chest, fell to the ground, and gasped. "Now I find where the brightness is. Jesus, through the narrow door I go. There is gladness." She died there, with her baby strapped to her back, a child grasping each hand.

"What the heck?" Taylor threw up his hands and gazed at the pitiful body lying at his feet.

John's guard dropped the bundle of loot he carried. "I'll keep the young'uns here 'til the others catch up with us." He unstrapped the baby from the widow's back and transferred the crying child to his shoulders. Kneeling beside the dead mother, he held out his arms to the sobbing children. "I'll hand these three over to that woman who lost her son. I wager she'll be glad to raise 'em."

Taylor nodded. "Good plan." He took a swing at John with his rifle butt.

John dodged.

"Let's go men. Daylight's burnin'. There's one more farm ahead with stock. I'm gettin' me a horse or else."

The afternoon sun beat on John's bare head. He forced his tired legs to keep striding. New Echota was still miles away. They trekked near the Coosawattee River.

The six remaining guards trudged along, strung out in a line, carrying their rifles slung across their shoulders, weighed down with stolen property. A heavy stand of trees towered down river about seventy yards. Their feet thundered on the wooden bridge.

Almost before the thought formed, John broke through the guard, arched into a shallow dive, and plunged into the river. As the water closed over his head, the thunder of rifles cracked.

CHAPTER 4

Kicking hard to propel himself, John headed downstream toward the trees. Had his arms been free, the swim underwater to the forest shelter would have been easy. This wasn't. Once he gained the trees, he could elude the soldiers. Then he would rescue Mother and Pris, and race for the ancient refuge of his people deep in the mountains of North Carolina.

Swimming to the trees was risky but no more dangerous than chancing Jeb Taylor would let him reach the stockade alive. Lúngs burning, he kicked. His ears buzzed ... his head felt dizzy. How far had he forced his way down the murky river? Light spots danced in front of his eyes. Finally, he surfaced.

He gulped a lung full of fresh air and shook water clear of his eyes. Still ten yards to go. His heart thudded—the river was no longer his friend. Shallow near shore, the water gave scant protection from the Kentucky long rifles many of the volunteers carried. Time to leap out and dash for the trees.

Someone thrashing through the brush behind him, made him glance over his shoulder. A handful of men ran along the side of the river, closing in fast. He mustered his strength, gained a foothold in the muddy bank, sunk his feet in solidly, and stumbled out of the water. He sprinted, zig zagging toward the forest.

"There he is. Shoot him!" A voice hailed from the bridge.

John thrust every ounce of strength into a super-human bolt for that last fifteen yards. His legs churned, but he didn't seem to be moving. His world tottered in slow motion.

The soldiers gained on him.

His chest ached.

Each breath whistled through his teeth.

Rifles cracked.

The ground behind his feet exploded into furrows, splattering his bare ankles with dirt clods. His skin tingled, spurring him with extra speed as he leaped into the cover of the trees. Then a stinging pain in the leg, the belated whine of a ricocheted bullet, and he somersaulted through a thicket. He landed on his feet and kept plowing through the underbrush.

Too close behind him came the thud of a soldier throwing his discharged rifle to the ground. Footsteps pounded on his heels. Pain burned his calf and forced him to limp.

"Got 'im! Come on, men, he cain't last long now."

Taylor, again. John dragged his wavering leg but couldn't maintain his pace. Pain streaked from his calf to his ankle and back up to his knee cap. His breath burst through his lungs in agonizing gasps. Just ahead, a deep ravine cut the earth. He gathered his strength for the leap ... Jeb Taylor wouldn't chance the danger.

But Taylor hurtled through the air, and his tackle caught John around the knees. He hit the ground in a bone-jarring tangle. Knocked flat, John tried to kick free. But Taylor's wiry, muscular body, slung sideways across John's back, pinned him.

Two other soldiers arrived and grabbed his ankles. Flat on his stomach, hopeless anger swirled through him. He let his head drop to the ground.

Jeb Taylor laughed long and loud, his weight making breathing difficult. He clutched John's hair and jerked his head back. Pain streaked through his scalp.

"Who's the best man now, Ross? Who's the winner?"

A third soldier ran up and yanked on Jeb's arm. "Come on, Taylor. Get off the kid. He ain't goin' nowhere now. Let's get him on into the stockade. Cain't you see he ain't got no fight left in him?"

"Yeah, Taylor." The soldier grasping John's left ankle released his grip and jerked his thumb in a northerly direction. "Let's go get them horses you been yakking about. The kid's had enough. Leave him alone."

Taylor gave John's head another jerk then stood. "Okay. Two of you men grab his arms and drag him back to the road. Then prod him or drag him, or whatever you got to do to get this here prisoner on over to the stockade. I'm going after them horses."

John grunted. If Taylor did find horses, maybe the animals would stomp the bully to death.

Two soldiers grabbed John's arms and pulled him to his feet. The world tilted, and he swayed. They half-carried, half-dragged him through the grabbing undergrowth back to the road. Once on the hard, dirt road, John could barely force one foot in front of the other. Pain burned a path down his leg from hip to ankle. His buckskin shirt sagged, dripping water.

His vision blurred.

The rhythmic clang of the blacksmith's hammer on the anvil sounded above the soldiers' muffled footsteps as they approached the outskirts of the village of New Echota.

As he entered the town's main street, hard-packed dirt changed into rounded cobblestones beneath his moccasins. They headed toward the Cherokee council house in the center of town where he often sat in on meetings with his uncle when representatives from the seven clans met to legislate. He'd been proud that his nation, under Chief Ross's leadership, patterned their government after the democratic government of the United States.

He frowned at the giant mushroom-like building. American democracy was no longer for him. Two years ago, the US ordered all Indians to vacate their land. But Uncle John advised the Nation to plant crops, spin cloth, and live as though nothing had changed.

One guard shoved John's shoulder. "Get movin'."

John trudged past familiar Indian homes, each with its own garden and orchard, plus the indispensable hothouse.

Strange how peaceful everything looked. Perhaps the soldiers hadn't begun rounding up the Cherokees who lived in town. New Echota bustled with people celebrating sah-looh-stee-knee-heeh-stah-steeh, the Green Corn Festival.

He stumbled and almost fell as he passed the traditional embankment of sand which formed a square in front of the council house. Inside the hard-packed sand area dancers performed ritual dances. Punishment poles stood at the four corners of the square where any person who made a commotion during a dance, which might continue for days, was tied by the wrists until the ritual ended. He'd always avoided making a disturbance. Didn't like public chastisement.

Yet today he'd become a public spectacle.

The soldiers guarding him stopped so abruptly that John stumbled. They gaped at someone inside the raised sand bank enclosure. John focused on a young girl in the center of the square who danced the Friendship Dance.

Ironic!

Breathing heavily, he leaned against one of the punishment poles. He wasn't so far gone he couldn't admire her beauty. She was a rare Cherokee, a full blood. Her skin glowed an elegant sun-toasted brown. She wore white doeskin, her short blouse attached to her doeskin skirt with engraved silver brooches.

The soldiers stared ... some with mouths hanging open ... and stood like statues as the girl gracefully performed the age-old dance.

From somewhere behind the council house, a brawny soldier, clad in a wrinkled uniform, his cap tilted on his large head, staggered toward the girl, knocking people out of his way. A leer contorting his face, the tottering man seized the dancer around her bare waist and forced her into a slobbery embrace. She wrestled one arm free and slapped him. He lurched, blood spurting from his injured nose.

"I'll teach you dirty Injun not to hit a white man!" The soldier pinned her inside a bear-hug, then dragged her, kicking and screaming, behind the council house.

John felt rooted to the cobblestones and hot blood pumped adrenaline into his veins. He tugged his bound wrists and glanced at the numerous townsfolk. Was there no man nearby with a shred of decency?

The onlookers stared, eyes wide. No man came forward.

A deep sigh worked up from John's chest. Someone had to help her. He rolled his eyes, pulled in a deep breath, lowered his head, and shouldered through the guards. But the soldiers closed rank and wrestled him back.

A voice thundered from the far side of the council house. "Soldier, take your hands off that girl! Your orders are … no molesting!"

John quit struggling and breathed easier. The command must have come from a man of authority. Perhaps General Scott himself.

Walking carefully straight, a grim expression plastered on his broad face, the subdued soldier strolled toward John's guards. He gripped the girl by the arm and pulled her along. He hiccupped, and the reek of whiskey assaulted John's nose.

The dancer, chin high, eyes narrowed, fought the soldier's grasp. Only the bright color in her cheeks and the pulse throbbing in her throat betrayed her distress.

The drunken soldier pushed the girl into the circle of guards surrounding John. "Take thesh prisoner on over to the stockade. I need a drink. Prisoners is your job. See you do it." He reeled away.

White people in the crowd gazed at John and the girl, as though they had never seen Indians before, as though they had not bartered with them, as though they had not neighbored with them. The sight of him battered and with his hands lashed behind his back didn't dampen the town's holiday atmosphere. He and the beautiful girl had become entertainment. People he knew gaped and murmured.

Did they think he was a criminal?

The soldiers-for-a-day militia trooped through the crowd, herding the girl and him toward New Echota's central well.

John licked dry lips. One soldier removed a lid of sawed boards. Another cranked the windlass, and a bucket creaked down. The man cranked it back up, brimming with sparkling water. John swallowed hard.

Soldiers crowded the well and elbowed each other for a drink. One man offered the girl some water. John stepped toward the well, but two guards forced him to shuffle back to the grassy area beneath a tree. He sank to the ground, pillowed his head on a protruding root, and closed his eyes. The surrounding noise receded, and the ache in his head lessened.

A sweet, husky voice nudged him from blessed numbness. "You look like you need a drink."

Even before he opened his eyes, he knew the voice belonged to the girl in the white doeskin.

She knelt at his side, a gourd full of water in her hand.

John wormed into a sitting position.

She held the container to his lips.

He gulped the water. As the cool liquid slid down his parched throat, he tried not to stare at her beauty.

Large brown eyes, shaded with long lashes, gave her face an exotic appearance. Her nose was slender above full lips, and thick black hair flowed down her back, reaching well below her waist.

"So, this is what a man saved from death feels like. Thanks." He sounded hoarse.

"Physical death, maybe." The undertone in the girl's voice hinted she had a different meaning in mind from his. "I'll wash the dried blood off your forehead, then I'll bring you more to drink."

Each word she spoke left a delightful impression in his weary brain. Taking a soft, wet cloth, she dabbed coolness on his forehead. If he'd been a cat, he would have purred.

She rolled up his blood-saturated trouser leg. "That's a nasty gash."

Cool water smarted his wound, and he jerked upright.

"Looks as if a bullet grazed you." Admiration brimmed from her warm gaze. "You tried to escape, didn't you?"

"Didn't succeed."

The girl left to refill the gourd. When she held the life-giving water to his lips again, he tried not to gulp. Her exotic eyes roused a strange sensation in the pit of his stomach.

"Why are your hands tied?"

"The militia considers me dangerous." He raised a wry brow, strengthened some by the water.

"I should think so!" Her brown eyes sparkled.

"Misplaced admiration. I'm not."

The guards drank their fill from dripping gourds, then milled around the well or lolled on the grass. With Taylor gone and so many townsfolk nearby to help catch him if he attempted to escape, his guards no longer seemed to care what he or the girl did.

She touched John's bruised forehead with her wet cloth, then washed dust from his blackened eye and swollen lip. "You fought them?"

He frowned. "No, I had no opportunity." He turned away. "I don't want to talk about it."

She touched another full gourd of water to his lips. "My name is Rachael Whiteswan." She enunciated as though English were not her first language. "I have seen sixteen summers. My clan is the Wolf."

A burst of disappointment soured the moment. He clamped his lips. He'd not admit he belonged to the Wolf Clan as well. What she didn't know wouldn't hurt her. He pulled in a deep breath. "Name's John Ross from Pleasant Acres."

"Oh!" A blush colored Rachael's sun-browned face. Long eyelashes nearly brushed her cheeks as she shyly lowered her head. "I didn't know. I mean, I couldn't tell." She glanced at the bloodstained, torn, sopping buckskin he wore. "Are you Chief Ross's son?"

He shook his head. "Nephew."

Her lovely face remained downcast. "You live near Spring Place in the mansion on the hill above the Conasauga River?"

"Lived in the mansion. They burned my home." He didn't attempt to keep the bitterness from his voice.

"Oh, I'm so sorry."

A horse and rider trotted toward the well. The sun in his eyes, John saw little more than silhouettes.

"Let's go, you vermin!" Sergeant Worthington shouted. "Break's over." He spurred Jasper toward the well.

John jutted his jaw at the lather foaming Jasper's withers.

Sergeant Worthington trotted Jasper around his troops, chest puffed out like a rooster. "Hurry it up. I ain't got all day." Jasper's hoofs clattered on the cobblestones as the sergeant's sidekick herded the other set of prisoners toward the well. The Indian men hung back to let the women and children drink.

Sergeant Worthington spurred Jasper toward where John sat. Just in time, John struggled to his feet and dodged out of the way of Jasper's hooves.

The sergeant did want him dead. Then there could never be a legal claim to the plantation Worthington had stolen. So, the winks to Jeb Taylor had meant to make sure John never made it to the stockade. He clamped his jaw. Well, he was alive. And he would keep on living. But Sergeant Worthington's harassment was hard to swallow, especially in front of Rachael. The more the sergeant hassled him, the more John squared his shoulders and held his head high, a deliberate gesture to get under Sergeant Worthington's skin

The sergeant ignored John's silent taunts. "Quick, men. Form these prisoners and their children into family groups."

The children's slumped shoulders and lax faces showed how tired they were.

"Herd them toward the meadow outside of town." He ignored their cries of hunger.

John leaned against the well support as the Indians walked past in groups, dignity in their postures. A guard prodded him with his rifle barrel until he and Rachael formed their own small group and joined the other prisoners.

Though more tired than he could ever remember being, drinking the water and meeting the girl gave him a second wind. To divert his mind from how much his wrists hurt, he spoke to the girl walking by his side. "Where are you from, Rachael?"

"High in the hills, near Stony Rock Creek. I came to New Echota for the festival. My mother taught me the Friendship

Dance before she died." Rachael spoke with a husky, matter-of-fact voice. "There aren't many girls these days who know the steps."

"We've lost too much of our Indian way of life. We were wrong to follow the white man's path." John frowned. "Warriors would have fought for their land." He stumbled but righted himself. "Father didn't cave in and let the army grab our land." A wave of respect washed over him, soothing some of his bruised feelings.

"Did they kill him?" Rachael shivered in the fading sunlight, then grasped his arm to help him limp along.

Suddenly, he wanted her to know the whole story. "Father must have realized he couldn't win. I think he tried to warn me away. If I'd been home, we would all have escaped on our horses. Instead, he fought alone. Not just today's detachment of soldiers, but the entire United States Army."

She tightened her grip on his arm.

"Father and Uncle John fought for our rights under the Constitution in Washington, but nobody cared. Today he fought with his rifle and lost again."

Rachael smiled a sad little smile. "If he had surrendered, would he be alive?"

John frowned and flexed his numb hands. River water had tightened the rawhide, and the bonds cut into his flesh. "If Father hadn't fought, he'd be a prisoner. I think he made the best choice."

Rachael strode beside him in silence. A few minutes later, she whispered, "I'm going to untie your hands. They're swollen and purplish looking."

He glanced at the soldiers surrounding them, weapons lowered or slung carelessly over a shoulder. Sergeant Worthington was nowhere in sight, and the militiamen looked tired. Some carried small children on their shoulders, and one man helped an older woman walk. Chattering townspeople clustered on both sides of the road. Way too many people crowded around to attempt escape.

"Thanks!" He turned his back so she could get to the leather binding. She struggled with the knots.

Several militiamen eyed them, expressions unconcerned.

"My knife's on my ankle," he whispered. "I don't think the militia consider me much of a threat now that we're close to the stockade. But be careful."

Moving stealthily, Rachael tried to extract his knife from his ankle sheath. They walked slower, but she couldn't reach the blade. He stopped. Rachael retrieved the knife and sawed at the taut leather.

"I'm trying not to cut you, but the rawhide sinks into your wrists."

When the thongs fell to the ground, he grinned. Flexing his shoulders and arms, he tried to work the stiffness out. His hands, swollen twice their size, were a strange, mottled color. His fingers were clumsy when he palmed his knife from Rachael. He dropped his weapon—he had lost his sense of touch.

A soldier stepped over and grabbed the knife. Other soldiers watched but made no move to retie his hands.

Rachael looked crushed. Was her expression due to the condition of his hands or about losing his knife?

"How are your hands now?"

"Can't feel anything, they're numb. My arms and shoulders hurt as if I've been tortured on the rack." He clenched and unclenched his hands, trying to restore circulation. "I owe you."

He sighed. "You showed courage risking yourself to help me. Look, Rachael, thanks for cutting my hands free, but you must be careful. These men don't play games."

His words didn't seem to affect her. She smiled as if she knew something he didn't.

"What? You don't believe me?"

"God will not permit me to die until it is his will that I go to be with him." She used both hands to smooth her abundant hair back over her shoulders.

He shuddered. Today, his heart had been ripped out, leaving a bleeding hole in his chest. "That's crazy talk! I saw death come violently today. How can murder be God's will?" Did this girl think she was immune to violence because she believed in God?

He hunched his shoulders. Still, if what he expected lay ahead for her, she would need all the encouragement she could get. For her sake, he stuffed his anger inside, sure his ears would pop. "Okay, so maybe you're right."

In front of them, a small boy began to cry. Rachael stooped to kneel beside him. "What's wrong, little one?" She stroked his arm.

"I want Mommy! I'm hot, and I'm tired." He ground chubby fists at the tears in his eyes.

"How about a horsey ride?" The soldier walking beside John grinned at the child. The boy smiled through his tears as the soldier swung the boy up on his shoulders.

Mrs. Echohawk looked back at him, her black eyes grateful. She already carried a baby on her back and a slightly older boy trudged at her side.

"What's your name, chief?" John asked the sniffing child who clutched the soldier's head with both chubby hands.

"I'm Little Eagle. Sometimes Ma calls me Joseph." He snuggled into the back of the soldier's neck.

"Little Eagle, you can ride the rest of the way." The soldier gave a playful prance.

The boy laughed and hammered his little fists against the soldier's collarbone. "Giddy-up, horsey."

Their bedraggled group finally reached the stockade. The tall enclosure ran through the center of a large meadow surrounded by thick forest. The prison looked formidable. Escape proof.

Suppressing a grunt, John gauged his chances. Slim to none. His shoulders slumped. Just last month when he'd come to town for supplies, the stockade hadn't been here. The raw staked prison looked about a hundred yards long with trees, sharpened and set picket-style into the ground.

The soldier slid Little Eagle to the ground and handed him off to John. "You take him from here."

The boy grinned up at John and clutched his good leg. "Are you my father now?"

Throat too tight to answer, John smiled and ruffled the child's dark hair.

"Come, Little Eagle," the boy's new mother called.

Little Eagle hugged John's leg tighter, then ran off to her.

John squinted at the prison. On all four sides of the stockade, the army pitched their tents in neat, parallel rows.

"Looks like a city living under canvas." Rachael shaded her eyes. "Those soldiers must be boiling hot in those tents when they sit inside during the day."

"Too bad." John rubbed his raw wrists.

Dusk caught up with them.

Two armed men, slouched on either side of the stockade's heavy, double doors, jumped to attention, the setting sun glistening on their guns. One soldier lifted the heavy latches and opened the doors.

John turned to glance back at the open country. A brilliant sunset of purple, pink, and scarlet painted the darkening sky. The glow bathed the rolling countryside, tinting the earth golden where sky and mountains met in purple haze. In the meadow, wild geranium, wild gooseberry, and trees entwined with wild grapevines taunted him with their freedom. He cleared his hoarse throat. "The end of life as we lived it."

"The white man can imprison my body, but not my spirit," breathed Rachael.

"Good thought. We'll see if your words turn out to be true." John took a last look at the familiar countryside, then together they trudged through the massive doors.

The tall wooden gates swung shut behind them with a heavy thud.

CHAPTER 5

Once the stockade doors slammed shut behind them, John hardened his jaw.

"Ho, Ross, don't fret about that plantation." Sergeant Worthington's voice floated from outside the barred doors. "I aim to take mighty good care of that beautiful property."

"You won't own it long!" John yelled so loud his throat hurt. He clamped his teeth, then pounded his fist against the undressed logs.

Hearty laughter leaked through the barricade.

John surveyed his prison. How soon could he escape? Two small enclosures, constructed of logs chinked with clay, extended into both ends of the stockade. Naked red clay lay beneath his damp moccasins. No meadow grass. No trees.

The tight pressure trapped inside his chest almost bested the set of his jaw.

The stockade teemed with people, noise, and foul smells. Babies squalled. Dozens of men stomped around calling to and hunting for wives and children. Women with furrowed brows, panic twisting their expressions, searched for children or husbands who'd been working the fields when the soldiers seized them.

John wedged his fingers into his ears to shut out the clamor. Prisoners of every variety, ranging from the very poor to the very rich and the very young to the very old trampled the clay. Some Indians wore night clothes, some tall hats, and others basic calico. White and brown people and all shades between milled together. Only a dazed look of bewilderment bonded the swarming humanity.

He scanned the crowd. Surely Mother and Pris arrived hours ago. He wove through the people, searching. As dusk darkened, he grew more agitated, and his pace increased. When the sun slid below the mountains, he still hadn't found his family.

A shot rang out.

Instant silence.

Soldiers pushed through the prisoners, separating the men and boys and herding them into one building and the women, girls, small children, and babies into the other. John hung back, inspecting the remnant of the crowd. Where was Mother? Still no Mother or Pris. A uniformed man prodded him with his rifle.

John frowned. "Okay. Okay." He stooped and entered the windowless men's building, the atmosphere, stifling. Dim light filtered in between the boards penetrating the darkness. The stench of human sweat pinched his nose. On the dirt floor, men and boys sat, legs hunched, sandwiched as tight as pickles in a glass jar.

He stumbled over prone and seated males until he found a space and squeezed between two men. A sick, dizzy feeling warned him to lower his head between his knees. Good thing his stomach was empty—the way it churned, he would have vomited. Then he would have had to sit in his own mess. Judging by the rank odor, someone else had not been so fortunate.

A tall boy stepped on John's hand, and pain shot up his arm. He began to shake—sweat poured from his body. The sea of noise slapped his ears. His stomach roiled from the foul air and the oppressive heat. The lack of space, combined with his pounding temples, threatened to make him lash out. He clenched his numb fists. He had to get out!

A hand touched his shoulder. A bass voice, soothing as a mountain stream, rumbled beside him in the dark. "A bit much, isn't it?"

John expelled the breath he'd been holding, and his rigid body relaxed enough to let his shoulders slump.

"The guards release us at first light," the comforting voice continued. "The secret to adjustment is to remain calm. Relax as much as possible—mind above circumstances. Take slow, deep breaths. You can overcome this situation. My name is Isaac Worchester."

John forced himself to breathe deep and slow. As his eyes grew accustomed to the darkness, he made out a form sitting next to him, leg jammed against his wounded one. Of slight build and short stature, the man wore a pair of eyeglasses perched on his nose. From the rich quality of his voice, John had expected a strapping man.

"I assume you haven't eaten." Worchester squeezed his arm. "The soldiers promised to give us our food allotment tomorrow at midday. I doubt it will be appetizing but should suffice."

At the mention of food, John's stomach cramped. He wrapped his arms around his middle to quiet the rumble. No food until afternoon? The tug of war in his empty stomach upped the pain in his head.

"Do you have any injuries, son?" Worchester's friendly voice probed.

"Yes, sir. I got a rifle butt in the head this morning ... my forehead feels like it's going to explode. Then an *old friend* took his ire out on me—shut one of my eyes and busted my lip. A bullet grazed my leg. Must not be too bad, but it's painful." John tried to shift into a more comfortable position but was wedged securely. "Other than ravenous, thirsty, dead tired, aching in every muscle, and having an exploding headache, I'm in good shape."

"I have some herbs. We'll make a poultice with my handkerchief and wrap it around your leg. Old Indian remedy." Worchester chuckled. "The bandage will help no matter how bad the injury. Did your wound bleed clean?"

"Yes, sir. Blood soaked my pant leg."

"Unfortunately, I've used my supply of medicinal herbs or I could give you something for your head. I'll brew a special tea tomorrow. The soldiers promised to let the girls gather roots for me."

"I'm grateful for your help, sir. Are you a medicine man?"

The low, rumbling laugh reminded John of pleasant times. "No, I'm as far from being a shaman as I can think of. I'm Reverend Worchester. Been a missionary to the Cherokee for the past five years. I was interested in their healing arts, so studied all I could in my free time." Worchester shifted position and took some of the pressure off John's leg. "Good remedies too. Without any hocus-pocus magic, I might add. Nothing mystical about the procedure. Just using the balms the good Lord provided."

John let out his breath. Odd. Worchester was the second religious person he'd met today. And liked. Had to be a conspiracy.

"I have permission from General Scott to lead a worship service every day starting tomorrow. Eight o'clock in the morning, the soldiers open the stockade doors. Those who wish to attend may leave under guard." Worchester's teeth gleamed through the darkness as he smiled. "The army allows us to sit under the trees. The girls stay within earshot, so they don't miss the sermon while they gather roots and herbs for medicine. I hope you will join us."

John shook his head, not swayed by the man's persuasive voice. Not here. Not today. He wasn't interested. "No thank you, sir. I'll drink your brew, and I don't mean to be rude, but I can't believe in your God. Not after what I've been through this day."

John fought through the blanket of sleep and a fog of pain.

Was someone watching him? He opened his eyes. The person knelt exactly where his senses pinpointed. Copper red hair, though grayed at the temples, gave the man a youthful appearance. Inquisitive green eyes peered through spectacles.

"How do you feel this morning, young man?"

The deep timber of his voice told John the man was Worchester. John pushed himself to a sitting position and touched his head. Fierce pain. The slightest movement awakened new twinges. "Ever have a war party dance on your head, sir?" His puffy lip made his smile feel crooked.

"Glad to see you have a sense of humor."

John scanned the log enclosure and raised a brow. He and Worchester were alone inside the hot, humid building. Sweat soaked his hair. Squinting at the sun bursting through the open door, he rubbed the back of his neck. How had he slept so late?

"You don't look any better than you feel. You have a nasty bruise covering your temple, extending down to your left eye. Your right eye is black, and your mouth swollen." Worchester stood up as though his legs had stiffened from squatting. "I got concerned when you didn't wake. I thought it best to return and check on you."

Unfolding his long frame by painful segments, John stood erect. The drab room spun, and the floor tilted. He leaned against the wall. When the dizziness receded, he took stock of the man who cared enough to look in on him. Worchester's bright head reached to John's shoulders. A warm feeling swept over him—he liked the man and his generous personality.

"You slept through today's service. The girls gathered a mixture of herbs and roots this morning while I preached. I fancy the brew they make will help that head of yours."

"That's handsome of you, sir. I appreciate your concern."

Following the shorter man, John stepped through the door. Sunlight hit him like a physical blow. He winced and squinted. Out of temper, his lips dry as the red Georgia dust, he ran a hand through his long hair. "My mouth tastes as if the militia marched through last night, followed by the pony soldiers."

Worchester laughed. "I've got just the thing for you. Follow me." The preacher waved his hand toward a campfire in the center of the stockade. Jon shortened his long steps to walk beside the pastor.

The stockade sounded quieter this morning, with most people lolling against the fence or walking about. But the high walls closed in, and he fought an enormous urge to pace the enclosure like a cougar in a trap. John shortened his long steps to walk beside the pastor.

Other faces reflected tethered irritability. Only Worchester had a smile and a word of encouragement for each person he passed. He led John to a campfire where a steaming kettle hung from a tripod.

John's stomach growled.

Worchester dipped a gourd into the simmering liquid which wafted a distinctly medicinal aroma.

John wrinkled his nose.

"Here. Like I said, this brew will help that head of yours." Worchester handed him a gourd full of the medicine.

The smell brought back memories of house calls from Mother's doctor, but this concoction had a different, distinctive odor he couldn't place. He lifted the gourd to his lips and took a sip. The tart taste, just short of being bitter, was wet—his dry mouth soaked in the liquid. Even before the gourd was empty, drowsiness calmed his caged-animal agitation. The sharp pain knifing his brain dulled. His taut nerves loosened and his knotted stomach relaxed. Through a haze of woozy relief, he watched Worchester walk away, probably on some other errand of mercy.

Now to locate Mother in this throng. Most of the anguished faces around him were those of strangers. Had Uncle John been wrong when he advocated no resistance? Perhaps the passive fatality of the Indian mind, which neither questioned nor complained but loyally obeyed the decree of their chief, brought its own destruction. Still, fighting back hadn't been possible. Soldiers had long ago confiscated the Nation's arms, and even the war chief committed to Uncle John's path.

A rough hand clapped him on the shoulder. Pain shot through his head.

"John, where's your uncle?"

He shoved off the hand and turned.

Micah Water Spider frowned at him.

John didn't have much use for the spare little Indian with the wispy goatee.

Micah's dark gaze darted over John's hair, his moccasins, his left arm, but never met his eyes.

The man was John's elder, so was due respect. "Good morning, Mr. Water Spider. The last I heard, Chief Ross still works in Washington attempting to remind the President that the US government granted our land to us in a legal treaty for as Long as Rivers Run. Two days past, I crossed the Oostanaula River, and the water ran high."

Water Spider grimaced. "We know how the white man breaks treaties."

"But Chief Ross holds a petition, signed by a majority of our brothers proving the few signers of the Removal Treaty are guilty of treason." Looking above Water Spider's head, John scrutinized the multitude. Where was Mother? Why couldn't he find her?

"Yes, yes. I am aware of these matters. I signed the petition. I thought you had received a letter." Water Spider's hand shook as he tugged at his beard. "Perhaps we shall be released soon. The authorities can't hold us long in this inhumane prison. Someone made a terrible mistake."

John shifted his stance. "I must find Mother."

The older man clutched John's arm. "Yesterday's Banner and Wig was full of America's fear that some states would secede from the Union. There were editorials on the slavery issue but not a word about our problem. What can Chief Ross be doing?"

"Uncle John wrote that President Jackson wields power now, and he refuses to see my uncle. However, as long as my uncle remains in Washington, we can hope for release." Not much hope. Since a circle of listeners clustered around them, John kept his true thoughts to himself. "Excuse me, sir. I'm seeking my mother. Have you seen her?"

Water Spider shook his head. His brow still furrowed, but his mouth now tilted up instead of down.

As John plodded through the enclosed stockade, he recognized an acquaintance here and there. He shook a hand or bowed, but his heart grew heavier. Whites married to Indians had been imprisoned along with their spouses. Had no one living on Cherokee land been spared? People he'd seen watching the Green Corn Dance last evening during the celebration looked as confused as he felt. Appeared as if not a person with one drop of Cherokee blood walked free in Georgia today.

But where were Mother and Pris? An unreasonable hope built inside his chest. Perhaps Mother had not been brought here. He searched the entire stockade, then stopped and reassessed.

There she was.

An arrow flew to his chest. Mother had not been spared. She blended into the background, sitting on the red clay dirt in a narrow strip of shade cast by the women's building. She leaned against the log siding shading her azure eyes from the sunlight. At least she wasn't wearing bedclothes like some of the other prisoners. She looked delicate and out of place. He'd never seen her sit on the ground ... not even on the lawn under the shade trees. A slave always brought a chair.

Dodging between milling people, he limped through the crowd toward her.

Her face lit with a smile, mother jumped up and rushed into his arms. "Darling, I recognized that unmistakable thrust of your shoulders. You look awful. But you're alive! I was so worried."

He hugged her. Could her slender frame withstand imprisonment? "Where's Pris?" His voice broke like a boy's.

"Rachael has her. I went out looking for you, and Rachael thought I might find you more easily if I weren't carrying Pris." Mother gave him a dazzling smile. "I don't know how this happened, but last night in that awful women's building I met the one person who could give me news of you. Such a relief to discover you are safe. I don't believe I would have survived last night without Rachael. She's a dear girl. Come, Son, sit and tell me everything."

They talked. John told her of his trip to the stockade, leaving out the harsher details.

She told him an officer had given her his horse, so her journey had not been so bad nor as long. Perched in the saddle in front of her, Pris slept through much of the trip. John avoided any mention of his father and their burned home. His mother didn't mention Father either.

Rachael joined them and settled beside Mother. Priscilla slept, a peaceful expression on her face, cradled in a shawl fastened beneath the toddler's small body and draped over Rachael's shoulder.

"Rachael and I became close friends during the night." Mother touched Pris's rounded cheek.

Warmth curled around John's heart.

The two women looked a study in opposites. Mother tall, blonde, her pale complexion like the petals of a white rose, appeared fragile but self-assured. Rachael, tall, brown-skinned, and shy, looked very much a daughter of the land.

Isaac Worchester strode across the compound to the center of the stockade. "Come, folks! Let us gather together for strength and encouragement from our Lord. General Scott has given permission for a second service since today is the Sabbath." The preacher motioned toward the double-gated doors.

Rachael rose, murmured something in Mother's ear, and her smooth, supple stride took her and Pris into the crowd churning toward the gates.

"Please come, John. Rachael tells me some interesting things I had not thought of before." Mother's sky-blue eyes looked expectant. "Besides, it's far cooler outside this stockade beneath the shade of the trees." She tugged on his sleeve.

Lines etched creases around her mouth where none had been yesterday, but the soft chin was set. Though his heavy heart rebelled, he reached for her slender hand and placed her fingers in the crook of his arm. They joined the crowd pressing toward the open doors.

One guard scrutinized them as they passed. The other uniformed man thrust his rifle against John's chest, shoving him to a standstill. "The rule is you give your word of honor you won't try to escape." He punctuated his snarl with another shove.

The soldier resembled a coyote with his pointed ears, skinny face, and long nose. John kept his expression impassive, gazing over the guard's head toward the woods.

"Certainly, we give our word." Mother used the chiding voice she reserved for gossipy females. "Our purpose is to hear the Reverend Isaac Worchester's message. That's why he is here in this overgrown pigsty. He's sacrificing his own freedom to minister to us." She looked the coyote up and down. "Not many men have such nobility of character."

Red flooded the guard's face. He lowered his rifle, caution in his expression.

The other guard scowled. "I don't like the looks of that breed. Kid ain't got all the fight beat out of him yet. He don't look to me like he's goin' to any church meeting." He shoved his rifle against John's chest. "Give me your word."

"You've got it."

"I'll have my eyes on you!" The soldier lowered his rifle and let them pass.

With Mother's hand tucked onto his arm, they strolled outside the massive double gates. The cool shade of the trees beckoned. He and Mother sauntered across the open ground toward where Rachael sat, her back resting against a tree, cradling Pris.

Rachael smiled.

John's heart hammered like a blacksmith beating on a fiery horseshoe. But the blood rushing through him made his forehead ache. They settled beside her, his mother sharing the tree back rest and John sitting cross-legged facing them, his back to the flock of sheep who watched the preacher.

The slight breeze outside the stockade and the shade of the tree cooled his hot forehead but not the anger blasting his heart. He squinted in the bright sunlight. Beyond the prison, miles of mountains stretched on in triple peaks. Though he saw them every day of his life, never did he look at those majestic peaks without feeling kinship. He mumbled aloud, "Spirits of the mountains ... worshiped by my Cherokee ancestors in the dim days of antiquity ...."

But he couldn't concentrate. Worchester owned a compelling voice. A man with a voice like his should be in Washington persuading government leaders, not here preaching.

Instead of listening, John focused on the soldiers. So, this was the army that defeated Great Britain, the most powerful army in the world. Not that impressive. Still, didn't seem as if those men needed the Georgia Militia. Maybe regular soldiers didn't like rounding up innocent people and locking them in prison.

The army and the rag-tag militia weren't mingling, each congregating in different groups over the meadow. John couldn't see the end of their bivouac. To his left, six men in unbuttoned uniforms pitched horseshoes. Stripped to the waist under the hot sun, they wrangled among themselves. Two broke away from the group to measure the distance between horseshoes. Faint voices, hooting and hollering, came from another knot of men wagering on the outcome of a wrestling match. Crowds hid the contestants, but dust swirled around the boots of the audience.

The army owned beautiful horses. Some were probably animals the militia confiscated. Sure enough, he recognized a neighbor's bay Tennessee walking horse, with his rocking-chair gait. A pale Arabian, its flanks lathered, galloped by. That jackass racing her in this heat must be one of those saddle boys from Washington Uncle John spoke about, all political pull and no practical experience. Four matched Morgan horses were tethered near two light howitzers. What did the army plan to do with those cannons? Use them on women and children?

A vein in his forehead began to throb.

"But He was wounded for our transgressions, He was bruised for our iniquities." The words Worchester spoke penetrated before John closed his ears again.

John returned his attention to analyzing his surroundings. The stockade was built solid—had to be about ten feet tall—with sharpened stakes and no visible break in the wall. No other guards posted except the two at the gate. They must be confident the prison was escape proof.

Several feet this side of the stockade, the Conasauga River splashed a rocky path into thick forest. The sound of tumbling waters whispered below Worchester's melodic bass voice. A swim would ease John's aches and cool his sweaty skin. Near the stream a group of girls gathered yarrow, wild lettuce, mustard greens, and wild onions. They looked lovely as they stooped among the tall grasses, but none compared to Rachael.

John wiped sweat from his forehead. How long could men be imprisoned with women before they crossed the line of morality? He wasn't the only man watching the maidens. Groups of soldiers sprawled under the trees leered at them.

John set his jaw and gazed beyond the guard.

Mountain laurel, wild indigo, crepe myrtle, and azalea grew thick by the river. If his thirst was not so urgent, the heat not so intense, his stomach not so empty, and the preacher's voice not so annoying, he might have enjoyed the scene. The blues, reds, and lavenders, lavish against the green grass, and the sparkling water presented a gorgeous view.

He glanced at Mother. She stared at Worchester, her chin cupped in her hand as though making an evaluation. Mother had a quick, logical mind. If the preacher engrossed her, he must be saying something worthwhile.

"He was oppressed, and he was afflicted, yet he opened not his mouth."

John ground his teeth.

"He is brought as a lamb to the slaughter, and as a sheep before her shearers is dumb, so he openeth not his mouth."

Worchester's words burned into John's chest, somewhere near the region of his heart. He clenched his fists. He gritted his teeth so tight his jaw throbbed. That's just what the white man's government had done! Cherokee were stupid sheep. Ridiculous to submit. He jerked to his feet.

Mother looked up, alarm on her pale face.

Rachael's dark eyes widened.

John strode away, moccasins slapping the grass so hard the bottoms of his feet smarted. Shoulders rigid, mouth tight, strong emotions chafing inside, he headed for the thick woods. He crossed the meadow and was about to enter the first row of trees.

Of course, we shall not try to escape, echoed in his mind. He couldn't bring dishonor to Mother. What would they do to her if he ran? Besides the woods bristled with more soldiers than a porcupine had quills.

He ground to a halt and turned back toward the stockade.

A flash of light reflected from the barrel of a gun.

The sharpshooter had him sighted.

CHAPTER 6

John's heart pounded, and his stomach tightened into a hard knot. The sharpshooter would have shot him down like a wild dog.

The coyote dropped his rifle to his side. "Tarnation! One more second, and I would a kilt you."

John sauntered the last few yards to the stockade, trying to relax his shoulders and appear nonchalant. "Sorry to disappoint you. No target practice today," he lashed out as he reached the gate.

"Blast and bewhiskered! Not today, but I'm a waiting. The only good Indian is a dead one." The guard's smirk sealed his promise.

John gnashed his teeth and held his head higher. Being treated as less than human rubbed his feelings raw. He must remain clear-headed and not give hecklers a foothold in his soul. He was as good as any man. Better than that coyote.

Inside, the stockade blazed hot, with no shade and no breeze whispering through the tightly picketed poles. Not a person here. Should have controlled his temper. He could be sitting under the trees. This place was an inferno.

Sticky with sweat, he pulled the buckskin shirt up exposing his chest. Several flies clustered over to light on him. He slapped them so hard a red mark rose on his skin. More than likely, the prison swarmed with flies because no sanitary facilities existed other than holes in the dirt behind the two buildings. Surely, they'd only be kept prisoners a few days at the most.

Shoulders hunched, he stalked past the women's building. Since the door stood wide open, he peered inside the empty structure. Identical to the men's but smelled worse. Must be the babies and small children. He scowled and kicked the wooden-planked door. A rat scurried out and ran away. A shiver spiked John's backbone. He had to get Mother and Pris out of here.

Moccasins scuffing in dust sounding like faraway, plaintive drums, signaled the other prisoners returning. Hundreds of Indians straggled back into the stockade.

As the last few prisoners tramped in, John meandered over to meet them.

A pair of oxen dragging a wagon stacked high with bulging burlap bags, buckets, and barrels rumbled inside. "Line up by families, you filthy redskins," bellowed a muscular soldier driving the wagon. "Git your grub and water."

"Him again." John clamped his hands into fists. Wouldn't you know the bull-necked driver who assaulted Rachael would be in charge of supplies.

The tall man's large head bristled with dark hair, and his rolled-up uniform sleeves displayed brawny muscles. Standing with his legs spread in the bed of the supply wagon, he crossed his arms and tapped a foot. "Name's Dread. Corporal Robert Dread. Come on. Hurry it up. You Injins get yourselves into family groups and form a line to git your grub."

The wagon master's narrowed slate eyes smoldered beneath a scowl until he spied Rachael. She stood alone, Priscilla sleeping in the shawl draped over her shoulder. Dread's flinty eyes gleamed as the hefty man dropped down on the wooden bench seat, one ratty boot on the brake.

On the ground near him, Rachael blushed and crossed her arms over her breasts.

"You ain't got no family, girl, so you don't eat." The bully leaned from the wagon and spoke in an intimate voice. "Unless you're real nice to me!"

Hate streaked through John's chest. He strode to the wagon, steeled his jaw, and glared into Dread's ugly face. "The girl is my sister by clan bonds. I'm responsible for her." He converted the slow accent of the Georgian highlands into a sharp, crisp staccato. "Don't you make the mistake of touching her. I know General Scott's orders. If you break his rules, I'll make certain you are court-martialed."

Dread's face turned crimson. Veins bulged in his thick neck. He sprang from the seat as though he intended to jump from the wagon and tear John apart. Instead, he gripped his huge hands behind his back. "Git in line, Injin. Looks like someone already beat me to thrashing the bejiggers out of you. Saved me the trouble ... this time."

His face livid, Dread hurled John's food rations in the dirt, barely missing his moccasins. He ladled water into a bucket, then thrust the bucket into John's hand, spilling a quarter of its contents. The puddle disappeared into the dry red dust.

John heaved the burlap bag over his shoulder. Carrying the bucket with his free hand, he nodded for his mother and Rachael, who carried Pris. Together, they hurried toward the opposite side of the men's building.

Rachael's brown eyes radiated gratitude. "Thank you." Her voice sounded husky.

John stopped to reposition the burlap bag.

His mother's brow wrinkled, and she fluttered her fingers against her chest. "John, please keep away from that horrible man. You've been a champion to the helpless since you were old enough to understand need. I'm pleased you came to Rachael's aid." She laid her hand on his arm. "But you must not be reckless. For my sake, don't ever confront that man again."

John tightened his lips. As if he had a choice. Brutes never hesitated to weld whatever power they possessed.

The wrinkles in Mother's brow smoothed as a gentle smile transformed her face. "I well recall the first time you displayed this facet of your personality. You were five. Three of our pickaninnies were tormenting a fighting cock your father had penned. You stood there like a little rooster yourself among those older children and made them stop. When I told your father later, he laughed. He said you'd think differently when you grew old enough to bet on a cockfight." She smiled and shook her head. "You got into so many scrapes."

John's cheeks burned. He started walking again.

"You never learned to walk away from trouble. That's why your father thought you would make a fine lawyer." Mother's expression looked almost happy as she recalled his younger days at Pleasant Acres. He'd have to remember how those memories eased her sorrow. At least for a time.

Pastor Worchester placed Mrs. Ross's hand through his arm and walked companionably beside her.

When had the pastor arrived? The preacher had an uncanny knack of springing up, seemingly out of nowhere.

"That was a commendable act, young man, but you may be in for trouble." The pastor wiped his forehead with a white cloth. "You've made an enemy. That soldier has the look of a vengeful devil. Best steer clear of him."

Worchester turned to Rachael, his voice tinged with fatherly tenderness. "Remember, my dear, you are a child of the King. He will protect you from evil. He is your hiding place and strong tower."

"Yes, pastor." She spoke to the missionary, but her exotic eyes lingered on John.

Heat crept over his face and neck. The hate strangling his heart lost its grip. "We'd best get busy with the food."

Reverend Worchester turned to remove a crying baby from an exhausted mother's arms.

John gripped the pastor's arm. "I'd like to apologize for leaving the meeting this morning, sir. I'm not in the habit of being so rude."

Worchester's lips curved into a sad smile. "These are difficult days. And I confess I prefer a man who is either hot or cold toward the Lord. I'm praying for you, John."

John ducked his head. Why couldn't Worchester be a friend without bringing God into every conversation?

Rachael adjusted the sling over her shoulder and moved Pris to a more comfortable position.

Mother's eager hands opened the burlap bag. "Flour, jerky, and dried beans. What does one do with these?" Her silvery voice reflected disappointment. "And whatever can this be?" With her fingertips she held out a thick white slab.

"That's hog fat. We will put it in the beans after they soak. This brown flour we will make into bread." Though she answered Mother, Rachael smiled at him. "Since I'm the sister in this family, perhaps you will allow me to cook."

"Oh, I am pleased to welcome you into our small family." Mother waved a helpless hand toward the food. "But how does one prepare these bountiful supplies?"

A crease marred Rachael's serene forehead. "I'm afraid John will have to get wood, plus a kettle, some dishes, a large spoon, and whatever else you can get your hands on from the wagon driver. Perhaps it might be wiser to ask Reverend Worchester—"

"No. I'll collect the firewood and utensils. You two stay away from that wagon. As long as we're in this confounded prison, I'll pick up the food supplies. I want you two inside the women's building when Dread is near." John jerked a thumb toward the wagon master.

Rachael smiled. "I don't ever want to face him again."

John straightened his shoulders, set his jaw, and strode back to the supply wagon. He stood, feet planted, hands on his hips. "I need firewood, cooking utensils, plates, and spoons."

The scowl above the bullish eyes deepened until Dread resembled a pugnacious giant. "What's your name, squirt?"

"Ross."

"Ross. Ross ... hmm. Where'd I hear that there name?" He scratched a sagging jowl. "By cracky, you're the chief's son." The man's grimace drew up into a snarl.

Chills shivered John's spine. "No."

"Oh." The wagon master's expression dropped. "Still, it might work." He spoke under his breath, "I'll make it work." Mulling a wad of tobacco in his mouth, he shifted the wad from one cheek to the other. "You rich, kid?" he whispered.

"Not now," John muttered.

A stream of tobacco juice spurted through large yellow teeth and splattered on John's moccasin. "Don't get uppity with me! Bet your ole man has plenty." A gleeful look contorted his ugly face. He threw the firewood and utensils down on John's toes.

John grunted but didn't move. Did the bully have some evil plan in mind?

CHAPTER 7

A monstrous black bull towered above John. Almost human evil gray eyes glared at his defenseless body. The animal snorted. Powerful front legs pawed the dirt, spewing up clods. John stood alone in an arena, every side enclosed by tall, impenetrable walls. Running the interior perimeter, he searched every inch for a weapon.

Flaring nostrils below wicked pointed horns plunged toward him as the animal charged. The bull's fetid breath scorched his face.

John jumped aside.

The bull played with him, charging, time after time. With each thrust, the horns just missed goring him.

John feinted, dodged, and ran.

Head down, the monster plowed straight toward him. John pivoted, his breath harsh in his lungs. The bull thundered past, horns ripping a gash in his shirt. Dripping sweat, heart beating faster than the thundering hooves, John backed against a wall, hands scrounging for a way of escape.

The bull roared toward him. This time the charging animal would win.

John jerked himself through darkness out of the nightmare. Lying in a pool of sweat, a crick spasmed his neck. He pressed himself to a sitting position on the mud floor and realized the door stood open, flooding the men's building with hot light. He wiped a hand over his wet face. After his dream, even the stark reality of prison seemed welcome.

How had he slept so late? Again. The ache in his head had eased, but he'd be grateful for more of Worchester's brew. He yawned, stretched sore muscles, then stepped to the open men's door.

The stockade gates burst open. Sergeant Worthington, Dread, and two armed soldiers strode inside.

"John Ross, front and center!" the wagon master roared.

John froze, one foot on the threshold. Was this another nightmare? Both Worthington and Dread!

The sergeant spotted him.

The crowd around the men's building melted away.

John stepped into the hot sunshine and faced the soldiers and his tormentors. Standing within ten feet of him, two soldiers behind Dread aimed Kentucky long rifles at John's chest.

"Come with us. Don't make no trouble," Sergeant Worthington ordered.

The guns looked as big as cannons. John gazed over the silent crowd until he found his mother, her face white and her azure eyes wide. Goodbye, Mother. If only he had time to tell her he loved her. He couldn't swallow over the hard lump clogging his throat.

Pris waved a chubby hand, her rosy mouth parting in a smile. Mother tightened her grip around his baby sister.

Forcing one foot in front of the other, with the surroundings as surreal as if he were inside his nightmare, he sleepwalked through the opening. The double stockade doors thudded shut behind him. He clenched his ice-cold hands to his sides, a hard knot twisted his stomach, and bile rose to his throat.

Dread's rough voice ratcheted to a higher pitch. "Git over to them trees there on your left."

Worthington grinned.

Dragging his feet, with Dread tromping on his heels, John obeyed, though the direction barely registered on his

senses. As they strode among the tents of the bivouacked
army, soldiers, lounging near their tents, stared at them,
curiosity stamped on many faces.

They passed into dense woods, well out of earshot of camp.

Was this the end then? Would they shoot him like they
had Father? How would it feel to die? Was there life after
death ... or nothingness? The uncertainty of what lay ahead
... the body so obviously lifeless ... he ground his teeth.
Where did life go? Disconnected thoughts whirled in his
mind.

Sadistic chuckling and snorts rose from the soldiers.

John raised his chin and stiffened his shoulders. Could
it be true God waited for him, to punish or reward? *God,
give me more time, and I won't fight you anymore.*

"That tree there." Worthington pointed to a tall magnolia.
A wicked-looking bullwhip leaned against the rough bark.

John's knees buckled. They weren't going to shoot him.
A shudder passed through him, and his empty stomach
clenched. But would they beat him to death?

"Ross, strip off your shirt." Dread's voice held a strange
note of endearment, a caressing undertone.

Fumbling at his buckskin with trembling fingers, John
pulled the shirt over his head.

Worthington picked up a coil of rope lying beside the
bullwhip and shoved John against the tree. Rough bark
scratched his bare chest. Dread, humming a monotonous
tune beneath his breath, stretched out John's arm on a
shoulder-high limb and Worthington bound his wrist to the
extended branch. John twisted his head to watch as Dread
jerked John's other arm out, and Worthington tied his wrist
to another extended limb.

Dread's gray eyes glistened. A trickle of tobacco juice
rolled down the side of his thick lips. "Where's the gold
mine, Ross?"

"Gold mine? What are you talking about?" John hated
the tremor in his voice.

"Your ole man's gold mine, of course. We got orders
to find the gold mines you Injins stole from us Georgians.

Where is it?" A smirk darkened the fleshy face. Dread knew there was no gold mine.

John clamped his jaws. His wrists hurt. His face felt tight. Hot. His breath came too fast. *Oh God, don't let them kill me.*

He turned his head and spoke to Worthington and the two soldiers standing on the opposite side of the tree. "There's no gold mine. The only gold around here is in the cornfields. I heard you Georgians think we found gold. I didn't believe the rumors that you've whipped Cherokee men and women to find imaginary gold. There isn't any. Dread wants an excuse to torture me because of the girl. And Worthington—" John spat at the sergeant's booted foot. "Stop them. They know there's no gold!" John barely recognized the hoarse, scratchy voice as his own.

Dread threw back his head and laughed, deep from inside his belly.

John twisted his head to face him.

Tobacco juice dribbled from the leering mouth. "No, boy, you got us wrong. Our orders are to find them gold mines." Dread turned his square face to one of the soldiers. "Right, Elkanah?"

A hand slapped John's bare shoulder. "Tell me where the mine is, and we let you go." Worthington's evil grin crinkled his face all the way to his squinting eyes.

"You might as well spill your guts. We'll beat the locations out of you anyways." Elkanah leaned his rifle against a tree, slid down with his back against the bark, and crossed his arms.

"There's no gold mine!" John jerked at the ropes binding his wrists.

Dread peeled off his own shirt revealing cords of muscles rippling over his torso. He stepped back, unfurled the bullwhip, and snapped the thin lash viciously in the air, leather cracking like a pistol shot.

A shudder started at the tip of John's spine and streaked to his toes.

CHAPTER 8

Teeth clenched, John braced himself. Sweat dripped from his forehead into his eyes.

Another sharp crack. The whip slashed into his bare back, shaking his whole body. He writhed as pain from his spine shot through every nerve.

"Look at that, sergeant. The first slash cut through to bone." Dread hummed a lively tune. "Lovely ain't it, Elkanah?"

"Do what you want with me, but Rachael won't come to your wagon again." John knew his defiance would enrage his two enemies, but the words boiled off his tongue.

Another sharp crack … another lacerating hack. John's legs turned to mush and wavered, dragging extra weight on his arms and wrists.

Dread's humming stopped. "Where's the gold, you arrogant pup?"

With the fourth lash, agonizing pain radiated to every part of John's body. His head drooped. The world seemed caked in a bloody film, and he lost count of the slashes. A scream stuck in his throat begging to be let out. He barely heard the whip-wielder's bass voice belting out his incongruous song. His legs no longer supported him, and ropes dug into his wrists. Would his arms be dislocated? He tried to stiffen his legs to relieve the pressure, but he had no strength. Pain, a living, breathing monster, clawed his body.

Out of wavering darkness, someone moaned. Then he recognized the rasping as his own groaning. Worchester's words floated to his mind. "He was oppressed, and he was afflicted, yet he opened not his mouth." Jesus was a better man than I.

John's thoughts fragmented. Unrelated bits and pieces swirled like a fitful dream until descending blackness covered him.

Something soft cradled his head. Was he a small boy nestled in his mother's arms? No, the fluff of a blanket tickled his nose. Except for the itching fuzz, his body was numb. He forced his heavy eyes open, and the world stopped spinning and righted itself. Stockade stakes surrounded him. Then pain smashed into every nerve. He clutched at the earth, his body shuddering.

"Water." The weakness of his voice shocked him.

Mother brought water and pressed a gourd to his lips. He drank, then turned his face toward the men's building, closed his eyes, clamped his lips, and furrowed his forehead to block the pain.

"Please let him have space. Please don't crowd so close. Please leave us alone." His mother's soft, southern drawl mingled with the shuffle of feet as the crowd surrounding him stepped back. A faint breeze ruffled his hair while sympathetic mutterings from the other prisoners grew faint.

Rachael knelt at his side. "John, I gathered several baskets of healing herbs after the morning worship and made a poultice. The packet will sting when I first lay it on. Soon the medicine will ease your pain. This recipe works for easing all manner of wounds." With gentle fingers, she laid the dripping poultice on his back.

His body arched, then went rigid, and finally relaxed as the anesthetic penetrated his lacerated back. He fell into an exhausted sleep.

The next days passed in a nightmare of pain. If only he had the gift of unconsciousness. But he remained awake and tossed on his mat, oscillating from excruciating pain to relief when Rachael, Mother, or the pastor renewed the poultice.

The three took turns nursing him. The morning of the seventh day, after a restless night with little sleep, he opened his eyes. Rachael sat at his side with yet another gourd of medicinal herb tea. He forced his rubbery arms to prop himself up so he could drink the bitter liquid. The hard edge of agony softened into a throbbing burn.

Rachael touched a cool hand to his forehead. "Now that you feel better, we can talk. This is the prescribed way of the medicine man. Talking helps remove your mind from the pain. Perhaps you can explain why we are being held prisoner."

John gazed into Rachael's brown eyes. So warm. So sympathetic and filled with a tender desire to alleviate his suffering.

Talking did not rank high on his priorities. But he respected learning about the medicine men and would try their talk remedy. "Cherokee trouble began back in 1802 when the American President Jefferson signed the Georgia Compact." John tucked his chin as passion tightened his chest. "That dastardly paper stated that the United States promised to give Georgia all the land owned by our Nation if Georgia agreed to give half her land to the United States."

Rachael's eyes widened. "But the Americans had no right. We Cherokee own the land, not they!" Blush spots appeared in her tan cheeks.

"True. The government planned to force us to give up our land. One way or another, the US did gain control of thousands of acres. Then Uncle John laid down the law. No Indian could sell or trade a single section of land to the whites under any circumstances."

"Yes, I know about that. Mother and Father Brown, the missionaries who took me in when my mother died, thought Chief Ross mighty in wisdom to make such a law.

They hated watching white settlers grab our land." Rachael touched a slender finger to her chin and cocked her head. "But we lived so far from town, we knew little of what was going on."

"Uncle John's law would have stopped the infernal land grabbing if Sharp Knife Andrew Jackson hadn't intervened. Three years past, he used underhanded methods to persuade a small faction of Cherokees to sign a Removal Treaty." John tried to keep the satisfaction from his voice as he added, "The three leaders of that illegal group paid with their lives for their treason."

"A little severe, don't you think?" Rachael's pretty face screwed with compassion.

"Severe! Their own tribe executed the traitors. My father's dead because of those men! We're here in this ...." John clamped his lips, not wanting to offend a lady's ears.

Rachael lowered her long lashes and gazed at the ground. "But didn't those three men do what they thought was right?"

"They were guilty of treason, so they paid the penalty. Now every Cherokee man, woman, and child will pay for what those men did. The United States ratified the treaty even though the American Secretary of War stated the edict was no treaty at all, because the agreement was not sanctioned by our great body of the Cherokees. My father was in the Secretary's room and heard him say those words."

"Your father spent a lot of time in Washington?"

John nodded. So far, the medicine man's remedy helped, talking did lessen the agony. "Yes, Father supported Uncle John. But Father thought Washington a dreary place with its muddy streets and bad weather. He was glad to return to Georgia. I wanted to accompany him, but he needed me to oversee our plantation. The last two years, I ran the plantation." John shifted on the pallet.

"Why are we imprisoned when the Americans have a worthless treaty?"

"Valid enough for Sharp Knife. He gave us three years to move to Indian Territory. Jackson declared Cherokee law null and void, and Cherokees had to obey Georgia law. We had no voice in any court. As a result, the whites flooded our property, staked claims on our land, and stole any livestock they could get their hands on. All our people who defended themselves were locked in prison."

Rachael nodded. "Now I begin to understand. But how can the American people let their president get away with this?"

"Jackson." When John spat the name, his back convulsed, so he forced himself to speak with less fervor. "Jackson contended the treaty was for the Cherokee good because he gave us more land west of the Mississippi than we own here. Of course, the Osage and other tribes own the promised land, but this seems to be a minor point with the US President."

"Land west of the great waters. The region away from the rising sun, called the land of death," Rachael whispered.

John nodded.

"How did the soldiers catch us by surprise?"

"Uncle John's in Washington right now with a petition signed by 15,665 Cherokees who protest the Removal Treaty. He believes in democracy, but his only weapon is public opinion. The American people as a whole are sympathetic toward us. Only men like Jackson, Governor Gilmer, and a few die-hard frontiersmen want us expelled." He sighed and changed position to ease his throbbing back. "We never imagined the Americans would send soldiers to force us to vacate."

"I don't understand. Why do Gilmer and Jackson want us to leave? Do they hate us?"

"Jackson's an old frontiersman. He remembers the massacres thirty or forty years ago when our Nation defended our land against the white invaders. Indians killed his family, something he can't forget. Gilmer and the Georgians are hungry ... land hungry and gold hungry."

John squirmed and writhed on his pallet. "Uncle John advised us to wait patiently for the white man to find there was no gold, then Uncle John was certain the whites would leave. Instead, they stole food and livestock."

Talk no longer took the edge off John's agony. "Uncle John's strategy was to let the white men take and take and take, because he thought in the end the white man would become embarrassed by their treatment of us and would leave us in peace on our land."

John scowled. "My uncle was wrong."

Rachael traced her finger in the red earth. "Might it not have been better to leave without resistance? To move to the new land before soldiers came?"

He had no answer for her—or for himself. "How can a man hand over land he owned and worked for generations? How can he not fight?" He muttered, more to himself than to Rachel.

He lay flat on his stomach, hands clenched. "Got any more of that numbing tea?"

"Herbs are brewing now. As soon as it's ready, I'll bring you a cup." Rachael's voice held a sob as she whispered, "Mother and Father Brown came yesterday."

John twisted his head and glanced up in time to see her stealthy movement as she wiped away tears.

"I talked with them at the gate. They begged General Scott to let them take me home. They promised to legally adopt me."

John raised a brow. "And?"

"General Scott refused. He said because they are both in their sixties, they are too old. For them, I tried to make light of our situation in here. To see them so unhappy, broke my heart."

John gritted his teeth to hold back a curse. Telling her of his rage at Scott's denial would not help Rachael.

"They brought fruit," she said in a calmer tone. "I saved this peach for you."

"You best eat the fruit. Might be the last you see for a long time."

She shook her head, the long dark hair splaying back to cascade over her shoulders. "No, I've had mine. This one is for you."

Despite pricks of new pain, John forced himself into a sitting position. He bit into the ripe fruit and let the cool pulp and juice drench his mouth. Never had a peach tasted so refreshing! He managed a smile. "Thanks, this is good medicine." He slid down to rest on his stomach.

"*Tsiwanihu tocu.* I speak the truth." A baritone voice spoke from behind John. "You no look good."

Rachael sprang up and took the newcomer's hand. "John, I'd like you to meet Bold Hunter. Bold Hunter, this is John Ross."

John craned his head to stare at a tall Indian with a muscular, athletic body who stood close to Rachael. Too close. The young man's shining black eyes beamed a zest for living, and his high forehead showed intelligence. His expression projected disdain.

John scowled. If only he knew Cherokee. How could he feel so annoyed when he didn't know the man? Tall and strong, Bold Hunter radiated fearless freedom. Judging by his darker skin and proud hooked nose, Rachael's friend was a full-blooded Cherokee.

The newcomer tucked a possessive arm around Rachael's waist.

John grunted. Why did this cock-sure brute have to appear now while he was flat on his chest? Where did he come from? Who was he to Rachael?

Numbness from the tea was wearing off. Heat sizzled from the ground. He was a slice of bacon frying on a griddle. He clenched his fists and writhed on the blanket.

"Excuse me, I must make another poultice." Rachael ran off.

"Cherokee not show pain. You not much Cherokee!" The young Indian's deep voice was laced with contempt. Then he turned and glided after Rachael.

John scowled. He had to get back on his feet. Fast.

CHAPTER 9

Time became irrelevant. How many days had he passed tossing and turning in continuous pain? As agonizing minutes ticked into hours, the talks and numbing tea failed to provide the relief they first gave.

Bold Hunter became a daily, unwelcome visitor.

John frowned and hoisted himself upright on his pallet. At first, he tried to be amicable and made his voice sound as neighborly as he could manage. "Thanks for helping Rachael make the poultices and herbal tea."

Bold Hunter didn't answer.

"I'm obliged to you for picking up the noon provisions. Your added food and water give us a little more sustenance."

Bold Hunter's cold, impassive expression didn't change.

John tried the smile that usually opened doors for him. "Might as well be friends—"

"No friends." The Indian's hard black eyes glowed, and his lips drew down at the corners.

John snapped his mouth shut, clenched his fists, and tightened his stomach muscles. A few days earlier he would have made good his reputation as a hotspur. Now weak as a newborn colt, the fire inside suffered a quick death. When he got on his feet, he'd show that arrogant full-blood the lay of the land. Blast the extra food and help the Indian gave. He'd make Bold Hunter a former member of the family.

Rachael busied herself rearranging her hair and ignored the stony silence between him and Bold Hunter. "John, after they whipped you, I asked Bold Hunter to build you a shelter from the sun."

John grunted.

"Your mother and Priscilla also needed protection to prevent their fair skin from burning raw inside this unshaded prison." Rachael smiled at him and then turned to touch Bold Hunter's hand. "Thank you for building the shelter."

John groaned.

"Bold Hunter used poles and bark peeled from the east side of trees to build this lean-to against the woman's building. He and a couple other men carried you and laid you under its shade."

John managed a nod and forced himself to be civil. "Thanks, Bold Hunter. I owe you."

Bold Hunter didn't respond, just finished digging a round trench for their campfire near the shelter.

Rachael laughed. "I dub this fire pit our summer kitchen."

Bold Hunter raised his hands and shrugged, a puzzled expression on his dark face.

"I'm referring to the small houses built outside large plantation homes where slaves prepared food during hot summer months."

Bold Hunter shook his head. "Too much civilization. No need."

John turned his back on Bold Hunter and shaded his eyes for a glimpse of blonde hair bobbing among the throng of dark-haired people milling the stockade.

When they weren't outside listening to Pastor Worchester, Mother and Pris sat with him beneath the bark lean-to. Today they were on some mission elsewhere.

As the days passed and John's back healed, he required less constant care. He spent his time lounging beneath the shelter watching Pris's childish antics and playing with her throughout the long days. He soon realized she was a little person, not just a baby, and was a delight.

Watching Rachael cook also highlighted his day. She kindled a fire on the smooth rock and swept the hard-packed red clay clean. When she finished, she laid a lump of wheat dough on a strip of cloth on the dirt, then covered the bread with a deep clay pot.

"Did you fashion the pot from clay along the riverbank? It's beautiful work." John touched the smooth texture.

Rachael blushed as she built up the fire. "Yes, this is one of my pots. Keeping busy helps time to pass. We use all the natural material the soldiers let us dig up or gather."

"You have considerable knowledge and skill."

"Thank you. Mother Brown encouraged me to learn as much Cherokee lore as I wanted."

John grinned. "Good thing for my family you did."

The blush on Rachael's cheeks deepened. Soon the aroma of baking bread cramped John's always empty stomach. Her face, rosy from the heat, Rachael lifted the clay pot, revealing the loaf browned to mouth-watering, heavenly-smelling perfection. Before the toasty bread had a chance to cool, the five of them devoured the loaf, using their fingers to capture the last crumbs.

When the stockade emptied for morning worship, John pushed himself into a sitting position. His back felt stiff and unnatural, but the pain had subsided to a continual, dull throbbing burn. Moving his back as little as possible, he rose to his feet. His head spun, and his knees wobbled like a Christmas pudding. He ground his teeth. When would he regain his strength? Leaning against the building, he willed his legs to hold him upright. After he took a few minutes to regain his balance, he walked, stiff as a wooden soldier, one arm braced against the building wall. He staggered the length of the building, then returned to his bed. Thrusting out his chest, he grinned. Good to be on his feet. His muscles were weak, but his back didn't feel any worse while he stood than when he lay flat on the mat.

"Can't take much more sun, though. Where's my shirt?" He folded his trembling legs, sat on the pallet, and clutched his head. The solitude of the hot, empty prison, his stomach always signaling a need for food, and his general weakness imprisoned him as much as the high stockade wall. He rolled down to lie on his stomach, rested his head on his folded arm, and closed his eyes against the brilliant sunlight.

Light footsteps approached.

Rachael. He opened his eyes to her fresh vigor and unbelievable loveliness. Did the squalor of prison life not touch her? Like the dawn of a new day, his heart lightened.

"John." She settled on the ground close to his side, one soft hand on his arm. "Do you believe a man is bound to keep a promise?"

He raised an eyebrow and gave her a quizzical half smile. "Any man of integrity keeps his word. A promise is not made lightly." What could she consider important enough to keep her from Worchester's sermon? He couldn't read the expression in her eyes. Ignoring the sting of pain in his back, he hoisted himself up to face her.

"After the soldiers carried you here," her long lashes lowered, "they dumped you on the dirt. Everyone got busy finding a blanket for you, getting what medicine we could, and erecting a cloth tent. I feared you were dying. You lay there so white and limp, with blood dripping all over you. I begged God to let you live. If he did, I promised to help you follow the Way of Life. Mother Brown calls accepting the Way, becoming a Christian."

John's cheeks burned. Like a hawk spotting a rat, his soaring spirit hurtled into a steep dive. She was more interested in his soul than in him.

"While I washed blood off your back, just before you regained consciousness, you began moaning and muttering."

A flush heated his cheeks and slid down his neck. How much more embarrassed could he feel? He stared at the fissures in the hard-packed mud. "What did I say?" He slapped at the ever-present flies that lit on his flesh.

She took his hand and smiled. "You said, 'If you keep them from killing me, I'll stop fighting you.' I think you were talking to God." Rachael spoke as though the words felt good in her mouth.

Her easy talk about God lessened some of the tension from John's shoulders. Was that all he said? He hoped so.

"You're right. And I mean to keep my word." His throat tightened. He ran a hand through his matted hair and forced himself to confess. "The thing is ... I just don't know how." Okay, so he didn't have much pride left, but he still balked at admitting ignorance.

Rachael's gaze concentrated on the open stockade door.

John sensed she saw something far beyond the door ... something he could not see.

"Have you ever been lonely?" Her husky voice was so low he could barely hear the faraway, plaintive note.

"I was before you came."

"I mean really lonely ... so lonely you felt you were an empty skin, a broken bowl. Once you were filled with warmth and love, but everything seeped out through the break in your life. No matter how hard you tried, you couldn't regain the security and comfort you lost. Your life was vacant."

"Losing Father feels like that. Except I'm more angry than empty."

Rachael's eyes lost their faraway expression. "A bowl of bitter water is fit only to be tossed onto the dust. The bitter waters can be turned sweet just as loneliness can become love."

John shrugged and grimaced, not bothering to hide his disbelief.

"I never knew my father." Rachael lowered her head. "He died before I was born. My mother was beautiful. Many braves competed for her moccasins to rest inside their cabin, but she refused them all. She said the Great Spirit punished her for her sin by taking my father before they married."

John swallowed hard. If so, he punished an innocent child too.

"My mother loved me. I was happy until she died. Then no family in our Wolf clan would take me because my mother's people refused to give me their name. I was only twelve ... even then, young men wanted me. But I was not willing to marry. I was afraid." Rachael gazed at her hands. "And ashamed."

Caught up in her story, John pictured the beautiful child, alone in the world. An outsider because of her mother's past. Her allure spurring braves into approaching her. Her fear and shame binding her.

"One young man was special. He hunted game for me. But when he brought the wild turkey, I could not eat. His attention only made me weep. Even though he did not walk The Way of Life, he persuaded me to go with him to the home of the white missionary many miles away." She raised her head and smiled a sweet little smile.

"The missionaries were kind, insisting I live with them. I stayed because I did not care what became of me. Then Mother and Father Brown told me the Lord Jesus wanted to come into my life and fill me with his love. I decided if this were not true, I would kill myself." Tears reddened her beautiful doe eyes. "I no longer wished to walk the earth. If God were real, he would have to prove himself to me. If not, I had poison in a small pouch tied around my neck."

John let out his breath. Had she really been so desperate? He couldn't picture Rachael taking her own life. Nevertheless, Rachael and he had different temperaments. At times, he glimpsed a brooding personality beneath her loving, helpful nature.

"I went upstairs into the cozy bedroom Mother Brown had prepared for me. I set the candle on the table and slipped onto my knees beside the window seat, my favorite nook in all the world. From there I could see across the orchard to the little white church where Father Brown preached." Her lips curved into a wistful smile. "The time was early spring. I remember the peach blossoms. I've never seen as many since then."

Her story seemed so vivid, John felt as if the scent of sweet peach blossoms actually tickled his nose.

"I was crying because I could not respond to the love Mother and Father gave me. I feared I would never be able to love anyone again. Then I closed my eyes and prayed, 'Jesus, will you come into my life?'"

A few seconds of silence elapsed. John cleared his throat. "What happened?"

"It's difficult for me to explain. I had an experience I don't want you to ridicule. I'm telling you all this because I promised God I would share my story." Her rounded brow furrowed. Sparks darkened her brown eyes to deep mahogany.

"But from that time on you were able to love." John finished for her, careful not to appear in any way as if he thought her story strange.

"Not only love ... ever so much more! Life is a beautiful gift. Eternal life enables us to enjoy it forever."

John didn't want to spoil her story, but his integrity forced him to speak. "Isn't just praying a little too easy?"

Rachael's eyes were wide, her face tender, her usually mysterious smile replaced by a smile of such love that John's heart raced. "Yes. Easy for us because Jesus paid the price. He died in our place and took the punishment for our shortcomings." She clasped his hand in both her warm ones. "Just like what you did. Because you protected me from the wagon master, you suffered instead of me. You took my place. I think even if you had known the wagon master intended to whip you, you still would have protected me!"

John gazed down at the blanket beneath his long, crossed legs. Would he have? Better he hadn't known the cost. For an instant, suffocating fear drenched him again. He'd been certain Worthington and Dread would kill him.

"So you see, becoming a child of God is a gift." Rachael tucked her hand under his chin and lifted his head. "Your part is to accept the gift the Giver paid for and freely offers. Will you take his gift?" She leaned toward him, her eyes earnest.

"I need to think. I'll let you know what I decide."

"Of course." Some of the joy faded from Rachael's face. "Whatever you say."

A sound, like wind rustling dry leaves, made them both look up. The prisoners entered the enclosure. Men trudged in, shoulders hunched, faces gaunt. Women, expressions strong with quiet fortitude, carried wet clay, herbs, and home-made vessels of water. Only the children seemed unaffected. They joined in running games or clung to an older brother or sister, faces raised in hope of a story. Yet, many adult expressions burned with hope.

John rubbed his jaw. Where did they find the strength? The hope?

His mother strolled across the compound toward them, looking out of place in the rude prison. Rachael must have combed Mother's thick blonde hair into the graceful spiral on top of her head. Her delicate green dress, now stained with perspiration and the lace at her wrists frayed, had been exactly right in her airy drawing room. Here, the cut exposed her pale shoulders and neck to the pitiless sun. Her green, high-heeled slippers looked too thin for walking on the rough ground.

John rubbed the tight muscles in the back of his neck. How could he take care of her?

"Your suffering has hurt your mother deeply."

"You read thoughts, Rachael?"

"Yours are written on your face." Rachael patted his shoulder. "Your mother is proud of your courage, but she hates the price you paid. Courage always costs—sometimes, a lot."

"But it's impossible to live with yourself if you're a coward." John heaved a sigh. "Um, did you tell Mother what you told me? About Christ, I mean?" Speaking the name was easier than he'd expected.

"Yes, the first night in the stockade. She was terribly depressed because your father had been killed. I explained how God cares for her no matter what man may do. She accepted God's gift of eternal life. I doubt she would have the strength to face this life without God's help. She's not physically strong."

John grunted, glad his mother had found help and had someone besides him to lean on. Responsibility weighed him down. Not that he could do much for her, but he worried. Still, when he got back on his feet, he wouldn't need anyone to shoulder his burdens. He could handle them alone.

"Your mother has been sewing a shirt for you from her white muslin petticoat." Rachael's brown eyes and sweet mouth held a mischievous gleam. "Your shirt's folded across her arm. Looks as though she finished it."

Mother reached his side, her smile radiant.

John took the shirt she handed him. "Thanks, Mother. But now you have no ... uh ... you know."

His mother's lilting laugh pealed out. "I have less need of an undergarment than you do of a shirt." She helped him as he raised stiff arms and struggled into the shirt.

"I thought Bold Hunter might offer you his shirt, although he's considerably larger. But ... he didn't." Rachael seemed puzzled at the young Indian's attitude and lack of helpfulness.

Hah. "He's not that much bigger." John grinned, pleased Bold Hunter hadn't offered. The thought of owing the big man another favor didn't sit well. What did Rachael see in the full-blood?

CHAPTER 10

Another scorching day. John sighed. He was thankful the slashes on his back were almost healed. He'd kept his promise to God. He wasn't fighting him anymore, but he wasn't drawn to God either. Not that he had the energy to fight. Yet, he had too much time to think about the things Rachael told him.

John lifted his arms and stretched. Today began exactly as each tedious day during the two and half months since Corporal Dread and Sergeant Worthington took their revenge.

He gritted his teeth. Yesterday he'd gotten word via the grapevine that Worthington had left the stockade to take possession of his new home. At least Pleasant Acres would never be the same beautiful plantation minus the mansion Father built.

John shook his head. He couldn't look back. The past was past. He had to direct his focus to the future. He had to survive. His family depended on him.

He wiped a bead of sweat from his upper lip. During the early days of imprisonment, the citizens of New Echota passing the stockade surely heard the clamor from the mass of prisoners living inside. Recently, however, he figured no sound from within the walls filtered outside. No babble of voices ... no crying of children ... no sounds of activity. All must be puzzling silence to town folks. Did they care if the people trapped inside lived or died?

He rubbed his abdomen. Dysentery cramped his innards and sapped his strength. He slapped his thigh. "One less fly." He snorted and flicked the dead insect off his buckskin. "Which is worse—the flies swarming the prison during daylight or the mosquitoes that plague us every dawn and evening?"

Neither Mother nor Rachael bothered to answer.

The sun and diarrhea sucked every ounce of fluid from him and his loved ones. His tongue stuck to the roof of his mouth. Though the days blazed hot, no one perspired. Languor settled over him like a heavy weight he could no longer lift. He lolled cross-legged in the dirt, watching people sitting in groups or lying motionless on the bone-dry earth. Few talked. Families reclined together, drawing comfort from the nearness of loved ones. Some lounged, backs propped against the stockade walls. Flies droned, someone moaned, another mumbled a prayer.

The double stockade doors creaked open for morning worship.

Back at Pleasant Acres, he wouldn't have bothered attending. Now, these services offered escape from boredom, the stench of human waste, and his nagging restlessness. People within the enclosure pushed themselves to their feet and shuffled out to relative cool beneath the trees.

Had to be at least a thousand prisoners jammed inside here. When would they travel to the Indian Territory? Even that action sounded better than this limbo. Why was the government stalling?

John unfolded his long form, picked up Priscilla, and held his arm out for Mother. She walked barefoot, having long since worn out her slippers.

Rachael rose from her seat beneath the lean-to and strolled beside his mother. Bold Hunter jumped to his feet and stuck closer to Rachael than a thorn on a rose. He took her free hand.

John glared at him.

Rachael frowned at both of them, loosed her hand from Bold Hunter's and fanned her face. She and Mother increased their pace.

Pris must have sensed the tension in his body because she stirred and gazed up at him with wide, blue eyes. John forced his muscles to relax and smiled down at her.

During the last few weeks, the soldiers allowed them all to bathe in the cool stream running through the meadow. John licked his dry lips in anticipation. Worchester insisted the women wash at one end, the men and boys at the other. Children under ten could swim with whichever parent or guardian they chose. Most of the guards gathered at the women's area, ogling the girls.

Mother looked exceptionally tired, dark bags sagging below her azure eyes.

He nodded to her and turned toward the men's side. "I'll take Pris into the water today."

"Thank you, Son." Mother straightened her shoulders and smiled.

With Priscilla hanging onto his back, he stepped into the cool water and strode toward the middle. The liquid swirled around him higher and higher until he stood chest deep. Each step diminished his anger toward Bold Hunter. Everything that Indian did got under John's skin.

Pris threw off her lethargy and paddled her small feet while she clung to his neck. John splashed her with cool water. Her petite body felt so fragile, but she wind-milled her hands in the water, splashing his hot face.

He scrunched a funny face for her, and she giggled. How he loved to hear her laugh. He kept the game up as her tinkling laugh spurred him into pretending to be a walrus and blowing bubbles underwater, ducking her under with him. Through filmy eyes, they shaped comical faces at each other. He took great gulps of water and puffed sprays out in a fountain for her, then swam backwards, her little body lying on his chest.

With her wet diminutive palms, she patted his face. "John, John."

"Everyone out. Let's go." The soldiers ordered.

Sprawled on the ground after their dip, John listened intently to Pastor Worchester.

Pris curled in her mother's arms for a nap.

John stretched full length on his stomach on the dried-out yellow grass beneath the trees. Without this outside-the-stockade time each day, he would have gone berserk. Even with the blades prickly on his skin, what a luxury to lie in the shade without someone's elbow in his back. And Worchester was interesting.

"Difficulty is a severe teacher," the pastor boomed to his congregation. "When wind blows on a tree, the roots stretch and grow stronger. So it is with us. When the winds of adversity blow, we stretch spiritually and grow strong. We shall not enter exile as weaklings. God gives us this promise."

> Hast thou not heard, that the everlasting God, the Lord, the Creator ... fainteth not, neither is weary? He giveth power to the faint, and to them that have no might He increaseth strength.

Pastor held up his bible.

> Even the youths shall faint and be weary, and the young men shall utterly fall. But they that wait upon the Lord shall renew their strength, they shall mount up with wings as eagles. They shall run, and not be weary. They shall walk, and not faint.

Worchester rumbled on. But John rehashed the words he'd just heard. To them that have no might He increaseth strength ... they shall walk, and not faint.

The promise echoed in his mind. After being whipped, he'd never regained his original strength. Then, the daily lack of food and the dysentery drained what energy he had left. What kind of strength did Worchester mean? Physical? Mental? Spiritual? Did he speak of all three? Whatever it was, he wanted it.

He rolled over on his back. The grass pricked through his petticoat shirt, but the tree overhead sported leafy green shade. Somewhere nearby a bee buzzed. An inchworm humped across the lowest limb. Salvation sustained

Rachael, and he needed what God offered. Before the worm traveled halfway to its destination, he decided.

He flipped back onto his stomach, buried his face in his hands, and closed his eyes. The scent of dry grass and packed earth filled his nostrils. "Jesus," he whispered. "I accept you. Thank you for dying for my sins and rising from the dead to give me new life. Will you give your strength to me?"

Peace settled over him. Vitality and joy flowed through his innermost self. His thoughts grew rainbow tinted.

This was real! Opening his eyes, he gazed at a new world. He was born again.

After the service, as people returned to the stockade, John whistled. Pursing his lips wasn't easy—nor was whistling with dry, cracked lips—but the joy inside had to escape.

Rachael stared at him, her mouth opened in a perfect oval.

He grinned.

The smile on her lips widened until her whole face lit. The invisible barrier between them dissolved.

Bold Hunter's fierce look hit John like a knife to the chest, but John threw back his head and couldn't stop grinning.

The following morning, during worship service, John stood in the stream again. The water rose to his chest. He was the only one being baptized. Because so many people had been baptized during the past weeks, armed soldiers strolled along one riverbank, weapons lying over their arms with open breeches, no longer curious or even insolent.

Bold Hunter lounged near them, lips twisted in a sarcastic smile.

On the opposite shore, Mother, Rachael, and Pris watched amid hundreds of believing Christians. Their faces reflected serenity which softened lines of hunger and weariness. As he stood in the middle of the river, water swirling around his torso, he sensed cool indifference emanate from one bank and warm love from the other.

Why had he waited so long to switch sides?

The trill of a meadowlark singing on a tree branch arching across the river caused his heart to swell with joy. Looking beyond the people to the rolling hills, to the fields laid out like a patchwork quilt over an uneven bed, to fenced-in farmhouses and yards, neat and tranquil in the sun, he laughed. He would not forget this day and certainly not this event.

Red hair shining in the sunlight, Pastor splashed toward him from the right bank.

John stood straight and tall in the center of the stream. Would the much shorter man have trouble immersing his tallest convert?

Worchester stretched as high as he could and placed a hand of blessing on top of John's head. "Have you received Christ as your Savior?"

"Yes, sir, I have." John let his baritone ring loud to both banks of people and beyond to the army's tented city.

"John McCormac Ross, I baptize you in the name of the Father, and of the Son, and of the Holy Spirit."

Pastor Worchester's words gripped John's heart as the missionary grasped John's two hands with one of his own, put his other on the small of John's back, and slid him into the water.

No problem dunking him at all. The Moravian missionary baptized him easily. John held his breath. If only he had surrendered and given his life to Christ as easily.

Worchester lifted John from beneath the water. "This baptism signifies your identity with Christ in death, burial, and resurrection. Walk now in a newness of life."

John automatically shook his head, cascading water from his thick blond hair in all directions. Not even sparing a glance at the hostile shore, he splashed across the wide river to stand with the other believers.

Pretty girls smiled at him, and the Christian men crowded forward to shake his hand. Despite his dripping clothes, Mother hugged him and Rachael looked radiant as a bride. John took her hand.

He felt a new spring in his step as he and Rachael walked hand in hand back into prison, his tall frame relaxed, moving with an inner air of confidence. Wearing his dripping buckskin pants and the thin makeshift shirt, a fresh life opened before him. Christ had made him a new man. Where was the rage that had sapped his strength? Gone!

Back inside the stockade, he noticed the blush on Rachael's cheeks did not pale. Her eyes sparkled unnaturally bright.

"Do you feel well?" John put his palm to her forehead.

"No, I began to feel sick just before you were baptized. I thought I was excited, but now I'm not so sure."

Her hair, falling so freely to her waist, appeared less glossy, and her rosy lips pallid. She raised a slender hand to her temples. "I have a blinding headache."

"Let's get you out of this sun and under the lean-to." He thrust an arm around her shoulder and hurried her toward the shelter.

She stopped mid-step, turned her back, then heaved.

John tried to help, but she shook him off. "Leave me. Go away," she begged between bouts of vomiting.

John stood, hands hanging at his sides. What could he do for her?

Rachael shivered.

John half carried her the rest of the distance to the shelter. He rustled up a gourd of water, gave her a drink, and ran to fetch his mother.

Mother knelt and examined Rachael, then straightened the pallet on which she lay beneath the peeled bark structure. "John don't come near. Stay away. I'm fairly certain Rachael has smallpox."

Like the talons of a hawk, fear clutched John's chest. Visions of Rachael's beautiful face marred with pox flashed before his eyes. "What of you, Mother? If you take care of her, you might catch smallpox. I'll nurse her."

"You can't, John. There are personal things you can't do. Besides, I need you to watch Pris. I'm afraid my baby's already been exposed, but perhaps not." Mother searched Pris's sweet face. Worry flitted over her features, quickly erased by an expression of forced cheerfulness John recognized. "Thank God, John, you had smallpox when you were ten and are immune."

John took Pris from his mother's arms and cradled her in his own. Her innocent blue eyes beamed love and trust. She smiled a tired little smile before her curly lashes dropped closed on her rounded cheek.

He carried Pris to the men's building on the far end of the stockade and rocked her tenderly in his arms. "What am I going to do with you?"

Bold Hunter strode toward him, weaving through the congested prison grounds like a cougar stalking food. "You turn into squaw. First you get Christian like old man. Now you become squaw." He spat the words as flaming symbols of scorn, then stood, arms crossed, broad chest heaving, lips curled into a snarl.

A flush started at the base of John's neck as heat spread to his face until the tips of his ears burned. He stared at his frayed moccasins. Biting his lip, he held back an angry retort. He was a Christian now. How did a Christian handle those taunts? He hadn't the vaguest idea, but he wanted to smash his fist into Bold Hunter's leering face. Hate tasted bitter on John's tongue.

The sudden tension in his body must have awakened Pris, and she started to cry. His every nerve longed to set her on the ground and teach Bold Hunter just who was not a squaw.

"You not even good squaw," Bold Hunter taunted.

Pris's crying screeched to a crescendo.

That did it! John slid the screaming child to the ground. Knees bent, hands half extended, he faced Bold Hunter. John tucked his chin. He was probably faster than Bold Hunter. But Bold Hunter was taller and outweighed him by more than twenty-five pounds. And the muscular Indian looked tough. But John raised his fists and danced in close.

"What's wrong with the little girl?" Isaac Worchester's voice boomed between the two of them.

John dropped his hands.

Bold Hunter stepped back.

"Looks like she's scared." Worchester bent over her. "Hush, hush, little miss. Big brother is right here. He will take care of you." Worchester lifted the toddler and placed her in John's arms.

John bit back his anger. His hands trembled so severely he almost dropped Pris. He turned his back on Bold Hunter's disdainful expression—branding John as scared and less than a man.

"John, Christ in you means his love is in you." Pastor thrust his hand on John's heaving chest. "Hate destroys. Hate is easy. Christ wants you to love your enemies and pray for them. Only a committed man can love as Christ loves." Worchester turned to Bold Hunter with a warm smile. "Son, I've been praying for you. I'm available if you want to talk."

Bold Hunter snorted. "I no need squaw power. I got big medicine power. Power from shaman to make woman love me." He glared and spat on the ground. "Ancient way of Medicine Man better than Christian way of white man." He jammed his arms across his chest, and his black eyes flashed.

Small hands wrapped around John's neck. Pris hiccupped and buried her face in the damp muslin clinging to his shoulders.

Worchester offered him a tattered blanket to make a sling for carrying her.

Pris tucked her thin legs around him. "Mama. Mama. Mama."

John turned his back to Bold Hunter and faced Pastor Worchester. "Is there any way we can get milk for Pris? She's lost weight, and I'm worried about her. The food we're given isn't what she needs."

"My daughter, Hope, arrived in town yesterday from Tennessee." Pastor tugged a soiled handkerchief from his trouser pocket and wiped his perspiring forehead. "Hope's fetching milk from our cow for the young children tomorrow. I'm to meet her at noon when the gate opens for the wagon master. We'll be certain Pris gets milk every day while Hope is here." He smiled. "One piece of good news. The military says we're moving out in September—we'll be stuck here only for a few more weeks."

John's spirits spiked. Any action sounded better than rotting inside the stinking stockade.

"I believe you two young men have cooled sufficiently. I have other sheep to tend." Worchester waved a hand as if blessing them both. As he walked away, he called over his shoulder. "Meet me at the gate tomorrow. I'll introduce you to my daughter."

Hmm. Was the red-haired preacher speaking to both of them? Did he invite Bold Hunter to meet his daughter? Why not? The girl was probably a missionary too … and someone needed to warn the arrogant Indian about eternity. Not that the obnoxious man hadn't already heard. No one who came near Pastor Worchester failed to hear.

After Pastor turned the corner of the men's building and was out of sight, John faced Bold Hunter. If he wanted to fight, John was more than willing. He deposited Pris gently on her feet and squared off.

Bold Hunter stepped back. "We talk."

John lifted Pris, settled her inside the tattered sling, and used his body to shield her from the sun's hot rays.

The scowling Indian hunkered down on the red clay and motioned for John to join him. "Bold Hunter not captured by soldiers. Come here alone."

"What? Why?" John squatted, facing the fierce black eyes and the challenging expression.

"Bold Hunter live near Rachael in mountains. Know her since young boy. Take her to live with white missionaries when she alone. She my woman. Before Bold Hunter come inside prison, meet Rachael outside stockade under trees while short man with four eyes preach. Tell Rachael come, escape to mountains, hide in caves. No soldiers find us." He scowled. "She no come. Say she must help white baby and mamma." Bold Hunter glared at the dozing child hanging in the sling from John's shoulder. "Bold Hunter can get Rachael away. Rachael no come. She needed here she say. She no leave Ross family."

John's mouth dropped open. Rachael could have escaped?

"If Rachael die, Bold Hunter kill Ross."

CHAPTER 11

Bold Hunter lifted his deerskin shirt. A rawhide strap fastened around his muscular chest concealed a sheathed hunting knife beneath his left arm. "Soldiers no search here."

John gnashed his teeth and set his jaw. Regardless of Bold Hunter, of Dread, of hunger, thirst and smallpox, he would survive this imprisonment and the removal to an unknown land. He would start a new life. He had to. For Mother. For Pris. And for Rachael.

Naked hate in the Indian's eyes raised hackles in John's chest. He would live his new life for the Lord. But love your enemies and pray for them? God asked an awful lot. He gazed, tight-lipped at Bold Hunter. How could he love this enemy?

A crowd gathered, their faces excited. "Fight! Fight! Fight!"

John's temper felt close to snapping. He clenched his fists. But fighting didn't show love. Slowly, he relaxed his hands.

Tension spread in widening circles around the two of them. Crowds of men and women formed an enclosure, urging them to settle their differences. John couldn't back down. He held his ground, lowered Pris to her feet, and raised his fists. Bold Hunter grunted, turned on his heel, and stalked off toward the women's building.

John wiped his forehead with the palm of a shaking hand. He dragged in a deep breath, then gazed down at Pris. She stared up, wide blue eyes questioning, and mouth open, her expression melting his heart. Using his thumb, he caressed Pris's smooth cheek.

He preferred fighting Bold Hunter to living with his disdain. But he didn't want to make mistakes in his new way of living. What made a Christian different? He knew how he was different inside, but did Christians fights? *God, you live inside me now, teach me what you want me to know. Looks like you'd better hurry before I make more mistakes.*

The peace of living in unity with God began calming his tight nerves. He pursed his lips and started to whistle.

Animation faded from the tired faces of onlookers as the crowd dispersed. A few glanced over their shoulders, eyebrows raised. Others smiled.

Bold Hunter didn't show up to collect their daily food supply. Instead, John noticed him hanging around the woman's building sticking as close as he could to Rachael. Would the arrogant man never leave her side?

John shook his head. After his whipping, Bold Hunter had picked up their rations from Dread. Since Bold Hunter didn't leave, this routine appeared to be John's task again. He squared his shoulders, sauntered to the food wagon and stood, legs planted wide, one arm curved around Pris.

"What's this here? A pretty new squaw in camp!" Dread stopped tossing down bags and grinned.

John's face flamed. He narrowed his eyes and settled Pris more snugly in the sling under his arm. Did the beefy man have to add humiliation to John's agony and days of pain? Hadn't flogging him been sufficient? John kept his expression a blank mask. But even this attitude seemed to spur Dread's sarcasm.

"Ain't this a nasty place for such a nice young squaw? You don't look very strong, Miss. Maybe somebody ought to take care of you 'stead of you takin' care of that papoose." The wagon master's wide mouth creased into a snarl, then pulled back over his yellow teeth. He shot a stream of tobacco juice that plopped wetly onto the front of John's white shirt, barely missing Pris's golden curls.

John clamped his lips, braced his legs, crossed his arms beneath the putrid splotch, and showed no emotion. He gazed up into the cold eyes. Evil in their deepest recesses flicked like the tongue of a snake.

"I'm waiting." The putrid chewed-tobacco odor on John's shirt wafted a stench that curdled his stomach.

"Tarnation! You can wait until I'm good and ready to ram these supplies down your gullet, squaw. I serve men first. Just mebby there won't be nothin' left when I get done." His broad face reddened. "Don't you come over here all high and mighty and tellin' me what to do like some big shot. Why, you ain't nothin' but a dirty half-breed Injin."

John pulled in a deep breath, clenched his fists at his side, and narrowed his eyes. He shouldn't feel loathing, but how much could a man endure and keep his self-respect? Love his enemies and pray for them? Temples throbbing, he forced his fingers to unclench and his taut face to relax. He widened his stance and waited.

Overhead the sun blazed.

Working with slow deliberation, Dread handed out supplies to the long line of Indians. The sympathetic looks coming his way didn't ease John's temper. Pris was hungry. He had to start the fire and bake bread for her. He glanced at the sunburned face half-buried against his chest and ground his teeth.

The sun moved higher in the sky before Corporal Dread finally finished. He picked up the oxen reins and slapped them on the backs of the patient beasts.

John stepped in front of the animals. "Hold on! Give me our rations."

"Ask me nice." The deep voice from the wagon seat cooed as if talking with a woman.

His family needed food and water ... the skimpy two meals a day had left them all hungry. And, because of her fever, Rachael needed extra water. Something snapped inside John's head.

Sliding Pris to the ground, he leaped aboard the wagon bed and grabbed two burlap bags from the dirty floor. Voice gritty, he commanded through clenched teeth, "Give me our water—I need extra because of sickness—or so help me, I'll see you get what you've been asking for!"

With amazing speed for such a heavy man, Dread shot out his foot. The heavy boot caught John in the chest and knocked him out of the wagon. He landed with a jarring crash flat on his back on the rock-hard clay. Writhing, he struggled to breathe.

Dread's harsh laughter boomed in the hot, still air. "Whelp! I can break you in half anytime I feel like it. But I'd sooner see you twiddling your thumbs inside this here stockade. I get a kick out of watching your hide turn brown while you roast." He bared stained teeth in a wide grin. "But one of these days I'm gonna get tired of waitin'. Then I'm gonna give you another taste of Ole Bess here." He flicked the bullwhip and the oxen jerked nervously. "When I do, I ain't gonna stop till your hide's been cut to ribbons. There won't be enough of your skin left to make a bow on a Christmas package. You got that, boy?"

Flat on his back, his chest heaving, John kept a tight grip on the food sacks.

"'Till then, I'm gonna keep you fattened up. You look as skinny as a starving wolf." With exaggerated helpfulness, Dread jumped from the wagon and carried two brimming buckets of water to John. "There, squaw. Don't say Corporal Dread never done you no favors." His eyes twitched as he planted a huge, dusty boot next to John's head.

Dread's sinister gaze looked itching to stomp.

On the ground beside him, Pris shrieked. When Dread raised a heavy boot, John curved his torso around her delicate little body. The big wagon master's slow-moving thoughts were written plainly on his savage face. Why didn't he stomp?

Pris cried.

Raw power dissolved from Dread's expression, and he assumed a guise of respect. The bull-like man offered a half-hearted salute, turned on his heels, and plodded back to his wagon.

Marching footsteps sounded. Two soldiers, blue uniforms bright with gold braid, strutted further inside the stockade.

John rubbed his chest. Ha! Top brass. So they're what stopped Dread.

He hoisted himself up and sucked in air, sending pain radiating from his ribs. He cuddled Pris, not attempting to talk. Gradually her choking sobs quieted. John cupped his hand and gave her a drink from one of the water pails. She smiled through her tears, hiccupped, then settled back against his dirty shirt.

He brushed at the red boot mark and the tobacco stain on his shirt, only succeeding in smearing both into muddy white. He staggered—his gait hampered by the baby—but managed to haul the food and water to their campsite and deposited them there.

Then he smacked his forehead. "Worchester's daughter!" He glanced at the stockade door. The big wooden gate still stood open. Grabbing a drinking gourd, he raced toward the gate, Pris jouncing against his chest. He had to get that milk!

Dread stood near the gate at the heads of the supply wagon oxen, talking with the two officers.

Face stony, John strode past them. He wasn't in any shape to meet anyone, but he'd given his word. And Pris needed milk. Chest burning, blood pounding in his temples, he broke into a trot and rushed to where Pastor and his daughter stood on the far side of a dusty wagon.

They turned in his direction. From where they stood, they'd obviously missed seeing his humiliation from Dread's treatment.

"You arrived just in time, John." The worry lines on Pastor's forehead disappeared. "The guards will close the gates soon. We've distributed milk to the other young children but saved enough for Pris. We've been waiting. What kept you?"

"Had a problem." He snapped his mouth into a thin line.

"Oh? Sorry to hear that." The rusty eyebrows puckered, then smoothed. He turned to the girl at his side. "Hope, this is John Ross. You recall, I told you about him."

Dread turned, locked eyes with John, and smirked.

John scowled. His breath came hard and fast. He grunted, hunched his shoulders, and clenched his fists.

The dimpled smile faded from Hope Worchester's face, and the warm lights in her wide green eyes turned distant as a mountain peak buried in snow.

"John, my daughter, Hope." Worchester's jovial voice sang with pride. Then, he frowned.

John sucked in a deep breath and rubbed a hand across the grit and grime streaking his face. A sinking sensation clenched the pit of his stomach. They must think he was rude. And he looked awful—angry, wearing a dirty shirt, threadbare britches, moccasins with holes so large his toes poked through, and his hair, stringy and uncut. He eased the scowl from his face, pulled at the collar of his shirt, and forced a smile.

"I'm pleased to meet you, Miss Worchester." His voice came out wooden, without warmth or enthusiasm. He thrust out a filthy hand for her to shake.

She was small. Her coal-scuttle bonnet stood even with his shoulder. And she was so clean and well dressed that she seemed to arrive from a different planet. A total contrast to the tattered people inside the stockade. The lacy mitts protecting her hands from the sun didn't belong in this stark world.

Hope Worchester's vibrancy radiated around her like a halo. She was stunning. Her green eyes sparkled vivacity. If she and Rachael stood side by side most eyes would be dazzled by Hope before noticing Rachael's dark beauty, though both women were enticing. Separately, they were admirable ... together, they would be awe inspiring. He swallowed and dropped the hand she hadn't taken. And he'd never been at a greater disadvantage.

Shifting from one foot to the other, he tossed his hair back from his eyes with a jerk of his head. For such a tiny person, Hope made him feel really uncomfortable. He should say something. But he stood there trying not to scowl, trying to cool his rage, and drinking in her healthy freshness. How many worlds ago had he been on the outside? At his fixed stare, color painted her cheeks, but he couldn't look away.

Character, courage, and determination showed in her strong round chin. Her steady gaze returned his stare so coolly. Passion showed in the curve of her lips. Hope Worchester wasn't the sweet, docile, plain preacher's daughter he'd expected.

"Your most humble servant, ma'am." He cleared his hoarse throat. Then flushed as he realized he'd already acknowledged her.

"This is Priscilla, John's baby sister." Pastor touched Pris's small hand. "John's caring for her while Mrs. Ross nurses those who are ill with the smallpox."

John shuffled his feet. If Pastor hadn't come to John's rescue, the missionary's daughter would have let him stand there all day blithering like a fool.

As Hope reached for Pris, her face softened into a sweet maternal look.

Pastor stepped between Hope and the baby. "No, my dear. I'm afraid the baby may have been exposed to smallpox. I'm sorry, but I must ask you not to touch her."

Hope scooted away, her face hidden in the shadow of her sunbonnet. She turned to fill a gourd with the remainder of the milk she had brought. "Give this to the sweet little girl, please, Daddy." She had a slight tremble in her voice.

Pastor poured milk into the gourd John held. Replacing her own gourd on the bucket hook, Hope half turned from him, but not before John glimpsed a wet spot glistening on her cheek. When she straightened, the tear was gone.

Pris gulped the milk John held to her lips. Her heart-shaped face looked content and she wrapped her small hand around John's finger. Behind him came the sound of shuffling feet and a muffled creaking.

"They're closing the gate. I'll see you tomorrow, dear." Pastor kissed his daughter's cheek.

Hope hugged her father. "Please take better care of yourself, Daddy." She turned to John. "A pleasure to meet you, Mr. Ross." The girl's tone suggested that it definitely had not been a pleasure to meet Mr. Ross.

John jutted his jaw. The girl could go to blazes for all he cared! Immediately he realized he did care. The prick to his pride hurt like an arrow to his chest. He couldn't remember when he'd wanted to make a better impression on a woman. Or when he failed more miserably.

She turned and walked toward the gate, her slender back stiff, her head held high, the strings of her bonnet floating behind her.

Pastor laid a heavy hand on John's shoulder. "Sorry, my fault. Timing was off and I'm afraid I built you up to hero status in my daughter's eyes."

"No, sir. Not your fault. I was rude." John kicked at the ground and gazed at Pastor's worn boots. "What did you tell her about me?"

"Oh, not so much. Just that you had been accepted at Princeton and how you saved Rachael from Robert Dread. Oh, and I told her you were a new convert and skimped on your own food to give more to the children."

John swallowed. "You laid on the praise a bit thick, didn't you?"

"All true, son." Pastor winked. "And I told Hope you were very respectful to women, seldom lost your temper, and were never in a bad mood."

"You didn't!"

"Afraid I did."

"So, when I had my mind on plotting revenge, she got the impression I didn't like her." John winced. He was the worst kind of idiot.

"Probably do her good. She's accustomed to having young men fall at her feet. You no doubt intrigue her."

"Aggravate her more like."

"Don't let her get the upper hand with you or she'll lose interest."

She was interested? Pastor must not know his own daughter. She wanted no part of him.

And, that stung.

CHAPTER 12

John frowned at Hope's receding back as she walked away. With a swirl of yellow skirts and scent of honeysuckle, she glided toward the gate, the sweet scent in her wake an inviting trail. As if they were royal escorts, a soldier fell in on either side, and each offered her his arm. Two other guards, silly grins plastered across their faces, stopped lingering near the gate and rushed to carry Hope's empty milk buckets outside.

John grunted.

Two other soldiers walked the missionary's daughter toward the door, their puffed-out chests and proud expressions betraying their eagerness. Infatuation seeped from the men's pores like sweat, obviously they couldn't wait to accompany Hope back into town. She turned a laughing face up to one of her escorts.

John scowled, and kicked a stockade stake, sending shooting pain up his leg. The double doors crashed together, shutting off his view. He slammed a fist into his palm. Why did he care? He cradled Pris in her sling and paced back and forth along the locked gate. There was no way to see through the tightly placed logs.

"Losing one's freedom is not easy."

John glanced behind him.

Pastor's green eyes crinkled at the corners as he peered over the rim of his spectacles. "I'm curious to find out what happened to you. You looked as angry as Moses thundering down Mount Sinai when you stormed over to meet Hope. I could see smoke curl out of your ears. Did you have another encounter with Bold Hunter?"

"That, plus one with Dread." John gazed down at his smarting toes. "When I went for rations, Dread made me crawl again." John cleared his throat. "Got to be more than I could handle today."

"I see." Pastor frowned and opened his mouth as if he were about to volunteer his services as the food supply man for the Rosses.

"Um, sir. Before you offer, I don't need any help." Nor pity. John leaned against the closed gate. "You have a fine daughter."

"Quite." Pastor dipped his head revealing gray among the bright red hair. "I notice she took you by surprise. She's flabbergasted people since she was a tot. She's a strong-minded girl." He straightened the lapel of his frock coat. "My parishioners expected her to fit into a specified mold. She refused. Hope called their presumption 'pristine, pure, and pallid.' She insisted on being herself in every way." Pastor folded his hands in supplication and gazed at the sky. "What can a man do?"

Was the saucy girl a thorn in this godly man's side? John rubbed the back of his neck. She sure pricked his own hide.

"I lost my wife when my daughter was born. Should have taken another wife. But the years swept by, and the right woman never came along"—Pastor winked—"though goodness knows, many a dear lady had designs."

John forced a smile.

"I sent Hope off to the strictest finishing school in Boston, but she wrote and begged me to let her come to Georgia to visit. She wants to help the Cherokee until we leave on the wagon train to the Indian Territory."

John swiped a hand over his dirty face. So, Hope wouldn't be around long. His shoulders slumped. Why should he care?

"I hadn't gotten the best of reports on her behavior at school." Pastor tugged out a handkerchief, wiped his forehead, and shook his head. "I missed her terribly, so I decided to let her come." Pastor's sigh trembled his cravat. "She took matters into her own hands, sold our household furniture, most of our clothes, and anything else she could get her interfering fingers on. She even held a couple of fund-raising bazaars. Used the money to buy blankets and clothes for these prisoners. She talked the government into issuing her a team of oxen, a wagon, and a driver ... and here she is. She bought a milk cow and finagled several gallons out of the army."

He gave a wry smile and straightened his spectacles. "I'm proud of her, but I'm worried too. While I'm locked up inside here, she's on her own with no chaperone. Between the two of them, I've ... well, let's talk about your problem."

"You have another daughter, sir?"

"No, a son. Just a bit older than you. He's here in the Regular Army. But that's a different story. Which gets us back to you. Who's doing your cooking now that Rachael is sick?"

"Me. I watched Rachael enough, so I think I can handle what little we have. And rustling up the rations gives me something to do. Mother gave strict orders to stay away from her and Rachael. After I prepare their food, Mother comes over to pick it up. She wants Pris kept out of danger."

"What about you? Have you had smallpox?"

"Yes, sir. When I was ten. Mother's nursing pulled me through."

"Happy to hear that. Rachael's not the only one who is sick. Quite a few of the children, plus some adults, have the fever. Several already have the spots. I fear we are in for an epidemic." Pastor shook his head so hard red spikes stood out. "I blame the unsanitary conditions in this place. I'll speak to General Scott to see what the army will do for us. The contagious ones must be isolated and given protection from the sun. This stockade could turn into a prison of death. Your mother is wise keeping Pris isolated."

John shifted his feet and rubbed his forehead to erase the frown creasing his brows. He'd heard about smallpox epidemics. Even with the best of conditions, people died. His head ached. The encounter with the Worchester girl had given him a headache.

"Man's inhumanity to man causes the suffering you see." Pastor's voice rang loud in the hushed prison. "The government must not have planned to keep everyone in prison this long, otherwise they would have provided better living conditions." He placed his hand on John's shoulder. "Your expression tells me you're still angry. You can't blame God for this. I think the prolonged drought made travel impossible."

"Then why doesn't God step in and do something? Why does he allow this suffering?" John kicked at a fissure in the baked ground.

"Ah, the mystery of suffering." Pastor ran his index finger under his cravat as if the tie were too tight, then took off his glasses and polished them on his handkerchief.

John gazed at the locked stockade doors.

Pris uncurled, stretched, and moved to a more comfortable position.

"I wish I knew all the answers to those questions." Pastor spoke as though he had been thinking over the possibilities. "I believe there are many reasons God allows suffering. I know a few of them from experience, a few of them by faith, and some I'm sure I'll never understand until I see my Lord. Why did God allow his own son to suffer?" He raised his graying eyebrows.

John shook his head. A muscle in his cheek twitched. "Why did he?"

Pastor rubbed his chin, his fingernails dirty from helping others survive their daily hardships. "The Bible says that Christ died for our sin. He took our punishment. The Perfect dying for the imperfect. I know God uses suffering to grow a Christian in his faith. When we suffer ... if we turn to Christ for help ... he will give us the strength we need." Pastor blew out a breath. "Suffering makes a Christian strong."

John let the words seep into his mind, cool water refreshing his thirst. The tired, middle-aged pastor never failed to give him what he needed. Here was a man who chose suffering so he could help the Cherokee ... a man who lived what he believed. The little pastor stood taller than any other man John had ever met.

"Still ... what about the people inside this prison who are not Christians?"

Pastor rubbed the red bristles on his chin. "Every man under the sun faces suffering sometime in his life. Suffering results from our own sin and from the sin of others. Sometimes this affliction makes a man turn to Christ, as you did. Other men turn away from God, growing hard and bitter. Look at Bold Hunter."

John glanced across the open ground toward the women's building where Bold Hunter leaned against the structure, his eyes on the lean-to under which Rachael lay.

Pastor continued. "John, I hope you will take every opportunity to tell Bold Hunter what Christ means to you. Bold Hunter worries me. He used to be a fine boy, but now he's full of hostility. There was a time, not so long ago, when he came close to accepting Christ. But he turned away." Pastor's deep voice dripped compassion. "If Bold Hunter doesn't turn to Christ, the hate in his life will destroy him."

John choked. Talk to the arrogant Indian? Pastor didn't know how much he asked.

The evening sun seemed as unwilling to set as John was unwilling to talk with Bold Hunter. The soldiers locked the men without active cases of smallpox as usual in the men's building. The suffocating blackness and stench frightened Pris, so John cuddled her in his arms and hummed to her until she slept. Then he peeled off his shirt, tucked the thin muslin around her, and settled her on the mud floor beside him.

Under cover of the darkness, he shifted to his knees and strove to get his mind off Rachael and the smallpox, the overwhelming heat, and the bodies packed about him. His meeting with Hope and the freedom she represented sent his blood thrumming with restlessness. Surely there was no worse torment in Hell than this. Although his lips remained closed, his heart stretched toward God.

Oh, God, please deliver us from this inhumane prison. He dropped his face into his hands. *Please relieve this gnawing hunger and everlasting thirst. Give us freedom to walk beneath the trees without someone pointing a gun at us, to smell clean air, to be alone.* He bowed until his forehead touched the mud. *Set me free from the daily humiliation of begging for rations. Give me safety from men who want to kill me.* The twisted knot in his chest felt ready to burst.

John opened his eyes. Nothing changed. He was still trapped, and the darkness remained thick, heavy with human odors. *God, where is the help you promised?* Hunger kinked his stomach. His gut ached. His dried-out tongue felt shriveled against his teeth.

Pastor's words reverberated in his mind, "They that wait on the Lord shall renew their strength; they shall mount up with wings as eagles; they shall run, and not be weary; and they shall walk, and not faint."

Timeless, eternal words. Promises to the Cherokee and the white man, to all men. God, the Creator, promised strength to any who wait on Him. "Thank You, Father, for your promises." John didn't care who heard his gratitude.

Muffled sobs came from somewhere to his left—hopeless cries, and the stifled sobbing had an instantaneous effect. All over the room young voices sniffled or moaned. A lump formed in John's throat. He swallowed hard. How could he help the children?

A faint voice in his mind answered. Having lived in the midst of Cherokees all his life, he knew the Cherokee were musical people, singing at weddings, births, deaths, while working the land, at the spinning wheel, rocking the cradle, pounding the corn, and during festivals.

So, John chose text the Pastor preached earlier in the day. He sang softly, his baritone filling the prison.

"Peace I leave with you,
Peace I leave with you,
My peace give I unto you,
Let not your heart be troubled,
Neither let it be afraid.
Peace I leave with you."

Catching the simple melody, men and boys joined in singing. The wonder and truth of the words encircled the room. The darkness, the heat, the stench, the loneliness, and the longing for home still occupied their minds, but now a sense of peace filled the room.

When the song ended, Pastor cleared his throat. "This reminds me of when Paul and Silas sang in their prison."

A young voice mounted above the hum of people sitting forward. "Please, let's sing some more. My mother used to sing me to sleep."

John's mind was a blank. What other words had Pastor given them? He shifted on the hard earth. He knew so little about the Christian life. "Pastor?"

Pastor began to sing a psalm of praise.

John crossed his legs more comfortably. Perhaps the singing would become a nightly boost, transforming the worst evening hours into a time of praise. Just before falling asleep, a new thought wormed its way into his mind. Perhaps the strength to endure comes as we reach out to help others.

Morning came in the usual way, but John welcomed dawn with lingering peace from the night's praises as he sat outside the men's building holding Pris in his lap. He stroked her soft curls pillowed against his chest. Since Mother left her, Pris clung to him, fussing if she were not in his lap or in his arms. She seldom laughed except when she played in the river. And she didn't ask for her mamma anymore. She seemed content as long as he held her but cried if he attempted to put her down.

A small lad shuffled to John. The boy stood in front, head hunched into his shoulders, and dug a bare toe in the dirt. "Will you tell me about Jesus?" His big brown eyes reached straight into John's heart.

"Sure, sit, and we'll talk man to man."

A group of boys followed the small lad and plopped down in a semicircle facing John. Hero worship shone on every grimy face. John's chest hurt as he looked at the thin, ragged youngsters, their faces so young and vulnerable. They should be in school. Enduring the heat and hunger were more than a man could bear. How could a child? He had to help these little ones.

He shared with them as much as he knew of the eternal story of God's love. They lolled in the blazing heat, eyes scrunched against the white light. Dull hopelessness, making their faces look older, slowly slid away as they responded to the truth of Jesus's love.

John finished speaking. He'd explained all he'd learned.

They gazed, wide-eyed, lips hanging open. A boy about seven, both front teeth missing, scooted closer. A sprinkling of freckles spread across his nose, his dark brown hair stuck out like straw, and his big brown eyes didn't waver. "I want to ask Jesus to come into my life same as you did. Will you pray with me?"

John swallowed and bowed his head. *Lord, help me do this right.*

The boy prayed, his childish voice quivering. "Jesus, please forgive my sins and come live in my life. Thank you."

Other voices joined his as some other little ones became children of God.

When the boy raised his head, his face sparkled, and he grinned from ear to ear. "Thanks, Mr. Ross."

John wet his dry lips and attempted to whistle. The little fellow tried, too—but with missing teeth, he could only produce a whooshing sound. John's dry cracked lips managed a thin imitation of his usual robust whistle.

"Uh, Mr. Ross." The oldest boy in the group, a dark lad with troubled black eyes, touched John's arm. "Are Indians not as good as white men?"

John bit his tongue, then squeezed his lips into a smile. Daily, he faced this question himself, struggling against his feelings of inferiority while penned inside the stockade and treated as less than human. Some of the soldiers worsened the situation with their name-calling. And Dread made his life hell.

"If the eternal God agrees to live in your heart, then you are worthwhile." John chucked the boy beneath his chin. "Does it matter what anyone else thinks?"

The boy straightened his shoulders. "That's right! Thank you, sir." He walked away, his head of matted dark hair held high.

After the others meandered away, John asked the one youngster who remained, one of the ones who had prayed, "What's your name?"

"Sitting Bear's my Indian name. Mother calls me Jamie."

"Jamie Sitting Bear, we're brothers in Jesus now. You come to me anytime you need help. Pris, say hi to your new brother."

Pris smiled a slow smile, her face like an angel's. "Jesus."

John grinned. He would never forget this precious word one-year-old Pris uttered. Or this happy moment.

CHAPTER 13

Someone was dead.

A crowd gathered near Pastor as he hammered a sign on a stud next to the stockade doors. John knew the Cherokee custom. When a person died, a leader tacked a notice on the church door, and the ringing church bell announced the death.

Here, there was no bell nor church door.

A low, wailing moan wafted from the area set aside for isolating women patients. A spasm of dread shot through John's chest. He rose to his feet, careful not to disturb Pris asleep in her blanket sling. Weaving through the people-congested enclosure toward the notice, he prayed. Not Rachael. *Oh God, please not Rachael.* Fear prickled his skin.

The stench of death hovered in the still, hot air. Four blanket-covered bodies lay side-by-side on the hard-packed mud near the stockade doors. John moved through the crowd to read the paper.

- Tim Takatokoh—age six months
- Sarah Raincrow—age four years
- Samuel Echohawk—age ten years
- Mary Matthews—age eighteen years
- Baby Matthews—unborn

Rachael still lived! John turned away from the pitiful line of bodies. He had to be alone. But he found no privacy.

Everywhere he went, someone filled the space, so he walked blindly toward the stockade wall, his lips clamped. A greenish tinge blurred his eyesight. He leaned his back against the chinked poles and slid to the ground. Holding his head in his hands, he tried not to surrender to the sickness churning inside.

All but one of those still mounds under the tattered blankets had been happy, carefree children. He remembered when they were chubby, full of life and health. Sammy Echohawk had vowed, 'When I get big like you, John, I'm going to have a horse just like Jasper.' The boy had so much determination. So much life. So much to live for.

Little Sarah Raincrow had been the pride of her family. A bright, inquisitive child, always asking questions. From playing ball to learning to weave, Sarah had been Johnny-on-the-spot, eager to participate. The last time he'd seen her in her own home, she stood by her mother and older sister, listening to the hum of the spinning wheel and the smack of the loom as they wove special material for Sarah's birthday dress.

Pris stirred in her blanket sling. John shook himself and jammed his hot forehead against the smooth timber of the stockade, hiding the agony twisting his face. He smashed his fist into the wall, glad for the physical pain.

"Why, God, why? They were so innocent. Why do the innocent suffer?"

Pris lifted her little arms, cupped her hands around John's face, and kissed him. Her hot fingers wiped the wetness from his cheeks. Then she wrapped her arms around his neck and hugged him.

John buried his face in her soft neck, and her golden hair tickled his nose. "I've got to get you out of this prison of death."

"What wrong, Unaka? You God no help?" Bold Hunter's voice sounded like the hissing of a snake.

John spun to face him. "I don't know much about God yet, but I do know He has the answer. What explanation do you have for all this?" He waved toward the bodies, the filth, the prison.

Bold Hunter's eyes shimmered with dark passion. "Thunder man no come for long time. He protect Cherokee. Me go to long man river. Have water prayer for people. Face east on bank of flowing long man. Wash in long man. Pray. Lay on bank long time. Have dream. Blue cloud covering Cherokee go away. White cloud come. Hear drum beats far away. Get louder and louder in head. Drumbeats stir in blood, in bones." Bold Hunter held his head high. His jaw squared and his eyes flashed.

"Now drums in air, all around, loud. Drums make Bold Hunter stand tall. Put on war paint. Make war dance. Women make war whoop. War food tasted. Put away. Take war trail, take bow, hatchet, long rifle, knife, get scalps. Avenge Cherokee dead."

John easily pictured an angry Bold Hunter leading a war party against the uniformed soldiers. He held up his hand. "Stop and think. For every white man killed, twenty will take his place. We are hopelessly outnumbered. And fighting won't bring back the dead."

Bold Hunter flexed his muscles. "Ross have yellow stripe down back."

Bam. Bam. Bam.

As he had each morning for the past two weeks, Pastor hammered a new list of the dead next to the one he tacked up the previous day. The old lists numbered fourteen, but today's list contained twenty names.

A crowd gathered. Pastor turned to face them. "Because hundreds of you are sick with smallpox, our journey to Oklahoma Territory is delayed until cooler weather."

A murmur, like wind through stalks of dry corn, whispered through camp.

The little pastor let his hammer slip to the ground by his worn shoe. "Take heart folks. We've only a few more weeks. Pray for cool weather."

John heaved a deep sigh and shuffled forward to read the names of those who would never leave the prison. Tears he no longer bothered to hide filled his eyes. His little friend Jamie Sitting Bear now lay safe in the arms of Jesus. Grandfather Raincrow also made today's list.

John glanced across the open yard to where the isolated sick lolled in an area beneath a crude pole and blanket shelter. Mother and six other women nursed the stricken day and night.

Each morning soldiers removed the dead and buried them outside the walls.

When John strolled to morning services, he averted his eyes from the growing cemetery.

Except for double rations of water, the guards offered no other help, staying as far from the prisoners as possible. The few soldiers who ventured inside had survived the dread disease in their childhood. Unfortunately, Corporal Robert Dread was among them.

Pastor caught up with John. "Good news! Rachael's improved. Her pox are dried up and falling off. She's going to live."

John flashed a real smile, his first since Jamie Sitting Bear had decided for Jesus.

"What's more, this morning Rachael sat up alone. She's thin and wobbly, but she's definitely recuperating."

"Excellent news, sir. I didn't think she had much chance."

"God spared her from scarring. Her skin's as smooth and clear as a newborn child's where the pox have fallen off. She told me she prayed that if God let her live, he would protect her from being pockmarked." Pastor shook his head. "Women. As if her being scarred could make a difference in how much we love Rachael."

"I can't wait to see her." John dabbed Pris's face with a bit of the precious water. "Why do some people live and others die? Why are some prayers answered, but not all? God's ways are more than I can figure out."

Still without answers, a week later John sent word to Rachael to pray for Pris. Fever raged in the little girl, and she couldn't keep milk down. She lay limp in his arms, her big blue eyes bewildered.

Mother came for Pris.

"Let me nurse her, Mother. She likes me to sing to her." John hugged Pris to his chest.

Mother's cheeks were sunken, dark rings circled her eyes, her torn dress hung on her thin frame almost to the point of being immodest, and uncombed hair straggled around her face. She gave him a wistful smile and a light kiss on his cheek. "No, dear, a mother needs to be with her child when she is sick." Her hot fingers patted his cheek. "I've missed her so dreadfully."

As his mother took Pris, John caressed his sister's golden curls and trailed his fingers over her arms "I hate to give her up."

All that long night John missed the little girl's sweet presence. His empty arms yearned to hold her. Next morning, before the wide gates groaned open, Mother walked to where he sat hunched outside the men's building.

He knew.

A weight crushed his chest so he could barely speak. "Did Pris suffer, Mother?"

She knelt beside him and took both his hands. "No, darling. Pris was sleeping. She woke up with a bright laugh, like she used to at Pleasant Acres. As if she were back in her own crib at home, she asked for her baby bear. Then she smiled, closed her eyes, and said, 'John, John.' Then she was gone." Silent tears flowed down his mother's cheeks.

In the days that followed, John kept checking to see if part of his own body had been amputated. Was he bleeding? His arms felt empty. He saw Pris's smile in shafts of sunlight under the trees. A whispered breeze across the back of his neck reminded him of her sweet breath when she hugged him. Many times, he stopped short of pointing out a pretty butterfly or flower to her.

She was gone.

Tears washed Pastor's once-lively eyes as he wrapped an arm around John's shoulders. "If we had no pain, we would need no Spirit of Christ to comfort us."

John gritted his teeth, clenched his fists, and walked away.

CHAPTER 14

The stockade doors opened. Outside, a long line of Conestoga wagons appeared to stretch on until they met the horizon. John gazed at the sky. "Mother, such a dark, overcast morning to mark this momentous date. I'll remember this day until I die."

His spirits soared. Freedom at last!

Leading almost a thousand other Cherokees, he trudged out through the tall prison gates. The early morning stiffness in his back eased as he, Rachael, and Mother hurried across the meadow toward the canvas-covered wagons. Bold Hunter ran to join them and reached for Rachael's hand.

Once outside the gates, a guard fell in on either side of John, matching his stride. John grunted. Dread pushing his advantage, being overzealous.

John looked behind him. The milling mass of captives attempted to keep families together and claim a wagon. Hundreds of soldiers, eyes alert, and rifles at ready, fell in to guard the prisoners surging from the stockade and congregating around the wagons.

John ignored his scowling guards and led Mother away from the wagons to the graveyard. They stopped at the recently dug grave, and he knelt beside Pris's tiny burial plot.

He prayed, then reached up and touched the simple wooden cross he'd constructed, and on which he'd carved

Safe in the Arms of Jesus. He buried his face in his hands. "I'll meet you in Heaven, sweet Pris." He stood and wrapped an arm around Mother's bowed shoulder. "How can such an impersonal piece of ground contain our sunny little girl?"

Mother's eyes spilled over. "She's not there. Only her precious body."

Rachael and Bold Hunter joined them. Rachael's lovely dark eyes streamed, and she embraced John's mother. Bold Hunter stood, face impassive. Waiting.

John swiped at the wetness on his cheeks. Much as he yearned to leave, his feet seemed rooted beside the small mound. And yet, Pris's lilting laughter sang inside his mind as if urging him to go—to go on to the new land. Go on to the new life. Go on to the new home. Still, pain rooted his feet beside her grave.

"Gotta get moving, fella. Sorry for your loss." The taller of his special guards motioned toward the waiting wagons. "But we gotta get goin'."

John sighed, nodded, and guided mother away from the cemetery toward the line of covered wagons where people scrambled aboard. How could he encourage Mother? He forced a smile and pointed. "One of those Conestoga's will be our home for the next six months or longer. They don't look comfortable, but they'll transport us out of here."

Mother offered a wavering smile through the tears trailing her pale cheeks. "Wherever you and I are together will be home. We'll manage quite well inside one of those wagons."

"Right." He used his thumbs to wipe the tears from her face, then tapped a water keg strapped to the nearest wagon. "We'll have water."

"Do you think the army will give us more food than we had in prison?" A crease deepened between Mother's brows.

John snorted. Huh. The government won't suddenly care about us. "Let's wait and see." He sauntered over to stare into the open rear flap of the closest wagon. "Barrels, bags, and boxes fill most of the interior." He slapped the wagon's wooden side. "But there can't be room for many people."

He stared up the road. The lead wagons were already moving, escorted by soldiers on horseback. "Looks like there aren't enough wagons for all of us. I don't see any blankets or bedding either."

"At least, cooler weather has finally come." Rachael lifted her face to the gray, overcast sky with more dark clouds rolling in. "Looks as if the drought will break at last."

John nodded. "Not an ideal way to begin our journey. At least, those wagons will shelter us. And we're headed to freedom."

He squinted. Beneath the clouds, a blue haze hung low over the Smokies making the lower range barely discernible. The higher elevation blurred in a purple mist. John lowered his gaze and spotted the soldier in charge of the moving wagon train. A hard knot clutched his stomach and he scowled. So that's the way this journey would go. He should have guessed. *God, give me strength.* He dragged in a deep breath.

"I'm sorry, Mother, but we can plan on getting the last wagon, if we get one." He sighed. "Corporal Dread's assigning wagons."

"God will take care of us." His mother perched on a smooth rock beneath a tall Magnolia tree and spread her tattered skirts around her ankles. Rachael settled at Mother's feet, Bold Hunter behind her, his hands on her shoulders.

John, his toes protruding from his worn-out moccasins, paced back and forth in front of his little family. Sure enough, he was right. The sun, hidden behind bleak roiling clouds, stood at high noon before Dread strode toward them, his muscles pumping.

The next to the last wagon rolled up the trail, brining a cloud of dust to settle over their small group.

"Leave it to the army to work with efficiency." John spoke loud enough for the wagon master to hear. "Takes them all morning to assign wagons."

Strangely, Dread seemed in a rare, good mood and ignored John's jab. "This here's the last wagon, and we ain't got enough Injun men left to help navigate it up and down those mountains, Ross." A smirk spread over Dread's face.

"You and thet varmint there." Dread nodded toward Bold Hunter who lounged against the tree next to where Rachael sat weaving a reed basket. "Will have to git this wagon to the Indian Territory by yerselves. Don't look to nobody else for help when the going gets rough. My soldiers got their orders." He sneered, showing tobacco-stained teeth. "If you two cain't get that wagon up them mountains by yerselves, well that's jist too bad."

On his way toward the wagon, John froze mid-step. Would the man never get his fill of tormenting him? All the other big Conestogas had four men assigned to drive them. The four men team's job would be back-breaking. He and Bold Hunter faced the impossible. No wonder Dread was in such a good mood.

Bold Hunter shot John a deadly look, then strode over to help Rachael scramble up the high step into the wagon. She climbed over the wooden seat, through the flap, and under the canvas into the wagon bed. Bold Hunter hopped up and perched on the wooden bench seat in front of her.

On the driver's side, John lifted his mother to the step— she was much lighter than she should have been. She bent and followed Rachael into the covered wagon's interior. John poked his head inside. Nine Indian children who probably lost their parents in the smallpox epidemic sat in two rows, their backs braced against the wagon ribs. Rachael and Mother had squeezed in beside them. All eleven were jammed into the wagon like pickles in a jar.

"We are out of the wind." Mother tucked an arm around the child on either side of her. "We can be thankful for the shelter." She glanced at each child. "Let's all pray for John and Bold Hunter. Since the weather cooled, they need warmer clothes."

The little voices rose in prayer. John leaped onto the wagon and dropped onto the driver's seat. As though the elements had waited for the last woman and child to be seated inside the wagons, the sky turned black. Wind rushed down the mountain and carried rain in waving sheets.

John sucked in the fresh clean scent, and energy seeped into every muscle. More wind ghosted into the valley, shaking tree branches, rustling dry leaves, and swaying the wagons. John raised his face to the wind, thankful the canvas overhang kept most of the rain off him and Bold Hunter.

A soldier leading a horse slogged up to Dread, handed him yellow oilskins, and the horse's reins. The beefy man slipped on the rain gear and hoisted himself into the saddle. Reining his skittish horse in front of the oxen, he pointed a thick forefinger at Bold Hunter. "You drive."

Dread turned to John and yelled over the wind. "You walk! Don't need that tall frame of yours adding weight to the wagon."

John slammed his fist into his open palm. Oh, he'd like to pound that grinning face. He exchanged places with Bold Hunter.

Bold Hunter shook as he unwound the rein from the whip socket. His fingers fumbled with the numerous leather straps. He spewed Cherokee below his breath. John scooted closer, adjusted the reins in Bold Hunter's hands, and demonstrated how to signal the six yoked oxen. "Have you never driven a wagon?"

"Bold Hunter no need learn drive wagon." He elbowed John away. "Bold Hunter smart."

Dread furrowed his bushy brows and slapped his hand on the whip attached to his saddle. "Walk!"

John glared at Dread as he leapt to the ground. Rain hit him with pounding suddenness, the pelts pricked like needles, soaking him to his skin. His feet sank into mud.

Dread turned his big roan toward the front of the train, then scowled down at John. "I got plans for you, Ross. When things get boring, I'm gonna have me some fun. In the meantime, you're gonna push your guts out and shove your shoulder through them wagon spokes until your flesh turns black, and you wish you was dead!" The veins in the bull-like neck stood out. He threw back his head and laughed. "You're mine until we reach Indian Territory." He lifted his bullwhip.

The hair on the back of John's neck stood up.

With a crack that opened a red stripe across the lead ox's rump, Dread bellowed, "Wagon, ho!" The oxen jerked forward and plodded into position at the end of the line of wagons lumbering away from the empty stockade, its tall open gates rattling in the wind.

Ignoring the rain, children leaned out the back of the tented canvas and waved goodbye to the land of their birth. To the life they had known. To the silent cemetery where their parents rested. To Cherokee land.

As the wagons jolted past the hundreds of freshly dug graves, John let rain wipe tears from his face. Parents, brothers, and sisters remained behind in those graves. Pris's sweet little body lay below wet earth. Pris's laughter still echoed inside his memory. If only he could feel her slight weight hanging from his shoulders.

The rain seemed to share the sadness of the exodus, weeping mighty tears. John hunched his shoulders against the chill. The October sleet pelted his skin and turned the clay beneath his almost bare feet blood red. He shivered, his linen shirt rain-blasted to his body. Strong winds plastered his blond hair to his head one moment and drove strands into his face the next. The lashing rain blinded him, so he could barely see Bold Hunter's clumsy handling of the reins.

The ruts in the road flooded, and John's feet skidded in the ankle-deep mud.

He tightened his jaw. He would get Mother and Rachael and the wagonload of orphans safely to Indian Territory. He would start a new life for them, knowing the strength from his new life in Christ would help. And he wouldn't let Dread break him.

Moving at a turtle's pace, their last wagon in the long train passed the Moravian Brethren Mission at Spring Place on the familiar road from Georgia to east Tennessee, three miles east of the Conasauga River. Would he ever travel this road again?

To divert his mind from the miserable weather and his dismal appraisal, John thought of the youngsters inside the wagons who must have attended the mission. They'd learned reading, writing, arithmetic, English, grammar, and geography. The girls had learned spinning, sewing, knitting, and how to make their own stockings. The missionaries taught the boys to farm, to make animal skin clothing, and to guide the horse and plow. The children would need those skills in the new land. If the hostile Indians living there made room for them.

John slipped in a rut, burying his knees in the mud, and jolting his thoughts to the treacherous road. He struggled to his feet and dodged an army officer on horseback patrolling the train who looked as happy to be on the move as the Cherokees.

John had to keep alert to dodge the Army horses splashing through the mud, trotting up and down the creeping wagon train. The soldiers' muzzle-loading rifles lay across their saddles, primed and ready, as though they expected every Indian man on the train to venture an escape.

Who would be crazy enough to slip away with one armed guard for every two weakened Cherokee men? John eyed the full-length yellow oilskins each soldier wore and tried to control his shivering.

He swiped rain from his eyelashes. At various spots along the train's length, a cluster of militiamen jugged whiskey. Probably their way to ward off the cold. They would be dead drunk by tonight, so he'd confine Mother and Rachael to the Conestoga.

The rain slashed into his face from the west. "Land of the Dead," he growled to the wind. The rain beat so loud he scarcely heard the friendly creaking of the wagon with its wet canvas slapping against the sides. He kept a sharp eye on the oxen straining their shoulders against the load. With heads hanging and ears fallen forward, they followed the wagon ahead. At least, since he'd learned to keep the wheels on the road, Bold Hunter shouldn't have much trouble driving them.

Lucky him. What appeared to be a company of cavalry rode about twenty feet behind their wagon. The tall blue hat emblazoned with the United States eagle identified them as they huddled under yellow oilskins. The jangle of their spurs, an occasional clank of a sword, along with the creak of leather from men on horseback robbed John of any notion of freedom. He was a prisoner. Still at the mercy of the US Government. Still hassled by Dread.

Snatches of the rider's conversation, bits of jokes flung his way by the wind, and ribald songs meant to cheer the soldier caused loneliness to curl inside John's chest. He trudged near the right front wheel of the groaning wagon. He dipped his head. He was alone, cut off from human companionship.

As the soldiers yelled back and forth from horse to horse, John picked up bits of the men's conversation, revealing the wagons headed toward Rattlesnake Springs, Tennessee.

He swung his arms and hunched against the wind but couldn't stop shivering. When had he ever been so miserably cold? Even the blasting heat of the stockade seemed easier to endure than this.

"Lord, give me strength." He glanced at Bold Hunter, reins taut in his brown hands, his body—except for his long legs—sheltered by the canvas overhang. Rachael huddled behind him, obviously taking warmth from his big frame, her head buried in his shoulder. Her glossy braids bounced with each jerk of the wagon.

Hands filled with leather reins, Bold Hunter threw him a smug smile.

Love my enemies. John concentrated on keeping his footing in the slick mud. *You really don't expect me to, do you, Lord?*

The wagon lumbered on for hours in the downpour. Mud sucked at John's feet, making every step a contest of strength. After wasting in prison for five months with insufficient food, this exodus required all his energy.

The wagon ahead bumped over wood. Then oxen's hooves clanged. John turned to Bold Hunter. "A covered bridge. Must be the Chickamauga River. We'll soon be in Tennessee. That mountain on the other side of the river will be tough to cross."

"Yeah."

John rested beneath the bridge's wooden roof until the horse soldiers riding behind their wagon forced him back into the rain.

The road narrowed and ascended the mountain. The wagon in front, pushed by four Indians, lurched slower and slower as the road angled higher. Inching up the steep ascent, the wagon ahead began to circle the mountain. Flooded ruts cut deep into the mud from preceding wagons provided no traction for theirs.

John slogged beside the wagon as it started up the mountain, then ground to a stop.

"Shove your shoulder to it, Ross!" Dread's voice cut through the dense rain.

John scowled. Blasted man sloshed back through the muck to check on me.

Corporal Dread sat on his roan, grinning down.

John wrapped his cold, slippery fingers around the large wooden wheel, struggling to dislodge the wagon from the mud. Too tired to more than glance at Dread, he grasped the slimy spoke and shoved. The wagon inched upward.

Bold Hunter handed the reins to Rachael and landed in the mud, splattering clods on a passing soldier's horse. He grabbed a spoke of the other rear wheel and rammed his shoulder against the wood. Together, he and Bold Hunter shoved the wagon until it ground through the ruts, inching up the mountain.

Mother opened the back flap and stuck her head out into the rain. "I think the children and I should jump out and walk. If we don't, I doubt the two of you can propel this monstrosity up that mountain."

"No, Mother, you and the children stay put." John gasped and took a minute to lean against the tailgate to catch his breath. "It's too wet and cold. You'd never dry out, and you'll all get sick. We'll shove this wagon up."

Mother frowned. "You've been drenched for hours. I didn't realize how thin you've become."

John glanced down. With his clothes plastered to his skin, he couldn't hide how much weight he'd lost. "Don't worry about me. Work like this builds muscles."

"But you'll catch pneumonia working barefoot in the rain." Her face contorted, and tears spilled from her eyes.

John laughed. "I won't run after it, and I won't let it catch me." He sure wasn't the well-dressed man who'd prepared to leave for Princeton. He didn't have any of the trappings of wealth now.

But he did have a calm center inside, a place of rock steadiness that diminished the reckless daring that had driven him when he lived at Pleasant Acres. In the past few months, he'd lost the cocky arrogance he'd not realized he had when he worked with the slaves. Pastor's words were true. God did give him the strength to persevere. "Go on back inside, Mother. I'm fine."

"I'm afraid I'm not reassured." But she pulled her head in and closed the flap.

He and Bold Hunter shoved and sweated. For every yard gained, the wagon rocked back a foot. Already his shoulders were tender where he wedged them against the spoke. They heaved the loaded wagon, inching it up the steep incline. Then the front wheels hung up. The Conestoga stopped.

Knee deep in muck, John's head reeled.

Dread's roan splashed down the mountainside. He pulled up beside them, threw back his head, and brayed like a hyena standing over a fresh kill. "You got a long way to go, Ross. One way or another, you ain't never gonna make it to Indian Territory. You'll regret the day you tangled with Corporal Robert Dread." With a vicious spur, he sent his roan back up the mountain, his laughter floating on the wind.

Shaking with cold and too tired to push himself to his feet, John knelt in the muck and gazed at his foe's retreating back. "Just shoot me now and get it over with."

He hung his head. Nothing that easy for him. A dozen lives depended on him.

CHAPTER 15

Hands slippery with mud, John rubbed his raw shoulders and leaned against the wagon, trying to catch his breath. "That's it. I'm through pushing my insides out on this Conestoga." His voice sounded raspy. "Either we get help, Bold Hunter, or we sit here."

A soldier, his yellow oilskins dripping waterfalls onto his Cavalry boots, dismounted from his horse and took a place in the center of the tailgate. The three strained together until the wagon lurched forward and snaked up the mountain.

Gasping like a steam locomotive low on water, John bent, hands on his muddy knees, back to the wind, and rested. The others did too.

"Don't I know you from somewhere?" John shoved wet hair out of his eyes. "You look familiar."

The man in oilskins was short, about five feet eight, but strongly built. Rusty hair hung limp and wet beneath his campaign hat. He had a frank, honest face which some might call good-looking and others rugged.

"Nope, don't think so. I'm from Massachusetts. Just arrived to police the removal. Company got in last night. Name's Jeremy. Jeremy Worchester." The soldier's voice sounded like a younger version of Pastor's.

"Ah! Now I know." John straightened and leaned against the back of the wagon. "Isaac Worchester's my friend. He mentioned he had a son who served in the army." John swiped at his wet eyelashes with his arm. "I don't think he knew you were coming here."

"Nope, our orders were secret. Most folks in America are riled up about this removal. General Wool resigned his commission because he objected to what Jackson's doing. 'Old Fuss and Feathers' took his place. Many people think stealing your land is un-American."

"I'm honored to meet you." John stretched out his hand and shook the soldier's equally muddy, equally wet, and equally cold hand. Their hands squelched out mud between their fingers. "And much obliged for your help." He leaned toward Jeremy and spoke in a low voice. "Guess you noticed Dread's been riding me hard. I don't want you getting into trouble with him for helping us."

"Don't fret about Dread. The saddle will be on the other horse when the wagon train conductor gets wind of this." Jeremy's square chin jutted. He braced his back against the canvas. "I've been eager to see my sister again. She's joined the train, too, I hear. Have you met her?"

Hope was on the wagon train? Interest flickered as an uncomfortable heat crept up John's neck. "She didn't go home?"

"She wants to help our father and the Cherokees in any way she can. I understand Pa and she have a wagon near the front." Jeremy shaded his eyes from the slashing rain. "Say, you sure don't look Cherokee. Are you?"

"Uh-huh. My dad was only an eighth Cherokee. My uncle is the chief." John shrugged and pain whipped through his shoulders. He ducked his head. Not a good time to think about his past.

A mounted soldier yelled, "Worchester, get this rig going! The others are leaving us behind. Close the gap."

"Help shove if you want us to move," Jeremy yelled back. "We need at least one other man pushing this wagon. Two more would be better."

The soldier grumbled. "You're always asking someone to do something he don't want to do." He dismounted, slipped in the mud, and cursed but took a place beside Jeremy.

No other soldier offered to help.

The day dragged on. John forced one tattered moccasin-clad foot in front of the other. Each time the wagon hung up, he struggled to carry his weight getting the Conestoga on the move again. Bold Hunter kept his side rocking along while Rachel worked the reins and urged the oxen on.

But could he shove this wagon to the top of this unending mountain? Just before nightfall when shadows hid the road, the muddy ground beneath John's cold feet leveled off. The wagon ahead halted on the narrow, twisting road.

"We'll make camp here, men." The word came down the long line of canvas-dripping wagons. Since theirs was the last wagon in line, John stopped at the crest of the mountaintop while others halted below on the long plateau.

The rain continued, sometimes slowing to a drizzle, but mostly driving hard, sending cold slivers into John's flesh. He gave up trying to build a fire. "Impossible." He watched as some of the kindling floated away.

He poked his head inside the Conestoga and found the interior damp and chilly. The women and children huddled together trying to keep each other warm, but each had a smile for him.

Rachael climbed over the seat and moved inside to sit between the youngsters. Hunched together on the front bench, John and Bold Hunter wolfed cold hominy grits. Cramped and wriggling with restlessness, the women and children remained inside the wagon. Each time they moved, the wagon swayed. The smell of wet canvas hung in the dripping air.

In the deepening darkness while John unhitched the oxen, the soldiers pitched their tents on any flat spots available, ate their rations cold, and climbed into what John was sure were dry bedrolls. A heavy guard patrolled the length of the wagon train. Appeared the commanding officer didn't want to lose any Indians on such a wild night.

John sighed. Easy to sneak away, but he wouldn't leave Mother … or Rachael … or the youngsters. And then, there was the haughty Miss Worchester. He hobbled the oxen where they could graze on whatever grass they found. Teeth chattering, he climbed up on the wagon seat and glanced at Bold Hunter. "Where do we sleep?"

Bold Hunter pointed beneath the wagon. John stared at the sucking mud. Water swirled through the ruts worn into the trail and slime and mud coated the wagon's wheels. Miniature waterfalls cascaded off the wooden frame, leaving a narrow space under the center of the wagon which offered a slight protection from the deluge.

Flanked by his two grumbling guards, John followed Bold Hunter and tramped through knee-high wet grass to a grove of trees halfway down an embankment. He and Bold Hunter gathered fallen fir branches and lugged them up the hilly bank to make a bed beneath the wagon.

John shook water off the boughs, scrambled under the wooden floor, made a branch bed, and pulled sprays over his shivering body. "Not too bad a blanket. Damp but keeps the wind out."

"Ugh." Bold Hunter grunted and reached for another spray.

Water cascading from the wagon swirled down the mountain, the wind howled unhindered at the crest, and the temperature continued to fall. Sheltered between fir boughs and out of the rain, John stopped shivering, but cold reached through the branches like a hungry wolf. His legs ended in lumps of ice. Oh well. Huddling back to back with Bold Hunter at least brought body heat.

Overhead, the rustling in the wagon stopped.

Mother, lying up there crowded with the youngsters, might finally rest. Try to relax as he could, still sleep eluded him. Which sounded worse, the drumming rain or Bold Hunter snoring. In the distance, a single wolf voiced a dismal howl.

John lifted heavy eyelids, then heard the music again. The bugle. Time to rise and shine. He groaned. Another day of downpour. They needed this rain last summer.

Bold Hunter stirred and snorted but didn't move.

Outside John's small oasis, soldiers clanked through their bivouac starting their day. Everything smelled musty and John's clothes clung like damp sacks. A hot bath followed by steak and eggs sounded good. Had it been years ago he took food for granted? No, just long months. Now he didn't know whether to rub his stomach or his feet. One rumbled. The others were numb. He waited until the last minute, then crawled from beneath the wagon, and stretched his stiff knees and back. A warm-up restarted his circulation.

Eyes drooping and face gloomy, Bold Hunter crept out the other side looking as tired as John felt.

The soldiers cursed and grumbled as they saddled their horses. "I sure didn't want to pull this duty," a tenor voice complained. "You can say what you want, but I say a terrible wrong's being done to these ignorant savages. We ain't got any right to make them leave this land."

"Not like we could do anything. Shut up and help me get these horses fed." A hand slapped the rump of a horse. "Orders are orders. When old Dan Webster failed to stop the removal, what can a poor grunt in this man's army do?"

Mother leaned from the rear of the wagon and handed out a burlap bag of oats. John fed and hitched the oxen, then hoisted himself onto the wagon seat and bolted down the cold hominy grits Rachael handed him.

"I'm sorry, but this is the best we could fix." Rachael ladled water from the barrel tied on the outside corner of the wagon and handed the cup to him. The cold tin chilled his hands.

Deep creases between Mother's eyebrows stood out starkly in the light of a single candle inside the wagon. "Did you sleep, dear? Were you dry? I worried about you all night."

"No need to fret, the fir branches kept me warm." John stretched his aching arms.

"So why the weary lines around your mouth and eyes?" Rachael's long hair straggled around her face, and dark circles underlined her eyes.

Mother brushed Rachael's hair into a braid and tied pieces of tattered lace to hold the strands in place. "The children are cold. We need blankets. Do you think the army will issue us some?"

"I'll see what I can do," he promised and then told all those inside the wagon about meeting Jeremy Worchester and how Pastor's son had helped.

In the distance, the bugle sounded for the wagons to roll. John jumped to the ground. His feet slid out from under him, and he landed on his backside in the mud.

Bold Hunter climbed into the driver's seat and sang out, "Ho!"

The well-trained oxen strained against the harnesses, and the wagon jolted forward.

John splashed through ankle high water on a road he could barely see. At least he wouldn't have to push going downhill. From where they camped on the crest, the distant mountaintops just visible through the drizzle looked snow-capped.

Clouds hung low over the road. In spots, thick fog made driving dangerous. But the oxen lowered their heads and tramped on, following so close to the wagon ahead that their breath plumed against the wagon's rear end.

Damp and chill settled with a vengeance into John's bones. He whooped a deep, dry cough that hurt his chest. The wagon began to descend but too steeply. The swaying canvas top leaned hard to the left side. Bold Hunter grabbed the wooden brake and slammed the stick down hard. But the brake yanked too fast on the left rear wheel. Sliding with incredible speed sideways over the slippery mud, the wagon load of people headed for the steep mountain drop-off.

CHAPTER 16

John sprinted toward the right lead ox. He pulled the nose ring to the right. "Gee! Gee! Gee!"

Stamping and snorting, the bewildered animal struggled to obey the repeated commands. The other oxen followed, then dug in their hooves and strained against the harness. But the wagon's weight dragged the animals toward the brink.

John planted his feet and hauled on both oxen's nose rings with every ounce of muscle. The animals heaved against the wagon, but the huge Conestoga kept sliding toward the cliff. The loaded vehicle tilted, stopped, and hung, its left rear wheel spinning crazily over the edge of the gorge. The panting oxen and the wagon straddled crosswise over the narrow road.

John took charge and bellowed above the screams inside the wagon. "Jeremy, grab the reins. Keep these oxen steady so they don't slide backward." He yelled at the officers assigned to guard him, "You two get over here and help me haul this colossus back onto the road."

The command in John's voice spurred the soldiers to dismount and spring into action.

"Mother, you and the children crawl to the front of the wagon and climb out. Don't panic. Everything's under control."

As Bold Hunter slid from the driver's seat, his mouth looked green around the edges. One by one, the nine youngsters climbed over the seat, down from the wagon into the mud and drizzle. Then the women descended.

John's mother clung to him, laughing her relief.

Rachael whispered in a husky voice, "We'd all be dead if you hadn't acted so fast."

Bold Hunter's eyes smoldered. His expression left no doubt he wanted to take John apart, limb from limb, and hang the remains on the nearest tree.

With the soldiers using ropes, horses, and manpower, John directed them to ease the wagon back onto the road. Since the wheel was bent but usable, the women and children scrambled back inside, dripping rain, and babbling their excitement.

The soldiers mounted their horses and took their places behind the wagon, two or three throwing respectful glances his way. John nodded. Maybe the riders didn't think he was such an ignorant savage now.

"That's a beautiful girl. Where's she been hiding?"

"She can warm my tent anytime."

Other Cavalry riders continued to stare at the tailgate after Rachael climbed inside.

John glared at them, shook his head, and raised his fist. Then he opened the flap and leaned inside the wagon. "Everyone settled?"

The children cheered.

"The children say you are a hero." Rachael's throaty voice floated above the hubbub of excited children's voices.

"My pleasure, ma'am."

Even damp, with her long black hair tousled, Rachael looked captivating. He could have stood there all day while she gazed at him, admiration beaming from her expression. "But you and Mother need to stay out of sight." He jerked his head toward the mounted Cavalry.

"Oh. Right." Rachael and Mother's voices blended. A blush spread over Rachael's cheeks.

"Come on, Don Juan, pin on your medal of bravery and sprint back here," Jeremy called. "We have to catch up."

John backed away, rounded the wagon, and hoisted his tired body onto the driver's seat. "This time Bold Hunter,

I'll drive. This treacherous mountain is no place for you to learn. Sit here and watch if you like."

Hunched beside him on the bench seat, Bold Hunter glowered in silence.

The oxen plodded down the narrow, twisting road. Just before the next hairpin turn, John applied the brake. The job of maneuvering the wagon down the steep road—slippery with mud, often obliterated by dense fog, and through the driving rain, left him exhausted and with an aching back. But at least he was mostly dry. At the bottom, he halted the team to rest.

Supper proved a repeat of the night before. When the rain let up, John trudged into the descending darkness to find Jeremy. He and his two jailors created plenty of noise in the darkness so no trigger-happy sentry would imagine he was trying to escape.

Jeremy had pitched his tent beneath an outcropping rock and hobbled his horse close by. He lay snug and dry inside his tent, eating his rations. "Have some." He held out a half-empty tin of beans.

"Thanks." Sitting cross-legged on the canvas floor facing Jeremy on his cot, half inside and half outside Jeremy's small tent, John wolfed jerky, beans, and a square of hard cornbread.

Jeremy reached inside his knapsack and handed John two biscuits.

John hunched his back against the renewed drizzle while his guards hunkered down in yellow oilskins on either side of the tent flap. "Do you think the army can supply us with some blankets? The women and children are cold."

"I doubt it, but I'll inquire." Jeremy rubbed his square chin and looked thoughtful. "Meanwhile, take my greatcoat to them. It should warm a few." He blinked blood-shot eyes. "I'll wager my sister stocked her wagon with blankets. Tomorrow morning I'll trot over to check. Been wanting to pay her a visit but haven't had the opportunity. I can't leave tonight because I drew guard duty and have to report in ten minutes."

"Much obliged." John coughed. Good thing he hadn't had to suggest Jeremy go to Hope's wagon for blankets. "I best be getting back. Thanks for the grub."

Next morning a heaviness settled into John's chest. His chilled fingers were so stiff they hampered his hitching the oxen. Fatigue dragged at his muscles. The rain slackened, and a lightening sky in the east promised clearing.

Bold Hunter appeared unaffected by the wet weather and sat ramrod straight on the bench seat.

John heaved himself up and called to the oxen. "Get up there, boys. Get up."

An hour later Jeremy rode up, saluting as he came abreast. He sat a horse well, looking jaunty, even in his oilskins.

John's spirits lifted, and he called from their slow-moving wagon, "Thanks for the loan of your coat. Four of the children slept warm last night."

Jeremy's face blazed. "Yeah. That's good," His voice sounded gruff.

The soldiers riding with him raised their eyebrows and started chatting among themselves. Jeremy saluted and rode down toward the head of the train, the other cavalrymen following.

From his vantage point higher up the mountain, John watched them trot down the road, along the valley, and toward the middle of the wagon train. The column stretched for miles ahead, but the mountain road held so many bends he couldn't see where the column began.

Finally, about noon, shafts of sunlight gleamed through the haze. Bold Hunter jumped to the ground. "Need to walk."

John inhaled, savoring the clean smell of the air. Even after the downpour, the land still bore testimony to the drought. Summer flowers were long since faded and grass showed bristly brown. Here and there a patch of yellow yarrow or white Queen Anne's lace provided color.

Rachael peeked out the front flap.

Should he chance the soldiers? Rachael needed fresh air. "Come on out and sit." John patted the hard bench seat. "You did a good job driving yesterday, but I'll teach you to drive with more confidence. I noticed you looked scared when Bold Hunter and I both had to shove this wagon up the mountain." He smiled.

Rachael didn't need coaxing. She slid out the opening and settled close, her long skirt touching his knee. He placed her fingers on the reins and demonstrated how to hold the leathers and signal the oxen, her hands warming his like gloves.

The sun burst forth and lightened the soggy air.

"You and Bold Hunter aren't very nice to each other." Rachael lifted a dark brow and gave him a sad smile.

"No. It's a delicate situation. Seems we both like the same girl."

Rachael blushed. "Please don't be enemies because of me."

"Do you and he have an understanding?" John didn't believe in skirting around a tree when he could climb straight up.

Rachael flipped the reins. "I've known Bold Hunter most of my life." Her voice sounded thoughtful. "He's very appealing—strong and wise, as well as kind."

"Are we talking about the same person?"

Rachael laughed. "He reads and writes Cherokee fluently. Not only is he an excellent hunter, he knows how to farm. He owned a nice farm close to the mission house. He wants me to be his wife."

John gazed intently at his hands, cupped around hers on the reins. "Do you want to marry him?"

"I can't, of course. He's not a Christian."

John's stomach jumped. "What?" He glanced at Rachael's averted face. "Why can't you? I don't understand."

"Jesus said we are not to yoke ourselves with unbelievers." A frown marred her smooth forehead.

"Oh." This was a new thought. He knew so little about following Jesus. He pondered on her words for a few minutes, then squeezed her hands. "Does Bold Hunter know why you won't marry him?" John tried not to sound grim. She was too good for the angry man.

"No. I don't want him to become a Christian just to marry me. I want him to become a Christian because he realizes he needs Jesus as his Savior."

John gazed into the distance. While he mulled over Rachel's words, the wagon hit a deep rut and tilted. He circled Rachael's waist to keep her from falling.

"Ho, John. We brought blankets." Jeremy's voice cut into their private world. He trotted close, his saddle laden with large blankets.

Yahoola! Beside Jeremy, Hope rode a dainty, gray Appaloosa mare. The dark green riding habit she wore reflected the emerald of her eyes. Red gold hair cascaded over her shoulders.

John swallowed hard, suddenly aware of the poor condition of his clothes. Mud caked his buckskin breeches from ankles to thigh, and the same red muck splattered his petticoat shirt thicker than spots on a dappled dog. His long hair matted down his neck, and his dirty feet stuck out in front of the driver's seat with embarrassing nakedness.

Hope nodded to Rachael and smiled. She ignored John and sat statue-stiff in her sidesaddle.

Jeremy stared at his sister, his mouth agape.

John tightened his arm around Rachael and covered both her hands in his free one.

Rachael smiled at Hope, and then glanced from Hope to John, eyebrows raised. No one spoke.

Hope glanced at John. Her expression sent darts penetrating through every barrier he'd built up to protect himself against this dazzling, unattainable woman. Though she'd never acknowledged her awareness, she must have noted his interest in her during those days at the stockade when she brought milk for Pris. He squared his shoulders. He was not about to become another of her tongue-hanging-out lap dogs.

He tried on his most ferocious look and emphasized his slow, Georgian drawl. "I'm aware this is presumptuous of me, Miss Worchester ... but didn't I part my hair to your satisfaction?"

"I really am not concerned about the manner in which you did or did not part your hair, Mr. Ross." Hope spoke distinctly, her words like icicles tinkling in the winter wind. "I merely made this call to offer you some warm clothes, but I notice you've found other methods of keeping warm."

Rachael blushed and tried to release herself from John's grip around her waist.

"Miss Worchester, may I present Miss Whiteswan." John kept his eyes steely, his Georgian drawl coldly impersonal. Jeremy's sister showed up at the worst possible time, but he wouldn't let her dictate where he placed his arm.

Hope's face softened. "I am pleased to meet you, Miss Whiteswan. My father has mentioned you many times ... in a most favorable way. I hope *we* can become friends."

Rachael smiled faintly. "It's an honor to meet you, Miss Worchester."

A pucker between his rusty brows, Jeremy gazed from Hope to John and back to Hope. He tossed some blankets onto John's lap. "I don't understand what's going on between you and my sister, but here's a blanket for you, one for Bold Hunter, and two more for those inside the wagon. Keep my greatcoat as well. I can manage without it."

Hope smiled. "Goodbye, Rachael." When she glanced at John, her cameo face tightened into a creamy mask. She handed a bundle to Jeremy, wheeled her horse, and galloped down the road toward the front of the wagon train. Mud from her horse's hooves splattered John's foot.

He clinched his jaw. What did he care if Hope Worchester thought he was more intimate with Rachael than he actually was? He lied to himself. He did care. Deep down. More than he wanted to admit. He cared far more than he should.

Jeremy spoke to no one in particular. "What in tarnation got Hope so riled?" He raised his campaign hat and raked a hand through his thick, rusty hair. "She had her claws out, but you sure had your spurs dug in. I don't know who scratched the hardest. You didn't tell me you two were such good friends."

John set his mouth and stared at the lead ox's rump.

Rachael wiggled out of his embrace. "Why did you keep your arm around me? Were you trying to shock her?"

Jeremy shot the bundle of clothes toward John, and they landed neatly on top of John's clenched fists. "Hope's been handing out blankets since she joined the wagon train. These and the clothes were all that were left. I fancied she'd been saving these for someone special, since she hid them under her wagon seat. Shows you how wrong a person can be." Jeremy wheeled his horse to leave. "Duty calls and all that. You know where to find me." He gave a quirky smile.

Rachael smiled sweetly. "Thank you, Jeremy. We really appreciate the blankets."

Jeremy grinned, saluted her, and left.

Rachael, her back stiff, her hands gripped in her lap, whispered, "She's the most beautiful girl I've ever seen. You're attracted to her, aren't you?"

John jutted his jaw. "What? She's worse than an onion poultice on my skin. I'm attracted to her like I'm attracted to a she-bear separated from her cubs."

"Um." Rachael picked up the bundle and opened the parcel like a precious gift. She shook each item out and held it up for him to see. Her voice sounded excited. "Here's a woolen shawl. It's for Charity, of course. Your mother will be so warm wearing this."

Rachael looked pleased as she extracted a heavy home-spun, long-sleeved shirt of robin egg blue. "Miss Worchester matched your eyes perfectly. It's certainly large enough.

She really did save these for you. No doubt she had to shop a long time to find this particular shirt." Rachael hugged John's arm, and bounced on the wooden bench, her face glowing. "No matter how Hope managed this, thank God, you've got a warm shirt."

John laughed, loosed his tight grip on the reins, and sat straighter on the hard bench.

"Look, here is a pair of buckskin britches, with the pelt turned inside. They're for someone very tall," Rachael teased. "Now how did Miss Worchester know your size?"

John's neck grew hot. The heat spread to his face. He slapped the reins and refused to look at Rachael. "Stop bedeviling me. How could she know my size? I only talked with her a few times at the gate when she brought milk."

"Those must have been amazing talks." Rachael's eyes twinkled. "Look, here's a pair of tremendously large shoes. Are your feet really this big?"

Rachael seemed to be enjoying herself. At his expense. Still, he loved seeing her pleasure.

"What are these called?" She dangled one by the laces.

He could no longer conceal his excitement. His grin spread across his face. "They're brogans. Like hiking boots, only better. Any socks?"

"Two pairs of heavy socks." Rachael held them up. "St. Nick could put loads of goodies in these if they hung by the chimney at Christmas."

John laughed, but his ears got hotter.

"Don't just sit there shivering. Change into these warm clothes." Rachael pointed. "There's a long stretch of valley ahead. I'll drive while you transform yourself into a charming gentleman." She poked him playfully in the ribs.

"So, when I get embarrassed, you aren't shy anymore." John winked and jumped off the slowly moving wagon. A couple hundred yards ahead a river meandered into trees. A perfect spot for a quick bath to rid himself of the mud, and then to change into the new clothes. He searched in front of and behind the wagon for his two-man guard. Where were they when he needed them?

He dashed back toward the river. Humph, a lot further from the road then he'd thought.

As he dashed toward the trees, the shouts, hoof beats, and creaking wagons of the train grew less and less audible.

He'd not have another opportunity. Seizing the moment, he shucked his muddy clothes, waded out, and stood chest-deep in the freezing water. Cold. But what a blessing to bathe. He ducked underwater, then broke surface, and shook spray from his face.

Behind him, a horse broke through the undergrowth.

A sudden knot tightened his stomach. He'd heard the wagon train and Calvary pass on down the road. Was Corporal Dread coming to make good his threat? He had been a fool to leave the wagon train, to put himself completely into Dread's hands.

CHAPTER 17

"Hey."

Startled, John looked up.

"You expecting a ghost or my sister?" Jeremy's bass voice sounded gleeful. He grinned, then slid off his horse.

John splashed cold water in his friend's face.

Jeremy laughed and shook his head, sending drops of water out in a spray. "I thought you'd be wanting a bath, so I brought you soap. Government issue. But if a cold shower's my thanks, guess I'll take my soap and leave." He pretended to turn back to mount his horse.

John lunged after him, half jerking Jeremy's foot from the stirrup.

"You've drenched me so I might as well join you." Jeremy laughed, one hand unbuttoning his tunic. He tossed his uniform, boots, and hat on the grassy bank.

"Never thought I'd be so glad to see your freckled face."

"Ha—scared of my sister, are you?"

"More likely scared of that red hair of yours standing on end."

Jeremy stuck his big toe into the river, then backed away. "Ow! You didn't warn me this water's only fit for Eskimos!"

"Come on in, lily-liver." John danced around in the waist-deep river trying not to let his goosebumps drive him ashore. He splashed Jeremy until his friend dove under the bone-chilling water to escape.

Both lathered, splashing, hopping, and flapping their arms to stave off shivering. John slipped on a wet rock, fell, and sprawled across the riverbed, only his bare feet floating above water.

Jeremy howled.

Before John surfaced, he grabbed Jeremy's ankle, yanking him facedown into the frigid water. They wrestled until Jeremy pinned him underwater. John whirled, released himself, and shoved Jeremy forward into deeper water, then stood. "What's the matter? Can't take it?"

Jeremy sputtered and lunged for him. They tussled until John started coughing. Shivering ended their roughhousing, but John stayed in a few minutes more to wash his hair.

"Dare you to stay in longer!" Jeremy hugged himself as he splashed toward shore.

John plunged ahead, then clambered on shore first, with Jeremy seconds behind.

They shook themselves like playful puppies and hustled into dry clothes.

Jeremy eyed John up and down and grinned. "Say now, you resemble a civilized gentleman instead of a savage Injun."

"You still look like a brutal soldier to me." John clapped Jeremy on the shoulder, then knelt to take a long drink from a spring of ice-cold water bubbling up from the ground before rushing into the stream.

The grin faded from Jeremy's freckled face. "We don't like this duty. Me especially. Gen'l Scott said this expedition'll take about six months. I'll be mustered out of the army after that, and I plan to stay in the new territory to help your people settle in."

John shoved a fist into the air. "Great news. I can sure use a friend once we arrive. Do you know anything about this territory we're headed for?"

"Nope. Just know the land is filled with Indians who aren't as civilized as you Cherokees. A number of different tribes—Apache, Caddo, Osage, and others." Jeremy combed

"God's called me to preach."

John worked tangles out of his wet hair. "Yeah? How can you be so sure?"

"Up until a couple of months ago, the last thing I wanted was to preach. I hankered for adventure." Jeremy tugged on John's arm. "Hey, don't break my comb with that thick mane of yours."

"Don't worry. You were saying?"

"A few years ago, a part of me yearned to do all the things I'd been taught not to do. So, I joined the army." Jeremy's green eyes watched John, as if gauging his interest.

"What did your father say?"

"Dad said"—Jeremy struck a pose and mimicked his father's voice—"discover what God wants you to do, then do it. You won't ever be happy until you find God's will for your life."

John chuckled. "You sound just like your father."

"I'll take that as a compliment." After pulling on his boots, Jeremy plopped on the grassy bank.

John stooped, trying to see his reflection in the stream. Maybe Hope would ride back to check how his clothes fit. He squatted beside Jeremy, his eyes on the sparkling water dashing over the rocky riverbed, his ears rejoicing at the sound of rushing waters, his skin tingling from the cold bath. Great to be relaxed and have a friend. "Did you find God's will for your life?"

Jeremy took a long time to answer.

John stretched out on the ground with his hands laced under his head and gazed at the clear sky where the October sun burned off the overcast. He inhaled, filling his lungs with the pungent scent of autumn. He'd almost forgotten his question before Jeremy began to talk.

"I asked God what he willed for my life. I prayed a lot. The only trouble was"—Jeremy knit heavy brows—"I never listened for his answer. Too busy planning what I wanted to do."

Brilliant red gold leaves rustled overhead. John's eyelids lowered. His muscles jerked as they relaxed. "What happened?"

"Got myself into a scrape. Started keeping company with the wrong crowd. Remember, now, I was looking for adventure. You don't find excitement in the army. Nothing but spit and polish, march and ride, routine jobs, maneuvers, saying, 'yes, sir—no, sir—right away, sir.' Got a bellyful in a hurry." Jeremy grew silent.

Sensing Jeremy seldom talked about himself, John opened his eyes and glanced sideways at his friend's strong profile. "C'mon, Yank, don't be tight-mouthed."

Jeremy sat, elbows on his knees, hands steepled under his chin. "Dad raised Hope and me strict. We never got away with mischief. Just work, study, and pray. He had a handful with us, though. I tried running off, and Hope had her own ways of getting around him." His lips curved into a smile, then his face turned grim. "Every time I ran off, Dad found me and dragged me home. He licked me with his belt until I thought having a stinging backside was the natural way of life."

John grinned, but Jeremy didn't. "Don't misunderstand me. He's a good father, but I think he worried because we didn't have a mother. She died when Hope was born. When I was a little shaver, I stole his big black Bible. I was going to find the verse he always quoted, 'Spare the rod and spoil the child'. I planned to slit it out of his Bible with my knife, but I couldn't find the sentence." Jeremy reached down and punched John's shoulder. "In all likelihood, we needed the discipline."

"I'll wager you did. And your sister, did he spare the rod with her?"

"She got spanked some. I got shellacked!"

A big grin spread over John's face as he pictured Jeremy's proud sister getting her backside spanked.

"When I turned sixteen, I ran off and joined the army. Dad didn't agree, but he let me go. He bundled Hope off to a straitlaced girl's boarding school and traipsed out here to become a missionary to the Cherokee. I thought he was crazy."

"And?"

"Darned if Army life didn't turn out to be just as strict—except for off-duty hours. Made the most of them. I drank and gambled and did everything else a man could think of. My temper landed me in fights. Once after a night of revelry I woke up AWOL and spent time in the guardhouse. Before I regained my senses, I came close to getting a dishonorable discharge."

Jeremy sighed. His matter-of-fact voice gained a layer of sadness. "I never let on to the other soldiers I was a Christian ... a carnal one. Three wasted years. Shocked my friends when I finally started reading my Bible." He plucked a blade of grass and played with it. "At first, they jeered and tormented me. They had tasted my temper before, so they baited me to get me mad. They'd hold me under cold showers or put manure in my bunk just before inspection." He pulled slivers from the blade.

"When they found they couldn't get me riled, they got curious as to why I was so different and started to ask questions." Jeremy's face lit like a harvest moon on a clear night. "That's how I discovered the adventure I'd been seeking. The real jolt came whenever one of them decided he wanted to become a Christian. Far more important than adventure, I have peace in my heart now that's more valuable to me than anything else on earth." He tossed the last sliver of grass and plucked another blade.

John nodded. "I feel the same peace now and again. But most times the peace seems elusive."

"I hated the Army, but I decided to be a career man and witness to the soldiers the rest of my life. Then we received our orders to guard this removal. Dad said prayer, peace, and circumstances guide a person into finding the will of God. Then God added his still small voice. This time I listened." Jeremy leaned an elbow against the grassy bank and sighed. "Isn't God good?"

John glanced down at his warm clothes. "Yep." He mimicked Jeremy's clipped New England speech.

"We'd best get back to the wagon. Part of our job is to hunt meat for your people. I noticed when you polluted the stream with my soapsuds, you could use more meat on your bones." Jeremy jumped up. "We don't seem to be doing our job." He strolled over to his horse and rummaged in his saddle bag. "I caught a couple big catfish in this stream just before you decided to head out here for a swim. Here are enough to feed those kids. And don't forget to eat some yourself."

"Thanks, Yank, I owe you. Again."

Jeremy looped his reins over his arm, and they strolled back to the moving wagons. "Is the beautiful girl on the wagon your girl?"

"No." John sketched him in on Rachael's trouble with Corporal Robert Dread, including Dread's latest threat.

"That's some adventure. I wondered about those scars on your back. I'll keep my eye on Dread. But I can't report a threat to my commanding officer. We'll have to sit tight until Dread tries something else."

"Maybe he won't. Perhaps he's all wind." Not likely, but he could hope.

They sauntered past the mounted cavalry trailing their wagon.

"Next time you decide to leave the train, let me know." Jeremy's voice sounded too casual. "My Commanding Officer takes a dim view of prisoners leaving unescorted."

John stopped short. He gritted, "So, you followed me to bring soap. Great story! You guarded me to prevent my escape. Would you have shot me if I had run?"

"Don't get steamed. We're friends. Someone has to guard you. Might as well be a man who likes your company. Better me than five guys who don't. I won't be your guard in Indian Territory, but I'll still be your friend." Jeremy's clear green eyes pleaded. "Try to understand my position and my duty."

John's anger fizzled like dud fireworks. "Fine, Yank. Next time I take a fancy for a stroll, I'll whistle Yankee Doodle."

Jeremy turned off to join the Cavalry following the wagons.

John strode to their Conestoga and found Bold Hunter and Rachael together on the wagon seat, cozy with shoulders touching and faces close in an intimate tête-à-tête, talking Cherokee.

He gave them a fierce look. Bold Hunter had no right to treat Rachael as his intended.

The full-blood smiled tenderly, his mouth close to hers, his animal magnetism obviously attracting Rachael.

Jeremy rode up and reined his mount to walk beside the wagon. "Make a nice couple, don't they?" He nudged John's arm.

"If a panther and a deer constitute a nice couple." John spat a sour taste from his mouth. "I don't trust that panther."

"Looks as if Rachael does." Jeremy rubbed his horse's neck as the animal reached down to nibble John's ear.

John raked his fingers through his wet hair. What should he do? He didn't want to create a scene in front of Rachael and haul the Indian down from the driver's seat. She wanted them to be friends. Pastor wanted him to witness to Bold Hunter, and John wanted to see the last of the big guy.

Jeremy pulled several huge catfish out of his saddlebag. "Have Rachael clean these. I'll stay behind to guard her, and then we'll catch up."

John grabbed Jeremy's sleeve. "Are you fascinated with Rachael too?"

"No, I'm trying to show you I'm your friend."

John swallowed, then nodded. He cleared his throat to gain Rachael's attention and handed her the fish. "Surprise! Can you clean these?"

Rachael pursed her lovely lips, and a twinkle lit her brown eyes. "What do you mean can I clean a fish? I filleted and cooked fish when I was five years old. You forget who you're talking with."

John nodded. Her teasing restored some of his good humor. "The fish is for you, Mother, and the children. Go on now and clean those catfish while they're fresh."

"First I've got to tell you. You look so attractive!" Rachael's voice bubbled pleasure. "The clothes fit perfectly." She tilted her head, her long hair flowing over her shoulder, and surveyed him. "But you need a haircut."

John lifted his arms to catch her. "Jump down. Jeremy has to stay with you." She felt light in his arms ... warm and very womanly.

Bold Hunter halted the wagon. "Bold Hunter go with Rachael. Clean fish fast."

"Uh, I want to talk with you. This seems an appropriate time—"

"Later." Bold Hunter flipped the reins, and the leather slapped John across the nose. The man's antagonism hit John like a rock to the gut.

"Nope, only one Indian at a time leaves this wagon train," the crisp New England voice interrupted.

Bold Hunter settled back into his seat.

Humph, Jeremy hadn't fooled Bold Hunter. Though the Indian didn't know why, he probably understood Jeremy schemed to get Bold Hunter alone with me. John sighed. Bold Hunter would retaliate.

Swinging up onto the driver's seat, John gathered the four sets of reins. "Ho!" he commanded the oxen, and the wagon jolted forward. Bold Hunter rose from the wooden bench and turned to jump down.

"Stay. We need to talk." John reached for his arm.

Bold Hunter scowled but plopped down on the bumping seat.

John tightened his grip on the reins. How to begin? The silence grew uncomfortable. Had Jeremy picked the wrong time? John licked his lips. Why did he let himself get sucked into these situations? The conniving redhead planned this being alone with Bold Hunter. John rubbed his jaw. Okay. He didn't know any other way but blunt. "You're not a Christian, are you?"

"No!"

Mentally, John wiped his forehead. Poor choice of words. Now, how was he to get the conversation rolling?

Bold Hunter sat stiff and straight as a rifle barrel, his stony expression grim.

"What's wrong with Christians?"

"Christians no have courage. Afraid. No take war trail. No take scalps. No fight soldiers." He turned a contemptuous face toward John. "Make friends with soldiers. That treason."

"Wrong. I'm not afraid to fight."

"Show Bold Hunter you no afraid. Then believe. Ross eyes full of smoke, ears full of rushing water, mouth full of empty words. When Bold Hunter see dead soldiers, believe Christian not scared like rabbit."

John's back stiffened. "God can give you love for your enemies."

"Ha, ha, ha." Bold Hunter's laugh roared contempt. "Jaybird sit on bush all day. Talk and talk. Who want to listen? You Christian, you scared!"

"I'm not scared."

But how could he prove it? John tightened his fists around the reins.

CHAPTER 18

Two shots reverberated some distance behind the wagon, interrupting their conversation.

John stood, pulling hard on the reins. "Whoa! Whoa there!" He glanced at Bold Hunter. "I think Rachael needs help!"

Behind them, the Cavalry Captain's voice rang out, "Follow me!"

John craned his neck to see around the canvas canopy. A quarter of the company wheeled their horses and galloped back toward the shots.

Bold Hunter jumped from the wagon. Three soldiers on horseback barred his way. "This is army business, Injun. Remain with your wagon."

Mother stuck her head out the front opening, and John handed her the reins. "Handle these." Then he hit the ground running.

Soldiers rode up from behind the wagon and surrounded him. "Get back up there and keep that Conestoga moving!" One soldier lifted his rifle barrel and threatened to club John.

He stopped, then slowly hoisted himself up to the driver's seat and took the reins from his mother's trembling hands. Bold Hunter jerked himself into the seat beside John, his coppery features set in a scowl.

John called to the oxen, "Get up!" The teams strained, then plodded forward.

Again, he leaned out and craned his neck to stare around the canopy and beyond the remaining guard, and glimpsed the investigative company trot off the road. The dust settled behind them. No further gunfire.

Mother leaned out the flap. "What's happening, Son?"

"Blast this captivity." John grimaced and tightened his fingers on the leather reins. "Rachael's in trouble, and I can't help her." He shifted restlessly on the springless seat.

Bold Hunter's scowl deepened.

"Oh, that's awful. The children and I will pray for Rachael."

"Thank you, Mother." John stretched out again, attempting to see beyond the wagon.

With a thunder of hooves and amid a blanket of dust, the soldiers cantered back. Jeremy, his uniform torn and dirty, led the way with Rachael perched in front of him on the saddle. His symmetrical face appeared lopsided and his mouth was puffed and bleeding. An angry red swelling half-closed his left eye.

John pulled back on the reins. "Whoa, there. Whoa." The oxen plodded to a standstill.

Jeremy rode up beside the wagon. "In you go, Miss." He clasped Rachael around the waist and boosted her over to Bold Hunter's extended arms. He teetered to reach her, then caught her and slid her onto the seat between them.

John glimpsed Rachael's pale face and wide, frightened eyes. "Best you stay out of sight, Rachael."

"Go inside." Bold Hunter's hands trembled as he helped her climb through the flap back into the Conestoga.

"My fault," John muttered. He turned to Jeremy. "You have the makings of a first-rate black eye, Yank." Easy to guess what happened. He'd feared for Rachael since they left the stockade.

Jeremy's explanation came thickly from his injured mouth. "Couple of wiseacre soldiers had bold intentions. They jumped her. I tried fighting them off, but they were keelhauling me. Rachael had the wit to fire my rifle to signal for help." He gasped and his chest heaved. "Best keep her out of sight whenever possible." He raked a hand through his disordered hair. Because of his swollen eye, his frown shifted one side of his face. "Should have known better than to let her leave the wagon train."

John nodded. "Reckon you didn't think out your plan too well."

"Forgot the fish in the excitement. I'll ride back for them." Jeremy patted his horse's neck and winked his good eye. "By the way, I'll live. Still have all my teeth. Thanks for your tender concern."

John grinned. "Yanks are tougher than army boots." He cocked his head and studied Jeremy. "I think I like your face better this way." He ducked Jeremy's wild swing.

Horses hooves rumbled and kicked up more dust. Escorted by soldiers on horseback, three men with disordered uniforms, bloody faces, and sheepish expressions trudged up the trail toward them. The company's captain rode up and met the soldiers. "Take those disgraces up front to report to the commander."

Surrounded by soldiers on horseback, the three men lowered their heads and, expressions surly, marched forward.

The sun hung low in the western sky when John halted the wagon to strike camp. He glanced toward Bold Hunter. "I reckon we're about two miles south of Rattlesnake Springs." He hopped down and stretched his tired muscles.

The children exploded from the wagon. Bold Hunter caught Rachael as she jumped from the wagon and shadowed her while they gathered sticks for a campfire. John shuttled inside the wagon and settled beside Mother on the rough boards. He spoke with forced cheerfulness. "Good evening, Madam. I happened to be in your neighborhood, so I decided to pay a social call."

Her pale skin was drawn tight across her face, and a spot of pink burned on each thin cheek.

"May I present my calling card?" He kissed her hand.

"John, dear, how warm you look! And handsome, too. God answered our prayer for warmer clothes." A smile lit his mother's face. "Rachael told me about the pastor's daughter. A lovely girl. You shall bring her here so I can thank her properly." A fit of coughing forced her to lie back.

John fluffed up a half-empty sack of hominy grits to serve as her pillow. "Naturally, I'll fetch the young lady if you wish. The shawl she brought for you is becoming."

"Thank you, dear, but I feel so untidy. I peeked at Miss Worchester through the flap while you were talking with her. Such fiery hair. And her complexion—I don't believe I've ever seen more luminous skin." His mother reached for his hand. "I think she likes you."

Humph! John tried to keep his voice from rising. "Likes me? Don't picture me as one of her suitors. She's a frigid New Englander, and I've no intentions of courting her. Sorry, but you can forget that impossible dream."

He shook his head. Lately nothing went well. Bold Hunter gained the bulk of Rachael's attention. John sighed. He had all he could handle transporting the wagon, the two women, and the children to Indian Territory. He was in survival mode and had no energy for anything else.

Someone stumbled against the water pail attached to the side of their tent on wheels. John stuck out his head as small feet sent up a dust devil. A short Indian boy scuttled away, ran to the adjoining wagons, and disappeared.

"Who was outside, dear?"

"No idea."

"About Miss Worchester?"

"Right. I'll escort her here so you can thank her. But don't get any ideas. She's not partial to me."

"Of course, she is fond of you. Any girl feels honored to capture your interest."

"Maybe in another life, Mother. Not now."

Mother gazed fondly into his face and traced her finger

down his nose. "You've got the patrician nose of my people." She smiled. "Did you know your blue eyes turn gray when you're determined and flash blue when you're angry? Even I dare not face you when you're furious."

She patted his cheek. "I've seen those eyes full of fun, laughter, and reckless adventure. But over these last months, you've disguised your sadness with banter. I know you worry about me." Her chest rose and fell with a sigh.

He moved away to stare out the rear flap and clench his eyes against his heartache. He couldn't lose Mother. "I need to check on Rachael's progress with the fish and see to the teams. We'll eat well tonight, thanks to Jeremy. You should rest until dinner is served."

He folded his cleaned and patched buckskin britches over the hominy-sack pillow to make a softer nest for her, kissed her forehead, and escaped out the rear flap. His new boots thudded on the ground. He strode across the road and into the meadow to feed the oxen, gather dry wood, and build a fire for the children.

Then he set out to scout for Jeremy. The need to be under constant guard irritated like rope chafing his wrists. After a futile search, John slipped into a thicket of trees. "Friend Jeremy, I'll have to go without you this once."

Blood surged in his veins—free! For the moment, at least. The feeling was intoxicating, and the quiet woods beckoned. His long strides took him deep into the green solitude. Sweet-scented pines moaned in the breeze while the forest, crisscrossed with gurgling mountain streams running over rocky beds, sang an alluring song. Entering a small glade, he gathered more dead wood. The children needed a roaring fire to warm them.

As if a sixth sense warned him of danger, the hair on the back of his neck bristled. From the direction of the wagon train, branches snapped, and hoof beats thundered on the grass.

"Good old Jeremy, hot on the trail." John turned, a grin on his face.

Corporal Robert Dread's big roan crashed into the arena.

CHAPTER 19

John dropped the wood in a heap—his heart thudded and sweat flooded his body.

"I knowed I seen you tryin' to escape." Dread's voice echoed around the small clearing. "Old Bess here'll have somethun' to say about thet." He shifted the large chaw of tobacco in his mouth. Unfurling his bullwhip, he pressed his horse close.

John backed away, the hair on his nape standing up. The whip snapped, hostile and wicked, cutting the air. He ducked, an instant ahead of the black snake, the wind swirling only a breath from his face.

Again, the whip lashed out, flicking hair from John's head, its backlash slashing the roan's flank.

The horse jumped forward and reared, forefeet windmilling, almost unseating Dread.

With a harsh jerk, Dread pulled the animal around, raking his spurs across the scarred sides of the plunging animal, then rode straight for John.

John sidestepped the flashing hooves. Still half in panic-freeze, his mind unlocked, then flashed into action.

Dread wheeled his horse, cracking the whip at John.

He dodged, but the whip cut through his sleeve, slashing his flesh. Pain jolted up his arm. Mind performing at high speed now, John calculated the distance the bullwhip traveled. He had no time for fear. He had to stay out of the whip's deadly reach.

Time after time the big man's bullwhip snaked out, and each time John danced away. His survival depended upon clear thinking. If Dread connected once, he would slash the blows so hard and fast John would have little chance. He had to act now.

Dread galloped toward him.

John calculated the risk. Now or never.

The whip streaked out.

John caught the lethal leather with his right hand. The whip cut into his flesh, pain flared through his hand and up his arm. Teeth locked against the agony, he used both hands and hauled on the whip with all his strength.

Dread fell from the saddle like a bear from a tree, losing his grip on the bullwhip.

John whirled the whip around and around his head, then released his grip. With a whistling noise, the whip sailed out of sight into the woods.

Dread wiggled to his knees, then floundered to his feet, his barrel chest rising and falling. He cursed, his slate-colored eyes narrowed to slits, his mouth thinned to a slash of meanness, his face crimson. A meaty hand reached to his belt and pulled a Bowie knife. "I'm gonna peel enough skin offen your hide to make me a new whip," he hissed like a rattler.

Shadows darkened as dusk fell, making footing treacherous. John laughed. Perhaps his Scottish blood, coursing from those ancestors who fought against overwhelming odds with wild fervor, gave him this strange exhilaration, firing every neuron in his brain. Now that the waiting for the inevitable ended, every muscle stoked him with power.

Dread crouched, knife deadly in his raised fist.

John circled away. A final ray of sun outlined the weapon, highlighting the razor-sharp double edges.

Dread lunged.

John pivoted, grasped his assailant's knife hand, and slammed Dred's wrist hard over his knee.

Dread grunted but held tight. His other hand grabbed for John's ankle.

John spun out of his reach—panting, gulping air. The incredible strength of the man! If Dread got hold of him, this fight would be over. Though the fever in his blood made him reckless, he realized the Lord provided the absolute control of emotion necessary for him to face Dread's murderous intent.

Again, the Corporal circled.

John backed toward the trees.

Sweat glistened on the older man's forehead. He spit out his tobacco, clamped his lips, and rushed.

John grabbed the thick arm, then, using the man's own momentum, flipped Dread over his back.

The huge man landed hard, like an overturned Conestoga but managed to lumber to his feet. As he limped forward, his breath shrilled between his teeth. He stood beneath the trees, swaying his bristling head back and forth like a wounded bull. Then he rushed again.

Evening darkened the tiny glen. John, unsure of his steps on the rough ground, circled away.

Again and again, Dread slashed at John with the knife.

Each time John dodged just beyond the razor-sharp point.

Finally, Dread's movements slowed ... his lunges grew careless.

John could barely lift his leaden arms in defense. Yet, he'd wear Dread down, throw him so hard he wouldn't be able to get up, then high tail it to the wagon train—let Jeremy handle the problem from there.

Dread made another reckless lunge.

John dodged.

Dread staggered off balance.

John dashed in before Dread could regain his footing and used both hands to clutch the man's knife arm at the wrist. Taking advantage of Dread's impetus, John pulled the bully toward his own body. In one swift movement he dropped to his back on the ground, kicked Dread in the stomach with both feet, flipped his legs straight, and sent Dread flying over his head.

Dread landed in a heap.

John groaned. He'd expected Dread to be heavy, but he exerted far more effort to throw the Corporal than he anticipated. John rolled over and forced himself up onto shaking legs.

The bull roared up again and brandished his long knife!

Waves of fear rippled along John's backbone. Was the man invincible?

Dread thundered forward, his lips clamped, eyes intent, with a look that spelled death.

John dredged strength from beyond his reserve. Again, using the man's own speed and weight against him, John twisted Dread's extended knife arm.

The heavy man cartwheeled through the air, landing on his chest. A loud thud. A long, low moan. Dread lay where he fell.

John panted, legs shaking but braced, ready for another attack. Minutes passed. "I know you're tricking me." John gasped, hands on his knees, fighting for air. "You want me close so you can get your hands on me. Won't work." He stared at the splayed-out body, a black shadow lying on the dark grass.

"What's going on here?" The voice behind John had the unmistakable ring of authority.

John's hands, braced in front of him for battle, trembled. Had to be a soldier. John kept his gaze on Dread.

A sword clinked. An officer. John dare not glance from the fallen hulk. "I came here to gather firewood, sir. Corporal Dread followed me and accused me of trying to escape. He knew I wasn't, but he took the opportunity of finding me alone to attack me with his bullwhip."

"You're kidding me!" The officer's horse trotted closer and leather creaked as he shifted in his saddle.

Eyes focused on Dread, John pointed to the trees. "You'll find his whip over there." He turned to face the dark silhouette of a soldier astride a horse.

The officer dismounted and checked the bushes, then held up the whip. "Then what happened?"

"Corporal Dread pulled a knife. I defended myself. He must have lost his wind when I threw him." Darkness prevented him from seeing the soldier's face beneath his cocked hat.

"I'm Lieutenant Whitsell." His sword clinked as the soldier turned back to Dread. "Corporal, your fun's over now." The officer leaned forward over the prone body. "This time you've gone too far. The army knows your fondness for Old Bess. Be assured, General Scott will have something to say to you."

Dread didn't move.

Lieutenant Whitsell stooped to poke the inert body. He stood and turned to face John. "Someone with more authority than Scott is holding Corporal Dread's court martial."

John stared, heavy hands hanging at his sides. "Sir?"

"Dread's dead. Looks as if he fell on his own knife."

John's insides somersaulted. "What?"

Lieutenant Whitsell walked over and stuck his pointed nose in John's face. "You killed him."

John's skin turned cold. He started shaking. A bright moon broke through the clouds, bathing the body in silver light.

"You're fortunate I arrived when I did, young man. It's obvious from this scene you're telling the truth." He waved at the trampled grass, the dirt on the uniform, and the blood dripping from John's hand. "But there will be an inquiry. You could be in serious trouble."

The lieutenant's voice blurred. The earth was spinning.

"I'll commandeer two men to witness the position of the body. You'll have to reconstruct the fight. How did you manage to best Dread?"

"Nagewasa."

"Isn't that an ancient Indian branch of combat?"

John nodded.

"Guess those moves worked for you." Lieutenant Whitesell's voice changed. "But you look like you're about to collapse. Ride Dread's horse back to camp. I'll be right behind you." He mounted his horse.

John stood frozen.

"Your face is as white as undyed muslin." The man leaned over his horse's neck and clapped a hand on John's shoulder. "I know how you feel. Felt the same way when I killed my first Indian." He gave a nervous laugh. "No offense. Get on over to the horse."

John stumbled to the roan. The saddle looked higher than any saddle had a right to look. Could he hoist himself up there? He heaved and forked a leg over the leather. Riding through the dark trees in the twilight with the officer's mount alongside touching his brogue, turned into a fantasy. The horse glided, his hooves never touching the ground. The trees swayed, reaching out grisly arms, and a mist swirled around him. He would wake soon and find himself trapped back inside the hated stockade.

"We're here. Climb down." Lieutenant Whitsell reached for the roan's reins.

John didn't move.

Jeremy rushed to his side. "His eyes look glazed, Lieutenant. I'll give him a hand."

When John slid off the saddle, his legs wobbled. He grabbed the horn and would have fallen, but Jeremy caught him, held him upright, and guided him to the dying campfire. Jeremy threw his Army blanket over John's shoulders and handed John a tin cup of steaming coffee.

John couldn't stop shivering and splashed the hot brew onto his knuckles.

The lieutenant clapped a hand on John's bowed shoulders. "I've got to make my report. Keep him here. I'll need his statement later tonight."

"Yes, sir." Jeremy set John's coffee on the ground and inspected his lacerated hand. "Break out the first aid tin, will you, Tom?" Jeremy called to another man.

John stared into the crackling embers and barely registered what was happening.

"Take a gander at this. What do you suppose made a cut to the bone like that?" Jeremy held up John's palm.

"Ya got me." Tom opened the medical tin.

"A bullwhip!" Jeremy cleaned the dripping blood from the wound. The deep cut ran across John's palm, severing the web of skin between his thumb and index finger. Small bones peeked through the mutilated flesh. Jeremy wrapped a muslin bandage around John's hand. "Of course. He's run up against Dread. Why does Lieutenant Whitsell want to see him again? Where is Corporal Dread? Here's another slash on my friend's arm. Toss me some more bandages."

John heard the conversation as if the words came from a distant well. Someone shoved another tin of coffee in his good hand. After swallowing his third cup, the unreal feeling faded. He let his shoulders slump. So tired.

Jeremy's voice broke into his fog. "How you feeling now?"

"Exhausted. I'm about to fall on my face."

Lieutenant Whitsell trotted up, leading Dread's roan. "Let's go, Ross. Private Worchester, you and a couple men come with us to retrieve the body. Fetch a horse for Ross."

Back in the glade with the flickering light from pine torches casting grotesque shadows, the dense darkness of the forest crowded in. John was closer to Hell than he ever wanted to be.

He had killed a man.

CHAPTER 20

With no moon, the sky was black when John halted the loaner horse next to his wagon and dismounted. Jeremy's boots hit the ground beside him. "The Lord takes you through the fires of purging more than most Christians I know." Jeremy steadied John as he stumbled. "He wants you for a vessel of gold."

John worked up a smile. "Tell me what you're talking about sometime when I'm not so trail worn." He gazed at the silent wagon. "Does Mother know what happened?"

"Yep. Sent word to her that you were all right. She was not to worry."

John rolled into his blanket and sprawled beside the crackling campfire. "I owe you again. Thanks, friend," he mumbled, almost asleep before his head touched the ground.

He opened his eyes to a sun peeking above the horizon. A clear November morning—blue sky, leaves brushed red and bronze, air cold and fresh, helped him wake. As he tumbled out of the blanket, his muscles knotted. Others refused to cooperate, forcing him to hobble like an old man.

Smoke curled up from the campfire, trailed overhead through low branches of the firs, and wafted into the brightening sky. The aroma of johnnycakes and coffee hung about camp. Judging from the gossip whispered around him and looks he received from guards passing by, every person on the wagon train knew his story. He hunched his shoulders and tried to ignore the soldiers stamping out campfires and upending tents as they broke camp. The smell of smoke and pine needles hung in the air.

Rachael handed him breakfast, her eyes soft and radiant. "John, you're—"

"Forget it, okay?" He wolfed his food, but the meager portion of grits and johnnycake didn't come close to filling the cramping emptiness in his gut. He hoisted himself to his feet and attempted to help Bold Hunter with the team but fumbled the leather as he worked one-handed trying to fasten the harnesses.

"I can't do much." His palm throbbed with pain even when he pressed his hand to his chest and held it still. Since he could barely handle the team, he climbed into the wagon to spend time with his mother and managed to roll up the canvas on her side to let her enjoy the lovely morning.

"John, tell me what happened last night. I've heard so many versions."

"What did you hear?"

"Everyone calls you a hero. Or even a super kind of hero."

"I'm not. I killed a man." He ruffled the fingers of his left hand through his hair. "Something about my attitude kept setting Corporal Dread off. Seems I rubbed him the wrong way—and now he's dead." John hung his head.

"From what I hear, the fight was definitely not your fault. The corporal was a known bully, and he had many enemies. Tell me the whole story."

Shortening how deadly serious the fight had been, he related quick details of what he preferred to forget. Before he finished, the bugle blew for the wagons to roll. He kissed Mother's thin cheek and climbed through the front flap and over the bench seat. Blast his limbs being so stiff and uncooperative.

Bold Hunter sat erect, clutching the reins in both hands. John lowered himself to the seat beside Bold Hunter. Neither mentioned the fight, and they rode without speaking.

Watching the muscular rumps of the slow plodding oxen soon lulled John into his own thoughts. He couldn't erase the image of the limp, unmoving body that had once been a living man. Though Dread was detestable in many ways, he was still a human being. John had deprived the corporal of life. He'd fought to survive, but never expected to hurt Dread. But he didn't initiate the confrontation. Nor could he have backed down. He'd been forced to fight or die.

Thank you, God. You gave me a cool head and strength to defend myself. Please forgive me for taking a life. Please remove this awful guilt from my heart and mind. After the initial shock, he'd had no time for fear. At least not until the end when he thought Dread was invincible.

He'd about melted to the ground in relief when the officer showed up and believed his story. *That had to be grace from you, God. Thank you for sending a man who knew what a bully Dread was and how much he liked to whip Cherokees.*

John gazed at the cloudless blue sky above the rugged mountain peaks. Maybe God used him to save other men and women from the corporal's cruelty. Or was he rationalizing to throw off his mantle of guilt? He rubbed the back of his knotted neck. He hated feeling lower than a rat.

Okay, then, what were the facts? Number one—Dread trapped him when he was alone and without a weapon. Number two—Dread attacked him. Number three—Dread fell on his own knife. Number four—an Army officer could have arrested him but didn't because of the corporal's well-known reputation of hurting people and because the trampled clearing provided evidence of a fight.

John shook his head. As if he'd performed some great service, the reaction from every soldier and civilian he'd passed this morning had been positive. True—the wagon master was an unpopular man ... correction ... had been an unpopular man. Deserving death or not, the image of Dread's limp body wouldn't disappear. How could he shed his awful load of self-loathing?

Do you forgive me, Father?

Pastor rode up beside John's wagon on the same pretty appaloosa Hope had ridden. "Morning, John. I heard what happened last night and came to see you as soon as I could."

"Thanks, Pastor. You know Dread's death was an accident?"

"Yes, John, I do. I want to make certain you don't experience remorse over the death. Satan loves to cripple God's children with a false sense of guilt. From all accounts and from what I know of your character, Robert Dread's death was indeed an accident."

John made a wry face.

"I visited General Scott before I came. He said to tell you the Army will not file charges."

John straightened from his slumped posture. "Thanks, Pastor. Telling me about false guilt lifts a burden from my shoulders."

"Glad to help." Pastor cleared his throat. "Thought I'd let you know I've encouraged our Indians to liken themselves to the twelve tribes of Israel leaving Egyptian slavery for freedom in the promised land of milk and honey. Seems to cheer them. They need all the encouragement they can get, for many are sick."

"I don't know much about the story you mention. Is it found in the Old Testament?"

"Yes. I taught about the Exodus when your people were first interred inside the stockade. Before you started attending our meetings."

"Sorry I missed those sermons."

An Indian John didn't know raced up. "Pastor Worchester can you come?"

"Be right with you." He turned back to John. "Take care you and Bold Hunter don't get into any altercations. You boys need to be friends. Look out for one another." He offered a salute to Bold Hunter, nodded to John, lifted his reins, shifted the appaloosa into a fast walk, then called over his shoulder, "I'm praying for the two of you."

Pastor trotted after the running Indian, past the slowly moving Conestogas, and towards the front. Soon dust and a bend in the road hid him from view.

Now, Lord. That's what I call an answer to prayer. Thanks so much more than I can say.

If God answered quickly, who was he to disagree? He had acted in self-defense. Time to accept the truth and move on. He shoved what remained of his guilt to the back of his mind and turned his thoughts to Pastor's words. So, they were headed to the promised land, were they? He hoped so.

Before the sun reached its zenith, the wagon train, surrounded by its mounted guards, approached Rattlesnake Springs, Tennessee. John received word they would camp here for several days to rest the oxen. He took a deep, relaxing breath and stretched his sore muscles. He could use the break.

As Bold Hunter drove their wagon into the outskirts of Rattlesnake Springs, John noticed another wagon train already camped outside the small town. Yesterday, Jeremy had mentioned seventeen thousand Cherokee Indians faced exile. Theirs was only one of twelve wagon trains, each carrying up to fifteen hundred captives, from Tennessee, Georgia, Alabama, and North and South Carolina. A regiment of infantry, a regiment of artillery, six companies of dragoons, plus four thousand militiamen guarded them. Probably not unusual to intersect with another train. Still, the sight lodged a lump in his throat. So many people uprooted from all they owned and knew.

Yet, the glorious fall day, coupled with the bustle of townspeople bantering with soldiers and militiamen, the busy campers, and the new arrivals setting up camp, sent excitement coursing through his veins.

As the last wagon in the train to rumble through town, John's Conestoga choked in the dust kicked up by the other travelers. Bold Hunter drove down the long main street, fenced by unpainted two-story buildings. A wooden sidewalk thronging with people, mostly men, stretched on both sides of the narrow dirt road. Horses crowded each other at the hitching posts.

Once their oxen plodded through town, Bold Hunter merged their wagon to the train circled in the large meadow and jumped down to set up camp.

Jeremy tethered his horse to a tree near their wagon and strode toward John. "Glad to see you looking chipper today. You're something of a legend you know."

"I'm considering changing my name to David," John joked, trying to overcome the remnant of guilt that would creep back and lodge inside his chest. "You know, fighting Goliath."

"You got any ideas of changing my name to Jonathan, forget it." Jeremy's twinkling green eyes belied his straight face.

"All tomfoolery aside, without God's protection I would have been slung across that horse you led back to the wagon train last night instead of Dread." John skidded down from the seat, his legs and back stiff, and joined Jeremy on the dirt road. The descent jolted every sore muscle in his body.

"Yep." Jeremy's wide grin flashed. "Think what a loss for womanhood your demise would have been."

John took a left-handed poke at Jeremy's freckled face. "Lieutenant Whitsell ordered me to stay with the wagons. I wish I could go in and view the town."

"I'm way ahead of you. Why I'm here. Thought you might want to sight-see for a spell. But don't get any ideas about slipping off again. Every soldier in my dragoon knows who you are now. You're under special guard, too."

"Oh, the price of infamy. I've been under special guard since I left the stockade, and that doesn't even include you." John winked.

Jeremy looked chagrined and ruffled his red hair.

"Come on ball and chain, let's go." Yes, he'd killed a man, but he was free from the wagon master's vengeance, and Rachael was free of Dread's constant threat. "I'd dance a jig right here on the grass if my muscles weren't so stiff."

As they hiked through camped wagons toward town, people they passed paused from setting up camp to stare.

"Why are they eyeballing us?" Jeremy smoothed his fiery hair.

John grinned. "You're a fine-looking guard with that lopsided mouth and black eye. I've got my hand bandaged to my elbow, hobbling along the street stiff as a British soldier. We resemble a couple of Jean Lafitte's pirates."

Setting his hat at a rakish angle, Jeremy hooked his thumbs into his cross belts and swaggered, glaring at any man who looked as if he might be too timid to fight. An old man hurried across the wagon and buggy clogged street to avoid them.

John and Jeremy laughed.

The town boomed with more people than the Fourth of July did with fireworks. Hogs had long since been routed from their wallows in the middle of the town's lone street. Families in a gala mood crowded into buckboards and gawked like country girls at the new encampment of soldiers and Indians.

Wearing curious or flirting expressions depending upon their age, the leading ladies of the county sat in elegant buggies, delicate fans waving, their faces half-hidden beneath coal-scuttle bonnets. Beside them, their husbands or fathers, clad in green or blue claw-hammer coats, drove.

After so much dust, rain, and wilderness, the sight looked colorful and smelled of perfume, manure, axle grease, and civilization. John couldn't keep a grin off his face.

Soldiers, blue uniforms shiny with epaulets and brass buttons, strode about with many a self-conscious swipe at their side whiskers. The doors of the town's one tavern swung constantly, and the wooden sidewalk trembled beneath so many feet. Town loafers sat idly in groups, whittling, spitting tobacco juice, and spinning yarns.

"Let's try the tavern. I'm thirsty." John started toward the swinging door.

"Best we don't. Not prudent." Jeremy grabbed his shirttail.

"Humph. You're a strict guard."

They walked up one side of the wooden sidewalk, crossed the dusty street, and strolled down the other side of the single main street. Too soon Jeremy gazed at the sun. "Time to go. Let's head to camp. I've got guard duty coming up." He turned on his heel, and they headed back toward the wagons.

Beyond the circles of wagons parked in irregular circles, yet almost linked together, drivers hobbled the oxen. Farther out, in loops like ripples in a lake, camped cavalry horses and artillery regiments. Some soldiers stood guard duty, while others wandered on various other missions.

As his new shoes crushed the meadow grass, John pointed to the encampment. "This seeming confusion forms a pattern. Everywhere your blue uniforms of the regular army maintain order."

"You got it. Order is the Army's first name."

John's skin crawled. "I feel naked among the officers' swords, spurs, and gold braid." He dodged out of the path of the baggy-trousered, coonskin-capped militia who totted muzzle-loading rifles. "I need my own firearm."

Jeremy spoke over his shoulder. "Ross, you're better dressed than the militia." He strode faster.

"Thanks to your sister."

"Sorry, didn't mean to embarrass you. Just meant you could be mistaken for a local, so keep up. Don't get any foolish ideas, okay?"

"Don't worry about me, Yank. I'm tied to the wagon train by stronger chains than the cavalry." John turned for a last look at the enticing town and followed Jeremy toward camp.

Staying close to their wagons and looking bedraggled, tacky, and hungry, the Cherokee huddled in family groups. Some, who dressed in baggy pants or tunics with turbans on their heads, looked like mystics from an eastern land. Others wore buckskin or otter. Hundreds shivered in summer-weight homespun. A good many walked barefoot.

John winced, reminded of how cold his feet had been before God used Jeremy's sister to provide his shoes.

Yet, the Cherokees maintained their innate dignity as they moved around their wagons. Though forced to remain in camp, they were not idle. The men whittled blowguns from river cane to be used for small-game and bird hunting. Others fashioned darts for the blowguns from locust wood, feathering them with thistledown.

Some worked with heavy rocks chipping knives from flint. The men were busy, and John knew they thought of food, not escape. They continued to obey the voice of Chief Ross who had ordered them to maintain a non-violent acceptance of their destiny.

John smiled back at the Cherokee girls, appreciating their beauty even after months of imprisonment. Tall, slender, vivacious, with graceful walk and brown, even features, Cherokee women sparkled even in captivity. The sprinkling of browns and blondes among raven tresses revealed the mixed blood from their mothers' marriages to traders and trappers. Some of them bent over campfires, preparing dinner, while others wove baskets from honeysuckle vines. Others dried medicinal herbs in the sun on lines they fashioned from wild hemp. No wonder so many soldiers lounged in the vicinity of the busy girls and women.

Many women took advantage of the camping respite to fashion pottery bowls. They dug under the topsoil for clay, dried it by the fire and pulverized the clay into powder. Then they mixed it with water. They coiled strips of clay, upward from the base to the rim, polished the surface with a stone, then fired the bowl.

A prickle of pride stirred in John's chest. His people's only resources were raw materials. Whatever they needed, they dug, cut, and shaped for themselves. Had the men been permitted to hunt, they could have brought back animal pelts to make warm clothing. Already the days were crisp, the nights cold and frost nipped the air.

He thought of the several hundred graves left behind in New Echota. Once again, the memory of Pris's arms wound round his neck, her sweet moist kiss warming his cheek, wrenched his spirit. His chest ached. How many other graves would sprout beside the trail to the new territory if his people didn't receive warm clothes before snow?

"Yank, are we sanctioned to hunt?" John pointed toward the thick woods that covered the hills surrounding Rattlesnake Springs.

"How can the army allow you captives to roam the forest? You could escape. Part of the militia's job is to supply meat for the wagon train."

"What about the skins? Do we get the pelts for clothes?"

"Couldn't say. The militia does pretty much what they please. Pelts bring a lot of money."

"Let's amble over toward the river." John nodded to the widest part of the rushing water dividing the town from the campgrounds.

Jeremy glanced at his pocket watch. "Just a few minutes. We can take a quick look."

Scores of children played beside the clear, fast flowing mountain stream. On the riverbanks, women washed clothes, carried water, and dug for clay, although hampered by the soldiers who meandered underfoot watching the girls.

"Glad Rachael stayed in the wagon. I don't relish any more trouble over her."

"Yep."

John pointed toward the river. "Jeremy, how about you cut a couple of long pieces of river cane?"

"Sure." Jeremy switched open his army knife. "You want to build a tent for your mother?"

"Something like that."

While Jeremy cut three straight six-foot lengths, John gathered other items he needed.

When Jeremy finished, his attention shifted to the young ladies. When a girl noticed Jeremy watching, she lowered her head shyly and turned gracefully away. Fewer girls were captive now because many had married militia or soldiers not tasked to accompany the Cherokees and had left the wagon train. But many girls had been raped by less virtuous guards. So, a young woman had to be careful, never knowing which type of soldier had his gaze on her.

Jeremy stood engrossed in the girls while John searched the rocky stream for large pieces of flint, which he pocketed. Now, where could he find wild hemp?

Jeremy startled with a jerk. "Ho, John, we can't idle here all day." He grabbed John's arm. "I've got to stand guard duty. I'll race you back."

"I fancy you'd be glad to race me today." John held up his bandaged hand and rested his other one on his sore back. "I can't run. I'm so stiff I can scarcely limp."

"I've got to high-tail it back or I'm in serious trouble." Jeremy knit his brows. He gazed at the off-duty soldiers lounging by the wagons. "Give me your word of honor you'll return to your wagon. I'm responsible for you."

"Word of honor. We're friends. I won't get you into trouble. I'll make it back to my wagon as quick as I ...."

Jeremy sprinted hard toward his post.

John chuckled as he watched the redhead dodge through the surging mass of people and animals, leaving startled gasps at near collisions in his wake. Hobbling as fast as he could, and balancing the river cane on his right shoulder, John followed.

Two drunken militiamen tried to help each other stand. Appeared, they'd lingered inside the town's saloon several drinks too long.

John smiled. Then he saw Hope. She had her back to him, but there was no mistaking her small form. He could circle her tiny waist with both hands. She'd replaced her sunbonnet with a perky green hat with a wisp of a veil. Her golden-red hair gleamed in the sunlight.

One drunk stumbled against her almost sending her into a passing buggy.

This opportunity was too good to let slip away. He limped to her side and used his most gentlemanly drawl. "If I may be so bold as to assist you, ma'am." With his left arm, he elbowed the drunks out of her path, then steered them on their course away from the wagons toward the militia encampment. They tittered on their way like two canoes wallowing in a gale.

She looked up, eyes wide with recognition.

He hid his amusement at the shock on her face "You shouldn't be standing here alone, Miss Worchester." He balanced the river cane on his shoulder with his injured hand and took her elbow with his left hand, then guided her away from the parked wagon. "It will be my pleasure to see you to your home on wheels." He steered her in the direction of his own wagon.

"Mr. Ross?" Her golden brows lifted. "How can you walk freely in this section of the wagon train?" Her dimples deepened. "You look so much the gentleman."

John laughed and savored her crisp New England accent. He avoided answering her question and added a Scottish burr to his drawl. Girls back home had seemed taken with the accent when he decided to use it. "Miss Worchester. I'm delighted I happened along at such a timely moment."

Her green eyes danced. "I believe I should escort you. Making certain you return to your own wagon. You are my prisoner, sir."

"Happy to oblige any way I can, Miss Worchester."

As they strolled, she appeared unaware of the stares from the soldiers, militiamen, and townspeople, and seemed accustomed to people admiring her. She glanced sideways at him, her dimples playing games around her lips. "I was expecting Captain Peterson." She turned to gaze behind her. "He promised to accompany me into town." She fluttered her long eyelashes. "But since you are here, I think it best I escort you to your wagon. I don't need a gun, do I?"

"A gun would be the least of your weapons." John tightened his grip on her elbow. For once she seemed to see him in a favorable light. "Although I am your prisoner, Miss Worchester."

A blush appeared on her cheeks.

"My mother would be pleased to have you call. She wants to thank you personally for your generous gifts." He piloted Hope around a passel of children playing jacks in the dirt beside their wagon.

"Oh, that's quite unnecessary. There is no need for thanks. However, I shall be happy to meet your mother. Father speaks of her often." She gazed at his bandaged hand. "I hope your hand is not severely injured. Like everyone else on the wagon train, I heard of your adventure."

"It's nothing. A minor cut." So that's why she was friendly today. The stories of his fight with the Army's bully made him a hero.

"I wish that were true. Jeremy told me your hand is sliced to the bone." She lifted her own hand to shade her eyes and gazed up at him. "I understand you and Jeremy have become good friends. At first, I found this hard to believe. When I met you, you appeared so fierce and angry, to say nothing of being rude. Jeremy never made a habit of being close to crude people. I don't mean to offend, but I had rather a poor first opinion of you." She smiled, showing her dimples brilliantly.

His stomach flip-flopped, and his body tingled.

"Now I see I was mistaken. Forgive me."

She was incredibly honest. No woman he knew had been so outspoken. And she seemed unaware of how her brother spent his first three years in the army. "No need to apologize." John nodded to a passing soldier who was staring at him. He lengthened his steps. "We met under trying circumstances. I was rude. I hope you'll forgive me."

Those green eyes that so easily prodded him to anger now gave him a warm quivering feeling deep inside.

"Hope, wait! Here I am," an anguished, male voice called from behind them.

John looked back.

The tardy Captain Peterson rushed toward them, his black hair falling in waves over a high forehead. He carried his hat in one hand and his sword in the other as he dodged between campers. When he caught up with them, his eager brown eyes sought Hope's.

Before the captain could utter another word, John spoke in as stern a voice as he could muster. "Captain Peterson, you left this young lady unescorted in a dangerous place. Fortunately, as a friend of the family, I rescued her."

The soldier's eagerness exploded into rage. "What?" The anxious face flushed. Turning his back to John, Peterson pulled Hope away. "I'm sorry, Hope. I arrived as quickly as I could. Lieutenant Whitsell was delivering his report. He was quite thorough and ran long."

John reached for Hope's elbow. "Miss Worchester promised to pay a call on my mother. I'm escorting her." He spoke as though the plan were confirmed.

"Is this true?" The captain's dark eyes questioned Hope's sparkling green ones.

"Yes, Matthew. What Mr. Ross says is true." She touched the officer's sleeve. "You may call on Father and me tonight and stay for dinner."

John tightened his grip on her elbow. Did she ever invite Indians to dinner?

For the first time, the captain appeared to notice John's identity. Peterson raised both dark brows. "Ross, what are you doing here?"

John let his voice ooze patience. "I thought I just explained, Captain. I'm taking the lady to visit my mother."

"You can't walk around anywhere you want. You're a prisoner." Peterson tore Hope's elbow from John's hand and spoke in an explosive burst of words. "From the report I heard, I'd vote to throw you in the guardhouse until you get dumped in Indian Territory!"

"I am under special guard. Didn't they tell you?" John disengaged Hope's arm from Peterson's grasp, and guided her toward the circle of wagons where his was parked.

"I'm sorry, Matthew," Hope called over her shoulder. "I really have committed myself. Please come tonight."

John hustled her away, leaving Captain Peterson glaring at them, his polished boots planted wide not two paces from a Cherokee rubbing sticks together to start his campfire.

She laughed as she gazed up at John. "You're rather accustomed to having your own way, aren't you?"

"Not recently."

With her dimples playing around her cameo cheeks, she appeared to have enjoyed their little drama. Despite their former misunderstanding, Hope seemed to be a likable person. She'd fallen into his scheme with the same fun her brother would have shown.

John turned and sent a triumphant grin back at the grim-faced captain. But the soldier's livid look sent an uneasy prickle down John's neck. Peterson appeared to be a man not to be trifled with.

As they approached the Ross wagon, a bright-eyed boy, Lone Feather, danced up to John. "Is this the girl you said nobody could force you to court? Is it, John? Huh? Is it? Is this the frigid New Englander? She's ...."

John's hand shot out, cutting off Lone Feather's words. He held the squirming child and hissed in his ear, "Not now! Go away!"

Hope's eyes flashed. "My first impression was correct. You are a crude person! I shall visit your mother because I keep my word. But I never want to see you again. Frigid New Englander, indeed! Let me tell you, Mr. Ross, New Englanders are as hot in passion as they are cold in loathing!"

The crisp voice sounded icy, distant, and ruthlessly final.

CHAPTER 21

John gulped and breathed a prayer. *God, I thought you were on my side. You know I care about this girl. And we were getting along so well. Why this?*

He rubbed a sleeve to wipe the sudden sweat off his forehead and glanced into the back flap of the wagon to make certain Mother was inside. She sat ensconced upon several grain sacks. Her eyes were closed, and she was alone.

John made a slight bow. "She's at home."

Hope shook off his helping hand, lifted her skirts, and scrambled into the wagon without a word or backward glance.

"Phew. That girl says what she thinks. No pretense with her." John slumped against the side of the wagon.

"Did I do something wrong?" Lone Feather's head hung almost to his chest.

"Rather. I would have preferred you asked me privately. Go play, will you?"

John's hands shook. Getting acquainted with Hope had been fantastic. But his hasty words bit him like a snake, ruining his possibility of any relationship. With his uninjured hand, he slapped the rump of an ox nibbling grass near the wagon.

The animal jumped, its brown eyes wide with confusion.

"Sorry." Why had he spoken words to Mother that could be overheard and repeated? John rubbed the nape of his neck where a muscle spasm had started a terrific headache, and the pain nagging his hand all day suddenly radiated into real agony. He would apologize when he escorted Hope back to her wagon or to town or wherever she wanted to go after she visited Mother. He'd make her listen.

Why did he have so much trouble with this particular young lady? Being in Miss Hope Worchester's vicinity was as dangerous as holding a torch near an open keg of gunpowder.

He paced the small area around the wagon. The campfire had died to glowing embers. Why was no one nearby? Where were the children? Where was Rachael? Bold Hunter was missing too. John stepped closer to the canvas canopy, trying not to appear to be eavesdropping. He could only hear a murmur of voices, spiced now and again with laughter. *They* seemed to be getting along well.

He slid his spine down the trunk of a tree and settled on the sparsely grassed ground. Lone Feather shuffled out of the shadows and plopped cross-legged, facing him, his mouth drooping.

John pulled his stash of reeds close, selecting the straightest piece of hickory rod to work inside the river cane. With his hand wounded, he couldn't use the knife he'd found buried in mud when he gathered the cane. "Perk up, Lone Feather, you can help me." He motioned the lad closer. "Use this knife to smooth the inside of this cane. My hand slows me so much I'm as clumsy as a bear at a tea party."

Lone Feather grinned and started work as if he knew how. John watched a few minutes, then he feathered the yellow locust shaft with thistledown.

"I'm sorry, John. I won't speak out like that again." The little fellow bit his lower lip.

"Forgiven. Hand me the other feather over there will you? I reckon you've done this before. You can make your own since I have enough supplies for both of us." John tousled the boy's dark hair.

Lone Feather grinned.

When John finished, evening shadows poked into the crannies under and around the wagon. Hope remained inside talking with Mother.

Bold Hunter arrived carrying a load of branches. He glanced at John, then tossed the sticks onto the campfire until the fire blazed.

John stood and bent over the fire to heat the canes. When they were supple enough for his satisfaction, he split one end in which to set the arrowhead and fletched the other with feathers. With Lone Feather's help, he lashed both arrows and feathers with sinews sliced from his worn-out moccasins.

Rachael stepped into the clearing from the same direction Bold Hunter had appeared. With potatoes aproned in her skirt, she'd arrived a few minutes behind the Indian. She bent over the cooking pot and sliced the tubers for their meal.

Apparently, the two had been together. John rubbed his aching forehead. He had strong feelings for both women. What was wrong with him? Aside from physical beauty, what attraction pulled him to each one?

Hope embodied everything he'd dreamed about in a woman—and much more. He'd never seen a girl more spirited—or difficult to handle. She lived her faith by putting her own life on hold to help the Cherokee people. She'd sold all she owned to buy the supplies the Cherokee badly needed and traveled alone with those supplies all the way across the country to meet the wagon train. No easy feat in these outlaw-infested, gun-for-hire days. Could his faith ever match hers? He frowned and grunted. Plus, with a snap of her fingers, Hope had every soldier in the guard dropping to their knees in front of her. How could he compete? He jammed a dart into the hard ground.

And darkly beautiful Rachael—with her raven tresses to her waist and her snappy, brown eyes—was a nurturing woman who cared for children and the sick. She expressed loyalty beyond human bounds when she chose to care for his mother rather than escape with Bold Hunter. Her strong

Christian faith radiated like the sun especially when she hadn't wanted Bold Hunter to become a Christian in order to marry her. But did she love Bold Hunter? John hurled a stick into the fire—logs scattered to the edge of the pit. He slammed his blowgun to the ground.

What chance did he have with either woman? He had to drive them both out of his mind.

"You look dejected, John. Is your mother worse?" Rachael's lovely eyes gazed at him from across the cook fire, a frown disturbing the calm of her forehead.

"No, the Worchester girl is inside talking to Mother. I'm waiting to walk her back to her wagon."

"Oh?" Rachael spilled some of the water she was pouring into the pot hanging over the campfire. Her face lost its usual calm expression, and her lips trembled.

Bold Hunter frowned, sprang up from where he sat on a log, threw more sticks on the fire, then thrust his arm around Rachel's waist. Disturbed by the Indian's familiarity with Rachel, John looked away.

He unfolded his aching frame, stood, and stretched his long legs, not attempting to hide the darts he had made. Armed with rifles, the soldiers now turned blind eyes when the prisoners fashioned crude instruments to hunt small game.

John strode from the campfire and scanned the landscape. In the west, the tree-clad peaks thrust up their rounded tips, row upon row against the skyline. As the sun slid behind the mountains, gold, pink, and purple splendor splashed the sky, then faded into bronze and gray. The reds and browns of the trees darkened into dullness.

A fit of coughing shook him.

The inside of the wagon had to be dark now. What was Hope doing? He paced the small clearing. Finally, the flap opened. Hope lifted her long blue skirts and climbed to the ground. Not sparing a glance in his direction, she headed for the line of soldiers guarding the wagons.

He rushed up to her and fell into step. "I'll accompany you to your wagon. It's dark and not safe for you to be alone."

"No thank you. I can take care of myself."

"But ..."

She pushed his offered arm aside, turned away, lifted her long skirts, and hurried toward Jeremy's post.

He dropped his empty hands. His head ached. His hand ached. Now so did his heart. He rubbed the back of his neck, but the spasm didn't release. He had no chance with Hope.

Did Pastor have any more healing brew for his headache? He wasn't about to risk seeing Hope to find a headache remedy. Banging his head against the tailgate sounded like a good idea. Instead, he hunched closer to the fire.

As darkness descended, cold seeped into his bones. After supper, he left the campfire to find Jeremy, John's two guards falling into step behind him.

Jeremy sat close to a large bonfire, drinking coffee with a few other soldiers. He motioned to the soldiers guarding John, who hung back in the shadows. "Come on over, you two. Have some coffee and warm yourselves."

He offered John a tin plate of hot beans and cornbread and a cup of coffee. "What's wrong, Ross? Run into more trouble?"

"Nothing's wrong." John devoured the food, then crouched in silence sipping the coffee, his eyes fixed on the ground.

"How's your hand?"

"Hurts."

"Yep. Reckon so. Want me to examine it?"

"I'm fine."

"You're full of sunshine and conversation. What happened?"

"Do you have a Bible?" John ignored the mocking expression of the soldier whose tent abutted Jeremy's.

"Yep. Looking for some reading material?"

John nodded. Then Jeremy sprang up, bent, entered his tent, ruffled around inside, and returned holding a small, black book.

"Study with me, will you? I need help understanding some of the meaning." John sipped the coffee, then set the empty tin cup on the ground. "Walk me back to my wagon. I've got to show up there before the change of guards."

When he, Jeremy, and the two guards reached the Ross wagon, Rachael smiled, hung her dishtowel to dry, and joined them. They settled on logs shoved close to the campfire's uncertain light. Two fresh guards arrived and squatted cross-legged near to the fire and the two off-duty soldiers tramped off into the darkness.

Jeremy thumbed through the Bible. "What do you want to read?"

"John looks sad tonight. Read something to cheer him." Rachael leaned next to Jeremy and guided his hand to the New Testament.

Hunched by the fire, chin on his knees, John idly traced a picture in the dirt. "You talked about fires of purging and vessels of gold. What did you mean?"

"I think Second Timothy, chapter two is what we want." Jeremy read the chapter aloud, then he explained. "Verse three tells us to endure difficulty as a good soldier of Jesus Christ. Verse ten says we must be willing to suffer if our suffering brings glory to Christ Jesus."

Rachel and John huddled close together, and he reached for her hand. The smooth, brown warmth nestled inside his as if they belonged together. Being near Rachael soothed the hurt from his encounter with Hope.

Jeremy shifted on his log, gazed at their clasped hands, · then stared down at the Bible. "Verse twelve promises, if we suffer, we shall reign with him. If we deny him, he also will deny us. When we think our suffering is hard, realize someday we shall rule and reign with Christ. So, we need to read the Bible to get to know God as our Father, then we can trust him ... no matter what happens. Trust is the key." Jeremy locked eyes with John. "If we trust God, we have faith he knows what is best."

"Trust?" Under cover of the darkness, John squeezed Rachael's hand. Was he wrong to have such feelings for two women?

"When we trust God, we know whatever happens to us is the best possible thing."

John had a sense Jeremy spoke of his lack of relationship with Hope, and his mixed feelings for Rachael. Were his conflicting emotions so obvious?

Rachael glanced at all of them clustered around the fire. "To me, trusting God is the greatest joy in the Christian life."

John coughed long and hard. After he gained control, he cleared his throat. "Jeremy, you're saying God makes no mistakes?"

"That's about it." Jeremy patted the cover of his Bible. "We have real security. Here's the part I had in mind last night. Verse twenty mentions the vessel of gold fashioned to honor Christ. A vessel of gold is one purged by fire so Christ can use the believer for the Lord's highest will. I see God doing exactly that in both your lives." He threw another stick on the fire. "Any questions?"

"I thought my sin was cleansed when I accepted Christ as my Savior." John rubbed his chin. So much yet to learn about this Christian life.

"To be purged is more than cleansing. Purging means to root out ... removing flaws which culture or environment engraved on a person. Weeding out the defect to shape a new personality for the Holy Spirit to use. God wants us to conform to the image of Christ. Purging is one way the Spirit transforms us into Christ's image. Most often the change happens over long periods of time, so God gets the glory not us."

Would God purge him for having strong feelings about two women? Torn between two women who already cared for other men trapped him in a personal prison. Maybe God was showing him not to let his heart get involved with either woman. Maybe God wanted his undivided attention. He rubbed his pounding temples.

No answer to this dilemma.

"I have another question that's plagued me for weeks. Why does God allow innocent babies to suffer? Why did my baby sister die?" John's voice cracked. He stared at the orange and red flames devouring the logs, sparks shooting to the black sky.

"Perhaps God intended to spare the child the suffering still ahead." Jeremy cleared his throat and swiped at his wet eyes.

Rachael wiped the tears glistening on her cheeks.

John dropped his head. "But Pris wanted to live. To enjoy life. To be loved and to love. Now she's gone. Why was she born, if only to die so soon? Why is there so much emptiness without her?"

Jeremy cleared his throat, and his voice sounded unsteady. "I don't have all the answers."

"I need answers!" John leaped up and paced around the campfire. "I can't accept events with no logical explanation and then say I trust God. How can a merciful God allow the innocent to suffer?"

"As far as Pris is concerned, you said she wanted to experience love and life to the fullest." Jeremy stood and put a heavy hand on John's shoulder. "And I believe that's exactly what she's doing. She has entered the place of absolute love. She's with God, who is love. How much more fully can a person experience love?" He squeezed John's shoulder, then let his hand drop.

John stared into Jeremy's serious green eyes. He was right. But more unanswered questions churned in John's mind.

"Suffering is the result of sin—directly or indirectly. As difficult as accepting suffering can be, pain is often necessary in God's plan to graft a spoiled human into his holy family. This plan requires a radical change." Jeremy closed the Bible.

"He's got a big job on his hands changing one John Ross." John stared at the circle of encamped wagons and the scores of campfires lighting the meadow. "Let me borrow your Bible, Yank? I can read during the day, and we can study together at night."

"Answer to prayer, my friend. Keep my Bible for a while, but I'll need it now and again. I've got difficulties of my own." He grinned. "Gotta go."

After Jeremy left, Rachael stood close to John, her beautiful face tilted up. "You're a tender person beneath that strong exterior." She touched his cheek with her warm fingers, smiled, climbed up, and disappeared inside the wagon.

He gathered his scattered wits.

Oh, God, am I a sinful man to be attracted to two women? If so, please forgive my sin and give me wisdom. And please don't let Hope hate me. Give me a chance to explain. Am I supposed to choose between the two of them or force my thoughts from both?

He threw more wood on the fire, wrapped his blanket around his long body, and stretched out near the heat. But sleep refused to come, and he shifted restlessly on the hard ground. The night's discussion and his trampled feelings swirled in his mind. His blanket was too short. Close to the fire was too hot, one side toasted, while the other froze. Farther from the fire was too cold.

Sleeping by a campfire seemed much like being caught between the two women who held his heart. Rachael loved him like a cherished friend, and Hope despised him. Wanting both and not being able to have either was driving him crazy.

Just at the point of sleep, a coughing spell wracked his body. From near the mountaintop, a cougar screamed, and the chilling sound revived another flow of thoughts. The general planned to leave Rattlesnake Springs tomorrow or the next day. He didn't have much time.

He lay on his back gazing into the velvet darkness. A mellow harvest moon shone brilliantly, casting deep shadows in the woods. The wagons stood outlined in the valley, but blackness spread behind them. Hundreds of campfires dotted the area. Indistinct forms surrounded each one and a deep hush filled the valley.

A soft, unnatural rustle caught his attention and he rolled over. At first, he saw nothing.

Bold Hunter slithered over, squatted beside him, touched his elbow, then whispered in his ear, "Bold Hunter go too. Go at dawn?"

"Two will be missed. No, I go alone."

Bold Hunter shrugged. "You no stop Bold Hunter."

John sat up. "When the guard changes, they talk with one another. Put the wagon between them and us. Head toward the river."

Bold hunter nodded, then slipped under his blanket. Soon his breathing grew deep and even.

Darkest night came, heralded by the screech of a mountain owl. The deep, wild, lonely cry roused a need, an aching, a desire. He tensed, his flesh tingled, and he tried to divert his thoughts, but thoughts of Hope drove him to his knees.

Lord, I've messed up with Hope, but I can't stop thinking about her. My feelings for Rachael run deep. Yet, I can't think straight when I'm near Hope. Being with Rachael seems right. My feelings for these two women are ripping me apart.

John tore at his hair.

Lord, I need help. What should I do?

CHAPTER 22

John rolled over on the hard ground. "Trust God," Jeremy had said.

A whisper, like the first breath of a cool breeze, pierced his soul. *Trust me.* John's heart quivered as the whisper grew louder. *I am the Lord your God. Lean on me.*

John's tension seeped away, and his passion calmed. His body relaxed and he slept until a cardinal's clucking high in a balsam tree woke him. In the lightening darkness, he folded his blanket and crawled on silent hands and knees away from the dead fire. With the wagon between himself and the guard, he stared across the clearing to the forest, then sensed a form slip up beside him.

Bold Hunter also carried a blowgun and darts, an unstrung bow, and a handful of arrows.

John whispered, "I'll go first. If I make it, I'll wait for you beneath those trees."

A gleam of sunlight filtered over the mountains. As the new guards tromped through the darkness toward him, John waited, frozen in place. The four guards greeted each other, resting their gun butts on the ground, their breath frosty in the morning's dim light as they talked.

John slid from shadow to shadow until he hid behind the adjoining wagon. Adrenaline drove his heart into double-time. He strained his eyes for a guard posted in an unexpected spot, then moved with swift, silent feet from cover to cover until he crouched in the trees. Nearby, a horse whinnied.

Bold Hunter touched his shoulder.

Though his muscles spasmed, he and Bold Hunter sprinted toward the rushing stream, feet pounding the ground as they followed the gurgle upward toward the mountains into denser woods. As John no longer heard muted noise from camp, Bold Hunter matched him stride for stride.

The sun rose in a burst of color, birds chirped a greeting to the day. Behind them, a distant bugle blew. Dew lay heavy on the grass, wetting John's shoes and the lower third of his pants. The crystal stream rushed over rugged rocks.

As they dashed along its banks, exhilaration exploded through his veins. Galvanizing to race in the early morning chill, to work through the smart of stiff muscles, and to relish the crisp air filling his lungs.

He and Bold Hunter raced past a waterfall shot through with sunlight diamonds from shafts filtering through the trees. How sweet the taste of freedom. Why should one man have power to hold another prisoner who had committed no crime? Wasn't there room on earth for all men to be free?

Winded, John stopped running and leaned forward, hands on his knees, panting. He pointed to a spot near a deepening of the stream, led Bold Hunter there, and dropped to the ground.

Both strung their bows and nocked their arrows. As John worked, sounds of the forest played a symphony while the calm beauty penetrated his heart and relaxed his frayed nerves. Sun shone warm on his head and shoulders while chipmunks and squirrels scampered to drink at the stream. He leaned comfortably against a tree, his eyelids scraping sandy eyes. Hard to keep awake after so little sleep.

The unforgettable fragrance of November—of dying things, musky scents of earth and moldy leaves—floated around him. A breeze rustled the leaves still clinging to the trees. Here and there leaves drifted down into dead mounds on the mossy ground.

Back at New Echota, autumn leaves fell on mounded graves. Would the memory always thrust darts of pain through his heart? Thinking of Pris turned his mind toward the Lord. Would the Lord want him here? Maybe he shouldn't have come. A flash of red brought his senses to full alert. A red fox, his nose high, scented them.

"Lord, bless us with game." Eyes wide, he searched the area. "Forgive us if we shouldn't have come. But you know the children need meat and warm clothes."

A buck stole to the water's edge. Silent as a fox himself, John stood. Muzzle lifted to the air, the deer sniffed. Under his breath, Bold Hunter repeated the Cherokee charm a hunter spoke before killing an animal. He asked the buck's permission to take his life.

Raising their bows, John and Bold Hunter each fit an arrow into their bowstrings, aimed, and with muscles straining, pulled the string taut and shot their arrows. Pain from John's injured hand jolted all the way up his arm.

At the crucial instant, the deer bolted. John's arrow fell short but Bold Hunter's penetrated the animal's front shoulder. Quicker than thought, the buck wheeled, heading for denser woods. John and Bold Hunter raced after the wounded animal.

John grinned as he ran. Fortunately, the deer chose to run toward the wagon encampment rather than further on up the mountain. At least, he wouldn't have so far to carry the carcass. He fought through the dense underbrush and low-hanging branches catching at his clothes, Bold Hunter at his heels.

The deer faltered.

John slipped and slid over slippery moss and jumped iron-like bushes obstructing his path. A misstep could send him hurtling down a steep gully. He floundered through a heavy growth of rhododendron and stumbled over the fallen deer.

The buck lay on his side, panting. Large brown eyes stared, wide with fright.

"He's mine!" Bold Hunter whipped his knife from beneath his buckskin shirt, stooped, and put the wounded animal out of its pain.

Suddenly the hair on the back of John's neck bristled, a sixth sense warning him of danger. With a spine-chilling screech, a cougar, ears laid flat against its head, tan fur bristling, leaped down from an overhead limb.

CHAPTER 23

John and Bold Hunter had not been the only hunters.

For a stunned second, John stood immobile, the cougar's scream ringing in his ears. He gauged the situation. Bold Hunter lay pinned flat on his stomach, helpless beneath the heavy cat's clawing, biting fury.

The Indian squirmed, protecting his head and neck with his hands and arms. His options limited, John slammed both fists hard on the cougar's head. The stunned animal stopped slashing but clung to Bold Hunter's hunched body.

John leaped onto the cougar's back, wrapped his long legs around the beast's body, hooked his right arm around the warm, pulsating neck, then grabbed the animal's sinewy foreleg with his left hand. He exerted all his strength, grappled the snarling cougar free, and rolled it off Bold Hunter's back.

Landing on his rear beneath the furious cougar, John hung on. He panted hard, exerting every muscle to hold the writhing cat and avoid the four wind-milling paws. If only he could get to his knife. The cat screeched and clawed the air, repeatedly turning his head, his bared yellowed incisors flashing too close, it bit at John.

Can't hold him long!

John's heartbeat sped. Roaring filled his ears. One by one, his fingers loosened their grasp on the thrashing, furry body.

What now, Lord?

Eyes wide, mouth ajar, Bold Hunter pushed himself to his knees and clubbed the cougar on the head with the butt of his knife. But the cat still squirmed. Despite long scratches down the outside of his arm, Bold Hunter slashed the cat's exposed belly. The animal's screech ended in a humanlike scream. His paws jerked, his head lolled to one side, heavy on John's arm. The round yellow eyes stared unblinking at the sun. Bold Hunter shoved off the dead weight.

John lay spread-eagle on the ground, gulping in deep, gasping breaths, his limbs drained of strength. Bold Hunter, right sleeve torn off and blood dripping from his arm, stared at him,

"We were lucky." John pushed himself into a sitting position. "Wrong, not luck. God stepped in. His strength ... not ours." He pulled in gulps of air. "If you'd lost your knife when that cat jumped you, we'd have gotten mauled, maybe killed. I couldn't have held the cat another ten seconds."

Bold Hunter's breath whistled through his teeth. He sat beside John. "Why you save Bold Hunter life?"

"When the cat landed on your back, I couldn't stand here and let you die." John's voice sounded more unsteady than he would have liked. A coughing convulsion shook him. When he regained his ability to speak, he stood. "Let's take a look at your injuries."

Bold Hunter turned.

John peeled the big man's shirt over his head, expecting to see the Indian's back slashed into ribbons. Instead, there were two deep claw marks on Bold Hunter's shoulders— where the cat's front feet landed and further down near Bold Hunter's waist, more bloody impressions left by the rear feet marred the muscular brown back. The wounds bled freely. The wildcat had also torn off a hunk of Bold Hunter's hair.

"Look for herbs like used on you back."

Under Bold Hunter's direction, John gathered herbs, then bound them over the wounds with wild grapevine. As John worked, the Indian talked. "Shaman witch doctor make strong medicine for Bold Hunter. Strong medicine for hunt. Medicine no work. Make strong medicine for love. Love medicine no work. Rachael no marry. Bold Hunter see God of white man stronger than witch doctor."

Even as John bound Bold Hunter's wounds, the Indian didn't flinch—just kept on talking. "Bold Hunter say Christian scared." He shook his head so hard his black hair haloed out. "Bold Hunter wrong."

John opened his mouth to speak but chose to keep silent.

"Bold Hunter hear you strong in fight with wagon master, see you strong in love, and see you strong in saving life of Bold Hunter. You no scared." Bold Hunter's eyes gleamed.

John shrugged. "I can't say I wasn't scared."

"You no have weapon to fight cougar. But you fight. You think you God help?"

"I didn't have much chance to think."

Bold Hunter cleaned the cougar's blood from his knife on the grass and skinned the beast. "Find sapling to tie animal on." He nodded toward the thinner clump of trees. "We carry to wagon."

By the time John returned carrying the sapling, Bold Hunter had the cougar pelt bundled.

Together they used grapevines to knot the deer's front and rear legs to the sapling.

Bold Hunter wiped his bloody hands on the grass, then, his jaw set, stood to face John. "Bold Hunter ready to take God of white man."

John dropped his jaw. Was Bold Hunter joshing? He re-tied the string that had loosened from around his long hair, then straightened his clothes. "Right."

Bold Hunter raised his black brows, shuffled his feet, glanced at the sun, and crossed his muscular arms over his wide chest, but didn't budge from where he stood.

"You mean now?" John wiped a sweaty hand on his leg.

Bold Hunter nodded.

John swallowed. Sweat dribbled between his shoulder blades. How should he do this? "Um. You know you've sinned, and God can't look at sin?"

"Bold Hunter do many wrong things."

Speaking of wrong things, he sure didn't want to say the wrong thing. "Just tell God you want to be his child. Then ask the Lord Jesus Christ to forgive your sins and invite him into your life ...." What else could he say? He didn't know any of the Bible verses Pastor and Jeremy quoted.

The Indian dropped to his muscular knees and raised his arms toward heaven. In a loud voice he prayed as he gazed at the brilliant blue sky, "Lord of John Ross, Bold Hunter want Lord Jesus Christ come into life. Bold Hunter want evil forgiven. Bold Hunter say yes to God of white man. Want God become God of Bold Hunter." Then the young Indian spoke in Cherokee.

Moved by Bold Hunter's sincerity, John dropped to his own knees beside the Indian.

When the wounded man gazed at John, his large black eyes no longer burned with hatred or contempt. Instead, the shine of worship lit them as God poured out his Holy Spirit upon Bold Hunter.

John blinked hard to disguise the strange softness that entered his heart.

Bold Hunter stood, placed both big hands on John's shoulders, and gazed into his eyes. "No barrier keep us apart. Ross lift heart of Bold Hunter when heart flat. From where sun now stand, we brothers."

John couldn't stop grinning. What a jubilant feeling. He understood now why Jeremy willingly withstood persecution from his fellow soldiers. Helping a person find new life in Christ was worth whatever the cost.

Bold Hunter slung the reddish-tan cougar skin over John's shoulder, then lifted the sapling supporting the deer's front legs. John shouldered the rear quarters hanging from the branch. With the deer swinging on the pole between them, they headed toward the wagon train.

As they trudged through the dense undergrowth, Bold Hunter stopped. "Wait!" He held up one hand, then lowered his end of the load and disappeared among the trees. What had Bold Hunter seen? John lowered the rear end of the deer, rested with his back against a large tree, and closed his eyes. Though his chest and hand ached, life seemed good for the moment.

Bold Hunter raced back. He carried a white eagle feather. "John Ross wear sacred eagle feather of brave." He attached the feather to a lock of John's hair, letting the symbol hang down the back, Cherokee fashion.

His hand still hurt, but the feather inspired a spring in John's steps.

Late afternoon sun cast long shadows when he and Bold Hunter approached Rattlesnake Springs.

"How we get camp? Wait for dark? Maybe guards not miss?"

John's wiped sweat from his face and pointed. "Too late. We've been missed. Take a look at those four soldiers guarding our wagon. No, we walk in like free men. Not many off-duty soldiers down there, so they must be searching the woods for us. If they've been looking for us all day, they'll be mighty resentful. We best go face the Army's wrath."

"Pray first." Bold Hunter dropped to his knees.

Heat flooded John's neck. Why hadn't he thought of that? He knelt beside Bold Hunter.

"White Feather pray."

John waited. White Feather? Oh him. He cleared his throat. "Thank you for sending the food for the children and for saving Bold Hunter. Father, help the authorities understand we are only trying to feed our people. We pray our punishment might be light. In Jesus name. Amen."

With the deer swinging gently between them, they strode into the clearing and headed toward the wagons.

Soldiers standing guard gaped.

When no one attempted to stop them, a surge of hope flashed through John. As they entered the encampment,

Cherokee women and children … old men and young, stood to their feet. Like a refreshing wind, new vitality radiated from their faces. The people chanted the century-old "Song of the Successful Hunt." The words rose and fell, growing louder as the he and Bold Hunter neared their own wagon.

John hadn't considered what their appearance might signify to the captive Indians. Clustered around the parked wagons, men and boys reached for their own homemade weapons. Waving them wildly above their heads, they chanted words John couldn't understand. Bold Hunter's deep voice rose above the multitudes as he joined in the ritual.

Never had John felt more attuned to his people. As a boy, he had dreamed of a similar hunt and the welcome home.

Suddenly, a detachment of armed soldiers cut through the crowd. "Break it up! Break it up!" They pointed their guns at the cheering people. The crowd waved their weapons and chanted louder. Two soldiers jerked John's bows and arrows from his hand while other soldiers seized the pole and the game.

Wide-eyed young soldiers with fingers on their triggers surrounded him and Bold Hunter. "You two, raise your hands in the air. Raise 'em high."

He and Bold Hunter reached for the sky.

A soldier stripped Bold Hunter of the knife in his belt, then turned to the crowd. "The rest of you Injins go back to your wagons!" The soldiers repeated, "Go on back to your wagons!"

More soldiers arrived and forced the captives to disperse. But as they returned to their wagons, men and boys held their weapons high, and continued the triumphant chant.

John clenched his raised hands. Obviously, the soldiers feared revolt. Because they couldn't speak Cherokee, the army didn't understand our people merely performed a vigorous ceremonial welcome.

An angst-faced soldier ordered, "Keep your hands high. We're taking you to General Scott's tent."

As John trudged the length of the camp, the chanting followed. Quick as a whisper from one person to another, the ancient song kept pace with them, like one candle lighting another until a great bonfire raged. The nervous soldiers cocked their guns and waved them at the crowd, their index fingers on the triggers.

John glanced at Bold Hunter. What wild thing was this? Matters had gotten way out of hand. He and Bold Hunter would pay for starting this commotion. *Lord, please don't let anybody get trigger-happy.*

He spotted Jeremy, ducked his head, and gave his friend a sheepish grin.

With taut face, mouth tight-lipped, and his eyes unfriendly, Jeremy looked John in the eye.

John let his grin fade. He was so tired, his body sagged. And he had to be in real trouble to incur Jeremy's anger. A fit of coughing convulsed him.

He approached the lead wagon. Soon, they would march past the Worchester wagon. *God, please don't let Hope see me.*

But Hope sat on her horse with an excellent view of their whole parade.

John's face burned. His ears burned. His neck burned. He set his jaw. Topped with a flaming face, his devil-may-care disguise probably didn't convince her. He met her gaze across the excited mob and stared into her moss-green eyes.

She lifted her small chin and pink spots tinted her cheeks.

Confused hurt pierced his heart. She's still angry. She thinks we tried to escape. *Why do you let this misunderstanding continue, Lord?* His hand throbbed and his arms felt so heavy he lowered them.

Immediately bayonets prodded painful darts into his back. "Keep those hands high!" a squeaky voice ordered. Long minutes passed. He and Bold Hunter ducked their heads and shuffled inside General Winfield Scott's tent. He would soon meet the man soldiers nickname, Old Fuss and Feathers.

John waited, arms raised. What manner of person was Scott? His headquarters looked immaculate. On the general's table lay several thick volumes, a trimmed kerosene lamp, quill and ink, and an orderly pile of maps as well as a stack of parchment paper, everything squarely in place. The general obviously permitted no disorder.

Despite his heavy arms and exhausted body, John felt awed. The general was a national war hero, a man of courage. John remembered the stories of how two horses had been shot from under Scott at Lundy's Lane during the Second War of Independence and how Scott had distinguished himself as the top field general the United States ever produced, a strategical genius.

General Scott strode into the tent with all the ceremony of arriving for a state dinner.

Two orderlies, as well as the guards on either side of the canvas door, snapped to attention, while the four guards surrounding John and Bold Hunter saluted, shrouding the plain tent in a formal atmosphere.

A sense of hopelessness crept over John.

The general's stern uncompromising face, with his thin mouth drawn down at the corners, gave him an expression of perpetual disgust. A hawk-like nose protruded beneath a pair of penetrating eyes.

Other soldiers entered the large tent, wearing full-dress uniform and gloves. Outside, the chanting stopped. General Scott pulled out a camp chair and sat ramrod stiff behind his desk, his steely gaze piercing John's practiced calm. Then the man blasted his gaze toward Bold Hunter. A soldier entered, seated himself at a smaller table, and dipped his pen into ink to record their words.

When the general spoke, his voice sounded unexpectedly kind. "Were you two the cause of this tumult?"

"Yes, sir." John lowered his arms.

"Names?"

They gave their names.

"John Ross, you say. Are you related to Chief Ross?" General Scott steepled his fingers, elbows on his desk.

"Yes, sir. He's my uncle."

Scott's impassive face didn't change expression. "You two caused considerable problems for the United States Army today. Half a company took double duty to search the woods for you. After my soldiers arrested you, you incited the Indians into a rebellious mob. Your actions may motivate more attempts to escape. This is a serious offense. The punishment for escaped Indians who are recaptured is the firing squad."

CHAPTER 24

The firing squad!

John's world lurched. His knees buckled, and sweat beaded his forehead. A spasm of coughing shook him. Heat turned into chills. He glanced sideways at Bold Hunter, standing straight and tall, a calm half-smile on his lips. John read his mind.

Bold Hunter's ready to die. He's not afraid, because he's a Christian now. John clenched his fists. But he wasn't ready to go! Too many things left unfinished. He had a wagonload of women and children to provide for.

The general's voice rumbled on. What was he saying? John forced himself to concentrate.

Scott sounded impatient. "I repeat, do you have anything to say in your defense?"

"Yes, sir." John tried to keep his voice steady. "Bold Hunter and I have nine orphan children in our Conestoga. Their parents died in the smallpox epidemic inside the prison at New Echota." His voice caught on the lump constricting his throat. "My baby sister died there."

He straightened his shoulders. "The children are barefoot and wear summer clothes." Blast the emotion in his voice. "They're cold, hungry, and some are sick." He stepped forward. "The orphans have grown thin, their bodies weak because they haven't enough to eat. They whimper at night when the temperature falls and the wind blows. Soon snow will come. If the children don't get warm clothes and more food, they will die."

John raised his left fist. "Over two hundred graves mark the beginning of our exile. If something isn't done, the journey from here to Indian Territory will be remembered by future generations as a trail of death."

Except for the slow flush that began beneath the rigid collar of his uniform and crawled toward his hairline, General Scott seemed unmoved.

John stepped closer to Scott's desk. "The children's plight pressed heavily on me, so I decided to provide my wagon with fresh meat and pelts for warm clothes." He nodded toward Bold Hunter. "My brother and I didn't try to escape. We left to hunt game for our people. Nor were we captured. On our own volition, we walked in from the forest carrying our game tied between us."

General Scott's thin lips barely moved. "And the riot?"

"Hope. My people are proud, self-reliant, self-governing, unused to captivity. Since they lost their homelands and many family members, they feel sad and disconnected." John jutted his jaw. "Seeing the two of us return from the hunt kindled hope in their hearts, so they chanted the Cherokee "Song of the Successful Hunt." Your soldiers didn't understand. They mistook the happy chanting for a riot."

Scott tapped a quill against his desk, his bushy brows knit into a deep frown. Minutes passed.

John coughed again. Each cough wracked his chest. His body felt on fire, sweaty and chilled, his energy depleted. He'd spoken his best, but would his honesty save their lives? The agony in John's hand sapped his strength. Exhausted, hungry, and light-headed, the tent whirled. He swayed.

The soldiers filling the room waited, their taut faces turned toward their general. The secretary sat with quill lifted.

Scott finally spoke. "You realized you would face punishment when you returned to camp, did you not?"

"Yes, sir." John widened his stance, balancing against the tilting room.

General Scott leaned back in his camp chair and crossed his arms over his chest. "Did it not occur to you that the militia would provide your wagon with meat?"

"Yes, sir. I asked one of your men if the mercenaries would furnish the pelts as well as the meat. He answered that the militia probably would not. We've been on the wagon train several weeks now. During that time, I've not seen any meat or pelts provided." John braced his legs against the desk to stop the tent from leaning.

Scott sat forward and grabbed the outer edges of his desk with both hands.

"What was the soldier's name?"

"I'd rather not say, sir."

Scott pursed his thin mouth and frowned.

John pulled in as deep a breath as he could without starting more coughing. Would he have to stand in front of those penetrating eyes forever? He stiffened his knees.

"I believe your defense. There will be no firing squad. However, leaving camp without guard demands strong disciplinary measures." Scott loosed his grip on the desk and rubbed his jaw. "On the other hand, your motives were good. Tempering mercy with justice is the American way, though you may find that difficult to accept." He stood and rested both hands on his field desk. "Your sentence is two week's discipline under one of our captains. That will instill in you both a high regard for obedience to the army."

John released a long sigh. "Thank you, sir."

General Scott dropped a heavy fist on his desk. "Ross, this is the second time my soldiers brought you to my attention. There had better not be a third."

"No, sir."

Scott turned toward the soldiers. "Guards escort these two to the medic. Then release them to...." He pulled a sheet of paper from the stack in front of his desk and peered at it. "Captain Peterson."

John groaned inside. That couldn't be good.

General Scott gathered a handful of papers from a corner of his desk, dipped his quill in his ink bottle, and stared down at the papers. Apparently, the general wanted nothing more to do with the two of them.

Four soldiers formed a guard, shuffled him and Bold Hunter out of the tent and to a wagon in the exact center of the train. The four ushered the two of them into the roomy hospital tent adjacent to the wagon where a slender man dressed in rumpled trousers and a wrinkled army shirt sat writing at a long table. In the glow from the hanging kerosene lamp, his strong features stood out in sharp relief on his thin face.

John blinked, trying to focus his gritty eyes. The man's furrowed forehead and head sparsely covered with sandy hair showed the doctor to be somewhere between forty and sixty. His uniform looked baggy and slept in. Seemed the doc took scant notice of his appearance, but his tent looked spotless.

Two cots clad in snowy linen waited along one end of the tent. Books packed in a carton, titled spines in view, beckoned within easy reach of the doctor's camp chair. Surgical tools were arranged, side by side atop white linen on another table. Bottles and beakers stacked in crates lined the end of a table where a chess set waited. The tent had the atmosphere of clean efficiency plus homey comfort.

The Doc's curious gray eyes appraised them. "You guards wait outside. Tell my aide to fetch you coffee." He waved toward the canvas door, a warm smile on his thin face making him appear years younger.

Some of the tension drained from John's shoulders.

"So, you're the men who caused today's ruckus."

John nodded.

"You're already a legend around here. But you look battle weary. Sit on the cot while I examine your friend."

John lowered himself to sit on one of the cots. A legend? Hardly. More like ... ugh, he was too tired to think.

The Doc lifted Bold Hunter's shirt and examined the claw marks, then glanced toward John. "Hmm, you used these medicinal herbs?"

"Yes, sir." John sagged full-length on the cot.

Bold Hunter stood compliant and uncomplaining while the doctor cleaned and medicated the wounds, then replaced the herbs on the deepest gashes, and bound them with white bandages. "I don't think these will slow you much."

Bold Hunter started to put his shirt on, but the doctor stopped the Indian's hand. "While you're here, I'll give you a thorough check. I'm researching the effect of captivity on the human body." After prodding, peering, and poking Bold Hunter, the doctor deposited his instruments on a tray and tidied them.

"What you find?" Bold Hunter pointed to the tray.

Doctor Smith handed over Bold Hunter's fringed, buckskin shirt. "You're a puzzle, young man. You're the finest specimen of manhood I've ever seen. Being a prisoner hasn't produced any adverse effect on you."

Bold Hunter looked impassive.

John smiled. He'd figured out his new friend. Bold Hunter reverted to that wooden statue disguise when he felt embarrassed ... and if he thought he'd lost control of a situation. Yeah, the guy had turned out to be a decent man.

The doctor turned to John. "You're next."

"I'm not injured." A spasm of coughing shook him and the cot.

"Hmm. Pale face, beaded with sweat, and a deep, harsh cough. Doesn't look good. Let's take a gander at your hand." Doc unwrapped the dirty bandage that extended to John's forearm, then whistled. The wound lay open, raw, and painful. Small bones gleamed through yellow pus, and streaks of red ran up John's wrist.

John's empty stomach somersaulted.

"You've got a nice little infection here. I'll clean this out, then sew you up." The doctor spoke as casually as if he were discussing how to sew a turkey after it'd been stuffed. "I need to stop that blood poisoning, or you'll lose your hand."

John grit his teeth. "Maybe being captured was a good thing."

"Obviously." Methodically choosing his instruments, the doc took two bottles from the crate and then poured a solution into a clean pan. With the graceful movements of an orchestra conductor, he selected an oversized needle, placing it at a ninety-degree angle. Then he lifted John's hand.

John gasped. The room tilted.

The doctor caught him as he slumped from the cot toward the floor. As though they were far away in a tunnel, he was vaguely aware as Bold Hunter and the doctor settled him back on the cot.

"The needle distresses the best of them. Strange, seems it's the big blades that faint when they see this instrument."

Bold Hunter grunted.

John forced his eyes open. The doc gazed at his needle much as a horse breeder might look at his favorite brood mare. The sides of the metal cot pressed into John's arms. Yet the bedding was so relaxing, he could doze if the other two would stop waving like grass in the wind.

Bold Hunter shook his dark head. "Bold Hunter thought White Feather strong in love, strong in war, strong in all things."

John fought to say awake.

"Better this way. It's a painful job." The doctor's voice came from a great distance. John winced and tried not to pull away as the doctor lanced his hand, forcing out pus. Doc began stitching the raw flesh of John's palm together. Burning pain followed each poke of the needle.

Through slitted eyes, John saw Bold Hunter's face take on a greenish tinge.

The Doc stopped mid-stitch. "Better look the other way, son."

Bold Hunter grunted.

"Get that blanket off that other cot and cover Ross."

An agonizing pain pierced the base of John's thumb, then the doctor slipped John's hand to soak in something cool and wet. The liquid stung like a thousand black ants. But he found comfort from the warm blanket lowered over his tired body as he watched Doc lift another bottle from the crate.

All cheerful bedside manner, the doctor slipped to his knees beside the cot and raised a tablespoon to John's mouth. "Open up." He poured the medicine into John's mouth.

John swallowed, and then choked as liquid burned his throat. "My hand hurts like blazes!" He struggled up and jerked his hand out of the pan.

The doctor shoved him back and forced his hand into the solution. "Lie still and take it easy. Surgery's all over but the soaking. Your hand will torture you for a week or so and then be good as new. Another day left untreated and you would have awakened with gangrene. I did a beautiful job, though I say so myself."

John lay back and rested his head on the pillow. His stomach gurgled.

"We'll have grub for you boys in a few shakes. Hope you don't mind army rations."

"Sounds good to me." John shifted into a more comfortable position on the narrow cot. "I could eat a dog about now."

"I assumed all Indians ate dogs."

He should offer a retort. Too tired to think, sleep took over.

John woke to someone shaking his shoulder.

"Here's your food." The aide handed him a plate.

John pushed himself up on an elbow and eyed the rations. Hunger jolted him wide awake. The scent of bacon and fresh coffee had him digging into the warm beans and cornbread. He saved the apple for dessert.

The sound of eating filled the hospital tent. John ate until the last crumb disappeared and could have eaten more.

He reached for a third cup of coffee. When he finished, he leaned back on the cot.

The doctor raised his brows. "I see your hand didn't slow your eating any. You two boys stow away a mighty amount of food." The doctor gathered the tin plates and set them outside the tent for his aide to wash. "Ross, you put more away with your left hand than most men do with both hands." He slouched in his chair, filled a pipe, lit a match, and puffed the pipe into life.

The scent of sweet tobacco wafted through the tent. "Bold Hunter, you can leave anytime. But I'm detaining you a while, Ross. I want to keep tabs on you until that blood poisoning's gone. Also, you need medication to cure your cough. We'll be hitting the trail tomorrow, so you'll ride in the medical wagon with me."

John rubbed his eyes. Unable to stifle a yawn, he turned to Bold Hunter. "Tell Mother I'm fine."

Bold Hunter nodded.

"And would you bring Jeremy's Bible? I left it folded in my blanket under the wagon."

"Glad to bring God's Writing to brother." The words must have loosened Bold Hunter's silent tongue because he started telling the doctor how John saved his life. Without embarrassment, Bold Hunter related how because of the way John lived, he accepted the white man's God as his God. While Bold Hunter talked, John propped his head on his good hand and fought to keep his eyes open.

The doctor's twinkling gray eyes grew serious, his attention on the dark, young Indian. His pipe died. Periodically he nodded, encouraging Bold Hunter to continue. "So, you end up here. I'd say you fellows are lucky to be alive."

"Not lucky. God protect."

The doctor unfolded from his camp chair, walked to the tent flap, and gazed over his shoulder at Bold Hunter. "Okay, young man, time to return to your wagon. Report to Captain Peterson tomorrow. You're fit for duty."

Dark had fallen when Bold Hunter left the tent. Two guards tramped after him, and the other two remained outside—one on each side of the hospital tent flap.

Doc lit a kerosene lamp and moved to where John sprawled on the cot. "Remove your shirt, Ross, I need to examine you."

Though John's eyes felt as if they'd been hollowed out with sandpaper, his vision bleary, he sat up, and tugged his shirt over his head.

"By the way, my name's Smith."

John nodded.

Doc Smith ran his hands over the scars on John's back. "Must have been some herbal healing here. I've examined other Indians who had been whipped, and your scars look rather good." He took his time examining John. "I've got medication that'll help the dysentery. Better take a dose now. You should have told me about that problem before we ate. You've got congestion in your lungs. Don't think it's gone into consumption though. You'll have to take it easy until I can get you back on your feet."

John gagged down a half glass of foul-tasting medicine.

"How did you lose so much weight when your friend's in such good shape?"

John shrugged. Research or no research, this man didn't need to know he shared his portion of food with the hungry children.

"Strange Bold Hunter didn't get dysentery. That would account for some of his normal weight. Was he overweight when we captured him?"

"He's lost some weight." John yawned. "I think he was accustomed to a stoic life. He ate and slept outdoors a good bit anyway."

"How about you? What kind of life did you have?"

John shifted his position on the cot. "Much like yours, I presume."

Doc raised his brows, then soaked John's hand in the solution again. John was close to sleep before Doc removed his hand from the chemicals and bandaged it. His thoughts drifted.

Hope saw his arrest. She must have a bad opinion of him again.

How could he change his impact on her? Why did he want ...?

CHAPTER 25

John opened his eyes to bright sunlight. Blast, he'd slept late. The doctor and his aides must have worked on tiptoes as they emptied the tent and loaded the medical wagon.

Doc chuckled and handed John a plate of biscuits and gravy. "After you eat, we'll soak your hand. So, you need to hurry." He set the solution beside the cot next to John.

As he soaked his injured hand, John gulped the delicious breakfast with his good hand.

Bold Hunter strode into the tent. "Here Bible." He laid the Bible on the cot beside John's empty plate.

"Much obliged." John lifted his hand from the soaking bowl and dried it. "How's Mother?"

"Not good."

John winced and rose from the cot.

Bold Hunter tapped his hand on John's arm. "Rachael take care Mrs. Ross." He grinned and chuckled. "Rachael happy Bold Hunter Christian."

The heavy breakfast he'd eaten rumbled in John's stomach. No doubt Rachael was delighted. But how delighted? He had to find out.

"Bold Hunter go. Learn to obey soldiers." He winked a dark shining eye.

"Yeah. Let me know how that goes."

Bold Hunter grinned again, nodded, and then ducked through the tent opening.

"Who's driving our wagon?" John called to Bold Hunter's retreating back.

"Fire-hair soldier drive until Bold Hunter finish punishment. Him keep soldiers from Rachael. Bold Hunter trust."

John pulled in a deep breath, and ten years slid off his weighted shoulder. Though Jeremy was angry, he remained a loyal friend.

Doc entered the tent and nodded toward Bold Hunter's disappearing back. "I see your friend is about to learn army discipline."

"So General Scott ruled." John stripped his cot. "Sir, do you have more medicine for a bad cough?"

"Yours?" the doctor bent to fiddle with the lock on the remaining trunk not yet packed into the wagon.

"No, sir. My mother's."

"Depends. Does she have a fever?"

"Yes, she's flushed. And she doesn't have much appetite."

"How long has she been this way?"

"Four days."

"I'll see what I can do."

"She's in the last wagon. I'm worried about her."

Doc Smith narrowed his eyes. "Is this a trick so you can escape?" The aide entered and carried John's cot outside.

"No, sir, on my word of honor. There's no deception."

Doc's warm gray eyes searched John's face, then he clapped him on the shoulder. "I'll take a chance you're telling the truth. Let's bandage your hand first, then we're on our way. My aide will take care of driving the wagon."

They ducked out the front flap just before the aide pulled the last tent pegs. Doc Smith carried his black medical bag, and the two guards posted outside the flattened tent followed them.

As he and Doc strode toward the rear, the wagon train moved west, coiling up the trail like a long, noisy, serpent. Wagon after wagon lumbered across the valley floor. Dust rose. Voices called out. Wagons creaked, and the odor of ashes, cooked food, and coffee from dead campfires, mingled with the odor of manure.

As John and Doc passed one wagon, a small Indian girl poked her head out the open end and vomited. Doc Smith removed a pad of paper from his medical bag and jotted a note. "I need to remember which wagon."

John nodded.

A nearby militia man hoisted his rucksack to his shoulders. "Them young'uns sure like to puke. They do that all day long."

John's old anger blazed. "Dolt! You drag these children away from their homes and don't give them enough to eat! If they're sick and hungry, it's your fault!"

The militiaman took a quick step back.

"Call Doc Smith when you see the people are ill." John so wanted to use his good left hand to smack the man. Instead, he bent to the child. "This nice doctor will come see you soon and make you feel better."

The soldier cocked a thumb at John. "Hey, Doc, who's he?"

Doc Smith spoke loud enough for the surrounding soldiers to hear. "Chief's nephew. Better do as he says, or you'll end up on the carpet."

John joined Doc, and they continued walking toward the tail end of the slow-moving wagons. He took a deep breath. "Were you ridiculing me, sir?"

"On the contrary. These soldiers know the Cherokee still obey Chief Ross. Though he's not on this wagon train, doesn't hurt to spread your name around, son."

John frowned. "Hmm. Maybe that's why we didn't receive much punishment."

"You're wrong there. General Scott is a just man. He wouldn't care if you were his own nephew. In fact, if you had been, he would have decreed a stiffer sentence. Don't think you got off light. Army discipline is rough on men who have difficulty obeying orders. If you disobey, Captain Peterson has free rein to do anything he wants with you. You'd better decide right now to do everything he says. Doesn't matter how silly the order, never talk back. Just respond with 'Yes, sir. Right away, sir.'" Doc halted mid-step. "I notice you aren't afraid to speak your mind. Better learn to keep your opinions to yourself around Peterson."

John shrugged.

Doc frowned. "With certain people, you must recognize when to speak and when to keep quiet."

"Sounds ominous." As they approached the last wagon, John took the lead. "Wish my discipline were under anyone else. Peterson's sure to be nursing a grudge."

"He'll work your tail off. I've decided not to release you from the hospital until your congestion's gone and your hand's well. You can't do much in your current condition until your hand heals."

"I'm grateful to you, sir. I've worried I might have to report now. I still have intense pain in my palm."

John spotted Jeremy's red head where he perched atop the driver's seat, driving the Ross wagon. "There it is. That last wagon. The young lady sitting beside the soldier is Rachael Whiteswan."

Doc smiled. "Well, son, you're traveling in pretty company. Is she your girl or your friend's?"

"That's what I'd like to know."

"Ah. So." Doc Smith winked.

Jeremy stopped the wagon. "Ho, John." He didn't smile.

"You behaving yourself?" John joked.

"More than you."

John helped Doc climb through the rear opening, then caught up to stride beside the driver's seat. Jeremy slapped the reins, his back rigid and his gaze straight ahead. "Get up. Get up, there."

Rachael beamed down, her smile warm and welcoming. "You've not broken the chain."

"Chain?"

"First Pastor introduced you to Christ, then you invited Bold Hunter. And now is his turn to forge a golden link of love."

"That's a nice way of expressing what happened." John grinned up at Jeremy. "Hold up a minute, Yank. I need to talk to you."

"I'll drive while you and Jeremy talk." Rachael reached over and took the reins from Jeremy's freckled hands.

"Thanks, Rachael." John sent her a look he hoped conveyed more than thanks. Her rosy lips smiled. Jeremy jumped down to walk, but his unfriendly face revealed cold, controlled anger.

A sigh worked up from deep inside John's chest. He sure made a mess of relationships. "Give me a chance to explain." If he had to plead, he'd plead. "I couldn't tell you I planned to go hunting. You'd have stopped me, or you would have had to report me. Believe me, I wanted to let you know. You're the best friend I have. Please don't be angry."

Jeremy's rigid jaw lost some of its tightness.

"I had to hunt meat for these children. I knew you'd stop me because it was your duty." John raked a hand though his hair. "Our expedition must have been God's will, since Bold Hunter became a Christian."

Jeremy's jaw relaxed, but his mouth still looked tight. "Yep. Bold Hunter told Rachael and me the whole story. Apology accepted. But I won't trust you out of my sight." Jeremy's shoulders rose and fell, then ended in a slump. "When you disappeared, my CO accused me of helping you escape. General Scott held me at headquarters all day for interrogation. Only by the grace of God did Scott allow me to drive this wagon while you and Bold Hunter serve your sentences." He scowled. "Those two Georgia legionaries who jumped me volunteered to captain the wagon."

John clasped Jeremy's shoulders in a walking hug. "Thanks, friend. I'm sorry you had to go through so much. I'll make it up to you." He glanced back at the swaying canvas canopy. "Did our family get the meat and pelts?"

"Yeah. General Scott made sure we did."

They fell silent for a few seconds, then John grinned with his idea. "So ... are you certain you don't want to change your name to Jonathan?"

Jeremy kicked a foot at him, missing purposefully. "Ho, you're gonna want to change your name to Samson before you're done. How'd you draw Peterson as your discipline?"

"Pure good fortune. Did you mention his name to General Scott?"

"Why would I? Did you know Peterson's a friend of Hope's?"

"So I discovered." John kicked a rut in the road. "When he was late meeting your sister in Rattlesnake Springs, I sent the captain on his way like a bad little boy. He didn't relish the embarrassment."

Jeremy's brows rose almost to his fiery hairline. "Was that the time Hope stormed into camp demanding Peterson take her to her wagon?"

John cleared his throat. "I offended your sister totally without intention."

Jeremy threw back his head and laughed.

"Nothing funny about what happened."

"I think so. You're like every other soldier in the company. You're sweet on my sister. Isn't Rachael enough for you?"

"Your sting's worse than a nettle!" Blast how this situation got under his skin.

"Ha! If Peterson knows you're interested in Hope, he'll ride you hard. I wouldn't want to be in your shoes. He plans to marry her. She keeps him dangling."

"Is she in love with him?"

"I doubt it. She's not found a man yet with love enough to hold her." Jeremy stopped John and let the wagon roll past. "Take my advice. Keep away from Hope. She'll break your heart!"

"Easy to stay out of her way. She has an exceedingly low opinion of me." John started walking. "What discipline do you think Peterson's devising?"

Jeremy quirked his lips. "Bold Hunter's grooming horses, shining artillery, drilling, and filling Peterson's coffee cup. Nothing too bad. Same things we do every day, except for the close-order drilling. We got plenty of that during garrison duty."

"Rachael ... help," a small voice called from inside the Conestoga.

"Coming." Her pretty face turned toward Jeremy. "Someone inside needs me."

"Right." Jeremy swung up into the wagon, took the reins from Rachael, and slapped the leather against the wide oxen backs. He grinned down at John. "Peterson'll probably concoct something worse for you. Want me to ask him not to kill you?"

John shook his head. "Best you don't get involved. He might turn out to be your brother-in-law."

Doc Smith appeared at the front wagon flap. "I'm done here. Let's go, Ross."

Jeremy called, "Whoa, oxen. Whoa there."

Doc climbed over the front seat, jumped to the ground, and fell into step beside John. John waved his unbandaged hand. "Thanks for everything, Yank. Take care of Mother and Rachael for me."

"Will do. Read the Bible I lent you all you can. When Peterson has your hide, you won't get much free time."

Matching steps with Doc, John strode toward the middle of the train and the hospital wagon. "How is my mother, sir?"

"I left medicine for two of the children." Doc's voice sounded solemn.

"But what about Mother?"

"Son, there's nothing I can do for her." He put a heavy hand on John's shoulder. "She's dying."

John stopped as if struck by a fatal arrow. Like dark shadows that flamed into crimson capitals, the words vaulted into his consciousness. *She's dying.* The burning words shot spears into his soul. "I have to go back to stay with her, sir."

"I'd like to let you, but I've been ordered not to release you to Private Worchester's custody. I'll arrange for another guard."

"Those two soldiers following us have guarded me since we left the hospital wagon. Can't you release me to them?"

"Right. I'll send your medicine. Soak your hand at least six times a day. Report to me—uh ... when it's over." Doc put both hands on John's shoulders. "I'm sorry."

The two guards on his heels, John ran back to Mother's wagon. Before he reached it, he dropped to his knees onto the side of the trail and lowered his head. How could he face her? What could he say? *Lord, please help me.*

One guard poked a gentle knee in John's side. "Best get on with it."

When John slipped into the wagon to sit beside her, his mother's face pinked with pleasure. He took her in his arms, trying to shield her from the bumps as the wagon lurched on the rutty road. He stroked her hair, and she rested her head against his chest, breathing a sigh of deep contentment.

"Rachael told me everything that happened." Her breath came in wheezing pants, her voice so low he had to strain to hear. "I couldn't be prouder."

He whispered in her ear, "I love you. No man could ask for a better mother."

"I'm glad you know, dear. I'm ready to go. I only regret leaving you."

John's throat closed, and hot tears pricked his eyelids.

"My departing will be harder for you than for me." Her words barely above a whisper.

The children sat unmoving and silent, staring at her with large, tragic eyes, their bodies swaying with the wagon's motion. He wanted to be strong for her, but the tears came. He scrunched his eyes, then wiped them with his knuckles. He pitied the children, how they lost their innocence too early and recognized the face of death. Inside the stockade they had seen the mask on their own mothers' faces. Most had red eyes from weeping.

With maturity a child should not have, they looked away, allowing him this last time with his mother. Her dying repeated the agonizing loss they suffered when their mothers died. Tears washed streaks down their dirty faces.

"Carry on the generations of Ross and bring honor to your name, my son," his mother panted. "Promise me to serve God all your life."

"As long as the mountains last, as long as the sun shines, as long as the rivers flow, I promise." John spoke the sacred Cherokee pledge for the first time in his life. While his heart tore into fragments, he held her light form in his arms.

She reached up to wipe the tears from his cheeks. "Don't become bitter, dear. I've lived a good life. I have a wonderful son. You didn't go to Princeton, but you've graduated with honors from the college of life. I'm happy."

How could he not feel bitter? "I'll do my best."

She was quiet.

For hours, he held her, listening to the rise and fall of her breath, stroking her hair, whispering to her from time to time. The sun cast feeble rays in the west, failing in its attempt to overcome gray clouds before his mother spoke again, her voice soft as a breath, "Look, John, how bright it is. The light dazzles!"

John saw no bright light, only his mother's thin face. The years fell away, making her appear as eager as a young girl on her wedding day.

"Oh, my beautiful Savior, I'm coming." Her voice sounded strangely far away, soft, clear, and musical, a bell tolling across the abyss between life and death.

Then she was gone.

John clutched her, desperately wanting her back. Her peaceful form lay against his empty, pounding heart. A closed door in his mind broke open, revealing his father's face, frozen into an expression of perpetual surprise. How unexpected his death. As far as John knew, Father had never received the savior. His death had been too swift.

Two or three children sobbed. He should do something for them. Instead, he stared into the gathering darkness until the wagon lurched to a standstill and the children crept over him and shimmied out.

John kissed his mother's cool forehead and gently laid her motionless form against the half-empty bag of hominy. Anger flashed through him. His mother dying in a Conestoga wagon. What a death for a McCormac!

His muscles stiff, he stumbled out of the wagon. A few feet away, a campfire sputtered to life, bringing light to the circle of children's faces gathered around the warmth. Bold Hunter returned for the night, carrying a bag of food for the children who clustered to him and scrambled into his lap. Rachel took the food and turned to prepare the evening meal.

John's anger faded. Mother's life hadn't ended. She had gone through the door of death to a new beginning ... a new adventure ... a new life. She'd looked so happy he could not wish her back to face the cold, the hunger, the unknown dangers of the land that lay ahead. But the agony of losing her ripped his heart.

And Father—

He shoved his haunted thoughts about his father back into the locked trunk behind the closed door inside his mind. He stooped to retrieve his blanket from beneath the wagon bed, then climbed back into the wagon. With gentle hands, he wrapped his blanket around Mother's slight body, maneuvered her through the open rear flap of the wagon, and carried her toward the woods. Jeremy and his two guards followed, each carrying a shovel. Rachel hurried to find Pastor. Bold Hunter stayed with the children.

In the gloomy dusk, John pushed his reluctant feet to the base of an ancient oak, deep in the forest beside a bubbling stream. He laid Mother's body between the root mounds of the big tree, grabbed a shovel, and tried to dig. But the ground was hard and his right hand useless.

Jeremy took the shovel, and his two guards used theirs. As the moon rose, casting dark shadows on the ground, the clink of shovels digging into the earth grated John's nerves. In the uncertain light, ivy hanging from the trees turned into ghostly fingers.

Had Father found the way of life? If so, he'd never mentioned the experience. John tried to shrug away his doubt. At least Mother and Pris were united.

The funeral sounds of the spade digging into the earth continued for what seemed eons. Finally, the guards jumped up from the grave and stood beside John. Jeremy handed his shovel to the nearest guard. Standing knee-deep in the shallow grave, he raised his arms to receive John's mother. Numb, disconnected feelings wound around John's heart. As if he walked through water, he lifted his mother for the last time, laid his cheek against the top of her blonde hair, stepped into the shallow grave, and laid her on the ground. He folded the blue shawl and spread the wool over her face. Moving like a much older man, he climbed out of the grave.

The first clods of dirt struck her. He groaned, turned aside, and tears coursed down his cheeks. Softly, her lovely alto voice hushed in reverence, Rachael sang a hymn. Her voice rose and fell, but John couldn't grasp the meaning. He saw only the beauty that had been his mother crushed beneath layers of dirt.

Pastor prayed, his face sagging with lines and furrows.

John groaned. How did a person without Christ face death?

Long after he reported to Doc Smith, the grating sound of the shovel echoed in John's ears.

Another precious grave marked the Trail of Tears.

CHAPTER 26

John couldn't shake off his deep sadness. Day after day dragged by with no relief as he stumbled through the motions of life but found no meaning.

Doc Smith did his best to help. But John seemed unable to respond. They broke camp each day and struck camp each night. He ate because the doctor urged him. Then he hauled one foot in front of the other, following Doc Smith on his rounds.

Near the end of the week, he and Doc sat warming themselves at the campfire, their backs toward the night's inky blackness. The two guards flanked them.

"John, where's the Bible you borrowed from the soldier with the hair red as a rusted gun barrel? I haven't seen you reading from it." Firelight flickered across Doc's face, pinpointing its angular planes.

"In the tent somewhere." John stared into the fire.

"Thought you planned to read the book often."

"Haven't felt like it." John sat with his head hunched and his elbows resting on his knees while the fire sparked and crackled in the frosty air.

Doc left the fire and rummaged in the medical tent. In a few minutes he returned with the Bible and a lighted lantern. Opening the Book, he leafed through the pages. "I don't know what to do with this book now that it's in my hands." Doc read aloud a passage here and there. "The words sound strange. The people mentioned belong to a different time and culture." He tapped the page with a clean nail. "I always thought the Bible wasn't meaningful in this modern day. It's a relic, old-fashioned, outmoded. Why do people bother to read it? One more passage, and I'll put the thing back in the tent." Doc cleared his throat. "This is from the last book in the Bible, the Revelation, in Chapter 21 verses 4-7."

As he read, his pleasing tenor voice rose and fell in meaningful waves.

"In the Book of Revelation we read: 'And God shall wipe away all tears from their eyes; and there shall be no more death, neither sorrow, nor crying, neither shall there be any more pain: for the former things are passed away. And He that sat upon the throne said, Behold, I make all things new ... I will give unto him that is athirst of the fountain of the water of life freely. He that overcometh shall inherit all things; and I will be his God, and he shall be my son.'"

John didn't change his posture. He didn't stir. He didn't speak. But his attitude shifted drastically. The door he'd closed in his mind against God flew open. The gentle, loving Holy Spirit began his work, filling the void in John's life with the love of God.

John bounded to his feet. "Thanks Doc. I've been a fool not to read the Bible when I need it most." Doc handed John the Bible, and they both ducked inside the tent and dropped onto their cots. That night John slept on the narrow cot without tossing and moaning.

The next day as the wagon train passed through Murfreesboro, Tennessee, Doc glanced at John. "The change in you is so remarkable, you rouse my curiosity." Doc Smith cupped his hand around the handle of his medical bag. "Time to start our wagon rounds, but you might be interested to know I've decided to research the effect of the Bible on melancholy."

"Good idea." He'd love to see Doc turn his life over to the Lord, and reading the Bible would show him the way.

That day, John's appetite improved, and Doc Smith didn't miss the opportunity to chide. "You're eating me out of lock, stock, and barrel. I'll have to requisition more food from the supply officer." Doc clicked his heels together, doing the crazy hop he performed whenever he was particularly pleased.

Time continued to pass, and John's spirits continued to rise. Most days, when not helping Doc, John settled in the medical wagon's rear, his long legs spread over boxes and barrels, reading Jeremy's Bible. No easy trick with all the bouncing.

One rare afternoon when Doc Smith was free from medical duties, he climbed into the wagon and made himself comfortable next to John. "You play chess?"

"Yes, sir, but I haven't played for a long time. I'm pretty rusty." John closed his Bible and leaned forward to watch Doc Smith open a trunk, remove a chess board, and set up the pieces.

Time sped inside the rattling wagon. "Checkmate!" John punched his fist into the air.

"I quit, boy! That's the third game you've won. I've had enough. I'll play you sometime when you're not so rusty."

When the oxen slowed, John stretched out his long frame, crawled to the front, and lifted the flap. "What now?" The day was cold, with overcast skies and low hanging gray clouds. He caught sight of Captain Peterson striding toward them, tall and dashing with his cocked hat and ankle-length blue surtout.

Peterson motioned the medical wagon to the side of the road.

Doc climbed out beside the driver and settled on the wooden bench. "What can I do for you, Captain?"

"Came to check on your patient, Doctor Smith." Peterson's bass voice sounded businesslike. "Will he be fit for duty tomorrow morning?"

"Want to take a look?" Doc waved a hand toward the wagon's interior.

"I do." Peterson hooked his thumbs in his pistol belt and frowned. "Get him out here. Make it snappy." He used two fingers to brush his long, black, side-whiskers.

John and Doc climbed from the wagon. John held out his right arm, and Doc unwrapped John's injured hand. "Needs another week, I'm afraid."

Peterson stepped closer, grabbed John's hand, and stuck his nose close as if his staring at the wound would speed the healing. "You're the doctor. I'll take charge of the prisoner five days from today. His hand didn't keep him from escaping the wagon train. He's got duty to attend. Only your say-so keeps him from the discipline." He spoke in a flat, expressionless voice. "This man's a piece of unfinished business." He pivoted. His tall, polished boots clomped no-nonsense as he walked briskly toward his waiting squad.

Doc rebandaged John's palm, winding the white cloth up to his elbow. "That's one disappointed man, son. Appears he's looking forward to getting his hands on you. How did you put a burr under his saddle?"

John leaned against the side of the wagon and cocked a brow. "I was indiscreet. I made a fool of him in front of a certain young lady."

"Girls fancy you, do they? Thought they might. Tall, handsome lad like you." Doc chuckled.

"Some girls."

Doc smiled. "Ah, young love. Reminds me of my own romantic past."

John worked up a smile and climbed back into the wagon. Staying with the doc another five days was a gift.

He needed the kindly companionship and adequate food and rest.

As Doc's aide merged the medical vehicle back into the train, John settled behind the chess board, its pieces leaded on the bottom. But he missed Jeremy ... hadn't seen his friend since Mother died. But Jeremy still drove the Ross wagon during the day and stood guard duty in the evening. Had to be hard doing double-duty, but his friend would never complain. Jeremy had one final day to drive before Bold Hunter completed his punishment and returned to the orphan wagon.

Long before time to camp, the wagon slowed again.

Had Peterson decided to show up early? John stuck his head out the front flap. A small boy of about seven, dressed in broadcloth, stood in front of them frantically waving them to stop. The aide called, "Whoa, whoa there." The plodding oxen stopped, lowered their heads, and lipped the sides of the road for grass.

The boy's clothes looked well worn, his stock torn, and his shoes full of holes. Wind blew his chestnut hair back from his shoulders. "Doctor, my mother is having a baby! Please come and help her." The boy shivered. His pale face appeared pinched and moisture dribbled from his small nose.

"Come along, John, fetch my bag."

The boy led them to his mother's wagon that had stopped at the side of the moving train. As Doc climbed in, John handed up the bag. "What can I do?"

Doc opened the flap, smiled broadly, and hoisted a small girl down. "Here, John, watch her until I'm finished."

She looked about three years old. Frightened hazel eyes stared at John. Chestnut hair hung in ringlets circling her small face. The fine blue muslin dress gave her no protection from the cold. "Are you the doctor? My mommy hurts." Her high-pitched voice formed the words surprisingly well.

"No, little one. I'm here to help Doc. He's inside with your mother. What's your name?" John opened his warm shirt, tugged her against his chest, and buttoned the shirt around her.

As she snuggled against him, her heart slowed its rapid beat. "My name's Beth. I like you."

John cuddled the fragile child and told her funny stories until her sad, wistful face crinkled and she giggled. How little it took to make her smile. His heart ached. Had Pris lived, she might have grown into a toddler like this.

The boy joined them, manfully trying to hide his shivers. "I want to laugh too." They sat in the protection of a large boulder, both children snug on John's lap, his shirt buttoned to warm them. An occasional moan sounded from inside the wagon. The children, warm and comfortable, soon slept. Time passed and John's muscles stiffened, but he wouldn't disturb the children.

What seemed like hours later, Doc called. The boy woke, silent and watchful, and John handed the sleeping Beth through the flap to Doc.

"Come in and meet the mother and her new son." Doc held out both arms for the girl, smiling when she snuggled to his chest. "Bringing a life into the world is the most rewarding aspect of this profession."

John handed the lad up to Doc, buttoned his shirt, and climbed over the tailgate. A young woman, covered with an army blanket, lay on the wagon floor. Her chestnut hair straggled in damp waves around the pale oval of her face. Smudges underlined tired hazel eyes, and tears clung to long, dark lashes. Not being a member of the family, John felt as if he were an intruder.

"I've never seen such a tiny baby. He's pretty." John touched the fuzzy, dark hair. In the last few months, he'd been around plenty of deaths. Welcoming a new life felt special. He'd forgotten how to experience joy and felt almost light-headed to witness the promise of a brighter future. Pricks of sensation seeped back into his numbed legs. Using a cup of precious water from the keg, he helped Doc clean the floorboards.

In a hoarse whisper, the mother said, "His name is Bryce, after his father. I wish your daddy could see you, Bryce."

"Mr. Hancock was in Nashville on business when soldiers took his family to the stockade." Doc Smith snapped his black bag closed. "Mrs. Hancock hasn't seen her husband since."

"Bryce didn't even know we were going to have another baby. I planned to tell him when he returned." Mrs. Hancock laid her head back against a cushion of flour sacks.

John leaned toward the young woman. "Who will take care of you and the children?"

"Send Teddy for my cousin Martha. He knows which wagon her husband drives. Martha lost her three children in the smallpox epidemic." Anxiety etched lines in her delicate face. "She'll help."

In the five days that followed, while his hand healed, John learned medicine as he assisted Doc. Despite their best efforts, an average of four to five people died each day. The sight of a wagon pulled to the side of the dirt road took on tragic meaning as more and more families stopped to bury their dead. The Cherokee began calling the westward journey The Trail Where They Cried.

Doc Smith's angular face grew more creases and furrows after each death.

On the morning of his last day with Doc, John thrust his legs over the side of the cot, hustled into his brogans, and stuck his head out the tent flap. A pale November sun filtered through an oak's leafless limbs and a cold wind blew from the west. The Cherokees called the west wind black, the wind of death. He sure would miss this wagon. He'd miss Doc. And the food. And the medical work.

"John, I need your help. Fetch a shovel. I'll dig." Doc made a hurry motion. Together they trudged to bury gentle Mrs. Hancock and Bryce, the five-day-old infant. Doc shook his head. "Pneumonia closed both their lungs."

What happened to the promise of life? Would anyone survive this journey to the new territory? John laid the mother's slender body in the open grave, stroked the baby's fuzzy head, then placed the child against his mother's breast. The small boy stood against the wind, his arm circled around his young sister. Sobs racked the children as another grave marked the Trail of Tears.

John hoisted Teddy on his shoulders and carried Beth in his arms to their cousin's wagon. Both children were silent. If they survived, they would shudder when they remembered the lonely grave by the roadside.

The remainder of the day, when he was free from medical duties, John searched the Bible. From an anguished heart, he prayed, "I can't understand all this suffering and death, Lord. I only know you are perfect love. You love my people more than I. Since you allow this tragedy, I can only trust you. Your ways are higher than my ways. Your thoughts higher than mine. Please help me tomorrow when I face Peterson."

CHAPTER 27

John pulled in a deep breath. Though the autumn sun topped the tall pines and sparkled the morning dew, turning the wagon camp into a mystical scene, his nightmare with Peterson would begin today. Even with the ordeal looming, the heavy scent of pine needles invigorated him. Thanks to Doc, he felt better physically than he had since becoming a prisoner.

He leaned against Doc's wagon savoring the morning coolness and sipping what was sure to be his last cup of hot coffee for two long weeks. Catching sight of Peterson, John set his empty cup on the wagon ledge. "Here comes the Falcon."

Captain Peterson, the bright yellow plume on his shako waving briskly in the air, stalked toward John. Peterson did resemble a falcon—slender, tense with suppressed ambition, his dark, piercing eyes dominated a face kept from being handsome by his hawk-like nose set above thin lips.

John lowered his voice an octave. "Looking for me?"

The captain jumped like a nervous rabbit. Peterson couldn't see him where he stood in the shadow cast by the wagon. And judging from the captain's startle, John's deep drawl caught the officer by surprise.

"Where's Doctor Smith?" Peterson's voice sounded harsh. "You're to be released to my custody this morning.

I haven't time to wait." He slapped his riding crop into his gloved hand.

"Doc's out on a call. He released me last night before he left. He figured he might be gone all night. He—"

"Released you last night!" His voice sharp and annoyed, Peterson scowled. "Leaving you unguarded? Of all the stupid, incompetent, presumptuous fools! This will appear on Smith's service record!" He tapped the riding crop against his leg. "Are you fit for duty?"

"My hand's pretty well healed, if that's what you're asking," John drawled. "And my two guards are in the mess tent eating breakfast."

Peterson's face purpled. The veins in his temples and neck stood out as if he were having a seizure. "Worthless guards, I'll have them court-martialed." His frown deepened and his chest rose and fell. "Mister, when you address an officer, your comment shall be 'Yes, sir' unless more is required."

Peterson's black gaze raked John from head to toe. He stood a few minutes as if silently counting to ten, then his voice changed. He spoke as though to a child. "For all practical purposes, you are now a private in the United States Army. I am your commanding officer." The frowning man stretched to his full height but had to tip his head to stare up into John's eyes. "Your job is instant obedience. Any disobedience will be severely punished. Do! You! Understand?"

"Yes, sir."

"Attention!" snapped Captain Peterson.

John stood as straight as he could, hands clenched at his sides. Blasted foolish standing rigidly erect because of this man's command.

Peterson crowded so close, his uniform brushed John's shirt. He circled John. "Get those shoulders back!" He cracked John between the shoulder blades with his crop.

No one seemed to notice them. In the tents nearby, soldiers guarding the wagon train broke camp. Others saddled horses, doused fires, and attended their duties, laughing, talking, and cursing, while John stood in the middle of the organized confusion like a wooden soldier.

"Suck in that gut!" Peterson drove his fist into John's solar plexus.

"Ooof." John doubled over and gasped for air. Next time he'd be ready for that move.

"Keep your chin down. Stand erect. You look like a wilted pansy."

John tightened his stomach muscles and braced his shoulders, the bones almost touching. He jutted his jaw. Well, he'd not expected a buggy ride in the park.

"Keep those heels together and eyes front." Peterson punctuated his words by striking John's calves with his crop.

John gritted his teeth. First easy lesson on becoming a soldier.

"I shall outline your duties once. Any slip up, and you'll stand double duty like any other enlisted man. Report to my tent at 0500 each morning for your day's orders. After serving my breakfast, pack my gear, load my tent, feed and saddle my horse, feed and hitch both teams to the supply wagon, and walk close order drill for a specified time." Peterson whacked the top of John's head with his crop and barreled on.

"During the journey, you work with the teams and wagons as necessary in fording rivers, ascending mountains, and the like. In the meantime, artillery guns must be cleaned and polished, teams hauling guns groomed, water barrels kept full, my white gloves cleaned, and my uniform brushed. My boots and saddle must be oiled and polished nightly."

Heat rose from John's neck up through his ears.

"Report to me on the hour, every hour, regardless of my whereabouts. When the wagons halt, pitch my tent, unpack my gear, and serve my chow. After mess, report to the mess hall for cleanup duty. At 2100 report for final instructions." Peterson tugged a watch from his uniform tunic pocket and tapped the round face. "I do not tolerate tardiness."

John gave a low growl. Did the Falcon think he was a Morgan horse? Peterson was no gentleman taking advantage of his power this way. John grunted. He'd expected bad. But this!

Peterson sauntered to the coffeepot suspended from the ramrod over Doc's campfire and helped himself, then stared morosely into the fire as he sipped his brew. A group of children playing a game darted near. Peterson started so violently he almost spilled the steaming liquid. He took a drink, raised his face to the treetops, and shrugged. Then he fished inside a trouser pocket, pulled out a dainty, silk square, and buried his nose in the embroidered handkerchief.

John stifled a grin. The Falcon's as nervous as a den of cougars. He's caught, dangling on the whim of a woman. John frowned, almost feeling sorry for Peterson. He'd not let that particular woman snare him. He had no desire to end in the same sorry condition as Peterson. A dart of pain stabbed John's heart. Or was he too late? Attraction wasn't a decision to be made, captivation was ...

He shook his head. He didn't need Miss Worchester complicating his life. He required all his energy focused on getting to Indian Territory with his wagonload of orphans and the two lovebirds on the front seat. But Peterson was his present problem. John relaxed his shoulders and took a step to start his tasks.

"Attention! Did I say you could move?" Peterson raised his crop and whacked John's head hard enough to make his brain smart. He didn't need those blows to create a headache. His headache developed the minute Peterson showed up.

Doc's aide cleared the camping area and packed the medical wagon. Still Peterson kept John standing at attention while the medical aide climbed into the medical wagon's driver seat. Peterson pointed his crop like a saber charge. "About face. March!"

John's cramped muscles responded slowly to the message from his brain. With untrained steps, he obeyed. Feeling like Peterson's toy soldier, John marched down the mountain path. At John's heels, Peterson called out orders.

With each step, John's rage built. With each command, Peterson trampled the remnants of John's pride under his polished boots.

John scowled. Jeremy preached God hates pride. Seemed God still had a bunch of arrogance to purge from one John Ross. Knowing this didn't help. Face burning, jaw and mouth set, John approached the captain's bivouac area.

Peterson walked in his shadow.

John grunted. Wouldn't you know, when things couldn't get worse, they did. The Falcon camped directly in front of the Worchester wagon. John's head pounded, and his clenched jaw hurt his teeth.

"Halt!" Peterson boomed with unnecessary loudness.

Keeping his eyes focused ahead, John sensed someone from inside the Worchester wagon scrutinized them. He hated this standing weak and powerless in front of Hope. Sweat ran between his braced shoulder blades. Peterson left him standing at attention, like a puppet waiting for his master to pull the strings. For ten minutes Peterson puttered inside his tent.

John's face burned, then chilled, then burned again. Sweat rolled down his temples.

Hope didn't emerge from her wagon.

He refused to care a whit what Miss Worchester thought of him surrendering to these humiliating orders. But his face didn't cool. He was certain his locked knees would give way, and he'd topple on his face.

"Fall out!" Peterson cropped him across both shoulders.

Guessing the words meant he was free to work, John rushed inside the officer's tent. Much larger than the pup tents used by the regular soldiers, the canvas rectangle held a single cot, a table supporting a whale-oil lamp, and a camp chair. A wash pitcher and bowl filled with dirty water stood on a large chest. Peterson's toilet accessories, along with a straight razor, brush, and strap, were strewn on a sturdy table.

John glimpsed his red, sweating face in a small mirror attached to the tent pole. Moving fast, he packed Peterson's personal items inside his travel chest, stripped the cot, and ran to the supply wagon parked near the rear of the tent, clearly marked with the U.S. Army insignia. The wagon ahead and Worchester's looked packed and ready to roll.

John moved so fast he knocked over a stool. Peterson deliberately kept him standing at attention so he couldn't possibly pack the captain's wagon in time. John sped back inside, folded the cot and the chair, shoved them under one arm and the chest under the other, then dumped all three into the wagon on top of already loaded barrels, boxes, crates, pup tents, and various other provisions. He rushed back and jerked out the tent pegs.

The bugle blared for the train to roll.

Working at top speed, he hitched the two teams of oxen, not stopping to feed them. Despite the chill air, sweat rolled down his back. The driver stood by wearing a hangdog expression and didn't offer to help. He obviously followed his Captain's orders.

The wagon train surged forward, a gap widening between the Conestoga in front and where Peterson's wagon should merge in. Behind Peterson's wagon, a soldier John didn't recognize waited in the driver's seat of the Worchester wagon. John bundled the tent and pegs still lying on the ground and threw them into the wagon. "Ready." Only minutes late, the soldier driving Peterson's Conestoga urged his oxen into the moving line.

John shivered, his sweat chilled by the rising wind. He glanced at a lone horse tethered under the willow. Had to be Peterson's. Where was the saddle? Oh no. He raced after the supply wagon and jumped aboard. Looking around in the dim light at the piles of goods, he spotted an English saddle half buried under pup tents. He dug it out and whistled. "Captain must be a man of means to own a saddle like this." John heaved the saddle over his shoulder, grabbed the bridle and blanket, and leaped from the moving wagon.

Not sure whether he miscalculated, or the saddle threw him off balance, he fell, sprawling on the road, the saddle on his back, directly under the nose of the left front ox pulling the Worchester wagon. The placid, brown ox's eyes looked him in the face, and he stopped plodding.

John glanced up from his ridiculous position.

Hope peeked out the front flap of the Worchester wagon, waved, and laughed.

Scrambling off the road on all fours, the ludicrousness of how he must appear hit John. He let his laughter float on the breeze. "I look like a saddled jackass," he called up to her.

"Ross!" Like a knife cutting cornbread, Peterson's sharp voice pierced the air. "You won't be laughing this afternoon when you do two extra hours of drill for not having my horse ready. Give me fifty!"

John shrugged and raised both hands. "Fifty what?" Did the Falcon want money?

"You address me as sir!"

"Fifty what, sir?"

"Push-ups, stupid. Hit the dirt!" Peterson pointed to a level spot abutting the road.

John dropped in the dust beside the trail. Wagon wheels crunched through ruts as they rolled by knocking dirt clods onto his back and dust into his eyes. His arms trembled when he finally reached fifty. He sprang to his feet, sprinted to Peterson's horse, threw on the blanket, cinched on the saddle, and led the handsome horse to the captain.

Dashing in his immaculate blue uniform, Peterson vaulted into the saddle. He sat easily while the horse pranced and pawed.

John tasted bitterness and felt the ripple of horse muscle beneath his thighs as he thought of his own spirited Jasper. Jeb Taylor better not have mistreated his horse. Not that John would ever see that miserable excuse for a man again.

Peterson rose in the stirrups. "Attention!"

Not again. John snapped into the hated posture.

A company of soldiers assembled by the road and awaited orders from their captain. The men stood at ease while Peterson briefed them. Then ... "Ross. Front and center!"

Now what? John sauntered the few steps to face Peterson, then stopped near the captain's horse and patted his glossy, black neck.

"These men are soldiers, trained, and disciplined in instant obedience. This training is vital. Any hesitation in obeying an order in battle could result in death for the soldier or for the entire company." Peterson turned in his saddle to face his men. "Men, this miserable half-breed Indian has two weeks to become a soldier."

The expected laughter boomed from the ranks. But not as heartily as the expression on Peterson's face demanded. He frowned.

"Kid don't even know how to stand at attention," a surly voice obeyed the implied command.

Peterson gave a tight smile. "Oh, I don't think you give Ross enough credit. Even a 'breed can learn simple maneuvers in two weeks. He might have a little trouble with right face and left face, though. That's a bit more complicated."

"They don't make Indians like they used to," another voice from a man trying to curry favor jeered. "Used to be when they wore a feather in their hairlock, they was someone to be scared of. Nobody in their right mind would be scared of this 'un."

"That feather's not regulation." Peterson pressed his horse against John, leaned down, and stripped the white feather from John's hair.

John set his jaw so hard his teeth ground together.

Peterson snapped the feather between his fingers, tossed the broken symbol to the dirt and walked his horse over the remains. "Cavalry training is tough." Peterson rode back and forth in front of John, urging his horse closer and closer, forcing John to step back. Then, as if the captain suddenly had an idea, he pulled a wad of bills from his uniform pocket. "I think a wager is in order. I'll bet any soldier here Ross doesn't make the grade. My money says he'll break under the stress of a soldier's life. Is there a man here who would like to put money on Ross? Who'll take me up?"

The men shuffled their feet and grinned. No one offered to bet on John.

Despite the crisp air, John's ears burned.

"Ten to one. What? No one willing to take those odds?"

"I'll oblige you and lose some money on the Indian." A young regular gazed at the dirt beneath his feet but dug into his pocket. "Been saving this Gold Eagle. Ten to one's too good to pass up."

John held himself rigid, his jaw muscles working, his face as taut as his back.

Peterson stroked his long mustache and smiled. "Very well. Ten gold pieces to one gold piece." He turned his horse and rode over to another soldier. "James, you hold the bets." He dug some coins from his uniform pocket. "You, Maxwell, because you gain if Ross survives the next two weeks—just so you can't help him—you scout ahead for the wagon train and keep your distance from Ross. If I see you near him, you automatically forfeit."

The private glanced from Peterson to John, frowned, and marched toward the first wagon, muttering curses.

"From now until noon, Ross, you will be drilled in the correct manner of marching and saluting." Peterson seemed to love stroking his long mustache almost as much as he loved humiliating John. Or was stroking a nervous habit? A tell when the officer was unsure of himself?

"From noon until 1400 you will fulfill your two-hour penalty drill. You will carry this rifle." He nodded to a soldier who tossed John an ancient musket, minus the flintlock. "Plus, a sixty-pound pack." He nodded toward a pack lying in the dirt near his horse's hooves.

"I'll bet he won't make it until 1400," a rough voice called from among the assembled soldiers.

"Dismissed." Peterson wheeled his horse smartly and cantered after the wagon train, leaving John standing in the road, swirling dust biting his eyes. The company strode after Peterson, singing one of their marching songs.

John sagged.

One remaining soldier, a gnarled sergeant chewing the dead end of a cigar, swaggered over. He pointed to the pack. "Load up. I'm Milo, your drill instructor. Think of me as the man you'll wish you never met. I'm the man you've gotta please."

John struggled into the straps of the heavy pack. Grasshopper would be a better name for the bowlegged DI. The man's jerky movements got on John's raw nerves. The drill instructor put John through one of the most grueling mornings he'd ever endured. While he learned to march, salute, and handle the musket acceptably, the pack chafed his shoulders raw and the marching rubbed blisters on his feet.

He'd beat that wager. Prove Peterson wrong. Make him lose his bet. But if Peterson's discipline proved more than John could handle, he'd never be able to face Hope.

Yet, if he had a choice, he'd endure whatever Peterson threw at him in exchange for not caring what little Miss Worchester thought. The caring bit into his heart like a plague of locusts in a tobacco crop.

Had to be his cursed pride.

CHAPTER 28

By the time the November sun reached its zenith, John wished he'd never humiliated Peterson. Despite the chill temperature, he was covered with sweat, dirt, and temper.

The drill instructor shared dried venison from his saddlebag. They squatted by the road and washed the tough meat down with tepid water from Grasshopper's canteen. The man moved to a big oak's shade, rested against its bark, and issued more orders.

At the end of two solid hours' drill, John's knees were butter. But he'd kept up appearances, and Grasshopper would never know how close John came to the end of his endurance.

Grasshopper jumped aboard his horse. "You'll have to shanks' mare it to the train. Cain't be more'n two-three miles down the road." He spurred his pony to a canter.

Though running downhill hurt his shins, John jogged beside the pony, the pack banging his raw shoulders. Propelling his exhausted muscles and spitting dust, he reported to Captain Peterson.

Peterson walked his horse beside the supply wagon. The captain's mouth looked grim, but his brown eyes sparkled like tumbled onyx. "You failed to report to me six times today, Ross. That entitles you to six consecutive nights of guard duty—midnight to dawn."

John flinched, then set his mouth, trying to squelch the anger boiling inside his chest. The man was a cad. He could not report every hour as ordered without disobeying other orders.

"Of course, I'll have a soldier guarding you during that time."

Lord, see me through this. John kept his face impassive, his hands relaxed. He'd not give Peterson the satisfaction of seeing his rage. Obviously, the man intended to provoke him to blows, then have him confined to cuffs for the rest of the journey. A sneaky way to rid himself of a rival.

John shook his head. Huh, a rival. As if he'd made any headway with Hope. *God, give me grace.* Nor could he do anything about Bold Hunter and Rachael. Why did he care so much? Losing Mother and Pris and being a prisoner must mess with his emotions. Before the last six months, he'd never cared particularly for any girl. Now he couldn't go three minutes without thinking of Hope or Rachel.

He thought mostly of Hope.

Peterson put John through his paces and whacked him on the head with his crop for every wrong move. A good quarter of an hour later, Peterson's lips drooped at the corners. Had the man expected John to be inept? This duty didn't take brains, just brawn.

"You have until 1600 free time." Peterson's voice edged annoyance.

"Request permission for a swim, sir." John kept his voice neutral. If Peterson knew how much he wanted to swim, he'd never get near the river.

Peterson raised a dark brow. "You want to swim the icy water in November?" He shrugged hard enough to make his epaulets crinkle his uniform. "Granted. Wilcox, get over here and don't let this vermin out of your sight."

John slipped aboard the supply wagon and helped himself to a bar of soap. As he strode away from the wagon train toward the river, a fat private waddled behind.

The forest oozed serenity. John tramped by the swiftly moving stream the train had followed through most of the mountainous trek. His tense, aching body unwound as he strolled along its bank until he found an area dammed by beavers where the water had to be deep. He and the fat guard were far enough from the wagon train so only a murmur of noise disturbed the tranquil wilderness.

Grunting and wallowing, Wilcox settled on the ground and pillowed his head on a small log, his squinty eyes following John's every move. Afternoon sun slanted through the trees and made shadows flit over his face.

John chuckled.

The round-bodied man carried a tiny dog in a pouch slung under his left arm. A rat-like face peeped at John. "This dog is a purebred Chihuahua." Wilcox's high squeaky voice contrasted strangely with his bulky body. He puffed out his chest. "No mixed blood in him."

John ignored the slur. "What's its name?" He unbuttoned his shirt, slipped it off, and hung it over a convenient bush.

"Her name is Duchess. She's from a royal family so we had to name her proper, didn't we, Duchess?" He tickled the dog's chin. "She hails from Mexico. I paid a lot of money for her when I was down there last year. We ain't never separated, is we, Duchess?"

John's shoes and socks went next, then he slipped out of his new trousers and folded them over a low tree limb. Feet bare, he stepped down the rocky bank toward the beckoning river.

"You really goin' to get in that ice water?" Wilcox's soft body quivered, making his uniform crease.

"Instead, should I order Captain Peterson to draw my water, heat it, and bring the buckets to my tent?" John tossed and caught the soap.

"I didn't ask for no lip."

John grinned and plunged into the icy water. His body tingled with the cold. He swam fast with powerful strokes—his fatigue, embarrassment, and anger washed off with the trail dust and dried sweat. He couldn't endure the cold long, so soaped fast, rinsed, waded out, and shook himself like a dog.

While he buttoned his shirt, he gazed at his guard. The stillness, combined with an overabundant snack, must have lulled the paunchy private into a sound slumber. Why had Peterson sent this fat, careless guard? John rubbed the back of his neck. Did Peterson want him to escape? Sounded likely. Probably Peterson wanted John to escape, the soldiers to run him down, and General Scott have him executed. The jealous man couldn't seriously think of John as a competitor for the lady's affection.

The tiny dog crawled out of her pouch and sniffed the bushes a few feet from Wilcox's relaxed foot.

After John pulled on his pants, he sat a few yards behind his guard and tied his shoes. He took a deep breath and smiled. Cardinals chirped on the top branch of a towering fir. Beside him, rippling water rushed in its rocky bed, and the meadowlark warbled her song, wild and sweet and lonely. Through the leafless branches, John gazed at the hazy hills. His throat constricted. He'd miss these mountains. Seen them every day of his life. They were strong, beautiful, eternal. Whenever he gazed at them, he felt reassured. Pastor said eternity will only have begun when the mountains are no more. Mother and Pris ....

"Yip. Yip."

Roused from his musing by the dog scampering somewhere behind the trees, John muttered, "That mutt's going to get herself into trouble if she strays too far."

Wilcox snored as loud as a gaggle of squawking geese, his fat cheek pillowed on his rifle. John sprang to his feet and followed the Chihuahua into a thicket. He listened for the dog's yip, but he made more noise than a bunch of pigs in a cornfield. His new brogues weren't as quiet as a pair of moccasins. Where was that mongrel? A series of yips led him deeper into the woods. John froze. Was that a voice? Treading on tiptoe, he peeked over a large boulder.

Miss Hope Worchester hopped frantically on one foot, her red curls bouncing in all directions, chasing the tiny brown dog. She lifted her green skirts, exposing white pantaloons and one small shoeless foot. The mischievous Chihuahua gripped a high-topped boot in her mouth—the shoe bigger than the dog. But Duchess eluded Hope's grasp, dragging the shoe beyond her reach.

John burst out laughing.

Hope dropped her skirts—her blush made her all the more alluring. She smiled as if not surprised to see him. "Please stop laughing and help me get my shoe from that pesky animal." Her smile revealed a deep dimple in each smooth cheek.

John assumed a gallant pose, with one hand on his heart and the other arm raised to the sky. "Sir Galahad Ross to the rescue, ma'am." He crashed into the bushes after the dog. Harder to corner than a rat, John finally backed Duchess against a wide tree. With the lady's shoe dangling from one hand and the dog clutched in the other he stalked toward Hope.

Several feet from her outstretched hand, he stopped. "What are you doing out here alone, Miss Worchester?"

"Thank you for my shoe."

He shook his head and assumed a thoughtful expression. "Hmm, here are the facts. The lady left the wagon train, came to a secluded part of the woods, and removed her shoes. The question is, why? Did she come to meet her lover? Or to spy on someone?"

The pink in Hope's cheeks deepened to scarlet.

"But who—?"

"I'm afraid what I'm doing here is none of your business, sir."

John made his voice sound serious. "If the lady wants her shoe, she must answer."

"Oh, you! You're worse than the dog! I might have known you couldn't be a gentleman!" Hope's emerald eyes glinted mischief. She hopped toward him. "Give me my shoe!"

John had meant to surrender the boot, but she'd just said the wrong thing. He grinned. How did she like him laughing at her? He loved this turn of the tables. "Come get it, if you can."

She lifted her chin, jumped, lunged, and kept grabbing for the shoe. He dodged away, her tinkling laugh egging him on. Her head only reached to his shoulders, so he easily held the shoe out of her grasp.

"You're the most impossible person I've ever met!" The bright smile and dimples belied her words. Again, she lunged against him, stretching high to get her shoe.

John stretched to his full height and kept the shoe out of Hope's reach. Peterson baited him to escape because of this girl. Two gruesome weeks he would be Peterson's slave because of this girl. The captain had gotten an excellent start making those two weeks unbearable because of this girl. Maybe, he'd even the score with Peterson. He slid the pup to the ground.

His eyes must have sent her a warning because she tried to back away. Too late. He captured her in his arms.

She struggled wildly. The ringlets flying about her slender neck tickled his cheek.

He cradled her face with one hand while he pinned her against his chest with his other. The shoe dangled near her back.

He kissed her.

Both small fists pushed against his chest. Then, she quit pushing, and her lips responded. The answer from her lips urged him on. He hadn't expected his own fierce reaction to her warmth and softness. Abruptly, he released her. His heart beat a wild throb. His breath came so fast, he dare not speak. She must not know how much the kiss affected him.

Hope didn't move away. She looked so inviting, her soft eyes wide, her rosy lips parted.

He forced himself to step back, keeping his expression nonchalant, as though it wasn't unusual to kiss a girl with his whole heart, being, and spirit like he just had. As though this kiss were an every-day occurrence ... as though he'd not just fallen in love. He took her hand, placed her shoe in it, turned on his heel, and strode back toward the river.

As soon as he marched out of her sight, he collapsed against the nearest tree and wiped perspiration from his forehead. What just happened? Jeremy warned him to keep away from Hope, 'She'll shatter your heart. Wherever she goes, she leaves a trail of broken hearts behind.'

Like a sucker punch, realization hit him in the pit of his stomach. He already cared too much for Miss Hope Worchester. That reckless kiss sealed his fate. Too late, he was caught as firmly as Peterson. And there was nothing he could do to escape.

CHAPTER 29

Fear hit John in the chest with the impact of a bullet. His own fault—the kiss had been his undoing. Why hadn't he kept his hands off? Emotions churning, he drifted through the woods back to where he'd left Wilcox.

Lying like a sow in the sun, his guard snored like a wooden door flapping on rusty hinges. Wilcox's wayward dog curled at his feet.

John chose a location behind a tree where Wilcox couldn't spot him and settled against a fallen log. He had to clear his mind. Quiet his heart. He reached inside his shirt, fished out Jeremy's Bible, opened the book, leafed through the pages, and furrowed his brow. A few minutes later, he buttoned the small book back inside his inner shirt pocket. Shoulders slumped, he sprawled against the rough bark, buried his head in his hands, and groaned.

"Face it, Ross, you've trapped yourself in a dilemma."

Duchess yapped at a sound only she heard. Wilcox grunted, his eyes flew open, and he lumbered to his feet. He gazed around and yelled, "Ross, where are you?" His squeaky voice trembled. "I'll wring your neck like Sunday's chicken if you've run away."

"Right behind you, Private," John drawled, then stood. "Enjoy your beauty sleep?"

Wilcox scowled. On his pudgy face, the attempt to intimidate looked comical. "Don't you go lying to Captain that I was sleeping on duty. I knew where you was. I got eyes in back of my head. Shut your mouth and march. It's high time we reported in."

Precisely at 1600, John braced rigidly at attention before Captain Peterson.

"Take care of my horse. He's winded. I just made the fastest trip back into Nashville this army will ever see." Peterson stroked his handlebar mustache, and a flush heated his lean cheeks.

John moved fast to water, feed, brush, and hobble the lathered horse while the captain strode up and down the road, tapping his crop against his thigh, his high boots stirring up dust.

John sprinted over to salute Peterson.

"Set up camp immediately. I've an important engagement this evening." Peterson knelt beside his saddlebag, pulled up the flap, and took out a mirror.

John laid out the tent, attached four stakes to the four ends, and used the sledge from the wagon to pound three tent poles in the hard ground. With his first tap on the fourth stake, the first two pulled out. Exasperating. Hair straggling in his face and sweaty, he finally hammered in the last peg and stretched the tent upright.

Sore knuckles from missing the pegs showed his haste made pain as well as waste. His wounded hand ached from gripping the sledge, and extra knots in his neck replaced any that had relaxed during his swim. Peterson's curt orders and his obvious happiness scrambled more than John's muscles. He could barely string two thoughts together.

The captain leaned against a pine tree and tapped his riding crop against his dirty boot. "That was the clumsiest tent pitching I've ever seen. You're a dolt. Now, move my chest nearer the door and my bunk further from the draft."

John clamped his mouth.

"Fetch hot water for my bath. This lady is special, and I want to present myself in the best light. She deserves the whole treatment." Peterson strolled into his tent, opened his clothing chest, and selected assorted clothes. "Make it snappy." The man began to hum, his voice a boring monotone.

John hauled a tin bathtub from the supply wagon, built a campfire near the tent, hauled buckets of water from the river, heated them over the campfire, and dumped bucket after bucket into the tub. Short on Christian love, he hoped Peterson scalded himself.

While the captain soaped, splashed, sang, and transformed the clear water swirling around him in the tub to dingy grey, John brushed the man's uniform and laid out Peterson's boots on a small bench. Searching inside the chest among Peterson's personal effects for black polish, John lifted a rolled sock and discovered a tiny box. He slipped open the lid. A ring, holding a large, square diamond, sparkled against blue velvet.

His heart thumped. He gulped a huge breath of air, slapped the lid closed, found the polish jar behind a stack of underwear, and slammed the chest shut. He twisted off the boot polish lid, dipped a rag into the black paste, and slapped the cloth against the leather so hard the boot flew out of his hands and landed on the canvas floor. Though he yearned to lob the boot at Peterson's head, John grabbed the polishing rag and, with a vicious swipe, ripped the cloth in half. A hard strike at the temple might take the man down.

Peterson raised an eyebrow, stepped out of the tub, and wrapped himself in a large towel. His humming grew louder. He wiped an imaginary speck from his mirror and with careful snips of his scissors trimmed his military style black moustache. The edges of his mouth turned up, giving him a self-satisfied cat-got-the-cream expression. Still humming, he honed an edge on his straight razor, then scraped his lathered face.

"You Indians should take more care about your appearance." Peterson removed a small comb from the top of his chest and groomed his dark, wavy hair. "If you had a haircut, you wouldn't look so much like a wild donkey."

John slammed the drawer shut on his thumb. Behind Peterson's back, he thrust his thumb into his mouth to keep from cursing and hopped around the tent.

Peterson's black eyes sparkled. "Hurt yourself, did you?"

John glared and wrapped his hand around his throbbing thumb.

Peterson sniffed four bottles of after-shave lotion, then chose one. He motioned for John to bring his clean shirt and uniform, all the while smiling like a Caesar about to receive his laurel wreath. "I won't be here for mess." He made no attempt to hide the triumph in his voice. With quick fingers, he buttoned his uniform tunic.

John scooped up Peterson's long boot and polished the rich leather.

Peterson buckled on his sword. "I'll handcuff you to the wagon."

Handcuff!

"I expect to be back quite late. You have five minutes to dump this bath water and make my tent orderly. Meet me at the supply wagon exactly at 1650. Oh, before you leave, polish my saddle."

John threw the boot violently to the tent floor.

"Handle my things with care." Peterson's lips twitched up at the corners. "And when I speak to you, you are to answer, 'Yes, sir.'"

"Yes, sir," John growled.

Peterson stomped his stockinged foot and picked up his riding crop. "What did you say?" He smacked his crop on John's shoulders.

John modulated his voice. "Yes, sir."

"That's better." Peterson stepped over to the mirror.

John ran outside, grabbed the saddle and the polish, and set to work.

Five minutes later, nails black with polish, he met Peterson in front of the supply wagon.

"Where's your bedroll?"

"I don't have one, sir."

"Incompetent. What happened to it?"

John remained silent. He'd never tell Peterson he buried his mother in his blanket.

"Sullen half-breed. That attitude will avail you nothing. If you have no bedroll, that's not my concern." He wrapped his greatcoat closer to ward off the rising wind. "Look inside the wagon. There must be something there to sleep under."

John climbed aboard. The temperature was a good ten degrees warmer out of the sharp wind. Peterson dropped in next to him and rummaged through the boxes, burlap bags, and stacks of other items.

"Ah." He uncovered an iron coupling in the tailgate and raised John's left arm above his head. A businesslike snap and cold, hard metal clamped John's wrist near the top of the canopy. Then he manacled John's ankle to the tailgate. His tormentor tossed an empty gunnysack over John's shoulders. Flour dust sprayed his face and John sneezed. Since the iron clamp made lying down impossible, he squatted on the wooden boards. At least the Falcon hadn't cuffed his injured hand.

"Your guard will wake you at midnight and stand guard duty with you. He will be relieved in four hours by another guard who will stand your remaining three hours with you and then return you to my tent. At that time, your daily duties will commence. This will be your schedule for the next six days. Any other foul-ups on your part and you'll spend your last week repeating this duty."

With exaggerated movements, Peterson lifted the tiny box from an inner pocket of his uniform, removed the diamond and held the sparkling gem to the light, then slipped the re-boxed ring back into his vest.

John tugged at his chains. Peterson was not only cocky ... he was cruel.

Peterson jumped out of the Conestoga, and John swallowed the anger burning his throat. From his viewpoint across the wagon and through the front canvas flap, he watched Peterson stride with confident posture over the frost covered ground toward the Worchester wagon.

John smacked the floor with his free foot. Flour particles and dust sprinkled his leg. If Hope accepted Peterson's diamond, she was sure to face his cruelty at some point in her marriage. He jerked on the manacles until the wagon rocked. Regardless of what Hope thought of him, he would make it his personal crusade to see that she didn't marry Peterson.

John gazed through the open wagon flap at thousands of stars pricking the black sky like diamonds parading down the path of the Milky Way until the swirling acid anger inside his chest ebbed. Half-sitting, half-lying, manacled to the top of the wagon and the tailgate, welts formed on his wrist and ankle. Fourteen very long nights to go.

A voice hissed from outside in the darkness. "Ross, where are you?"

John scraped his elbow against the rough boards. "Up here, in Peterson's wagon."

"Move over."

John scooted as far from the opening as the metal cuffs allowed.

Jeremy vaulted inside. "Peterson did a job on you with those handcuffs. The guy sure hates you. He's over at Dad's camp making calf eyes at Hope."

"Glad you came."

"Looks like Peterson gave you a rough day."

"You could say that."

"I calculated he would. Here's a blanket. I was sworn to secrecy. I cannot tell from whence it came." He grinned and winked. "Me, I think you're getting too soft to sleep in the cold. Doc Smith played your nursemaid too long."

"Huh. You try to stomach the foul medicine Doc doles out."

As Jeremy tucked the blanket around John, warmth eased into his chilled body.

"Are you sure Rachael and the orphans don't need this blanket more than I do?" John sneezed again.

"Nah. The children have warm moccasins from the deer's pelt. Rachael's pegging and softening the rest of the skin and making coats for them." Jeremy lifted a corner of the sack. "Flour sacks—?"

John's stomach gave a distinct growl. "The Falcon flew off before I had a chance to eat."

Jeremy slammed a fist on top of a nearby keg. "That scoundrel!"

"Shush. Peterson will hear."

Jeremy lowered his voice. "I'll forage something from the mess tent. See you after." He climbed through the flap and dropped to the ground, returning a few minutes later with lukewarm coffee, cornbread, beans, and dried venison.

Thank you, God, for such a good friend and for this food. Using his uncuffed hand, John dove into the feast.

"Rachael and Bold Hunter send greetings. The kids are in good spirits."

"Um." John swallowed another mouthful.

Jeremy leaned against one side of the tailgate. "I think Rachael still prefers your company to Bold Hunter's."

John choked on a piece of cornbread. With his casual words, was Jeremy probing? What did he want to know? Had Hope asked her brother to sound out John's feelings for Rachael?

Jeremy grinned.

John bit off another bite of cornbread. How could he keep his friend from getting more suspicious? And how did things stand between him and Rachael? He'd never told Rachael he belonged to the Wolf Clan. As such, he was considered by clansmen to be too close a relation to wed her. Not that he'd let a distant blood relationship get in his way ... if he discovered his feeling for Rachael was love. Or were the ancient rules correct? Did he love Rachael more like a sister?

"How do you know Rachael would rather be with me than Bold Hunter?"

Jeremy smirked. "Anyone with two eyes can see. You collect all the female hearts."

"Hah! Not. True." John frowned. His hurting heart had to know. He took a long swallow of cold coffee, then tried to sound casual. "Speaking of females who don't like me, how is Peterson progressing with your sister?"

The smirk remained on Jeremy's good-natured face, and he winked. "Can't tell. Peterson might be special, or he might be just one of the herd." Jeremy shook his head. "More soldiers buzz around Hope than flies around cold buttermilk on a hot day. Dad says chaperoning her is a full-time job. He's vexed. She enjoys all the attention."

John stopped eating.

Jeremy handed John another piece of jerky. "It's like this. Hope spent the last four years in a girl's finishing school in Boston. Wasn't even allowed to meet a man after church, much less have one call on her. So, she's enjoying herself making up for lost time." He squeezed John's shoulder. "Besides, she doesn't encourage them. She happens to be the only unattached white woman on the train."

John ate, but the food no longer held his attention. Visions of Hope surrounded by handsome soldiers in smart uniforms spiraled through his mind.

"You're not very talkative tonight." Jeremy gathered the empty tin plates and stacked them.

"Sorry, I'm tired."

"You'd better get some shut-eye. I've got guard duty from 2100 until midnight. I'll check in on you tomorrow night."

"Thanks, Yank. Looks like it'll be a long, cold night. I have guard duty from midnight until dawn." John shifted his arm to relieve the pressure where the handcuff cut into his wrist.

"What! Graveyard duty with three extra hours? Peterson's a dirty player. Serve him right if my sister trapped him into permanent wedlock. Be just what he deserves."

A bolt of pain shot into John's heart, and he didn't join Jeremy's laughter. "Listen, Jeremy, Peterson's cruel. You should discourage Hope from seeing him."

"Give Hope some credit. She's got brains behind that pretty face."

"Yeah, but—"

"Take my advice. Forget you ever met my sister. I don't want to see your scalp hanging from her belt."

"Yeah."

After Jeremy left, John shifted restlessly, searching for a semi-comfortable position. Though his hand was numb, his wrist still burned and his shoulder ached. How long had he been trying to sleep? His tense body wouldn't relax. He strained to catch the sound of the captain's boots on the frosty ground. The slower the minutes ticked by, the more his wrist hurt.

A shadowy form nudged John. He must have dozed since he hadn't heard the soldier approach. Had to be midnight.

The soldier twisted and turned the handcuff, trying to unlock the cold metal and chaffing John's wrist, "Guard duty, if I can get you free." Finally, the metal cuff clanked to the floor.

In the inky darkness, stumbling over roots, rocks, and other unknown obstacles, John followed the soldier. He massaged his wrist and as circulation returned, pins of sensation pricked his hand and foot. Heavy black clouds obscured the moon and stars. The wind blew so cold John shivered and stomped his feet to get the blood running through his chilled body. The eerie silence, broken only by the whining of the wind hurled against the wagonloads of sleeping people, made him jittery. The rhythmic clomp, clomp, clomp of feet as he and his guard trudged their perimeter around the wagons sounded like a funeral march.

John hunched against the chill air, the hand not hefting the useless musket shoved deep into his pocket. Despite the cold, he had to fight off sleep. His head nodded as he marched, locked in frozen darkness while endless minute followed endless minute. Had time ceased to exist? Was this what eternity would be like for those who refused Christ—endless, dark, and without hope.

More Hell. He couldn't force thoughts of Hope from his mind.

A new man relieved the guard pacing with John. Only three hours left. As long as he moved, his feet wouldn't freeze. His eyes kept closing, blinking against the sand rubbing his eyelids raw. Eventually, the darkness thinned.

I'm bone-weary. Lord, I need that strength you promised. The prayer whirled round and round in his sluggish brain.

The bugle trumpeted, and he realized dawn had come. He knuckled bleary eyes. "Guess I must have been asleep on my feet." He stumbled and his latest guard grabbed his shoulders, turned him north, and marched him to Peterson's tent.

John bent and entered. The warmth from the portable firepot seemed too hot. Peterson sat at the table writing, his uniform impeccable. Had the Falcon gone to bed at all? The piercing black eyes looked inscrutable. Had he been successful in his campaign?

He didn't look up. "Bring my breakfast immediately." The feathered quill scratching on linen paper echoed his strident voice, the command taking more than a minute to penetrate John's sleep-numbed mind.

"What's the problem, half-breed? Don't you understand English?"

"Yes, sir." John blundered from the tent and followed the scent of food. Inside the warm, delicious smelling mess tent, he helped himself to a bowl of mush and a few rashers of bacon.

"Here, have some more. You look like the walking dead." The sympathetic cook nodded toward more side meat as he rattled dishes, preparing Peterson's tray. A few minutes later John set the tray in front of Peterson.

"Clumsy fool! You spilled my coffee." Peterson picked up his knife and fork. "Those bloodshot eyes tell me learning to be a soldier is too much for you, 'breed. You'll never make the grade."

"Yes, sir." John tightened his lips. Had Peterson been successful or not?

Peterson picked at his breakfast. "Stop standing there like a drunken sailor. Get to work. Polish the howitzers before we pull out. They're covered with mud. I want all ten of them spotless before you pack up my tent this morning."

"Yes, sir." John sprinted to the artillery wagon, the run and cold air like a shot of coffee stirring him awake. He worked hard and fast but again was late packing the captain's tent, saddling his horse, and reporting in.

"Give me fifty!" Peterson's face was crimson.

John handed over the horse reins, then dropped. Fifty push-ups proved easier this time.

"Sergeant O'Neal, Private Ross needs to stretch his legs. Accompany him on a five-mile run up the mountain. He'll carry a sixty-pound pack. Double-time!"

"Permission to ride, Captain?"

"Granted."

O'Neal's horse was lathered at the end of the five-mile run. So was John. Sweat covered him from his wet hair to his damp toes inside his boots. Under the backpack, his new shirt dripped and his shoulders ached. Again, he reported in late.

"I warned you, Ross. Guard duty from midnight until dawn until the day you're released. Shape-up!" Peterson's sharp eyes darted over John. "Appears you're not tired yet. Since it's almost lunch break, when the train stops, you are to inspect each wagon and fill each water keg from the river. I want the job completed before lunch break ends. This will be a daily duty."

John grimaced. Hard as he tried, he couldn't help wincing. "Yes, sir."

Peterson turned to John's guard, who was dismounting. "Sergeant O'Neill, see to it."

The Falcon worked John through lunch. The man had no mercy. Perhaps he hoped John would drop dead in his tracks.

"We're crossing the river soon. For the present, you work at the ford. I want you to lead each team across. You're responsible for the safety of each wagon."

John heaved one of the heavy pack's shoulder straps off his right shoulder.

"No, leave the pack on—that's your uniform. From here on, you and that rucksack are not to be separated." Peterson chuckled. "A heavy pack will slow you down if you try to run off again."

Sergeant O'Neal frowned. "Forcing the kid to wear a rucksack and work in the icy water all day seems harsh even to an old drill master like me."

"You want to trade places with Ross?"

"No, sir. Whatever you say, sir."

The days dragged on ... not from boredom but from exhaustion. Peterson's constant demands nearly brought John to his knees. The six-hour graveyard duty became a nightmare of endurance. Any free time John received during the day he spent inside the supply wagon, stretched over uncomfortable boxes and barrels in exhausted sleep. Peterson made sure John never caught more than a few hours, day or night. The kindly cook sought him out and handed him food and water whenever he neared the mess tent. John ate on the run, gobbling scraps between jobs.

Sympathetic wagon drivers filled their own water kegs before John made the rounds. Even O'Neal turned a blind eye. Each night Jeremy brought food, often John's only meal. Did Peterson plan to starve him if he couldn't work him to death?

The man wore his frustration as a permanent scowl.

One cold night, John dozed in the wagon without having eaten. He figured Jeremy had been detained by duties he couldn't leave. Though his stomach touched his backbone, he slept.

"Up and at 'em, soldier." John's guard awakened him.

He squinted at the moon. "You're an hour early."

"Peterson's command." The less than chatty guard unlocked John's shackles and bodily hauled him from the wagon into the frosty air.

John stood, still more than half asleep. The guard strapped the sixty-pound pack on John's back and marched him double-time to his post where a campfire glimmered. When he reached the fire, a plate of cornbread and beans and a cup of hot coffee waited. He stooped down and reached for them. As he touched the plate, it disappeared ... the warm fire dissipated into cold air. As yellow fingers of light painted gold in the east, he hallucinated several more times before his guard duty ended.

All that day, Peterson dogged John's footsteps. He never gave him a moment to eat or rest, working him through the evening and into the night. Then, just before he sent John to guard duty, Peterson braced him. "Attention!"

John did his best.

Peterson smacked him on the head with his crop. "Before you walk out of my life tomorrow morning, I want you to know Miss Hope Worchester accepted my diamond."

John's stomach quivered, and his heart seemed to stop beating. Darkness wavered before his eyes. But he refused to show emotion, keeping his face taut, his hands clenched at his sides, and his shoulder blades pinned back so far they nearly touched each other.

"Never, never, never let me see you near Miss Worchester again. Or I will cut you down with my sword."

CHAPTER 30

Was the bugle sounding taps or reveille? John's thoughts fuzzed, his mind barely functioning. He concentrated, sorting through the notes swirling through his exhausted brain. Reveille. The past six hours had been guard duty then ... not another nightmare. How many days left? This discipline couldn't last much longer. He massaged his temples. Neither could he.

His guard grabbed his arm, pointed him toward Peterson's tent, and left.

John gazed after the departing guard, then turned, followed a mouth-watering aroma to the mess tent and stepped inside. Coffee. He lifted a thick porcelain cup from the makeshift sideboard, poured in hot liquid with the smell of chicory, and took a gulp. Too hot ... scalded his tongue ... mind still muddled. He swallowed another sip, careful not to burn his tongue again, then set the cup back on the rough wooden table.

Must show-up at Peterson's tent or the Falcon would slap on more work. John forced his aching feet outside and trudged toward his enemy. Every muscle revolted, his hands blue with cold, and his right palm throbbed. He pushed through a crowd of soldiers clustered around the open doorway.

After he entered the captain's tent his eyes watered from the unaccustomed warmth. Face flushed and raw from the wind, he tried to assemble a coherent thought.

Peterson stood just inside the front flap, feet planted, crop raised. "Attention!"

His blurry form looked every inch the Falcon, perched, ready for the kill. John snapped his shoulders back and went rigid, the automatic response kicking in before his sluggish mind caught up with his action. "What do you say, Sergeant? I won. The half-breed looks dead on his feet." Peterson puffed out his chest and stroked his handlebar mustache.

"That he does, sir." The sergeant stood next to where Peterson waited, crop flicking against his thigh.

"I'm savoring this moment, much as another man might take pleasure in an excellent steak dinner. Ross dared mortify me in front of Miss Worchester." Peterson strolled to his camp chair, lowered himself into the seat, and leaned back, a half-smile on his face. He laid his crop across his knees, reached for his pipe, and took his time performing the lighting ritual.

John swayed.

Peterson puffed. For ten minutes he smoked, forming a blue cloud around his head. Footsteps and mumbling voices told John the men from Peterson's unit gathered closer to the open flap and watched.

John remained at attention.

"Ross completed his discipline with reveille this morning," one soldier whispered.

"Looks like he suffered," another answered.

"Captain Peterson, you gonna keep your part of the wager?" The soldier's tone sounded tentative.

"Of course. I committed myself. I still have time to break Ross. He's all but out on his feet."

The tent floor tilted, but John held his ground. He would not allow this man to win. And he would never tolerate Peterson marrying Hope. Never. No matter what he had to do to stop him.

Peterson removed his pipe and blew several concentric rings of smoke. The woodsy scent wound itself around John's nose.

"Ross, you're the sorriest excuse for a soldier I've ever encountered. You're clumsy, slow, and lame-brained. Never punctual. It proved impossible to penalize you for all your blunders and disobediences. If I had done so, you would stand guard duty from now until you turn fifty." He sniffed. "There's nothing in that half-breed body of yours to shape you into a soldier. You've confirmed my opinion that Indians are an inferior race."

John maintained his stony expression, concentrating on Peterson's voice. But separating the meaning of his words from the rumble of his voice took too long. Was he asleep on his feet, eyes wide open?

The captain shot up, kicked back his chair, and glared. Peterson's eyes hypnotized John—a fly before a praying mantis. John kept his feet rooted and his knees relaxed else he would fall where he stood.

Peterson paced around John, his Calvary boots slapping the floor, setting a thrum inside John's head. "Ross, you're losing your self-control. It's only a matter of time until you break." He chuckled. "Get to it. Retaliate. You want to take vengeance—tell me where to get off. Do it!"

Chaotic echoes inside John's brain grew louder. What did Peterson say?

A soldier poked his head into the tent from where he stood among the group of men watching outside. "Speaking of time, you've run out, Peterson. Looks like you lost your vendetta. You won't break this young man."

"Shut up, Jones!" Peterson threw his pipe on his desk, and the bowl cracked. Eyes wide, he glanced up and down the tent until his gaze landed on his white gloves lying on the bunk. He leaned over and jerked them up. "Ross, a gentleman doesn't ignore a challenge! Are you man enough to face me?"

John's mind grasped for meaning. What had Peterson roared?

Captain Peterson slapped John across the face with the gloves. John faltered backward, then regained his stance. "Now what do you say? Defend yourself!"

Peterson's slap and loud voice penetrated the fog, but John focused his gaze straight ahead. In the past, he would have punched the captain—pummeled him until his anger was spent. Now, as a Christian, he would not. Instead, he smiled.

Deep purple spread over Peterson's face. "Out!" He choked and pulled at the collar of his uniform, gulping air. "Get out! You're released! Never step foot into my tent again!"

John backed toward the tent flap and stumbled out.

Men slapped him on the back.

"Pay up, Peterson. You owe me," a voice called above the hubbub.

Movement and cold air semi-roused John. The cook took him by the arm and led him toward the mess wagon. "Indian, those were the smartest moves you ever made. I watched the whole thing. If you had struck Peterson, he'd have had you behind bars before you could say your name. Striking an officer is a grave offense in this man's army."

Thank you, God, for keeping me from doing anything stupid.

"Get on in here, Ross. I know you're hungry." The cook plopped a plate of food on the table. "Have some beans and bacon on me. I got a few minutes before we start this wagon rolling." Cook tugged his arm.

The friendly touch woke John enough to bolt down the food and accept a second helping. Comfortable and his belly no longer aching, he drifted into a pleasant daze. The cook draped a blanket over John's shoulders and headed him in the direction of Rachael's wagon. He stumbled on legs that barely supported him. As the icy wind snatched him, he tightened the army blanket around his shoulders.

Bold Hunter raced toward him, grabbed John's arm, heaved it over a muscular shoulder, and all but carried him to their wagon. Rachael scurried on all fours inside their wagon and made a bed for him. "Dear John, you look half dead with those dark circles beneath your eyes." She took his hand and drew him to the pallet. "You can tell us about your ordeal after you sleep."

Wedged among the children, John collapsed. The children's chattering welcome created a rosy haze and even the wagon jolting felt comfortable as he dozed off. At one point, he realized the wagons had stopped, but he immediately went back to sleep.

Someone shook him. From the depths of sleep, he heard a voice. Rachael jostled his shoulder. "Wake up. It's time for supper."

"Need more sleep." John rolled over and faded back into darkness.

Sun shining in his face forced John's eyes open. Rachael shook both his shoulders. "You've slept for hours. You must eat."

Thick with sleep, he stuck his head through the tailgate flap. The sharp, afternoon air cleared the spiderwebs from his brain. As his vision cleared, he looked around. In the distance, the frosty ground of the ancient hills resembled old men covered with white hair. Wagons had formed a circle across the rolling terrain and groups huddled around a blazing campfire near each wagon. Judging from the familiar smell, the families ate their traditional food from bowls filled with Canahomie and Indian bread.

John smiled. Like him, his people survived.

His people. Two different worlds, white and Indian. He fit into both. Under the cultural differences, beneath the color of the skin, apart from their roles as capturer and captive, all were brothers. Most were good men, some bad. Brown or white, each had needs, hopes, ambitions, desires, heartaches. God waited for each man to choose him.

Though he hated Peterson, he must forgive the man. Perhaps as Peterson traveled this difficult trail, he would select a different path and turn to God. John sighed. Except for Sergeant Dread, he'd never met a man who needed a Savior more.

John scuttled from the wagon and strode to the campfire.

"Eat, John." Rachael placed a warm bowl in his hands. "I'm sorry, we ate our rationed meat a few days ago, so supper is scant."

"Thanks. Smells great."

Rachael sat on a log and patted the area beside her. "Now tell us your discipline was not as horrible as the rumors we heard." Bold Hunter hunkered at her other side. With John's head feeling large as a pumpkin, he answered his friends' questions about the past two weeks.

"Captain not chain Bold Hunter. Not hit with crop." He shook a fist. "Bold Hunter not see captain more than— one—two time." He held up two fingers. "Obey Sergeant." He shook his head so hard his long hair switched across his shoulders. "Peterson not bother with Bold Hunter."

"Water under the bridge." John stifled a yawn and stretched. After he rested, he would confess his hate to God, then come to terms with what he had to do to keep Peterson from ruining Hope's life. "Good night all, I'm off to bed." He rose and turned toward the wagon.

Twigs crackled. Footsteps tapped on the nearby road. John pivoted, but he didn't spot Hope until she stepped into the circle of light from the campfire.

Rachael giggled. "John, you should see the expression on your face. Glassy-eyed and with your mouth hanging open, you bring to mind a hooked fish."

He knuckled his gritty eyes. How right she was. He corrected his expression and smiled. How did Hope's presence instantly arouse every sense?

"I came to express my gratitude, Mr. Ross, for saving me from that savage animal in the woods." Hope held out a package. "Please accept this gift from Father."

John took the bundle without realizing what he did until the weight warmed his hands. "I was only too happy to be of assistance, Miss Worchester." Although he wanted to dance a jig, he only permitted himself to smile. He worked to keep his expression blank, fervently hoping to hide his inappropriate feelings. After all, Hope was engaged. He touched his forehead in a salute. "If the opportunity should present itself again, I would be most gratified to repeat the entire procedure." John emphasized the last four words. Thunderation, his thoughts spilled from his mouth before he could keep his tongue silent.

Hope seemed at a loss to speak, but her dimples gleamed impishly in the firelight. Her cheeks blossomed red.

"Should the event recur, I feel certain I would not be called away by duty in such an untimely way." John folded his arms across his chest. Engaged or not, he meant every word. The thought of another kiss made him tingle from head to foot. Caution be hanged.

Rachael's dark eyes glowed with fun. "Hmm. Sounds like a mystery. Would you two please explain what you are talking about?"

For a second, John panicked. Hope had a dreadful habit of saying exactly what was on her mind.

She thrust her hands behind her and took a step back. "Some other time, perhaps. I must leave now. Father's vexed with me. Seems it's not proper for me to walk about at night visiting my friends. But I did persuade him to invite you to dinner tomorrow evening."

Rachael waved her hand, including him, Bold Hunter, and the nine children seated around the campfire. "Thank you, we'd love to come."

"We can celebrate. Rachel, have you told Mr. Ross the news?" Hope smiled.

John's knees weakened, and he leaned against a tree, his heart thumping against his rib cage. Was Rachael about to announce Hope's engagement to Peterson?

Hope rushed off before John could offer to accompany her. He stared after her into the darkness.

Rachael's voice sounded amused. "Dear John, how hard you try to hide your feelings. Perhaps if you hadn't been surprised by Hope, you would have succeeded better. Go ahead, look. What's inside the bundle?"

John grunted and tore at the paper. A white mackinaw! The desperate problem of how to survive in the steadily dropping temperature was solved for him, but what about the hundreds like him with no coat? Working as quickly as his stiff fingers allowed, he slipped on the heavy coat and buttoned out the biting wind.

"The coat fits well, a bit snug in the shoulders." Rachael ran her hand over the material and smiled.

He had forgotten how warmth felt. At least the people in his wagon wouldn't freeze. Rachael wore a cougar skin coat from the catch, and Bold Hunter draped a blanket he gotten from one of Peterson's men around his large frame. The children each wore new mid-leg deer moccasins. Between them, they shared the two blankets, and Jeremy's greatcoat. And now, they had the blanket the cook gave him.

"What's to celebrate?" John braced himself. May as well face the answer now while darkness veiled his expression.

Rachael resembled a well-dressed cupid, her cheeks aglow. Why should she be so happy to announce Hope's engagement? Bold Hunter glanced sideways at John, gave him a friendly slap on the shoulder, and strode into the darkness.

"Oh!" Now he understood. Not Hope. "You and Bold Hunter …."

Rachael took John's hand and wrapped it inside her own soft, warm ones. Her mouth trembled, but her eyes sparkled.

Thunderation! Was she going to cry? An empty place in his heart hurt. But joy was there too. He loved Rachael, and Bold Hunter was a brother in Christ. How could he not be happy for them? A shred of relief trickled into his heart. Deep inside, he'd known for a long time Rachael belonged with Bold Hunter, but refused to admit the truth.

"I know you care for me, John. How could I not know? But I love you like a sister does a brother."

John swallowed hard, then worked up a smile. "For the beautiful bride." John cupped Rachael's face between his palms and kissed her on each cheek. "You two have my blessings."

"We'll name our firstborn son for you." Her dark eyes shimmered. "John Ross Hunter."

Later, curled close to the campfire, John felt he'd lost an important part of his life because of his own actions. If he hadn't led Bold Hunter to the Lord, Rachael would never have consented to marry him. Rachael's engagement left a vacant place, the one she had once held in his heart. He rolled over to toast his back. Still, he wouldn't want Rachael to wed anyone else.

But her decision left him feeling lonely. He'd lost both the women he loved.

He writhed on the ground, trying to get comfortable. Yes, the more he thought of Rachael and Bold Hunter being married, the happier he was for them. But with Rachael's future assured, he missed Hope with a physical pain that hurt all the way to his toes. No question but that he was in love with Hope. When she was near, the debonair John Ross vanished, his place taken by a bumbling schoolboy.

But Hope was engaged to Peterson. The anguish in his heart grew so intense he vaulted to his feet and paced the area beyond the campfire. He could not get Hope out of his mind.

Brutally frank, she had a temper coupled with a strong will. Obviously, she was dedicated to God, or she would never have undertaken the torturous wagon train to unexplored Indian Territory. From their stolen kiss, he learned hot blood flowed in her veins.

But she was enamored with Peterson. Could she be such a poor judge of character? One way or another, he'd make certain Peterson didn't get near her. John thrust his hands deep into his coat pockets. Even with Peterson out of the picture, what chance did he stand of courting Hope? Every soldier on the wagon train could offer her more than he. And each man was intent on doing just that. He had no future. No money. Nothing but the clothes on his back, and they had come from her. The old bitterness clamped his chest like a too-tight coat of armor.

He paced until the burlier of his two guards gripped him by the shoulder and stopped him. "Whatever's got you so riled up? Forget it and go to sleep."

John folded down to sit cross-legged close to the fire. He propped his chin in his hand and stared into the crackling flames. He'd confront one problem at a time. Hope had Peterson's diamond. First, he would call Peterson out. One way or another he would stop Peterson from marrying Hope, help her see the kind of man her fiancé really was. Then what? From what he'd seen, Hope collected men like trinkets for a Christmas tree.

"Hit the rack, kid."

John nodded at the guard and stretched out on the ground. Though warm inside his new coat, he tossed, sleep eluding him until well into the night.

The bugle and sounds of breaking camp woke him. Must be morning. He'd never felt so touchy and irritable.

Rachael spooned two extra fried cakes onto his tin plate. "It's a beautiful day, John. Warm for this time of the year. The wind died in the night and isn't blowing for once."

John scowled at the bright sky. "Won't last long. Good things never do."

By midday, John's sour spirit still weighed heavy.

Bold Hunter handed John the reins, hopped down, and walked off. "Black mood make poor company."

Rachael climbed over the seat and took the reins from his hands. "I've never seen you so grouchy. Go on back inside and catch a few hours' sleep. I'll drive."

"Best idea yet." John scrambled inside and curled into a corner.

That evening, John couldn't find anything to say while the group walked to the Worchester wagon. He dreaded seeing Hope—dreaded seeing her happily wearing the huge diamond Peterson gave her. A deep sigh forced itself up from the bottom of his lungs. Once he settled with Peterson, he wouldn't let Hope add him as another ornament in her collection of men. He would avoid her. He had to protect his battered heart. Survive.

CHAPTER 31

Pastor held out his hand. "John, good to see you."

John shook the warm hand. Pastor pulled him over to a camp chair next to his beside a roaring fire and offered a steaming tin cup of coffee. "Join us ... you're like one of the family."

Jeremy arrived and stationed himself in a vacant camp chair on John's other side, while Rachel walked to the cook fire to help Hope. Bold Hunter, grinning like an Indian whose rain dance had been answered with a downpour, sank into a camp chair on the opposite side of the campfire. The nine children, chattering and giggling, sat in groups on the ground.

John wrapped his fingers around the tin cup to warm his hands and frowned. Pastor looked fatigued. The man who had become like a father had aged during the last month. "For the past two weeks, I've been out of touch with the news. Are the people still responding to the gospel, Pastor?"

Worchester set the coffeepot back on the tripod hanging above the fire and stared over the rims of his glasses, his green eyes grave. "My contact with the people is on a one-to-one basis now, son. I only conduct church service on Sunday mornings. We are fortunate the army does not travel on Sundays. Still, that short time doesn't come close to filling the people's needs in these difficult times. As many as ten people die each day, and we still have hundreds of miles to travel. Sad to think ... the worst of winter is ahead. This forced removal is the blackest deed the American government has ever committed." Pastor shook his graying head. "The shame is the Indians only wanted to be left in peace to live in their homeland."

John's shoulders slumped.

"But I don't have to tell you two boys about the Cherokee desire for peace."

John and Bold Hunter nodded. The gloomy conversation didn't appear to take the edge off Bold Hunter's obvious joy.

"Nevertheless"—Pastor gripped his Bible and tapped the book on his leg—"the people are turning to Christ in greater numbers than I have ever experienced in twenty years of pastoring." He stood. "Let us thank the Lord for their acceptance and for our food."

Everyone joined hands and bowed their heads. After the blessing, Rachael and Hope scurried from one to the next, carrying steaming bowls of thick stew fresh from the cook pot.

John lost the conversation's trend. Hope looked so graceful strolling around the circle, her red hair gleaming in the light from the campfire, her expression serene and sure. Her lips were downright enticing ... her mossy eyes hid mysteries. What was she thinking? Was she expecting Peterson? Would the tyrant show up any minute? John coughed. If Peterson arrived, he would leave.

Jeremy poked his arm. "Did you hear me, John?"

"Sorry, what was that?"

"I discovered by way of the grapevine that Chief Junaluska, the man who saved General Jackson's life during the Battle of Horseshoe Bend, after he saw his people rounded up by Jackson and forced to leave, commented ..." Jeremy stood, gazed toward the night sky, and spoke fiercely, "'O my God, if I had known at the battle of the Horseshoe what I know now, American history would have been differently written!'" Jeremy bowed and sat down.

"You're a gifted mimic." Hope ruffled Jeremy's hair.

The small group lapsed into silence. The sighing wind reminded John of the Cherokees moaning for their lost loved ones. Grief, misted with ghosts, swirled about their little party. Yet, only a few white people were to blame. There were others, like the Worchesters, who loved the Cherokees.

Rachael rose, walked to the wagon tailgate, and returned to serve more hot cornbread to the eager children.

Hope served second helpings of the stew. "Everyone looks too serious for a celebration." She hung the pot back over the campfire, twirled her flowing, green dress in a circle, and smiled. "Dad, can't we liven things up? Why does everyone have such a long face? We're warm, we have enough food, we're among friends, and God loves us. We have much to be thankful for."

"You're right, my dear." Pastor turned to Rachael. "Share your wedding plans." Heartiness in Pastor's voice sounded forced.

John relaxed against the canvas back of the chair. Rachael and Bold Hunter looked happier than he'd ever seen either of them. Yes, their marriage was the right thing. Good for everyone.

As Bold Hunter sat with straight shoulders and puffed-out chest, Rachael explained their plans.

John's thoughts drifted. What were Hope's wedding plans? Like it or not, he had to talk with her. Warn her. After he did, she would hate him more. The conversation moved around him, but he wasn't part of it. He was an outsider. His poverty set him apart from his captors, the men who could marry Hope. Not him. He was a man without a future.

Shortly after the meal ended, a handsome soldier appeared. "I'm looking for Miss Hope."

John frowned. Didn't the man know she was engaged?

Pastor frowned and shook his head.

But Hope stood. "Hello, Sam." She walked with the newcomer into the shadows outside the circle of wagons.

Gloom settled over John like armor over an old war horse. What was she doing with that soldier? Would he be a guest for dinner tomorrow night? John hunkered down in his camp chair.

He had no chance with that beautiful, lively girl. He bowed his head. He would avoid Hope. Why let himself be hurt? He had nothing to offer her, no knowledge of what his new life would hold or how he would make a living. Even if she broke her engagement to Peterson, what could he offer her?

Yet he would do all he could to prevent her marriage to Peterson. That was a given.

His thoughts drifted to concern over Hope's conversation with the soldier. Why was he here? Why had Hope agreed to speak with him? To keep his worry in check, John counted the stars and reached one thousand nine hundred and ninety-nine before Hope returned.

She strolled back into the circle of light, a worried pucker creasing her forehead, her arms clasped in front of her waist, her expression almost frightened. Had the soldier warned her about Peterson?

"That's right, Dad." Jeremy's voice nudged John's thoughts back to the conversation.

"It is up to every Christian on the wagon train to show Christ's love. The men in my dragoon have been talking about what Drowning Bear said." Jeremy glanced at John.

John nodded. "I understand he's the leader of the Lower Towns Cherokees in North Carolina, and a noted orator."

"Drowning Bear had a vision and banned liquor from his peoples' territory back in 1819. He read a translation of Matthew, then reported, 'It seems to be a good Book—strange the white people are no better after having read it so long.'"

Jeremy shook his head. "Then my friend Tom spoke up, 'Too bad old Drowning Bear didn't know Jeremy here.' Then they all laughed. Made me uneasy. I don't know if they joshed or meant what they said."

"Red-haired soldier strong in heart, honorable in tongue." Bold Hunter made a fist and clapped his chest.

Jeremy blushed so red his freckles disappeared.

"Many of my people go to place of long rest." Bold Hunter tucked his arm around Rachael. "We pray they go with Christ."

The wind rose in a sudden gust that sent embers arching from the fire. Rachael rose. "Time for bed, children."

Pastor stood. "Let us depart with a prayer. Heavenly Father, in these difficult days we pray everyone on this wagon train—Cherokee and soldier—will face their need of your Son as their savior. In Jesus's powerful name, amen."

Rachael gathered the children to her, wiped messy faces and hands, and parceled out blankets, shawls, and the greatcoat.

As John rose to leave, he stole a quick glance at Hope. The firelight illuminated her face, even highlighting a sprinkle of freckles scattered across the bridge of her nose. Enchanting. He'd love to trace his index finger down her dainty nose. But did her preoccupied expression indicate she thought of the soldier? Or, of Peterson?

A gust of wind arose without warning, threatening to douse the fire.

"Father, I must speak with Mr. Ross alone." She patted Pastor's arm. "I will be only a few minutes."

John's heart pounded. His resolution to avoid Hope melted into the campfire at his feet.

CHAPTER 32

With his guard reduced to Jeremy following his stint with Peterson, John and Hope walked into the darkness behind the wagon, far outside the circle of the cook fire. They stopped, and he stood so close to Hope he inhaled her fresh scent.

"I'm frightened." Hope's voice was barely audible above the rising wind. The angry gusts caught her hair, whipping strands around her face. She shivered and gathered her green cloak around her. A strand of her brilliant red hair touched his neck, sending a shock to the tips of his fingers. Hope stepped even nearer as the wild weather tried to drive them apart.

A whisper of voices and an occasional laugh drifted from the other side of the wagon. Hope resembled a fawn who wanted to run because she sensed danger but didn't know where to flee.

With a longing springing from deep within that was almost physical, John hungered to fold her into his arms and protect her from the night and from her fear. If only he had the right to hold her, to protect her, to let her lose herself in his arms.

"What are you afraid of?" His voice sounded throaty, dragged up from deep within his chest.

She turned her face away. "Matthew Peterson threatened to kill himself." Her voice sounded small and tremulous.

John stiffened. The unexpected news held his mind in a net. "Why?" He couldn't reach in and extract a better response.

"I returned his engagement ring."

As tension seeped from him John staggered, then regained his footing. The familiar freedom of soul he'd experienced when he accepted salvation flooded over him. Forgiven. Forgotten. Gone. Hope was free of Peterson.

But was she? Peterson still maintained a hold over her. He'd reduced this lovely, spirited woman into trembling, pale-faced panic. He stepped away. "Why did you take his ring?" Anger sharpened his tongue.

She met his black look, and her chin shot up. Fury evaporated like water seeping into dry earth. Whatever Hope had done, she was having a hard time explaining. She shook her head.

"Doesn't make sense. Why take the ring and then return it?"

"I ... I feared if I didn't receive his ring, Matt would ...." She faltered, then lifted a determined face. Her lips quivered.

Heat pulsed through John's body. Whatever precarious position she put him in, he would undertake. Whatever she asked from him, he would give. He would probably die for this woman at Peterson's hands.

"Matt had you in his clutches. I feared he would take his wrath at me out on you if I didn't accept his ring. I watched him work you day after day when you were exhausted and shaking with cold. I'm so sorry, I couldn't send you the coat sooner. Matt would have known the gift came from me. He would have made your situation even worse."

John swiped at the perspiration beading his face. What was she saying? She took the ring because she worried about him?

"Matt suspected I cared about your well-being and what happened to you, so I took his ring, hoping he would be less harsh with you. Then, last night, after you were free of him, I returned his diamond." The full moon bathed her raised chin and flashing eyes with glowing light. "Tell me I did wrong."

John shoved his hands deep into the pockets of his mackinaw. His mind whirled. He turned from her and stared into cold moonlight and stark black shadows.

She cared for him.

Yet he loved her too much to ask her to share his life with its uncertain future. Bold Hunter and Rachael had skills that would help them create a home in the Indian Territory. They understood how to wrench produce from the land and how to build a shelter.

He knew only how to control slaves. How to oversee. How to give orders. In the Territory he would be ... what? His future had no promise. He had no way to provide a home for the most adorable woman on earth. Plus, he had nine orphans to care for. Hope was an angel to imagine they had a future together.

John braced himself, then faced her. "No, your actions came from a pure heart. I appreciate what you did." He cleared his throat. "Did you tell Peterson why you returned his ring?"

"No, of course not."

He tried to sound as impersonal as if she weren't the single most important woman in his life. "What do you want me to do?" Despite the howling wind, sweat streamed between his shoulder blades. "Did you tell your father?"

"No. I dare not. He never approved of my seeing Matt."

"Jeremy?"

"Jeremy would preach at me. Then he'd blunder over to Matt's tent and get himself in trouble. Matt's crazy enough to shoot my brother."

"So, you came to me, not caring if I blundered over to Peterson's tent and got myself into trouble." John kept his voice rough. She must not suspect that he would do exactly that. And hang the consequences.

"If I didn't care, none of this would have happened. But Matt can't hurt you now. You're not under his command like Jeremy. Don't you see?" She clasped her hands together.

"Besides, I merely want you to keep a watch on Matt. You're acquainted with his habits. If he does anything suspicious to make you think he's going to kill himself, you could stop him." She gazed at her feet, tears sparkling on her cheeks. "I'm so sorry I even looked at Matt twice. I didn't suspect him to be the kind of man he is."

John clasped his hands behind his back. How easy it would be to wipe her tears and whisper, "Whatever you ask me to do, I will do."

Blast it! Shadow Peterson? When the captain saw him lurking, he would destroy John, not kill himself. And broken engagement or not, Hope had no knowledge of how dangerous Peterson could be—not to himself but to anyone who opposed him. "I doubt Peterson will take his own life."

"I don't." Hope's small hands curled into fists. "Matt's very rich. He's never been denied anything in his life."

John swallowed. "If you think Peterson's in danger, I'll watch him." He knew the Falcon wouldn't remove himself from Hope's life simply because of a broken engagement. Inside his mackinaw pockets, John clinched his fists. He couldn't offer Hope marriage, but he would risk his life to keep Peterson away. A self-centered man like Peterson would never kill himself.

John clasped her shoulders and stiffened his arms. "You'd best go on to your wagon. The wind's bringing ice and rain." How he longed to hold her, protect her from the cold as she had done for him. Caress her flaming hair and kiss her down-turned lips until they burned with his love. He gave her a tiny shake, released her shoulders, and stepped away. If she didn't leave, he would kiss her senseless.

Her face crumbled.

John's resolve shattered and fell into a pathetic heap at his feet. He stepped toward her.

Too late!

She had turned and sprinted to the other side of the wagon.

CHAPTER 33

The following day brought good news. John smiled. Because of his and Bold Hunter's fetching the deer earlier, General Scott ordered the militia to provide meat and pelts to the Cherokee. Yet even as he delivered the meat to his wagon, he thought only of Hope. She avoided him. He groaned. No help for hurting her, he'd done what had to be done for her ultimate good.

He kept his word. Every second he wasn't driving the wagon, he maintained his watch on Peterson. On occasion, Peterson caught sight of him loitering in the vicinity of his tent, talking with his soldiers. The captain didn't appear to care.

Once John glimpsed Hope and pivoted off in the opposite direction. Being near her was too much like a starving man viewing a feast he wasn't permitted to devour.

Several weeks passed before he saw Hope again.

A blanket of snow covered the rolling hills outside Golconda, Illinois. Sleet had fallen before the snow, and John worked hard to keep the often-fishtailing wagon from sliding off the frozen trail onto snow mounded ground.

Wagons, creaking and groaning, added their complaint to the wails of the living for their dead.

The train halted south of the Ohio River near the mouth of the Cumberland River. John shivered in the bitter cold as each team and wagon was ferried across. He and Bold Hunter erected a temporary camp while they waited their turn to traverse the icy river and, once across, added their wagon to the wagons and tents blossoming on the far bank of the river.

Burial mounds multiplied.

A bleak setting for a wedding.

In response to Rachael's oral invitation, a small group of friends gathered adjacent to the bridal pair's wagon. No festive finery or decorations adorned the area. Rather than candles lining the aisle of a church, icicles sparkled from boughs of every tree. Snow-covered bushes ornamented the hill where the bride and groom stood. A dull wintry sun arrived just before the ceremony—God bestowing his blessing. The wind changed, blowing from the south. The Cherokees declared the white wind brought peace and happiness.

Pastor officiated, with John acting as best man and Hope as maid of honor. John couldn't take his gaze off Hope's rosy face, but she refused to look at him. He smiled, congratulated the couple, and engaged in small talk, hiding the pain tearing his heart. During the brief ceremony uniting the young couple, tears filled many eyes. Surrounded by death, this wedding symbolized hope for the future.

Bold Hunter placed an intricately carved silver band on Rachael's finger. "Many years past, Bold Hunter understand Rachael like Christian weddings at mission. Bold Hunter carve marriage band when turn sixteen summers and Rachael twelve. Bold Hunter carry ring from that day. This day, after five winters pass, Bold Hunter take Rachael as wife."

After the Christian ceremony, John witnessed the ancient Cherokee rites for the first time.

Bold Hunter—tall, brown, his face beaming happiness—offered Rachael a ham of venison. "This show Bold Hunter keep home filled with meat from hunt."

John acting as Rachael's nearest of kin, handed her a handful of corn on the cob. Rachael's hands trembled as she placed the offering in Bold Hunter's open palms. "This shows my willingness to be a good wife."

John sighed. Too bad the Cherokee custom of three days of feasting and fun following the ceremony was impossible. But he felt relieved the couple hadn't waited until they journeyed to the end of the trail to wed. John kissed the bride's cheek, then shook hands with Bold Hunter. "Welcome to the Wolf Clan. We are official clan brothers now, bound to help and protect each other until we die."

Pastor closed his Bible. "Seems a strange policy for males to leave their homes and kin to join the wife. Our American custom is quite the opposite."

John clasped his hands behind his back and nodded. "Yes. The lineage of chief is also handed down to the chief's sister's son, rather than his own. When the chief dies, his sister's children inherit the chieftaincy. Cherokee heritage is traced through the woman. Bold Hunter makes a sacrifice marrying Rachael, as she has no family lineage." John winked. "Although I'm certain Bold Hunter does not consider marrying Rachael a sacrifice."

"Ross speak truth. Bold Hunter think wife in Christ more important than clan bonds."

Guests surged forward to take Rachael and Bold Hunter's hands and give their blessings and hopes for a long, happy life and many children. Hope presented a large bag of cornmeal, her best wishes, and kissed both Mr. and Mrs. Hunter.

John held his breath, but she didn't even glance at him before she disappeared in the direction of her wagon. The sudden stab to his heart was brutal. After Hope left, he wandered over to the campfire, sat on a log, and dropped his head into his hands.

With the exception of today, he'd kept an eagle eye on Peterson—from as far into the wilderness as he dared roam. Peterson had made no move to take his own life and thus far had stayed away from Hope.

The day grew too frigid to remain outside the protection of their wagons, so the other guests did not linger. Many were barefoot, and bloody tracks followed them in the snow.

John glanced toward the wagon that had been home for the past three months. What now? He couldn't sleep there. Since the weather had turned freezing, he, Bold Hunter, Rachael, and the children had squeezed into the wagon to sleep. With his two friends married, he would be as welcome as a mother-in-law on a honeymoon. He leaned against a tree and wrapped his mackinaw tighter. He'd sleep outside next to the campfire. Others did ... so could he.

Jeremy bounded over the snow like a red-headed jackrabbit. "Sorry I couldn't make the wedding. Got stuck with guard duty."

"The wedding was uplifting, and both bride and groom are elated. Too bad you weren't there, but you were missed." John's mouth twitched. Jeremy looked so full of news he was all but jumping up and down. "What's up?"

Jeremy's green eyes snapped. "Captain Peterson overstepped himself this time. The entire camp's agog."

Oh, dear Lord, did he actually carry out his threat and kill himself? "Don't aim the gun without shooting it." John joked through stiff lips.

"Did you know Peterson and Hope had a fallout? I think the captain's trying to make her jealous. He's keeping a Cherokee girl in his tent!"

John passed his hand wearily over his face. More trouble. He rubbed the new spasm in the nape of his neck. "Against her will?"

"Nope! And is she a beauty! Carries herself as regally as the Queen of Sheba."

John doubled over with laughter, and tears glistened on his cheeks. He hadn't laughed so hard since—memory failed him. The release from his burden of keeping an eye on Peterson, coupled with the exquisite vengeance of the Lord, had him so lighthearted he fell to his knees and rolled in the snow.

Jeremy grinned, and threw a snowball that caught John in the face. "What's so funny?"

"Peterson's in for a surprise with a Cherokee woman. They have the final word in a family. She'll dump him if he doesn't suit her. There's no divorce. The girl merely leaves if the man is not everything she wants. Women have complete equality with men. Did you know the women decide when the warriors go on the war trail? Sounds like the Falcon's headed down the war trail and he doesn't even know it!"

Jeremy chuckled. "Peterson got what's coming to him. This charmer's got him ransacking all the enlisted men's tents for clothes for her people."

"The Falcon has his wings clipped now. In trying to save his pride with Hope, he's fitted himself with a hood and leash. Cherokee women hunt with falcons and know how to keep them tamed."

"I was told she's a beloved woman. What's that?"

John's grin widened. "A beloved woman takes her husband's place in battle after he's killed. With her courage, she earns the distinction of making future decisions in the rule of the nation and is welcomed in the council house. The beloved women sided with my uncle to avoid war against the Georgians and advocated passive resistance. That woman's husband must have been killed during the roundup because Cherokee haven't been at war for over thirty years. And if she's young enough to interest Peterson, the woman was probably born after the Creek War."

"Sounds like quite a lady."

"She must have fought the soldiers some way. Maybe she's fighting them with another technique now." He and Jeremy chuckled and poked each other's shoulders.

"Ho, John, I almost forgot. Doc Smith sent his congratulations to the newlyweds. Said since there's so much sickness, he needs assistance in the medical wagon. Wondered if you'd like to come and help him out." Jeremy slapped John on the shoulder. "Besides, the sly old fox said you'd probably feel embarrassed with your girlfriend married to someone else, right under your nose."

John's face burned, but he grinned. "Thanks, Yank. But Rachael's not my girlfriend. She's my sister by clan bonds."

"Glad you finally got that figured out." Jeremy winked and left.

John trudged to Doc's wagon. "I'm deeply grateful for the opportunity to assist you, Doc. I'm an extra mouth at the Hunters' wagon now. He's an expert driver now, and he and Rachael don't need me around."

"My pleasure, son. I crave an assistant. I've got my hands full and then some."

John settled comfortably with Doc, once again warm, well-fed, and enjoying the older man's friendship. He shadowed Doc on his rounds, and Doc trained him. Each day the pain in John's heart sharpened as he caught glimpses of Hope. But from the time he opened his eyes to the gray, sleeting skies until sleep locked his lids the minute his head touched the cot's pillow, he remained busy tending the growing number of sick Cherokee.

Late one night, he slogged toward Doc's wagon. His lower back throbbed from bending over a sick child, his feet were ice-cold, and his stomach growled like a suspicious dog. Darkness descended earlier and earlier, and he judged the time must be near six. In the dark, he stumbled over a root, fell to his knees, and his medical bag rolled down an incline. Served him right for not carrying a lantern.

Placing one cautious foot in front of the other, he felt his way down the hill and found himself near the edge of a small lake. As he bent to pick up his bag, he heard the babble of voices and almost fell into the lake. He caught his balance and turned.

Hope's voice. What was she doing so far from her wagon? Did she need help?

He tiptoed closer.

She stood in a circle of brightness cast by a lantern hanging on a limb above her head, her back turned toward him. A shaft of light made her red hair glow. She wore a long dark blue coat that clung to her narrow waist, flared over her hips, and brushed the grass at her feet.

A physical ache wracked his chest. Hiding behind a tree, he grasped the rough bark to keep from running to her. A sliver of bark stabbed under the nail of his index finger, but he barely registered the pain.

A tall soldier faced Hope, his hands holding hers—an officer, judging by the glint of his sword in the lantern beam. He leaned forward as if imploring her.

John tried to turn away, but his feet remained planted as deeply as the big tree's roots. Hope didn't need him nor would she want him spying on her.

The voices stopped. The soldier pushed his sword aside and knelt at her feet.

John choked until every breath rasped in his throat. He had to get closer. Had to know what Hope would say. He dropped to his stomach and crawled forward until he could hear the officer's words.

"Please, Hope, I would consider it an honor if you said yes."

John wiggled close enough to see the white of the man's eyes as he gazed up at Hope.

"But, Obadiah, I'm—"

"Don't give me an answer now. Think about it. I can wait until you're ready ... as long as you need ... well, until we reach Indian Territory. My company's scheduled to return to Atlanta, and you can ride back in style as my wife." He rose to his feet and tucked an arm around Hope's small waist. "I own a large home on a nice piece of property near the city center. I'm certain you'd love my mansion. Don't give me a hasty answer. Think of all you'd gain. You'd be the belle of Atlanta, and I know you would love my family. I'm crazy about you. I don't think I can live without you."

John had thought the anguish in his heart couldn't hurt any worse, but he floundered with newfound pain—even deeper than before. Hope deserved a home like the soldier offered, and a husband who could provide it.

He dropped his face into the grass. If she married him and remained in the wild Indian Territory, she might get an arrow through her chest. And if she found him spying on her tonight, she'd hate him. Yet he held his breath. And waited. And listened.

CHAPTER 34

John clutched the grass with both hands. He wanted to kiss Hope, caress those tender lips with his, inhale her sweet fragrance like a peach tree in full bloom. He yearned to feel her soft arms wrapped around his neck—he had to stop torturing himself. Would she accept the officer's proposal? The man crowded close to her, his shoe touched her toe, and she spoke so low John could not understand what she said.

The officer walked her toward where her father had parked their wagon. By the slump of the man's shoulders and the way his head drooped, John guessed Hope hadn't given him a definitive answer.

John beat a fist into the ground. Six months past he could have offered Hope his plantation along with all the love bursting his heart. He rose slowly to his feet, brushed off the dirt and grass, and trudged up the hill, back to where he'd parked Doc's medicine wagon.

Why had he let Hope stomp away the evening she asked him to keep an eye on Peterson? Knowing the answer didn't lighten John's mood. He clamped his jaw.

John buried himself in his work. But acting indifferent to what his heart told him grew more difficult. As the days ground past, he discovered he had an aptitude for medicine. Doc trained him meticulously. John learned Doc was one of the new breed of liberal doctors who refused to bleed a patient. Instead, Doc taught him to keep the surgical instruments sterile.

John woke one morning with patients already overflowing the medical tent. Children sat on the canvas tent floor all in a row, watching him with big eyes. He slid off the cot, shook the wrinkles from his clothes, and slipped his stockinged feet into his brogues.

Doc handed him a cup of strong coffee. "Son, time you took responsibility for your own patients. There are too many for me to care for."

John gulped the hot coffee, and the caffeine jolted him to instant awareness. "Whatever you say, Doc. If you think I'm ready."

Doc handed him a long list of wagon numbers "I need you to visit these wagons. If you come across something you can't handle, send for me."

John nodded. "I'll do my best."

"There are eggs still warm in the mess tent. I asked the cook to save them for you. You've time to eat before the train rolls."

"Thanks, Doc." John slipped into his mackinaw.

After the train stopped to camp late the next afternoon, John erected the hospital tent, built a fire, carried in water from the river, set the pot over the fire, and sterilized the instruments he'd used that day in the scalding water. He packed the instruments in clean linen and entered the warm tent.

Bringing a burst of cold air with him, Doc rushed in and collapsed on his cot in the corner. John handed him a cup of fresh coffee. "What about it, Doc? Will you build a cabin when we reach Indian Territory?" John lowered himself into the camp seat facing Doc. His mentor had bags drooping beneath his eyes and his sparse sandy hair was mussed. With new lines etched into his forehead, the forty-year-old appeared closer to sixty.

Doc dribbled honey into his coffee. "Huh. Not me. Why do you think I'm training you? When we reach the end of the trail, I'm returning home to my wife and children. You'll be the doctor for the Cherokee. I'm not staying in that hostile, unexplored land to get an arrow in my chest and lose what hair I've got to a scalping knife."

John nodded. He'd been thinking hard about what he would do to eke out a livelihood when he reached Indian Territory. He had an aptitude for medicine, and doctoring sounded better than anything else he could imagine. "I'd hoped to assist you, before venturing out on my own."

"You're ready. On and off, I apprenticed you for months, and you've learned all I can teach you. Trouble is, you'll have a bunch of patients who can't pay you. Hard to make a living that way."

"Yeah. I believe you're right about that."

"You can take your wages out in labor. Probably ten or twelve men you've kept alive will be more than eager to build you a nice log cabin. Others will help you put in a garden. I'm not a betting man, but I'm willing to wager you've never done either."

"Um. No. I'll admit, building a cabin has been a concern."

"I'm leaving the medical wagon and my tent for you. That'll keep you sheltered until your cabin's built."

"Doc, your kindness opens a whole new future for me. I'll never be able to thank you enough."

"I'll supply you with all the necessary equipment. I've sent word to my wife to send you the newest medical books. My gift to you. You'll make a fine doctor, John. I'm proud of you."

John clapped the older man on the shoulder. "That's the best news I've had in six months."

Doc laughed. "I've got five daughters back in Georgia and no sons to take up the mantle of doctoring. I'm delighted I have you to carry on the practice with the Cherokees. Before I met you, I thought the Army would order me to stay in the wild land you're heading for." Doc leaned against his pillow, pulled out his pipe, and soon the sweet aroma of tobacco swirled through the air.

John couldn't stop grinning. He had a future. He had a livelihood and means to provide for a family. Tiredness forgotten, he paced the tent. He had to share his good news with Hope. If only he wasn't too late.

Doc lounged on the cot and puffed his pipe, his smile erasing the aging lines that made him seem so much older. As if he could read John's thoughts, he shrugged his shoulders. "Don't think doctoring will be easy—it's a hard way to earn a living. Some patients can't pay with any more than thanks. Most women won't settle for that kind of life."

John sprang over to refill Doc's coffee cup. Huh. Was his eagerness to see Hope so obvious? Doc always had a way of knowing what John yearned for. He set the pot back on the camp stove and stuck his head out the front flap. The sky had darkened and promised sleet or snow. But he couldn't wait. "Hey Doc, I need some time off."

"Heading out to visit your red-headed girlfriend?"

"I'm going to try. She doesn't like me too well." That was an understatement. "But I've got to talk with her." He ducked out the canvas door flap.

His heart drummed so fast he panted as he strode within eyesight of her wagon. Pastor had set up camp, and Hope bent over a large kettle using a long-handled spoon to stir something inside. Her coal-scuttle bonnet hid her face. Both were wrapped in coats.

Jeremy walked toward them carrying a bundle of branches and twigs for the campfire. Jeremy's horse neighed from where he had tied the animal to a nearby tree.

Yank spotted him walking to their camp. "Ho, John. You've been too busy to call on your old friends?" He grinned.

Hope hung the spoon on a hook outside the big kettle, strode to the rear of the wagon, and out of sight.

"Yeah, Doc's been working me hard. Too many people are sick for even Doc and me to attend. He gave me a few minutes off so I could visit y'all."

"Ha, see Hope, more like. Day and night there's been a regular path cut to our wagon by soldiers. You sure you want to join the parade?" Jeremy dropped the firewood next to the fire. "I told you not to fall for her. I warned you she would break your heart."

"Maybe I came to see you."

"Don't kid me. That lovesick expression on your face tells the whole story."

"Okay, fine. Has she said yes to any of the soldiers?" John didn't breathe.

"You'll have to ask her yourself. She doesn't tell us much."

John grunted. "Is she planning to return to Tennessee at the end of the trail?"

"Like I mentioned, you'll have to ask her yourself."

"I thought you were my friend."

"I am. That's why I warned you off." Jeremy pulled a log near the fire and plopped down on it. "Nobody wishes Hope would make up her mind more than I do. I've had my fill of seeing those suitors don't try anything physical with my sister." He shook his head. "She's a handful. You fellows would be better off to forget her."

"I won't try anything with her, Yank. You can trust me." John settled on the log a few feet from Jeremy.

Jeremy smiled his familiar crooked smile. "I sure would hate to have to bust that handsome nose of yours if you did. But brotherly duty and all, you understand."

John thrust his hands wide. "I won't touch her. I need a few minutes alone with her."

"This runs against my better judgment." Jeremy rose and walked to the rear of the Worchester's wagon. "Hey, Hope. John Ross wants a word with you. Be easy with him, will you? He's my friend."

Walking with a slight limp, Pastor approached.

John stood, and they shook hands. Pastor beamed at John. "Hello, son. We haven't had the pleasure of your company since Rachael's wedding. Good to see you."

Hope strolled toward him, stopped on the opposite side of the fire, and peered at him, her bonnet shading her eyes. John pulled in a deep breath. Was her expression distain ... surprise, or ...?

"Hello, John." Her sweet voice sounded strained.

"Might I have a few words alone with you, Hope? Perhaps you could walk with me."

Pastor's bushy grey brows furrowed. "It's cold, John. Don't keep her out too long. I don't want her getting sick."

"Okay, Pastor. I'll only detain her a few minutes."

Then she was walking by his side. To keep Jeremy from bounding to her rescue, John clasped his hands behind his back and edged her toward the meadow next to the circle of wagons. "I reckon you're still angry with me?"

"You were rather rude. But Jeremy told me you kept your vigil on Matt, until"—she paused and slipped her gloved hands inside the sleeves of her coat—"until Matt took that Cherokee woman into his tent."

"I don't think he ever planned to kill himself."

"Perhaps not."

"I'm sorry I was rude. I had a lot on my mind." John raised his coat collar against the biting wind.

"I'm sure you did."

"I had to say things I didn't want to. And I couldn't tell you what was in my heart."

"But now you can?"

John nodded. "Doc's training me to take over his duties when we reach the end of the trail. He's supplying me with all I'll need to set up practice in the new territory. He's leaving to head back to Georgia to his wife and kids."

Hope tripped over a buried root.

He steadied her.

"Doctoring this multitude of people will be a huge job and keep you quite busy."

Dear God, I'm not getting anywhere. He had to tell her what was in his heart even if his confession dropped him square in the middle of being another ornament on her tree. "As Doctor Ross, I have a livelihood and a future." He swallowed and locked his hands behind his back.

She untied her bonnet, pulled it off, and her glorious hair fell to her shoulders. Her face, rosy pink with cold, looked incredibly beautiful. Her large eyes, green as summer meadows, opened wide with ... questions? What did she want him to say? The lips he'd dreamed about for months moved close, open and inviting.

He couldn't think.

Her brow puckered.

He'd never felt this way about any other woman. His yearning to tuck her in his arms and kiss her ached all the way to his toes. But what did her frown mean? He wanted ...

"I'm glad for you, John."

She was glad for him? Did that mean she had plans for herself? Had she accepted someone else's offer of marriage? He had to know. He blundered on, "Once we arrive, will you be staying in Indian Territory?"

She wrapped her arms around her waist and stared at the row of ruts barely visible in the deepening dusk. "I haven't yet decided what I shall do."

A late arriving wagon had jiggled by and almost drowned out her soft answer. The two men on the driver's seat stared at them, curiosity on both whiskered faces. "You got another one of those guys asking you to marry him, Miss Hope? Seems like you get two a day." The driver snapped the reins on the oxen's broad backs. "If this one gives you trouble like the last one did, just holler ... I'm Johnny-on-the-spot for you. Captain Peterson ordered us to keep tabs on you."

John's gut clenched. Peterson again. "I'm not giving her any trouble," he growled.

"See that you don't. We've been watching you." Since the wagon didn't move, John figured the two men obviously didn't plan to leave.

Footsteps pounded up behind them, then David Elk Horn thrust his small hand into John's and tugged. "John, Doc Smith needs you bad. He says come now!"

John sighed. If only the world would go away. He needed to be alone with the woman he loved. She was so close. If his hands had been bound, he wouldn't have been less able to touch her. Could she not read on his face what he longed to say?

She smiled—a sad little lifting of her lips. "I think it might be best if you leave."

"But, Hope, I ...."

"Oh ho, so you're the new doctor we've heard good things about." A male voice spoke from the wagon. "I'm Jake Rivers and this here's my brother Tom. We just started driving Captain Peterson's wagon."

John nodded and turned back to Hope.

She shook her head. "Now is not a good time to talk. Perhaps later ..."

David pulled his arm "Come on, John!"

As if even the weather conspired against him, heavy flakes of snow blasted down from the gray, overcast sky. Jeremy rode into the meadow and dismounted beside them. "Um, John. That snow's sticking, and Father said Hope should immediately return to our wagon."

John scowled. "Later then." Snow mixed with sleet pelted his face as he watched Jeremy lift Hope to ride in front of him on the saddle. When they reached the wagon, she slid to the ground, lifted her long skirts, and scurried to climb in.

Why hadn't she encouraged him? She must have anticipated what he hoped to say. Had she accepted one of the other offers and hadn't wanted to tell him in front of so many people? Did she not experience the same passion for him as he felt for her? He had to see her again. Soon.

"John ..." David jerked on his hand and shivered, his light coat scant protection from the sleet.

"Tonight, Hope!" he called above the wind and driving snow.

Had she heard?

CHAPTER 35

John couldn't keep their date. He worked through that night and the days following almost without sleep. Many people suffered pneumonia and related ills. Numerous babies chose this time to be born.

As John labored from wagon to wagon, the train rolled through southern Illinois. In its wake, blackened areas from campfires, bloody footprints in the snow, and silent unmarked grave mounds linked together in a chain of death. The wagon train rumbled on until the people reached the mighty Mississippi opposite Cape Girardeau, Missouri.

In a free moment, John gazed at the glistening water. The river ran high, clogged with ice. He stood on a hill and watched as the train circled wagons and made camp on the east side until the river cleared enough to cross.

During the first evening camped there, he worked all night, successfully delivering a live baby, with both mother and child doing well. No one else inside the wagon lay ill and the family had blankets, plus some coats donated from sympathetic army regulars. John prayed this baby and his mother would survive. He promised to check tomorrow and keep a close watch on the newborn, dreading to face another loss like Baby Bryce.

Following the difficult delivery, joy of a new birth died the instant John stepped outside the wagon. The hair on the back of his neck prickled at the strong sense of apprehension whipping through him. He shuddered.

As he picked his way through the darkness to the medical tent, his steps echoed in an eerie stillness. At the entrance to the tent, he turned and glanced around. What was wrong? The first touch of color lightened the eastern sky. If his reckoning was correct, this was the first day of the New Year, 1839.

Hoping daylight would dispel his uneasiness, he turned to watch the sunrise. As the dawn tinted the Mississippi, mist rose from its surface, giving the water a ghostly appearance. Weak sunbeams slanted off the ice-bound ripples, revealing how cruelly cold the night had been. Wind howled across the plains, promising another frigid day.

The bugle's lonely sound announced the morning. But the sleeping forms around the dead campfires failed to stir. John rubbed the back of his neck, a feeling of unreality swirled around him like the vapor over the river. He turned the collar of his mackinaw up to cover his cold ears. The dark wagons draped in their white canvas shrouds like so many ghostly ships lost on a pathless sea, stood in sharp relief atop the crusted snow. Like a portrait frozen in time, the uncanny silence framed a picture of desolation.

The reality of what had happened—which his subconscious already knew—penetrated. John trembled. Cherokees sleeping beside the dead campfires would never wake. Hundreds had frozen to death during the night.

Oh, Father God, I pray you kept Hope and Pastor safe inside their wagon. And thank you Father, I'm praying, believing you kept my little family snug inside our wagon. Thanks so much for the blankets and coats warming Rachael, Bold Hunter, and the children.

John resisted entering the pot-bellied stove warmth of the medical tent, gripped his medical bag tighter, and turned back to the horrific scene.

Hours later, bone weary, John hacked the frozen ground as the sun relinquished her place in the sky. Here the earth was not red like his native Georgia, but brown and bleak. The task of burying the dead had taken the day. And yet more remained, their bodies frozen to the soil.

Resting his cold hands on the shovel, he gazed at the dormant sod. The seed of a growing conviction, planted when he saw his father die, germinated, and sprouted. The scene of death he witnessed today brought the thought to fruition. Uncle John had been wrong in his strategy of passive resistance against the removal. His nation should have left voluntarily, resettled peacefully in the new territory, and begun life anew out of reach of the white man whose greed for land and gold exceeded that of a hungry wolf.

A time must come in the future when white and brown would live together in peace, when the white violators of the treaties and the Indian wars and raids were not so vivid in the memories of both peoples.

Uncle John had been right to fight for the Nation in the courts and in Washington. But when the irrevocable decision had been made for the Indian Removal by more powerful people, further resistance had been senseless.

To relocate family by family within the time set by the Americans, at a convenient season when children were well, when mothers had borne their babies, and families were together, taking their possessions with them in a practical manner would have been inexpressibly better than this forced march with its aftermath of death. If only foresight were as good as hindsight!

Still, through the suffering, anguish, and death, God had been with them. John rested his foot on the shovel's edge. He permitted President Andrew Jackson's evil decision because God gave mankind free will. Yet, even in the evil situation that decision caused, God had been here among them, working everything out for good, bringing many people to the Savior.

Of course, the United States must take her share of guilt for the decision to relocate thousands of people. Their greed for land and gold, and their failure to provide the necessities of adequate food and shelter …

"John!" Suddenly, in a flurry of green and red, Hope was in his arms, sobbing against his shoulder.

The shovel fell to the frozen ground, and he grasped her cold hands. Her lovely eyes looked swollen and red, and cold pinched her pale skin. Even in her present state, her riding habit stained and torn, she was beauty and love without equal.

"Why Rachael? Oh John, why Rachael?" Her voice muffled against his chest, tightened with anguish.

How had Hope found out so quickly? He had just learned of Rachael's death an hour past. His eyes filled with tears as he thought of Rachel, God's missionary on this journey who would not continue her work in the new land. The whys in his mind crumbled like dead autumn leaves, tiny, dry fragments against something grown strong, solid, and unyielding in his innermost self. "I don't know why, but I know God … and that is enough."

He held her while she sobbed her sorrow in the circle of his arms.

After she quieted, he stroked her hair. "Rachael had love enough to surrender her place in the wagon to a dying child and her mother while Bold Hunter had gone to gather more firewood. He was almost frozen when he returned at dawn and found her.

"But Rachael had so much to live for! She could have been such a help in the new land. She and Bold Hunter had great plans of opening an orphanage. Surely she would have been more useful to God alive than dead." Hope's voice quivered and her hands shook.

So many times on this trail, John had been plagued by the same questions. What answer could he offer?

"I read in Jeremy's Bible that God's ways are higher than our ways. We comprehend so little with our finite minds. Now, I'm convinced Christians whose missions on earth are completed are taken to be with the Lord. He makes no mistakes." John kissed the top of her head. "This is God's world, and God does things his way. We may think we have a better way, but we don't have a world to rule."

Peace settled over her pale face, her mossy eyes grew serene, and her grip around his neck eased. "Thank you."

"The pain from our losses will lessen with time."

"Yes. Father said as we walk though the shadow of the valley of death, Jesus becomes closer than we've ever known him."

"Bold Hunter has amazing faith for such a new believer. He has accepted Rachael's death." John tugged Hope so close, he felt her tremble beneath her heavy coat. "Bold Hunter's greatest regret is if he had received Christ years earlier, he and Rachael could have married, escaped to the mountains, and hidden in the caves of North Carolina."

"They were in love for such a long time." Hope smiled a tremulous smile.

John used his thumb to wipe tears from Hope's cheeks. "I've tried so hard, for so long, not to love you. I couldn't help myself." He touched her slender throat just above the fur collar, feeling her rapid pulse, then tipped her face toward his.

Her long sigh misted in the cold air.

He kissed her. Her lips warm and sweet beneath his. A thrill raced from his lips to his heart. He kissed her until her warmth thawed the cold he'd fought all day. He kissed her again … and forgot the world of death.

"I love you, Hope."

"Oh, John, I've been in love with you since the first time I saw you sitting outside the stockade with that rebellious expression on your face, listening to my father's preaching. Did you know I asked him to introduce us?"

He answered her with another long, satisfying kiss. "Marry me, my darling, my delight who has answered no to so many men. My own love. My beauty, who loves *me*."

She pursed her mouth to say yes, but he stopped her answer with his lips.

CHAPTER 36

John welcomed the early spring weather. After seven months of grueling travel, the wagon train, still traveling the Old Military Road, rolled into Indian Territory. He drove the medical wagon with Hope, his bride, by his side. They entered the beautiful Elbon Valley between gentle hills watered by five clear rivers.

"This is beautiful land, but these undulating hills are not our familiar Smokies." John halted their wagon.

"No, but this looks like an agreeable place."

An intense longing hit John as he viewed the inviting land. He gripped the reins so tightly the oxen bent their necks to stare at him with wide brown eyes. "I miss my parents, my baby sister, and my clan sister." He watched the train wind ahead of him as the thin, bedraggled people entered the new land.

"I know." Hope slipped off her sunbonnet and tossed her head, loosening her hair to flow free in the gentle breeze. "But think of how many people, though torn from their ancestral home and their loved ones, have found faith in God."

John's throat tightened. He released the brake and followed his people into the land, then turned to look back. Behind him, scattered over a nine-hundred-mile trek, remained the graves of four thousand Cherokees.

"We are a new family now." He reached for Hope's hand. "Ahead offers a new beginning. A goodbye to tears." He squeezed her fingers. "This will be our baby's birthplace."

EPILOGUE

And so it was that every person with even one-thirty-second Cherokee blood living on Indian land in Georgia, North and South Carolina, Tennessee, Kentucky, and Alabama was exiled across the Mississippi to unexplored land which belonged to other Indian tribes, most of them wild, unlike the civilized Cherokee.

Twenty-five years following the Trail of Tears some of the bloodiest battles of the Civil War were fought on what had been Cherokee national land. The battle of Chickamauga won by Confederate forces, and Chattanooga, Missionary Ridge, and Lookout Mountain won by Union forces to open the way for Sherman's devastating march on Georgia, bloodied the old Cherokee lands.

Hope and John's two sons, Jarrett and Jordan, and their daughter, Jerusha, missed those battles but fought the Civil War on opposing sides in the Indian Territory.

Another generation passed in Indian Territory—now called Oklahoma—outlaw gangs roamed, and Jarrett's grandchildren discovered oil on Cherokee soil.

And once again, the white man coveted their land.

Continue the saga by reading Jarrett Ross's story, *For Such A Time As This*. Chapter 1 is included below.

Anne Greene

FOR SUCH A TIME AS THIS—THE STORY OF JARRETT ROSS

By Anne Greene

Chapter 1

November 1859—Tahlequah, (Taw-a-quaw) capital of the Cherokee Nation in Indian Territory.

Jarrett Ross slammed the axe into the tree. The tree bent, and he used his foot to topple the sapling. He pondered—could a small decision irrevocably change a man's life? The thought hovered in his mind. Decisions needed to be made after serious consideration, but he was a seat-of-the-pants guy. Granddad Worchester often warned that a hasty decision could thrust a man toward a direction he would not choose. Why ...?

The rhythmic beat of hooves grew distinct. Jarrett dropped the razor-sharp axe ... the blade missed his foot by a miracle. He raced to the split-rail fence and stared up the dirt road. At the crest of the hill, an Indian astride a piebald pony thundered into view. With a rush of wind and a splatter of dirt clogs, he swooped toward Jarrett. The Indian pressed both fists against his temples, forefingers curled forward to simulate curved horns, then galloped past and out of sight around the bend.

Jarrett raced toward the back door of the two-story log house. "Buffalo sign! Runninghorse just gave the buffalo sign!" Before his foot touched the stone step, the latch lifted from inside, and his younger sister's elfin face peeked out.

"I wish you weren't going." Ten-year-old Jerusha swiped her long, blond hair out of her sky-blue eyes and turned up a woebegone expression. "It's dangerous."

Jarrett pulled his sister outside and tossed her into the air. She squealed. He slid her to the ground and slammed into the house. "Mom, the Osage scout is back! Runninghorse found buffalo!"

His mother stooped near the open fireplace stirring venison soup inside a black kettle suspended over glowing coals. The delicious aroma set Jarrett's stomach grumbling. He'd come to appreciate Mother, the woman his village called Hope Ross—with an emphasis on Hope.

She straightened, turned, smoothed her red-gold hair, and adjusted her apron over her long calico skirt. "You're like a thunderstorm sweeping across the prairie. Calm down." As she smiled, dimples dented her cheeks. "I think it's getting too cold for you to go."

Jarrett laughed. "Takes more than cold to stop me." He grabbed her slender waist, lifted her feet off the plank floor, and whirled her around the large room.

"Cold hands off, please. You're giving me a chill." Pink colored her clear skin, and her green eyes glistened.

Jarrett strode across the room, boots thudding on the wide wooden boards, and shoved his hands near the fire. "I've got to get away. Find excitement. See what's happening in the world. I can bring back enough buffalo steaks to feed us for months."

Hoof beats and buggy tires rattled on the dirt road. "There's your father."

The buggy, drawn by the high-stepping brown mare, clattered past the oversized living room window, and continued toward the barn.

"I'll go unhitch ..." Jarrett sped across the room and banged out the front door.

Dark followed Jarrett when he walked into the house from the cold. He shed his mackinaw and rubbed his chilled hands. Granddad Worchester, Mom, Dad, and Jerusha waited around the table set with white cloth and pewter and lit with bayberry candles.

"Hurry, Jer. Supper's getting cold, and I'm hungry." A frown puckered Jerusha's usually sunny face.

With cold water from the oaken bucket, he scrubbed off the smell of leather and horse and oats and slid into his chair. After Gramps prayed, Dad recounted his day of medical rounds and whose baby he'd delivered.

Conversation flowed around Jarrett in a warm, gentle stream. He perched on the edge of his ladder-back chair, one foot hung over a rung, the other tapping the floor, and spooned stew into his mouth. But the savory food didn't calm his rocky insides. He'd let Dad eat, then tell him. He'd planned this for weeks. Dad had to agree.

Finally, Dad pushed aside his empty plate, pulled his coffee cup toward him, and settled back into his chair. "What's on your mind, Jarrett? You have a run-in with the wrong end of a porcupine? You've been pulling out splinters since I came home."

"Sir." Beneath the tablecloth, Jarrett gripped his hands together and tried to stop jiggling his leg. "I need to leave tonight. Right now." He couldn't keep his words from tumbling over each other. "The Buffalo Dance has started." He scooted back his chair, jumped up, and paced the room.

Dad unbuttoned his brown frock coat and sipped coffee. His gray-streaked blond hair shone like silk in the candlelight. "Not a good idea. Hunting buffalo is dangerous. Plus, the buffalo range is on Pawnee land. They kill Osage hunters." Dad's face held a mixture of pride and reluctance. "You remind me of my father. He had your spirit of adventure." Dad shook his head.

"We need the meat to get us through the winter." Jarrett stopped midstride. "Because of the drought, our harvest was poor this year."

Granddad Worchester laughed his low, rumbling laugh. "Well, John, you can't expect to keep your colt tied when he's ready to run. Won't do him any harm seeing the way of the Osage. He's a good Christian lad." Gramps' faded green eyes twinkled behind rimless glasses. "A hunt's dangerous, but Jarrett can handle the challenge. He won't get another chance to bring us steaks before he heads east to college." He shook his white head. "Maybe never again."

Dad shoved his chair back from the table. "I don't know if Hope can manage without you, Jarrett." He glanced at Mom.

Before they could collaborate against him, Jarrett fired all his shots. "I've split more than enough wood to last a month, and I'll only be away two weeks." He faced his father squarely. "Fences are mended, corn's in the silo, pig's butchered and hanging in the smokehouse, cows are in the barn, manure's shoveled out, and the cabin's chinked for winter." His words jerked together as they would do when he was excited. "Work's all done. I drove in a wagonload of supplies from Tahlequah last week."

"I don't like your being gone so long. With Jordan at college, me on the road for days, and you chasing buffalo, your mother's—"

"I'm here with Hope, John." Granddad Worchester adjusted his spectacles. "And I've prayed about this for several days. I think God wants Jarrett to go."

Jarrett laid a thankful hand on Granddad's shoulder.

Dad stood, a resigned expression on his face. At six-feet-one, he towered two inches above Jarrett. "Then, God bless you and take care of you. Don't bring shame to the Ross name."

Jarrett grinned. "Trust me, Dad." He took the stairs three at a time to the loft he shared with Jordan when his brother was home.

Fragrance of drying herbs hanging from the rafters filled the room. Moonlight filtered through the window illuminating bunches of sweet basil, bloodroot, St. John's Wort, and dill, which Mom gathered and Dad used as medication for his patients.

Jarrett pulled off his old flannel shirt, yanked on his leather hunting shirt, shoved his pistol into his belt, and snatched his empty saddlebags. He clattered downstairs, kissed everyone on their forehead, and headed for the front door, grabbing his mackinaw from the door peg before he bolted outside.

Moonlight transformed the ranch into a world of shadows and patchy light—eerie and exhilarating. Jarrett inhaled the crisp scent of frosted leaves and packed earth. He lifted his arms and stifled a hoot and holler. He was free. No more ranch chores for two weeks, and even better—he'd go places he'd never been. The thought of danger made him grin.

He jogged down the path to the barn, his exhaled breath visible in the air. The barn welcomed him with its sweet scent of timothy hay, blue-stem grass, manure, and the soft breathing of horses.

"Hello, Sampson. Good boy. Ready for a run?" He saddled his horse, then with a creak of the saddle and a clatter of hooves on frozen ground, he headed for the Osage Village.

By the look of the night sky, the position of Orion announced the time to be close to midnight when he pulled Sampson to a stop at the edge of the village. The area looked ghostly in the moonlight with grotesque shadows flitting between tepees.

He leaned across his saddle horn, breath coming fast, and gazed at the confused bustle. Laughter, songs, and loud noises floated through the darkness. Unfamiliar aromas rose from campfires tended by women.

Adrenaline surged through his veins and left him tingling. He tapped his heels against Sampson's ribs, and trotted forward among the tepees. Where was Horse? Pungent smells and odors other than those coming from cook pots, assaulted Jarrett's nostrils. A multitude of dogs rushed his pony's hooves, nipping, snarling, and biting. Jarrett circled Sampson around a large tepee where three women stood at the door flap arguing like witches over a cauldron.

"Osage women quarrel constantly," Horse had warned.

Jarrett pressed his knees in Sampson's side, eyes sweeping the array of teepees. He caught sight of his new friend talking with a group of braves.

Bells tinkled on Horse's moccasins. He sported a leather shirt and leggings and wore a long, buffalo robe draped over his wide shoulders. When he moved, a necklace of bear claws and teeth swayed around his muscular neck. Rings dangled from brown ears, and two eagle feathers stuck out of his long, black hair, signifying Horse had stolen ponies from his enemies. Firelight flashed on something at Horse's waist.

Goose bumps shivered Jarrett's arms. Horse carried a war hatchet. Only an Osage who killed could carry a war hatchet. Nerves tightened along the base of Jarrett's neck. The deep shadows, a new arrogant expression, and the weapon transformed Horse into a stranger. Jarrett fingered the pistol in his belt.

He waited for Horse to notice him, while his mind adjusted to the knowledge that his scout friend had killed a human being. Horse looked wild. His black eyes gleamed in his bronze painted face. He yelled in Osage to his friends and brandished his war hatchet. Then he saw Jarrett. Tossing his head like a wild animal, he shouted the short barking yips of the Osage victory cry.

The Indian rushed over, kicked the dogs snarling around Jarrett's stirrups, and grasped Jarrett's arm. "At last you come."

"Pleasure to be here." Jarrett dismounted, his heart thudding.

"Come, friend. You late. Ceremony begun."

Jarrett tied Sampson to a tree behind the large teepee. Together he and Horse raced toward a blazing fire spewing thick smoke to the dark sky. Black clouds moved in, hiding the moonlight. Everything outside the fire's light disappeared into darkness.

"Buffalo great medicine." Horse pointed to the red stripes that ran from his forehead to his chin. "Good you come!"

Jarrett shrugged. "Yeah." Maybe not. Horse seemed a stranger with his hawk nose painted red and tossing his war hatchet from one hand to the other. Jarrett tried to shake off his uneasiness.

"You face easy to read as wampum. You want be Indian." A wide grin spread over Horse's face. "Careful. Maiden think you make good husband. Think you look soft. Think you no wallop with tent pole when she bad!"

"Don't talk crazy!" Jarrett poked his friend on the shoulder. "Who wants a wife?"

They skirted behind a large circle of seated men until they found an opening, then Jarrett followed Horse's lead and dropped to sit cross-legged beside him by the fire.

Women in colorful dress danced around the mammoth blaze, their long skirts whisking near the shooting flames, and exposing trim ankles. Okay, this wasn't bad. He liked to watch women, and four or five were young and pretty.

Beneath Horse's hooked nose, his mouth thinned. "Strict rules for Dance. Horse no look good in Osage eyes if Woodcarver no act well." Horse pointed to poles planted at four corners around the circle. "Punishment poles. If Carver no act well, move at wrong time or get up, guards tie you to pole, much high, much hurt, until sun rise. Much bad medicine."

Jarrett stiffened his spine and straightened his leather shirt. "No worries. Trust me."

Horse frowned and sat ramrod straight, face impassive, black eyes fixed on the fire.

Fifteen braves assembled before the mystery lodge. Each wore the head and horns of a buffalo, had a buffalo robe draped over his shoulders, and carried a bow and a lance. Women quit dancing. In a single line, the braves circled the huge fire. Each brave imitated a buffalo, lowering and raising its massive head, and bellowing in hoarse tones. Other Indians hunched cross-legged around the fire's perimeter, beating drums. The wild, exhilarating drumming quickened Jarrett's racing pulse.

Without turning his head, Horse murmured, "Brother Buffalo Great Medicine. When dance end, Brother Buffalo say he give Osage Brother him life. Buffalo keep Osage from starving through winter." With his erect, impassive posture, Horse seemed unaffected by the wild drums and wilder dancing.

Jarrett's blood thrummed with the drums and the dancers' silhouetted forms leaping about the flames. The bounding animal-like figures danced and chanted, tossing their horned heads to the hammering cadence.

Horse leaned close and whispered, "Drum beats are breath of Great Spirit. Osage in tune with Great Spirit. Let Great Medicine enter body."

The chanting and drumbeats crept into Jarrett's nervous system. Heat ignited his body. He was one with the night, one with the dancers, one with the buffalo.

Hours later the pounding morphed into a throbbing headache. Cold from the frozen ground seeped into his feet and spread through his body. He shivered. His leather hunting shirt was no match for the cold. He rubbed circulation into his legs and leaned toward Horse so his whisper could be heard above the pounding drums. "How about taking a stretch?"

"No move in circle. Give offense."

Jarrett stiffened his back. This rivaled a fourteen-hour day behind a lonely plow.

"Soon Horse dance. Watch, that one tired." Horse nodded toward a dancer.

The brave bent lower and lower. Another brave jumped up, drew his bow, and hit the sinking brave's buffalo robe with blunt arrows that thudded against the robe with a hollow sound. The brave fell to the ground like a wounded buffalo.

Indian women hovering outside the ring rushed to the fallen brave, grabbed him by his heels and dragged him into the night. The drums never missed a beat, nor the dancers a step as fresh braves replaced exhausted dancers.

Women danced about the fallen buffalo brandishing knives and making motions of skinning and cutting. Beaded buffalo and doe skin, flashing necklaces and earrings, and bright feathers gave the women festive, colorful beauty.

They chanted, their voices blending in a low moaning note and rising to a piercing crescendo.

Jarrett folded his chilly hands under his arms and hugged himself. He examined the seated Indians, all Osage men with paint on their faces. Many carried war hatchets, and all sat incredibly still. Only their black eyes moved, watching the dancers.

Out of the corner of his eye, Jarrett noticed the only other white man, sitting between Horse and a big Indian. A trader, by the looks of his clothes. The man appeared to be about thirty, stockily-built and unshaven, with the muscular arms and shoulders of a blacksmith.

"Who's the white man next to you?" Jarrett whispered.

Horse scowled, eyes fixed on the dancers. "Plenty bad man. No should be here. Sneak into dance. Osage no want."

"Why?"

"Him smuggle whiskey. No look."

Suddenly, Horse leaped to his feet and joined the dancers, shooting his arrows at a tired buffalo.

A sharp poke in his ribs jerked Jarrett's attention to the trader, who scooted closer. Though the unsavory man sat cross-legged, he towered head and shoulders over Jarrett.

"Have a snort." Saliva trickled from the corner of his mouth.

Jarrett shook his head.

The massive elbow poked him again. The man reeked of whiskey and dirty socks. "Come on kid, have a snort. It'll warm you up."

"I don't want any." Jarrett clinched his fists. He'd stopped lesser men with his glare.

"Thash no way to talk to a man's trying to be friendly."

The women's rising chant covered his loud voice.

"No." As Jarrett answered, the crescendo fell to a low chant. Every eye in the circle of immobile men turned his direction and glared. Bronze hands tightened around war hatchets. Horse missed several steps. Jarrett's face and neck heated.

He turned his shoulder from the sour smelling bully. At five feet eleven in his boots and weighing one hundred sixty-five pounds soaking wet, Jarrett attracted every bully looking for a fight. He sighed.

"You'll thansh me for this." A brawny arm enveloped Jarrett in a bear hug. With his other arm the trader lifted a jug, shoved the lip to Jarrett's mouth, forced the jug against his teeth so hard, he had to open his mouth or lose teeth.

He struggled in the giant's grip. Like a rushing stream, liquid flowed into his mouth. No choice but to swallow. And swallow again. And yet again. The liquor burned all the way down his throat into his chest. Some spilled down the sides of his mouth and over his shirt-front. He choked, gasped, and sputtered. His eyes watered, and liquid dripped from his nose. Still the trader forced him to drink.

Jarrett fought the iron grip.

DEAR READER,

I hope you enjoyed *Trail of Tears* as much as I loved writing about John, Rachael, Hope, Bold Hunter, and Jeremy. Thank you for joining me on this journey of love and faith.

Trail of Tears is one of my favorite stories because the novel is based on history. Almost everything that happened to John happened to many of the Cherokee people.

This is a story of ordinary people who do extraordinary things, a theme that often occurs in my books. I pray you will join me as I continue the Ross Saga, with stories of Jarrett Ross and of Jerusha Ross, plus Jeremy Worchester's story.

I hope you enjoy the first chapter of the next book in this series, *For Such A Time As This*, the story of Jarrett Ross, John and Hope's second-born son.

I find it such a pleasure to speak with my readers. Please visit with me at www.AnneGreeneAuthor.com, and www.facebook.com/AnneWGreeneAuthor.

You can also subscribe to my newsletter so we can keep in touch. I enjoy discovering what you think about my books.

Thank you for reading *Trail of Tears*. Please consider telling your friends how much you enjoyed this book and post a short review on Amazon or Goodreads. Word of mouth is an author's best friend and much appreciated.

HUGS,

ANNE

ABOUT THE AUTHOR

Anne Greene's home is in the quaint antiquing town of McKinney, Texas, just a few miles north of Dallas. Her husband is a retired Colonel, Army Special Forces. Her little gold and white Shih Tzu, Lily Valentine, shares her writing space curled at her feet. She has four beautiful, talented children, and eight grandchildren who keep her on her toes and running.

Besides her first love, writing, she enjoys travel, art, reading, and way too many other things to mention. Life is good. Whether contemporary or historical, her books celebrate the abundant life.

Anne is a multi-award-winning author. Her latest book, *Shadow of the Dagger*, makes her twenty-third published book and won the Christian Market Book Award for Book of the Year. If you enjoy a short read, you'll love her novellas: *A Crazy Optimist, Recipe for a Husband, Lacy and the Law, A Williamsburg Christmas, Her Reluctant Hero, Mystery at Dead Broke Ranch, Avoiding the Mistletoe, Lord Bentley Needs a Bride, Keara's Escape, Daredevils, Spur of the Moment Bride, A Christmas Belle, The Marriage Broker and the Mortician, A Groom for Christmas, A Texas Christmas Mystery, Texas Law, Love at Christmas, Brides of the Wild West, One Groom Is Not Enough, and A Smaill Voice. Hatteras Lighthouse Mystery* released in October.

Anne loves writing about alpha heroes who aren't afraid to fall on their knees in prayer and about gutsy heroines. Her Women of Courage series spotlights heroic women of World War II. Book One is *Angel with Steel Wings*. Her Holly Garden, Private Investigator series blasts off with *Red Is for Rookie*. Enjoy her award-winning Scottish historical romances, *Masquerade Marriage* and *Marriage by Arrangement*. Anne hopes her stories transport you to awesome new worlds and touch your heart. Buy Anne's books at https://www.amazon.com/Anne-Greene/e/B004ECUWMG. To learn more of Anne and to view her art and pictures of her extensive travel, visit her at www.facebook.com/AnneWGreeneAuthor. To view Anne's books go to www.annegreeneauthor.com/anne-s-books.html. Join her newsletter for fun, events, and give-aways at www.AnneGreeneAuthor.com.

BOOK CLUB DISCUSSION

1. What were your thoughts as you read about John's predicament at the beginning of the story?
2. If you were heading up a wagon train, what would your rules be?
3. What did you think of John's battles with Dread, the wagon master, and Captain Peterson?
4. Did John or Hope remind you of anybody you've known? And who was it?
5. The faith element was important to the story. How did faith weave its way through the main characters' stories?
6. What is your reaction to the real-life event of the Indian Removal?
7. What was your reaction to John and Hope's romance?
8. If you were on the wagon train, would you have forgiven the US Government?
9. What do you think was the author's purpose in writing this book?
10. Which scenes did you find particularly compelling?
11. What parts of the book gave you pause? What parts did you find startling? Troublesome? Were there parts of the book you thought unique, thought-provoking or disturbing?
12. How does the cover convey what the book is about?
13. What themes did you detect in the story?
14. How did the book make you feel?

15. What did you think about the ending?
16. What do you think a sequel should entail?

Feel free to email me at: annewgreene@gmail.com with your thoughts.

OTHER BOOKS BY ANNE GREENE

Angel With Steel Wings, Book I, Women of Courage series

Red Is For Rookie, Book I, Holly Garden Detective series

Shadow of The Dagger, Book I, CIA Operatives series